ARJUN'S PATH

RELEASE DAY SAGA
BY RYAN MATTHEWS

RELEASE DAY

KANO'S GRASP

ARJUN'S PATH

ZEPHYR'S HOPE

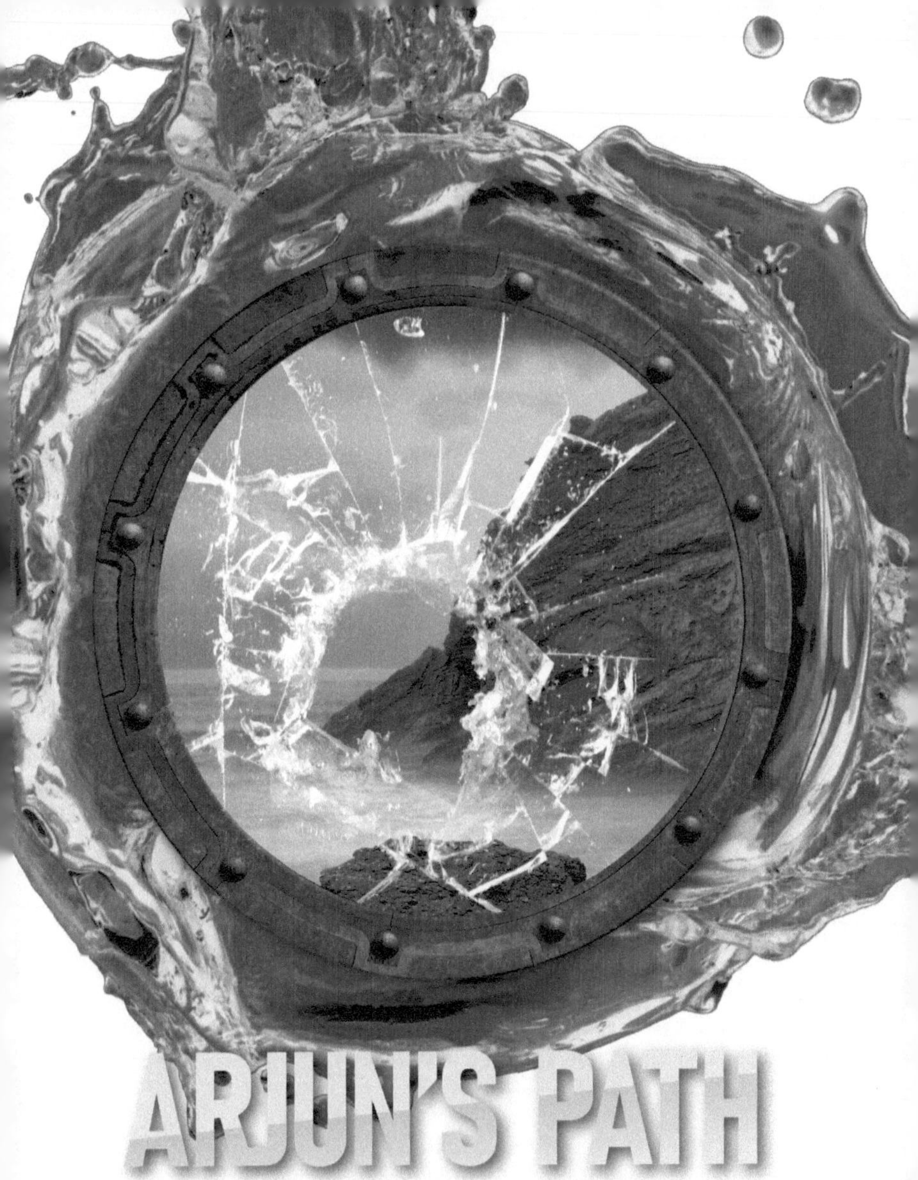

ARJUN'S PATH

RYAN MATTHEWS

All rights reserved. Published by Battlehill Press.
Friendship, Tennessee.

www.battlehillpress.com

Layout and cover design by Ryan Matthews
Images used under license from Shutterstock.com.

Library of Congress Control Number: 2023906267

ISBN 979-8-9865388-5-3 (paperback)
ISBN 979-8-9865388-6-0 (hardcover)
ISBN 979-8-9865388-7-7 (ebook)

First Edition: June 2023

For Bennie, my grandfather, who I will forever associate with ginger ale and chicken nuggets.

CHAPTER 1: HERA

Can't this thing go any faster? I thought as if I could will the vintage aircraft to slice through the desert air with more speed. I stared out the narrow cockpit window, already scratched from the abrasive winds. Far below, the undulating form of a desert borer gyrated through the sand. Despite being larger than the plane, the creature's rippling wake vanished no sooner than it began, leaving little trace of its passage. The rare Arthropod was one of the myriad reasons the local transporters clung to the hard-packed earth rimming the Syrian Desert's expanse.

I'd spent most of the ten-hour flight alternating between co-piloting and nursing our wounded. Their conditions were dire, but I was optimistic about their survival *if* given proper medical treatment in time. For that, this old beast would have to get a move on, but we were straining her ancient engines and exhausted crew as it was.

We'd spent the last thirty hours awake, leaving us running on fumes just like the antique that carried us. I was so proud of my husband, Samson. He'd insisted on manning the stick the entire flight, save for the sporadic moments I could convince him to take a much-needed break. Fatigue chomped away at our already ragged edges as we pushed through the final stretch of our flight to Pod Baghdad.

Given the emergency condition of our passengers, we'd only stopped in Pyramid City long enough to refuel before we were back up in the air once again. I could've spent hours staring up at the forlorn structures that, even half buried in sand, still dominated the landscape. *When we regain control of the surface, I* will *see them in their full glory.* Digging them up would be a massive undertaking, maybe less if we could enslave inverts to help. I harrumphed, pushing the thought far from my mind as quickly as it had entered. I wanted them gone. I'd rather dig out the pyramids with a hand trowel than let a single damn invert linger on our planet.

I lost sight of the worm and stared back at the cluster of gauges, blinking out the blurriness accumulating at the corners of my vision. Other than one of the engines running a little hot, the plane had performed remarkably well on her first flight after a centuries-long hiatus. I'd worked well into each night of the past few years rebuilding, restoring, and rechecking every minute component of the entire airframe. I'd be furious with myself should anything preventable break. *Sekhmet* was a well-oiled machine, but no amount of tinkering would keep her from acting like a five-hundred-year-old woman, even down to a little oil incontinence from her radial piston engines.

I turned back to check on the gravely wounded scattered around the cabin, wishing I could troubleshoot and repair them as easily as a mechanical system. Without the advanced skills and equipment necessary to deal with their egregious injuries, my medical training proved vastly insufficient for the task. After yet another cursory glance across the craft's analog gauges and a light stroke on Sam's thickly bearded cheek, I rose from my cramped seat in the cockpit.

"We're a little over an hour out, babe," he said, rubbing his eyes before tugging up the zipper on his beige gilet. "God, I can't wait to get some shut-eye."

"I know," I said, giving him a squeeze. "I don't care if we're ten minutes out, if you need me to land this behemoth, I will."

He nodded absentmindedly as I removed my headset and walked down the cramped fuselage now packed with bodies and reeking with the stink of death. After their initial harrying during takeoff, the Arthropods—the bane of all life on Earth—had left us alone once we'd reached cruising altitude. Aside from the defunct electromagnetic-field-producing antenna bugs, the flying inverts were thankfully limited to low altitudes, usually not venturing above several hundred feet.

Our plane—humanity's *only* functional aircraft—had been found preserved in a derelict museum in Pyramid City and lugged back to our home in Baghdad. Unlike the technological marvels humans had possessed upon the alien's arrival, the sky-fairing old lady had never possessed the technological upgrades which had proved so damning after the Arthropod Landing. Once the invaders had started spreading, their electro-magnetic-field-producing abilities thrust humanity back to the Industrial Age, making advanced circuitry useless and radio communication impossible. For the last four hundred years, that's how we had lived. I'd never known anything else. Aside from what I'd been taught in my history lessons, it was just the way of things.

I crouched next to one of the passengers seriously suffering from the Shock, watching her chest slowly rise and fall as she slept. I brushed the curly, sand-colored hair out of her face. Her breathing was regular under the influence of the sedative keeping her unconscious. When she'd been dragged aboard, she'd fought us vigorously every step of the way, unaware that we were trying to help. Something unbelievably traumatic must have happened to her. Her psychological wounds would run as deep as the others' physical ones.

I nodded to Remi who was checking the pulse of another's wrist. Krista, I think her name was. We'd managed to obtain a few of their names before they slipped off into unconsciousness. She and the others had been sedated for the long journey back to Baghdad. Heaven knows they needed the rest. The sedation might be the only thing keeping many of them alive. We had field-bandaged Krista's severed hand. She'd need a blood transfusion like Omar, whose flayed back we'd haphazardly stitched back together among the turbulent currents. It just needed to keep him alive until he could get proper care.

Rico sat at his turret, patiently keeping an eye on the skies for anything unexpected, a dark cloud of concern weighing heavily on his face. I was grateful for the fresh air blowing in from the gun ports, without which the sickening odors that wafted around the cabin would be overwhelming. I debated on comforting him but opted not to attempt a conversation over the roar of the engines without a headset. I knocked on the bubble of the turret, checking in on Ahmad, who responded with a thumbs-up and a grin from his inverted position. It still amazed me that he could tolerate being upside-down for so long.

I squatted next to the girl who had the medical kit. Unknowingly, her inventory had helped save her companions' lives. Even after being outfitted for a rescue, the plane's medical supplies hadn't been sufficient to handle the grievous injuries the passengers had sustained. *Ariadne, that was it.* She'd been the one Ekon had mentioned specifically by name. I adjusted the compress across her back, now purple from a substantial impact. I'd stabilized her until her spine could be examined, but there was nothing I could do on board if she was bleeding internally. I wiped the tear rolling down my cheek with the back of my hand. *They're just kids, no younger than Remi or Rico.* They were resilient though, having come this far. To think they were on a mission to end the war—a mission that would be delayed until they'd recovered. Even if Pod Baghdad was as far as they reached, they'd brought down the aerial network! They were already heroes.

My eyes fell on the large bulky pack lying on the decking. Samson had said it was a bomb of some sort. One that could destroy the Hive. I couldn't imagine a life without the inverts, but not for lack of trying. They'd been on Earth for so many generations that no living human knew a life without them. I knelt next to the twins. The slimmer one was badly burned; whether it was from our napalm or an exploding pill bug was unknown. Once airborne, Remi and I had painstakingly removed his jumpsuit, which had melted into his skin, before liberally applying ointment and cooling wraps to the front of his body. His face would carry permanent scars. Like the others, with the ten-hour delay in treatment, infection would now pose the biggest threat.

His brother, the larger of the pair, lingered on the brink of death. I felt his clammy head as he slept restlessly on the uncomfortable fold-out cot. The bone arachnid's sting on his shoulder had been in and out. If not for most of the eight's venom spilling out behind him, he wouldn't have stood a chance. When the stinger was withdrawn, some residual venom must have been released into his body. I'd administered a vial of the antivenin our researchers had developed, but his condition wasn't improving, likely because I'd been so late in giving it.

I realized that I was resting my arm on the body of the dead girl and jerked back suddenly. Remi, sensing my discomfort, grabbed my hand and squeezed it. Her help with the triage had been all that'd kept me sane over the last eight hours. Her ink-black hair, no longer composed, hung all over the place, frazzled by wind and stress. Letting go of me, she returned to the short, blond-bearded citizen. He'd been unconscious when he was brought in. Like Ariadne, he'd sustained massive bruising and was likely bleeding internally, though the fact he was still alive gave me much-needed hope.

Their dark-haired leader, Huck, was the only one of the group with minimal injuries. After being brought on board unconscious, he'd awoken mid-flight during the fuel stop. After another exam, he'd refused all sedatives and painkillers. I'd reluctantly agreed, making him promise to stay out of our way and rest. I glanced at him, doing my best not to let my gaze linger. His eyes were open as he leered at the brown blanket covering his deceased friend's face. Instead of sadness, he was filled with fury, despite having survived the catastrophic, near-death experience. I couldn't blame him. He was surrounded by dead and dying companions, hurtling through the air with strangers on what was quite possibly the first flight in centuries. I paced over to him, stooping to keep from hitting my head on the ribbed ceiling. He craned his head up to meet my eyes.

"Need anything?" I yelled over the ambient noise.

The question felt forced and superficial. He sat there for a lingering moment before sluggishly shaking his head. I almost touched his hand, but thought better of it. I was a stranger to him. *Who am I to console him?*

"Hera," yelled Samson.

With a nod to Huck, I made my way to the cockpit and donned my headset.

"We're beginning our descent," he said, rubbing his eyes. "If they're stable, I could use you up here."

"They're as good as they can be. Barring anything unforeseen, I think they'll make it."

"That's the best news I've heard all day," he said. "I radioed in. Abu said Minister Lafet nearly spewed out her coffee when my voice came over the radio. They're going to have the tug waiting with an emergency convoy at the end of the strip. That'll get them inside quicker."

Thank the universe Minister Okoro had the foresight to have the engineer man the radio. Sometimes his preternatural senses were downright creepy. I watched as Samson's practiced hands pitched the plane downward, ignoring the newly filled airsick bag he'd attempted to hide by tucking it down under his legs. I hoped with experience, his motion sickness would pass.

"Look alive, back there," he said. "A few thousand more feet and things are going to get interesting again."

"Bring it on," said Rico, flatly.

Even through the static, I could tell he lacked his typical enthusiasm. It was hard for any of us to act normal when our passengers were in such poor shape. All the excitement of the initial flight had vanished the moment we'd come across the ambush that had nearly claimed our passengers' lives.

"I'm locked in," said Remi over the click of her belts. "They're as stable as I can make them."

"Thanks, Remi," I said.

My stomach lifted upwards as the ground came closer. I might not get airsick like my husband, but the sensations of flight were still foreign. No matter what I told the others, I would always have concerns over *Sekhmet's* airworthiness. Fatigued materials and manufacturers' defects were aspects of the plane's age that I'd never completely trust. That and sheer chance.

"Flaps down," said Samson, as he banked to line up with the runway now visible in the distance.

To facilitate the initial population of Pod Baghdad, the United Territories of Earth had built the pod adjacent to the old city's airport. When the transporters showed up with the plane, Minister Okoro had optimistically insisted that a runway be excavated and prepared for use. Over the next few years, teams were dispatched on sorties to clear and maintain the field, losing a great many lives in the process. This landing would only be the runway's second use.

I watched as the ground transitioned from the infinite beige of the desert to the luscious green of the jungle as we flew over the river, indicating our arrival. I still couldn't get over how empty the expansive blue sky of the Eurasian Territory looked without the aerial network.

"We've got incoming," yelled Rico.

"I see them," said Samson. "Hera, get the gear down."

"It's down," I said after slapping the lever and seeing the tail dragger's dual indicators glow green.

Ahead, a cloud of hook beetles was hurtling toward us. Resounding gunfire filled the air as the port and starboard guns opened up on the enemy. The extensive vibrations created by the loud projectile weapons always posed the risk of attracting more inverts, but with any luck, we'd be inside the pod before any showed up.

"It wasn't this bad in Pyramid City," said Remi.

"Ekon said it would be rough," yelled Samson, resisting the urge to take evasive action in an effort to get us on the ground quickly. "He said the inverts don't like our passengers."

"Wait! They think?" asked Remi, slinging her turret from side to side to shoot at the hook swarm. "How do you like that, you bastards?!"

"They must have planned the ambush after we—" I began. "Sam!"

The sudden maneuver flung me to the side as Samson severely banked the plane to avoid a hook's kamikaze run. The sound of shattering glass turned my stomach end over end.

"We lost Ahmad!" Rico said, cursing. "The turret's… gone."

"Dammit!" I yelled. "Level out! We're going to crash!"

"Hera, Hemant's convulsing!" yelled Huck from the cabin.

Dear God! I grabbed the controls and helped right the plane just in time for the landing gear to hit the tarmac. The impact jarred me to the bone. More cursing from the gunners.

"I just broke my wrist," yelled Remi.

The plane bounced into the air a few meters before returning to the ground, slightly more smoothly this time. I heard Samson mutter a thankful prayer.

"We clear?" I asked over the headset.

"Maybe," answered Rico. "The ground troops are helping keep the swarm at bay."

"Remi, Rico, help me get the injured off. Sam can manage the plane," I said.

Sam arched an eyebrow as he pulled the plane to a stop. Judging from the complaints of the airframe, the impact and hard landing hadn't done anything good to the aging aircraft. I threw off my buckles, gave Samson a thank-you peck on the top of his head, and ran back to check on Hemant. My heart leapt into my throat when I saw the hole where the turret had been. I suppressed the grief and turned to Hemant, who was still convulsing.

"We're almost there," I said to Huck. We'll get them to our best medics immediately."

"Please," he said, tearing up. "I can't lose him."

No sooner had the plane come to a stop, Remi had cracked the side door. The medics from the convoy greeted us as they jumped aboard, cramming the plane with bodies. They said nothing, but their grimaces relayed their distress. We offloaded the wounded and dead through the narrow opening, almost throwing them onto the stretchers of the carrier. With a final wave at Samson, who was already hooked to the slow-moving tug, the carrier lurched towards the pod's main gate. As the tailgate closed, I could tell the old warplane was no longer in any better shape than our patients.

CHAPTER 2: HUCK

My head was pounding when I woke. I pried my sleep-encrusted eyes open, desperately trying to figure out where on Earth I was. Pushing through the pain, my mind caught up with reality. *Holy hell, I'm on an airplane! What in the…* I realized it wasn't just my head, but everything that hurt. I lay prostrate on the vibrating bunk, trying to part the shroud veiling my memory. I vaguely remembered fighting. It was hopeless, but then… the plane arrived, saving us! *Ariadne.* I shot into a seated position and almost blacked out.

"You're safe," a soft voice said, her smooth accent wrapping around me like a warm blanket. "You must take it easy though."

I leaned against the fuselage and waited for my vision to clear. When it did, I was staring at a beautiful woman with a long, thick braid dangling down over her shoulder. Her angular features and forest-green eyes gave her a rugged beauty.

"I'm Hera," she said, checking my vitals. "How are you feeling?"

I started to turn my head to look for the others, but Hera forcefully held my gaze to check my pupils.

"Huck," I said. "I'm alive. My head is throbbing like I've been hit by a war hammer. I feel like every bone in my body is bruised."

"They may very well be. You were lucky to get out of there alive. Many of your friends are in worse shape than you. Huck, I'm sorry. I don't know how to tell you this, but one of your companions has perished."

My heart did a flop in my chest as I frantically searched the room for Ariadne.

"It was a young Asian girl, Huck. I apologize. I don't know her name."

"No. Not Mei!" I said, shaking my head in disbelief. "She's too strong. She can't be dead. Are you sure?"

"I'm afraid so," she said, squeezing my hand. "She's gone."

Tears welled up in my eyes. I hated the inverts with an intensity that bloomed more every day. They could all go to hell. I'd be delivering that bomb. I'd carve every lost friend's name in its casing too. In my anger, I'd missed half of what Hera had said.

"…be alright once we get help. Do you want anything to help you sleep? Anything for the pain?"

I shook my head. I wanted to feel my anger. My pain. If I could've weaponized it, I would've sent them furiously clawing back to their burrows.

"That's fine, but I must ask you to remain in your bunk and let Remi and me tend to the others. We have medical training."

I nodded. Hera smiled and stepped away to check on them. I identified Ariadne among the unconscious bodies and relaxed when I saw her breathing calmly. *Thank the universe.* I looked at each of my companions in turn, my gaze lingering as long as necessary to find any sign of life. We were in bad shape. I looked at Mei's form, lying under a brown blanket that covered her from head to toe. The side of her arm was just visible from the side.

"Mei," I whispered. "I'm sorry I let you down."

The hours crept by as the plane hurtled through the air. Under different circumstances, I would've been mesmerized by the marvel of engineering, but all I could think about was Mei. Zeke would've flipped out to see an airplane in person, much less fly in one. The Arthropods had stolen so much from humanity. It was never enough to satisfy their unending appetite. They just kept taking, and taking, and taking. I began to rock forwards and back in an attempt to calm myself.

"Hera, I think we need a sedative back here," said the girl I assumed was Remi.

"No!" I said, then more calmly. "I'm okay. Really."

Remi cocked an eyebrow at Hera.

"You sure?" Hera asked.

"Yeah. I'm just pissed. Really, really pissed."

Hera nodded and reluctantly returned to her duties as Remi crouched down next to me. Her dark hair, disheveled from the chaotic rescue and aftermath, provided a stark contrast against her pale skin.

"I know loss," she said, her hardened eyes revealing the truth in her words.

"The trick isn't simply getting over it. Nor is it pretending it'll never happen like Rico over there. Embrace it as inevitable. As long as those bastards are out there, death is always lurking around the corner for each of us. It caught your friend. It'll catch you. Until then, remember her life, and don't forget to live yours."

She left, without looking back. My eyes fell to Liesel, then to Ariadne. Thousands of kilometers still stretched between us and the Australian Territory where the Hive was located. The idea that we'd continue to elude death was fanciful at best. Furthermore, it was also unlikely that any of us would be returning from our mission. *We're all going to die.* It wasn't pessimism. It was a moment of complete clarity. I could die scared, alone, and useless—or I could die valiantly, ensuring a better world for all those who came after me. Mei's death would continue to weigh on my conscience, but I would redirect all my emotions to bringing down the invading alien scum.

As the flight dragged on, adrenaline faded into a distant memory, but a deep-seated hatred of the inverts smoldered in my psyche. When Samson announced our descent, I felt a burst of excitement, knowing my friends could finally get the medical help they so desperately needed. As if on cue, we were bombarded by another wave of hooks just before landing. I examined the hull. The thin metal would do little to slow their razor-edged beaks. *What else could go wrong?* I thought stupidly as Hemant began to shake uncontrollably beside me. *Dammit! Can't we get a freaking break?*

"Hera, Hemant's convulsing!" I yelled.

She and Remi were powerless to help, both occupied with their duties. I did my best to comfort him through the bone-jarring landing. Everything was a blur. Strangers whisked us from the plane and into a personnel carrier outfitted for our injured. I was directed to a seat as the others were strapped down and assessed. After an injection, Hemant's convulsing finally subsided. As the carrier's door lifted into place, I could hear Hera cursing to herself about the aircraft's condition. Just when I thought things might settle, the carrier's gunner started yelling.

"Incoming multipedes!"

"Protect the plane at all costs!" yelled Rico, slicking his dark blond hair back out of his face. "Sam's alone out there!"

The strange sound from above was less like gunfire than one of the well drills back in Pod Horizonte. My eyes widened.

"You like that?" said Rico. "It's a minigun, though there's nothing mini about it. It fires faster than you can think. The problem is it blows through ammo like you wouldn't believe. It uses hydraulics to—"

A violent blow to the side of the carrier interrupted his passionate explanation.

"With all of our fire protecting the plane, they're turning on us," said Hera. "Keep your fire on the plane!"

I cringed inside. The plane was of paramount importance, but so were my friends. Regardless, nothing but silence came from the turret above.

"What the hell are you doing up there?" Rico yelled. "Open fire, dammit!"

Nothing. Rico stood and glared up into the turret, his chiseled face distorted in disgust.

"She's dead," he said. "The blow must've snapped her neck."

He wrenched the gunner's frail body down from the turret and unceremoniously dumped it on the floor. Now wasn't the time for pause. He flung himself up into the narrow seat. As the gun's barrels began to whir, there was a second, thankfully smaller, impact.

"Can this thing go any faster?" yelled Remi.

"I've got it to the firewall," yelled the driver. "We'll be there in another minute or so."

"In another minute or so we'll be dead!" she fired back.

Moments later, the sun's bright light filtering into the carrier through the ventilation slats darkened as we rolled into the entrance and down the incline into the safety of the pod. I let a small sigh escape. We'd reached the second pod. Far from unscathed, we'd done what few others had. I held Ariadne's unconscious hand as the locals cheered about their plane's successful arrival. The boom of the pod's massive main gates sealing shut resounded through the thick panels of the vehicle. Some of the tension dissipated from my shoulders.

There was a shuffle of activity as the door lowered and my friends were rushed off to the nearest medical district. The pod's high-ceilinged staging area bore remarkable similarities to that of Horizonte. The towering walls bore numerous repaired cracks where age had weakened the concrete, making the battle with climbing vines as never-ending as the war above. Even in the heat of the climate, moss found purchase in the dark corners light couldn't quite reach. I climbed out of the carrier, closely following the convoy of gurneys and I was stopped by a familiar face.

"Young Huck," said Ekon, embracing me. "I am sorry about the poor shape of your friends. Ekon assures you, they will be under the care of our best medics. Ekon knows you're in a rush, but please allow Ekon to take a moment of your time. This is Prime Minister Halima Lafet."

"It's a pleasure to meet you, Huck, though I wish it was under different circumstances," said Lafet. "Deputy Prime Minister Okoro, or Ekon as he prefers, has been singing your praises since his arrival. It was he who insisted on the inaugural use of the plane to rescue you and your friends."

"Thank you," was all I could think to say given the turmoil of emotions raging inside of me.

After enduring Zabu's cruelty in Pod Kano, Lafet's kindness was a welcome reprieve from the tumultuous experience I'd had. Beneath her crimson hijab, her warm, freckled face was soothing in a way that made me hesitate to depart from her company.

"Now, we've taken enough of your time, dear. We'll debrief you when you've had time to settle in. I'll do my best to keep this one out of your hair," she said, rolling her eyes as she gestured towards a shrugging Ekon.

She rested a motherly hand on my shoulder, urging me to walk with her.

"I'll escort you to where we took your friends. Don't worry about talking. Trust me, I can fill the air just fine on my own. I wanted to thank you for what your team has done. The journey you've made already rivals some of the most daunting since the pods' inception. The analysts inform me it was you we have to thank for the collapse of the aerial network. You and your friends are welcome to convalesce here as long as you have the need. We'll secure your weapon in the vault. You have my word that it will be released to you when you are ready. I'm sorry you had to deal with that asshole in Kano."

I looked at her in surprise as we crossed the catwalk to the Nucleus.

"Oh, I know Zabu. Prime ministers all communicate through the transporters. He's been a piece of work since before his questionable rise to power," she said, shaking her head. "No one could stop him. Anyone who stood in his way always turned up with a slit throat. As the years went on, he became more and more unhinged. Eventually, he stopped responding to my communications. It was only through the back channels that we kept up with the dismal affairs in Kano. Ah, here we are."

We arrived at a hatch so meticulously cleaned that the rough edges from its casting had been worn smooth by the years of excessive polishing. Marked as the entrance to the administrative medical district, the hatch proved to be a strange juxtaposition amid the other rust-pitted entryways lining the corridor. Lafet was truly giving us her best care.

"Thank you, Minister Lafet, Minister Okoro," I said, nodding in turn.

"You've earned the right to call me Halima. And everyone already calls him Ekon, even himself."

Surprising me yet again, she opened the hatch for me.

"Go on in. They'll be expecting you. You have unrestricted visitation rights. When you're ready to debrief, let one of the medics know and they'll contact me."

I nodded again and stepped into the bright medical facility as the door gently shut behind me. Amid the flurry of activity, medics darted back and forth between their only patients—my friends. Unlike the sand-strewn walk down from the staging area, the clinic was perfectly sterile. The scents floating on the air were a mix of sanitizers, body odor, and stale coffee. Our injuries appeared to be the most interesting cases this facility ever received. From the back room, Hera emerged to greet me.

"They'll want to examine you too," she said. "Just because you're in the best shape doesn't mean you don't need care."

"Can you do it?" I asked, already trusting her.

"I'm going to insist that they do it. I'm trained, but not to the level they are. These are the best docs in the facility. Let them see to you."

I nodded. Hera led me back to a tilted bed and gestured for me to climb on. Part of me hesitated to soil the immaculate sheets with the grime that covered me from head to toe.

"It's going to be fine, I promise," she said, pulling the curtain around me. "Slip off your jumpsuit and relax as best as you can. I'll let them know you're ready."

I removed the light armor first, which popped off with crackles as the crusted blood and hemolymph let go. Then I peeled off the jumpsuit bottoms with some effort, my sore muscles offering little in the way of help. I was struggling to pull the top over my head when the medic came in.

"Here, let me help you with that," he said, gently tugging the foul-smelling fabric upwards. "I'm Medic Erik. Lie back, please."

I lay on the bed in my briefs and let Erik poke and prod me from head to toe. Through the gap he'd left in the curtain, I watched the other medics as they went about their duties. Amid the looks of concern, there was an air of optimism that gave me some relief. When Erik had completed his examination, he rolled his stool to my side.

"You're in better shape than the others, but you need rest. You've got substantial bruising and you're running a slight fever which, accompanied by the redness and swelling, indicates that the wounds on your face and chest are infected. I'll give you some antibiotics and a topical cream, but there's little I can do for the scarring."

"That's okay," I muttered. "I'm alive and conscious."

The man grinned with a smile that didn't reach his eyes, patted me on the leg, and stood to speak with an orderly who promptly walked off. When the orderly returned to my bedside, he made me swallow a few large pills. As he applied an ointment to my wounds, I dozed off into the best rest I'd had in weeks.

CHAPTER 3: KOLYA

"Yes, yes," I muttered, smiling. "That's it!" I scribbled down the new insight into my notebook, its stained pages now barely adhering to the aging binding. There was nothing that could escape my attention. *Nothing!* Sometimes I was flabbergasted how these profound ideas still came to me, even after all these years of near reclusivity. These Arthropods… they were something else. Magnificent. Remarkable, in fact. Fighting them from Pod Munich to Pod Baghdad had left me with little respect for the violent creatures. However, over the decades since, my discoveries had dramatically reversed my opinion, increasing my appreciation for Earth's newest inhabitants.

"Munich," I said, scratching at the decades-old scar that adorned my leg.

Just uttering the words left a sour taste in my mouth. I reached for my cigarette, but it had long since turned to ash, like so many of the others that filled the cast glass tray.

"Full of idiots if you ask me, Sveta. Always poking fun at me, they were. But who first theorized the Queens' existence? Me. Once the full extent of my discoveries is known throughout the remaining pods, everyone alive will appreciate my worth."

I rolled the chair back away from my desk, listening to the groan of the wheels.

"Remind me to oil those later."

I peeled myself from the seat, admiring the piles of paper and refuse that cluttered my desk. *Someone should clean this place.* I rubbed my bleary eyes and made my way to the bed, kicking the detritus littering the floor out of my path. Collapsing onto the greasy mattress, I kicked the boots off of my feet, listening to them clatter to the floor.

"Another day in the books," I said, nodding off.

●●●●●●●●●

Knock. Knock.

"What… What?" I mumbled, forcing myself awake as the banging continued. "I'm coming."

I rolled out of bed, making my way to the door, rubbing the crust from the corners of my eye and wiping it on the chair back. I pushed the button that opened the hatch and saw my pimply, pale-faced lab assistant.

"What is so important that you felt the need to disturb my much-needed rest, Andrei?"

The fiery-haired boy was a moron, but he could be of some value when I needed him to fetch an artifact or text during my frequent visits to the vault, the archive for the historic materials from before the Arthropod Landing.

"They're here!" the boy said.

"Who's here?" I asked, my patience dwindling.

"The ones everyone's talking about. The group that brought down the aerial network!"

"Oh! Why didn't you tell me, Andrei?"

"I…I am, sir."

I shoved him out of my way and into the corridor wall, heading straight for the Nucleus medical district. The prized guests would undoubtedly be there, secluded from the public, as was Lafet's way with her little treasures. She could be such a selfish wench.

"Sir," said Andrei. "Your boots."

I looked down at my unshod feet, my socks embarrassingly stained. I made a mental note to order Andrei to do my laundry and ducked back into my apartment to retrieve my boots. I made my way to the upper levels as fast as my atrophied thighs would allow, barging through the bustling crowds to the exclusive administrative medical district, typically set aside for pod elites. Shoving open the doors, I blew past security, finding their silly protocols as nothing more than a thorn in my ass.

"Sir, you can't go in there," someone said behind my back. "Sir!"

Haven't they realized who I am? Good help must be impossible to find. Forget security. This was a matter of the highest regard. These people had just affected the most significant change in the Arthropod War since it had begun in earnest. *There!* Ahead was the entrance to the ward. I fumbled around in my pocket for my unrestricted keycard, feeling for its distinct punched metal form. When I felt its familiar groves, I jerked it out, dropping it to the floor along with half the contents of my lab coat.

"Dammit," I said as I fell to my knees to collect my things.

Once I had collected everything, I saw my reflection in the pair of black boots that appeared in my view.

"Nasser," I mumbled, standing.

The man always reeked of analgesic and hair oil.

"Kolya," said Nasser, sternly. "I'm surprised you deigned to grace us with your presence. To what do I owe the... *honor?*"

"*Researcher* Kolya," I corrected, "And you know perfectly well why I'm here, Nasser. I need to see them. I must know what they've learned."

"That's impossible. Lafet's orders. It'll have to wait."

Nasser cracked a smile, taking pleasure in turning me away. The arrogant bastard. His shriveled little mind couldn't comprehend how important this was. I pushed him aside, thrusting my way to the panel. I never made it. From behind, someone walloped me with a security baton. I fell to my knees, grasping at my lower back.

"Leave, Kolya. *Now.* I don't care what your clearance level is. They *will* not be disturbed. By you or anyone."

I paused long enough to regain my breath and pulled up my shirt, craning my neck to see where I'd been attacked.

"That's going to leave a bruise!" I said.

"You're lucky that's all, breaking through security like that," said Nasser, brushing his slick hair back into place. "They'd be in their right to put you down."

"They wouldn't dare!"

"You're right. They wouldn't. You have value, but you overstep your bounds, as always. Now, get the hell out of here, or I'll make sure you leave with more than a few bruises."

"You disgust me," I hissed.

"Consider it returning the favor," he said. "Gentlemen, see *Researcher* Kolya out. Perhaps to the showers."

"I can take care of myself!" I said, jerking out of their grasp.

"Then see that you do."

I readjusted my lab coat, which was in shambles after the interaction, and began the walk of shame from the area. My attempts to learn something had been woefully unsuccessful. I glanced back over my shoulder and saw the two guards pacing behind me, whispering. *They think they're quiet, Sveta, but I hear every word. I don't smell, nor am I useless. Those wretches! They wouldn't have a fraction of their knowledge if not for me. Now they're laughing. Insolent, little...* I looked at the security station. There were the new arrivals' belongings, unattended.

I glanced back at my escort, who was too busy mocking me to pay attention, figuring me out of their way. Nestled on top of the items was a notebook, by the look of things, a journal. *Eureka!* With a flick of my well-practiced wrist, I grabbed the book off of the pile and had it nestled within my lab coat before anyone was the wiser.

"I'll see myself out, gentlemen," I said, pleased with the bounty.

"Whatever, old man," said the taller one.

"Your time will come," I muttered as I left the Nucleus.

●●●●●●●●●

With eyes bloodshot, I finally closed Arjun's journal. *Fascinating! Bloody fascinating!* I shuffled to the kitchen and found an old loaf of bread, flicking off the roach that lingered on the slice I'd never finished the day prior. I rotated it, looking it over for mold. When I found none, I dusted the slice off with my hand and took a bite. *Stale. What a shame.*

I'd spent hours pouring over the invaluable research held within the pages of Arjun and Ciro's journal. They'd carefully documented every new finding and species they'd come across in their challenging journey through the Latin and Saharan Territories. I had enough new information to last many years to come.

"True scientists, they were, Sveta! It's such a pity that we lost Arjun's companion, Ciro, to such… unfortuitous circumstances. It's clear from Arjun's writing that the boy really cared for his friend. I would like to know more about these creatures that leave slime trails and their system of digestion. This is the first I've heard of such creatures."

I pulled a new pair of clothes and undergarments from my drawer. I couldn't remember the last time I'd changed, so it was long overdue. If I was going to meet this Arjun, I'd want to be somewhat presentable when I did so.

"I haven't forgotten, Sveta. Get off my case. I'll remember to ask about the spine back, mantis wraiths, and dart beaks as well."

It was hard to keep all the new creatures straight—Nightmare, wraiths, mashi—I rather liked that one. It appeared that for every given name, the Arthropods all possessed a nickname that was easier to bandy about.

"I know I'm old, but I can manage their little lingo."

Sveta would be the death of me. These days, she was the only one I talked to. She knew me better than anyone else. Perhaps even better than I knew myself.

"And no, I don't know how I'm going to get past Nasser. With any luck, he'll be off duty."

I sighed, staring up at the lonely fluorescent bulb that illuminated my crowded space with its dim greenish hue.

"I don't know," I said, shrugging. "Maybe we need to go outside again. There's just too much I can't glean from the texts. I don't care if I'm old. I'll get back into shape quickly enough. I'm sure my *shashka* is around here somewhere. I just need to sharpen it. Maybe swing it a few times in the arena."

I dug through a pile of rolled, dry-rotted maps in the corner and found my old sword. When I tried to draw it from the sheath, the blade felt gummy. Something must have leaked into it over the years. It would need to be oiled. I'd been a formidable warrior in the past. I could be again.

"Don't laugh at me. It's called muscle memory, and it'll return in time."

I wiped the blade with a reasonably clean rag, making sure to discard it afterward in case my blade had any of its residual poison, my particular *modus operandi*. Its shine was still just as vivid as it was decades ago. It felt good to have it in my hand again, as though part of my body had been missing.

"Why, you ask? Because this is our chance to prove ourselves.

You've watched as I've done every bit of this research. The Queens are as real as they are intelligent. No, of course, we can't reason with the drones and soldiers. They're as dumb as their human counterparts. We must reach the Hive! Convince them that there are other humans like us. Smart humans. You'll see. We'll live symbiotically and transition into something new—a daunting force the universe has never known!"

I tucked in my shirt. *A shower!* Ah, it'd have to wait. This was far more important.

"The warhead? No, that won't be a problem. We can't rightly go blowing up our potential allies. Leave their weapon to me. Years from now, Arthropods and Earthlings alike will be singing the praises of Kolya and Arjun—the humans who established peace."

CHAPTER 4: ARIADNE

"**A**riadne? Ariadne, can you hear me?" a friendly voice asked.

I rolled my head to the side and forced my crusty eyes open. The light was blindingly bright. It took several blinks for my vision to clear. When the fog receded, I was staring at soft eyes set within a warm face, her thick braid hanging down over her breast. It was the woman I'd seen boarding the plane just before blacking out.

"There you are," she said, her accent soothing. "The medics told me you were coming around. I wanted you to see a familiar face, though we've yet to be introduced. I'm Hera."

"Ari—," I sputtered, my throat as dry as the desert I'd escaped. Hera passed me a tin cup of water.

"Take your time. You've been through a lot."

I took a deep swallow of the glacially cold water, which almost sent me into a fit of coughing. I took gradual sips, feeling it awaken my appetite.

"My name's Ariadne. Thanks. For the water. And for saving all of us."

"You're welcome. What you are doing… It's very important.

Word of your journey is spreading as fast as the Arthropods. For the first time, people are allowing themselves hope. The Collapse, as people are calling the fall of the antenna bugs, is the first real sign in centuries that they can be beaten. And that was you!"

In her excitement, her accent became even more pronounced. One of the passing medics gave her a stern look. She paused and looked down.

"I'm sorry. I've been getting carried away lately."

I had never thought of myself as any sort of heroine, but even after what we'd been through, I was determined to see the mission through. Giving up now would feel like a slap in the face to all those who'd died to ensure our success. I took another sip of the water, more for distraction than thirst.

"How are you feeling?" she asked, changing the subject.

"Ravenous," I said.

Hera released a melodic laugh.

"We'll get you some food soon. Let's see how you do with fluids for the moment. Aside from hunger, how are you?"

I began wiggling my toes, slowly working the muscles up my body. Everything seemed to be in order until I reached my chest.

"Oh," I moaned audibly when I tried to take a deep breath.

"Gentle," said Hera. "Your ribs have some minor cracking."

The memories flooded my brain like a Latin-Territory deluge. The battle, the plane, the injury, the others—Mei! I rocketed up to the screaming complaints of my ribcage.

"Where are they?! Where are my friends?! Are they okay?"

A medic appeared at my side with a syringe. Hera gave him a glare that would drive an Arthropod away. Placing her hands on my shoulders, she gently lowered me back into bed.

"It's okay. The others are resting. Their injuries are grave, but they will live," she said, pausing. "Do you remember what happened to Mei?"

I nodded slowly, tears already blurring my vision. Hera squeezed my hand. I resisted the urge to jerk from her touch but allowed myself to relax into her comforting embrace.

"How bad are they?

"Are you sure you're ready to hear it?"

I nodded. "I'm trained in medicine. I like to think I have a strong constitution."

"That I noticed. Your kit helped save your friends' lives. You should be proud of that."

I beamed as much as the pain and concern would allow. Hera took a deep breath.

"Hemant is the most serious. He received the bone arachnid antivenin in time, but he's still unconscious. We won't know until he wakes if there was any lasting tissue or brain damage. Thankfully, the sting was in and out."

The beaming feeling vanished as quickly as it had begun. I couldn't image going on without Hemant. I couldn't put into words how badly I wanted him to pull through.

"Do you wish me to continue?"

I nodded, using my hand to hold in the sobs.

"Krista lost her left hand," she said, slowly shaking her head. "Even if we'd found it, reattaching it would've been impossible. We have prosthetics, but to be dead honest, they're useless on the surface. The better bet is to learn to cope single-handed."

I started sobbing. "I can't... I can't hear anymore now. I was wrong. I can't think clinically about my friends. I need to see them."

"No one is expecting you to, Ariadne. You've traveled thousands of kilometers with them. Of course you're close. That doesn't make you less of a medic. It makes you human," said Hera, looking me in the eyes. "As far as seeing them, they're mostly unconscious. Not to mention, you aren't fully dressed."

For the first time, I noticed my lack of clothing. Covered only by a thin medical sheet, I wasn't exactly hiding much. I rolled to the side, feeling the back. The material was held closed only by thin cloth straps. I groaned in frustration.

"I'll tell you what. Why don't I pull the curtain back so you can see them?"

I nodded, sniffling.

Hera rose, elegant in her simplest moves, and drew the curtain back. Like me, my companions were all wearing similar sheets. Each was sleeping calmly under the influence of narcotics as their attendants passed to and from their bedsides. Even battered and bruised, it was good to see them all.

"Thank you, Hera," I said, hearing the ball bearings trundle down their track as she closed the curtain.

"Where's Mei?"

"Her body's been taken to cold storage. It will remain there until you are ready to perform your choice of rites."

"Thank you," I said. "After the last pod we were in, I can't begin to tell you how much I appreciate all of this."

"I might not be in administration, but we hear things. Rumors keep people alive as much as sustenance. Some keep in touch with the residents of Pod Kano. If there's any truth to the stories, it sounds horrible."

"Horrible wouldn't be an adequate word for it."

"Well don't dwell on that now, okay? Like your friends, you need to rest. I'll leave you alone. With any luck, everyone will be up and about soon enough. Maybe then we can move you to more comfortable lodgings."

Hera stood and left, ducking through the privacy curtain. Despite having just woken up, my eyes were already heavy from the conversation. With the medication surging through my system, I had little trouble dozing back off.

·········

I woke to a start. Someone was yelling excitedly in the clinic.

"But I have to speak with him!" a gruff voice yelled.

"You know you can't, Kolya! You can't even be in here," said one of the normally placid medics. "Shall I summon the guards again?"

"You must tell me when the one called Arjun wakes."

"Fine, but get the hell out of here. You're causing a disruption."

The footsteps faded, accompanied by a receding grumbling. Within moments, the curtain was withdrawn along its noisy tracks as the flustered medic came to check on me. His unfamiliar gaunt features were magnified by his obvious lack of sleep.

"What was that all about?"

"I'm sorry, Citizen…" he said, glancing at his chart, "Ariadne. He's just one of our researchers. He's quite knowledgeable, but can also be incomprehensibly difficult. Somehow, it seems the extensive field journaling of your companion has made its way to his hands. He's riled up by its implications. Look at me, forgetting all of my manners. I'm Medic Nasser."

"Wait. Arjun's awake?" I asked, leaning forward as my ribs reminded me of their injury.

Nasser shook his head, slicking back the gray hair that fell out of place.

"Arjun has been looking forward to sharing his discoveries, but if he's not awake, how did Researcher Kolya get his journal?"

The medic choked out an icy laugh.

"Kolya has never been the most scrupulous of scientists. Word's gotten around about you. I'm sure he snuck in and stole it while no one was paying attention. I apologize on behalf of Pod Baghdad if that's the case. Which I have little doubt it is."

"He stole it?! Are you going to report him?"

The medic shook his head. "We stopped reporting him years ago. It did little good. He's insufferable as it is when he's in the best of moods. We wouldn't tolerate his behavior, but as previously stated, he's quite knowledgeable."

I grimaced at the idea of someone digging through Arjun's personal effects. It was an invasion of his and Ciro's privacy since many of their discoveries had been made together. Once I was in better shape, this Kolya had some things to answer for.

"How is Arjun?"

"Arjun has sustained heavy scarring up and down his anterior, especially his face," the medic said with no bedside manner. "Aside from some tugging of the scar tissue, he'll have full use of his appendages, but the burns will permanently discolor his skin's appearance."

"Is anyone awake?" I asked, feeling the sting of tears.

"As a matter of fact, yes. Huck is up and milling around. He can reliably be found underfoot, refusing to leave your sides," he said, checking his notes again. "Liesel is alert, but minimally responsive due to overwhelming trauma. We've sent for a counselor. Mental health care is not my forte."

I resisted the urge to make a sarcastic remark.

"Mathias has awoken, but we are keeping him on bed rest until his cerebral swelling diminishes. Everyone else is still in a medically-induced sleep. Omar will likely be the last to come out, his posterior injuries are so extensive he should be grateful he's alive."

Even with his lack of empathy, Nasser could tell that I had reached my max of information. After some uncomfortable prodding to my ribs and scratching a few notes, he vanished through the thin curtain.

"Medic Nasser?" I asked.

"Yes," he said, sticking his head back in.

"Could you send Huck in next time you see him?"

Nasser nodded. Minutes later, a familiar face appeared and I all but sprang from my bed.

"Stay there," Huck said, gesturing me back.

He came to my side and hugged me tightly. I needed the hug so badly, I forgot about the pain in my ribs and my lack of clothing.

"I'm so glad you're okay," I said sobbing, taking in the healing scar across his cheek.

"I'm glad you are. I've been pacing back and forth for hours. I think the medics are getting a little annoyed with me. I've been drinking enough coffee for you and Hemant both. I feel like I could walk to the Australian Territory right now."

I laughed hard enough that I remembered my pain vividly.

"Well I'm not leaving without the others, so you can forget it," I said, smiling.

"Then it's going to be a while. Medic Erik said it could take up to two months of traction before Omar is ready to move."

"Jesus. How bad is he?"

"They flayed open his back, Ariadne. I heard the medics talking. All of his skin and muscles were there, but it took them days to stitch it back together."

I was aghast.

"How long have we been here?" I asked once I'd collected myself.

"I don't know. A few days maybe?" Huck said. "The lighting in this facility never changes, so I can't keep track of the days. I've been judging time by the medics' shifts. Erik is the head during the day and Nasser at night. Probably because he's a vampire."

I laughed. Even with the twinge in my side, I felt human again.

"He said Liesel and Mathias are awake too."

We heard a clamor, and Mathias yelling, "What does a guy have to do to get a bloody beer around here?!"

"Mathias is, well… Mathias," Huck said, shrugging. "He's ready to leave, but they said he'd be risking further injury. He had some colorful remarks earlier about their prognosis."

"I'm sure he did."

"Liesel," Huck began, rubbing the back of his neck like he did when he didn't know how to proceed, "Liesel's got the Shock pretty bad. I can't get through to her. She just stares at the wall. Anytime someone touches her… she freaks. I'm surprised she hasn't woken the others."

I held his hand, and for the briefest second, saw a flutter of hesitation before he returned the squeeze.

"I'm sorry, Huck."

Huck nodded, his look returning from somewhere far off.

"They said you're doing well. Hera said as soon as you get released, they have some nice apartments set aside for us. I'm hoping they're like the good ones we had in Kano before everything went to hell."

"That would be nice. Wait. You said 'you're hoping.' Why aren't you going to the apartments? You could get a decent night's sleep."

"I have to stay here," he said. "I've been the only one up. I don't want anyone waking up without one of us around. When you and Mathias are more mobile, I think we should stay in shifts as the others awaken."

"That's a good idea," I said. "Did you hear the exchange between Kolya and Nasser?"

"It was hard not to. I think Arjun has his work cut out for him when he wakes up. I hope they hit it off like he and Dieter did."

"I don't know about him, genius or not. Nasser said Kolya stole Arjun's journal."

"That explains a lot of their conversation," said Huck. "Maybe he did it with good intentions."

That was Huck, perpetually the optimist when it came to people. If the man was as smart as Nasser purported him to be, his wisdom might prove critical to our mission. Perhaps he deserved a chance to explain his actions. I heard a soft dong over the speakers for the first time since my arrival.

"What's that?"

"Shift change. Erik should be coming on."

As if in premonition, Erik stuck his head in to check on us.

"Am I interrupting?" he asked.

"No, we were just chatting," I said, as Huck slid his hand from mine.

"Great. I have exciting news for you. After looking over Medic Nasser's findings, we are ready to release you, provided you come in for some periodic physical therapy."

Huck turned to me with a grin.

"You're free!" he said.

We heard Mathias getting into an argument with an orderly and the clatter of a thrown bedpan.

"I do wish you would take that one with you. We may dismiss him early under your care," Erik said, winking at Huck. "I'll start Ariadne's discharge paperwork."

CHAPTER 5: HEMANT

The three months that passed since our arrival at Pod Baghdad had crept by agonizingly slowly, most of it in recovery. It'd taken a month longer than expected for me and Omar to heal enough to even consider leaving. With any luck, by now the inverts thought us dead. Maybe they'd leave us alone for once in their miserable lives. Our unexpected convalescence worked out given the extensive damage the *Sekhmet* had sustained on her landing. Halima, the prime minister, had done everything in her power to make our stay as comfortable as possible. It proved to be a far different experience than either underground city we'd come from. I still felt heart palpitations from the close encounter with the eight's venom, but Medic Erik assured me that though annoying, it was a benign symptom that would likely bother me for the rest of my life.

"Damn, I hate inverts," I mumbled.

"Darn tootin' right," said Mathias from my side.

It was good to see him with his color back. Since Mei's cremation, he'd sunk even further into depression, but lately, there was a bit more pep in his step. With full bellies, we headed back to the relatively luxurious apartments that Halima and Ekon had provided. When we arrived, we walked into the large circular common room to join our friends. The space was well kept, but like everything else, its degradation was obvious. Even with Halima doing her best to run a far more civilized and fair society, she couldn't fight entropy. Like every other pod in the world, Pod Baghdad was falling apart—a silent motivation to press on to the Hive. We'd caught the others in a fit of laughter as my twin brother Arjun stared on blankly, not understanding what everyone had found so funny.

"What did Kolya say this time, Arjun?" I asked, surreptitiously checking how his facial burns were healing.

"He thinks it's possible to ride the desert borers," he said, straight-faced. "It's an interesting hypothesis and he has some theories about how to do so. Apparently, they travel quite fast."

"I think someone's listened to the Tales of Arrakis one too many times," Omar choked out through a laugh.

When I stopped guffawing, I asked, "Arjun, granted, I have never seen one, but what would make riding a burrowing invert that could gulp a cargo hauler seem like a good idea?"

"Kolya thinks that we could restrict its movements to the surface. There are transporter stories about a man who rides them. He says if—"

"Since when have the transporters' tales been a reliable source of information?" asked Mathias. "They're a superstitious lot, prone to exaggerate the most mundane of details."

"Arjun," I said. "Remind me again how long it's been since Kolya's been outside of the pod."

"I don't see how that's relevant."

"Arjun, how long?" asked Mathias.

"Thirty-two years."

"*Mmmhmm.* And do you really want to trust a guy who lives like a bloody duner himself?" I asked. "You told me how he has to worm through his own apartment between stacks of archives and rotting food. The guy probably has ninety percent of the city's paper pulp in his bedroom."

"He just knows that one aircraft isn't sustainable in the long term."

"What's sustainable is getting these ingrates off of *our* planet so that we can travel it however we damn well please," said Omar, leaning back on the futon with Krista snuggled up in his lap.

Her handless arm now bore a different mark. She and Omar had been marked with the emblem for the Protected. A rare mark I hadn't even known existed until Ekon proposed its use. It placed a sword over the theta tattoo marking those previously labeled as banished as having done an act of significant merit to expunge their sentence.

"Here, here," said Mathias, standing. "Let's get rid of the bastards. Who's ready to go?"

No one moved.

"Are you freaking kidding me? You've gotten too complacent among your soft bed linens and tasty square meals," he said, rolling his eyes. "We have a world to save! Or have you forgotten? And this wasn't even my mission!"

"He's right," said Huck, grabbing Liesel's hand and smiling at her. "We're ready—in mind and body. Liesel has grown quite adept with the pole sword in our downtime."

"Ugh," said Remi, falling back dramatically on the cushions.

Since Ariadne's waking, she and Remi had become fast friends. It was good to see a semblance of normal life returning. They did little self-care things for each other, as simple as back rubs or hair braiding, that there was no time for on the surface. The downtime in the pod was good for all of us. In addition to the psychological help that Liesel had received, dating Huck had also been good for her well-being. They made a cute couple, though secretly, I thought he was a better fit for Ariadne. Not that it was my place to tell him that.

"Look," said Huck. "The plane's ready, so we don't have to saddle up some duners like Kolya wants."

"Darn," said Mathias. "Really had my hopes set on that."

"If everyone's in agreement," continued Huck, "we'll talk to Halima and Ekon in the morning and start the mission prep."

Despite the choral groan, I knew no one was giving up.

"I'm in," I said standing. "There's no way in hell I've come this far just to stop now. I promised myself I'd shove Dieter's bomb up their asses and I plan to do just that."

"You know I'm in," Mathias said, jumping back up. "I've been twiddling my thumbs waiting for you pansies to sack up. I owe them all a special death for taking my girlfriend."

I grinned. Mei was never Mathias' girlfriend, but no one cared enough to correct him. He had immensely cared for her before she died—a feeling she never had time to reciprocate. *Who's to say what wouldn't have been?*

"Someone has to take care of you slobs and your boo-boos," said Ariadne, laughing. "I'm ready as I'll ever be."

"You know where she goes, I go," said Krista, thrusting herself up with her good arm.

Omar stood resolutely and gave a mock salute. He'd been spending hours a day divided between physical therapy and weapon training to regain his muscular function and adapt to his altered range of motion. The guy had some serious grit. During Omar's recovery, we received word of the former prime minister of Pod Horizonte's death. Despite the guy having been a real asshole, Davi Carvalho had been Omar's father. His response had simply been a scoff, though from time to time, he looked more distant than usual. If Carvalho's death had affected him, I doubted that he'd ever admit it.

Liesel stood slowly, rubbing her hands. "I think I'm ready. I haven't had anywhere near the amount of training you guys have had, but I know you'll watch my back. Nothing will be more effective preparation than traveling on the surface."

"We'll take care of you," said Huck. "I promise."

All the eyes in the room panned to Arjun's now two-tone face. He looked different with a wide swath of unpigmented skin diagonally across his face, but underneath, he was the exact same awkward genius.

"What?" he asked. "Did you think I wouldn't be joining you?"

I laughed, tussling his hair.

"You think Sam and Hera are ready?" I asked Remi. "And Rico?"

"You didn't ask me if I was ready," she said as I noticed for the first time she no longer wore her arm cast. "I am, by the way. As far as the others, Rico isn't about to sit out of a fight. He's been itching to be back in the thick of it. Hera and Sam know how important this mission is. They'll be ready when you are. I can't promise Sam won't barf the whole way to Bhopal though."

I laughed, shaking my head. I still couldn't get over the fact that one of the only two known pilots in the world got motion sickness.

"Sounds like it's settled," said Huck. "Ariadne, Hemant, and I will go talk to the ministers in the morning and plan our departure."

"Live it up while you can," said Omar stretching.

Huck and Liesel left for their nightly stroll. With a slap on Krista's rump, Omar carried her off, giggling, to his and Mathias' apartment.

"Guess that means I'm bunking with you guys tonight," said Mathias, dealing out a round of poker for Arjun and me.

Arjun always kicked our asses, but we enjoyed bluffing him. After several hours of losing, the game lost its flare and the three of us left Remi and Ariadne alone in the common room for some much-needed shut-eye.

•••••••••

After a hearty breakfast prepared by Mathias, I left the cozy apartment that had begun to feel like home. It was nice to only be worried about my recovery and enjoying a privileged life, though the night's sleep had been restless knowing what the coming day held. Today would mark the beginning of the end of our time in Pod Baghdad. We would willingly venture back into hostile enemy territory—Earth's surface. With a sigh, I drew the hatch closed, stepping out into the hallway a few minutes before I was supposed to meet up with Huck and Ariadne. As soon as I turned, I collided with Remi, emerging from Ariadne's room. Judging by the look on her face, I'd caught her by surprise. She regained her composure, and dashed down the corridor.

"Not sure what that was about," I muttered.

I let my feet guide me to the railing around the central shaft and rested against it, admiring the hum of activity that never ceased in a city this size. My thoughts drifted to Pod Bogotá and how many lives had been lost in one deadly moment. It was still strange to me that the inverts hadn't bombed another pod. *If they can destroy us so easily, why don't they?* I was briefly tempted to ask Kolya, but I preferred avoiding the man. His hygiene was deplorable, his fingers sticky, and he was more self-inflated than Yanus. Sometimes I swore I could hear him in a conversation with himself. At least Arjun understood him.

Arjun. God, I wanted nothing more than to beg him to stay here. He could even check in with me periodically over the radio. With the aerials all but extinct, radio communication was reemerging, though still in its infancy. So many of the external vehicles weren't equipped with transceivers, nor were there enough to go around. On hearing of our success, Pod Wuhan reconfigured all of its technological production to stamp out communication devices to be dispersed all over the world. Of course, with the waning quality of materials, they were begging other pods for fresh metal, rubber, and plastic. All of which had to be transported over the ground, which was a dangerous, and often unsuccessful, endeavor.

Arjun had already made it clear he was on this mission for the duration. Our extended stay actually encouraged his feelings. Before Memo had tasked us with his mission, Arjun's plan after Release Day had been to stay in Baghdad and study with the world's foremost invert experts. Once Arjun and the researchers met, it was them who clamored to study with him. The three months in the pod had provided him with ample time to share his work with Kolya and the other scientists. Though I didn't like how Kolya was rubbing off on my brother, their combined intellect was a force to be reckoned with. However, in addition to being a genius, the man held some controversial opinions.

"Boo!" shouted Mathias.

I turned to him, unshaken as ever, the grit making it impossible to sneak up on anyone.

"Well you're no fun," he said. "Soaking in the sights?"

Despite the administration's efforts to maintain the pod, the sand from the surrounding desert was ubiquitous. Its lack of accumulation illustrated how two pods that had been dealt similar hands by fate managed their living conditions. Pod Kano under Zabu's rule had turned its back on the health of the city. By comparison, Baghdad embraced its population's well-being, using it to add even more meaning to the existence of its residents. Halima and Ekon made a great team, making everyone feel as though they were each an integral piece in the war against the inverts. "There are no small jobs," she would always say.

"Yeah. I'm trying to absorb all the peace I can before heading back up there," I said, pointing to the large portholes only a few levels above, watching the motes of dust drift through the natural morning light.

"I don't blame you. All this tranquility will vanish when the first invert rounds the corner."

"Don't remind me."

Mathias chuckled and slapped me on the back.

"Hey, we've survived this long, and now they're blind," he said, tapping his temple. "I'm sure they know we're in here, so we can probably expect an ambush, but we'll shake them off like we always do."

"The thought of an ambush isn't exactly comforting."

"Nah. Just means we know to come out swinging. The way I figure, we finally have more communication than they do. We have the upper hand. They'll be just as deadly, but disorganized. Hell, in a few weeks, we'll be sitting on the smoldering crater of the Hive, drinking hooch out of their bloody skulls."

I laughed, my voice booming through the shaft. "If it's okay with you, I'll take my hooch from a cup and as far from the radioactive fallout as I can get."

"Fair point," Mathias said, smiling. "I'm going to round up some supplies while you guys do the politicking."

"Later, man," I said, pushing myself up from the railing as Huck and Ariadne approached.

"Morning," said Huck.

"Morning," I said. "You guys get any more sleep than I did?

Each shook their heads.

"Okay, then. This should be fun," I said, clapping my hands together awkwardly. "You guys ready to go see the ministers?"

Two nods later, we were walking to the Nucleus elevator in silence. I wasn't used to leading the conversation, so it was pretty quiet. When we neared Halima's office, an aide reached us.

"Good morning," he snapped. "The prime minister would like to see you on the bridge. If you'll follow me."

"The bridge," I muttered to Huck and Ariadne. "This is new."

The bridge was the command center of each pod. It was a secure location that very few individuals were privy to. Located on the topmost floor of the Nucleus, it was the only portion of the pod that extended above the city's subtly conical surface. If the rumors were to be believed, the bridge had a 360-degree view of the surface and tube monitors to keep up with the inner workings of the 100-level city. Getting to see the bridge wasn't just a privilege—it was an honor.

The aide led the three of us through scrutinizing security, up a ramp, and through large armored doors into a room buzzing with activity. The circular room was mesmerizing, its built-in lights paling to the natural light streaming in. A light haze of pipe smoke drifted up from the numerous engineers' stations as they devotedly monitored the pod's myriad systems from their antiquated consoles. Each panel was covered with toggle switches, large knobs, warm-hued lights, and tube monitors displaying their staticky grayscale feed. The consoles' sides were scuffed and dented from decades of use and never-ending repairs.

I shook my head, thinking back to something Arjun had said. Supposedly, before the inverts' arrival, humans had more technology in their pocket than existed on the entire bridge. I still found that hard to believe, but my brother assured me it was the truth. Shortly after the Arthropod Landing, humanity's advanced technology had become worthless under the inverts' planet-wide electromagnetic shroud. The First Builders had been forced to revert to long-obsolete technology when they'd designed the pod. Everything had been constructed with the simplest hard-wired technology. Now, even with the field gone, it would be decades before humanity caught up with its past.

"Our young trio," said the deputy prime minister. "Ekon has awaited your arrival. Welcome to Pod Baghdad's bridge. This is a new occurrence for you three, yes?"

We nodded.

"Ekon thought it might be. You and your companions are heroes and deserve to be treated as such."

I blushed under the praise. I was actually more uncomfortable with the ceremonious treatment than being left to my own devices. Ekon led us to where Halima was looking out from one of the scratched, squat windows that peered over the grimy surface of the four-century-old pod. She turned on our approach.

"Good morning," she said, smiling. "How do you feel about flying to the Hive?"

CHAPTER 6: SAMSON

The hot coffee tasted flavorless in my mouth, just as the idea of flying did. I'd spent my life dreaming of being a pilot, soaring above the clouds as free as any human could be. My daydreams, however, had never included vomit. I loved everything related to flight, but here I was, so anxious that I was sick to my stomach before my feet left the ground. I could almost hear my father laughing at the irony. He'd always been so critical of my decision, instead wanting me to take over the family restaurant. In a way, I was thankful he wasn't still around to see my failing or his small establishment's closure. I felt loving arms encircle me from behind and soft lips kiss the back of my neck. I caught the faint whiff of grease and citrus that always hinted at my wife's presence.

"You'll be fine, Sam," said Hera, nestling her cheek against my back. "I've built you a good plane. I personally safety-wired every nut and bolt on the airframe. Not to mention, Remi and Rico are the best aerial gunners around."

"They're the *only* aerial gunners around," I added, still feeling the loss of Ahmad.

Hera forced a laugh. "True, but we've put them through the wringer. That flight into the Saharan Territory got pretty darn hairy."

"Yeah, but we're talking about flying three times further than that with half the armaments. At a minimum, we're looking at a dozen fuel stops to the Hive. That's not even considering the return trip. We don't even have the squirt gun anymore. I'm not great at math, but even I know those odds suck."

"We can do this, *mon nounours*, with or without napalm," she said, squeezing tighter. "You'll be pleased to know that I spoke to Greenskeeper Cleo. She's made you an herbal supplement that she claims will reduce your nausea."

"Hopefully it doesn't taste as bad as her last tincture. I'd almost rather puke," I said, chuckling as I turned to face her.

Hera gave me a look of disapproval.

"Thank you," I said. "I don't know what I'd do without you."

"I do. You'd be the disgruntled manager of a sweltering kitchen, trying to fulfill your father's legacy instead of your own. You belong in the skies, Sam. *This* is your legacy. You've earned your right to fly this bird. You're going to do it so well, even he would be proud. But just so you know, you're my hero before you ever take off."

"I love you," I said.

"I love you too," she replied.

"It's just that there are so many unknowns. Even without the Arthropods watching our every move, not finding a clear spot to land at the pump houses could be what does us in."

"Sam," she said, taking me by the shoulders. "*Sekhmet* was a warplane. She can land almost anywhere that you have the confidence to do so. There is a plethora of pump houses between here and the Hive. She can go so much further on her tank than any ground-based vehicle. If we can't land at one pump house, we'll find another."

"I know the facts, but this is the most daunting thing I've ever done in my life," I said, tearing up. "Even more than asking you out the first time."

"Ugh. You're hopeless," she said, playfully shoving me away and making a show of rolling her eyes. "You'll be great. Now, suck it up, and let's go see what Halima has up her billowy sleeves this time."

I laughed, blinking away the tears.

"Anywhere with you, *mon amour.*"

•••••••••

I'd been on the bridge only twice in my life. The first time was when I'd been chosen for pilot training. The second was when I had been dispatched on the Saharan rescue—my first mission. The significance of striding onto the bridge for a third time wasn't lost on me. I refused to let any of the morning's doubt show on my face, but Hera held my hand, giving me the extra boost I needed. As we walked toward the narrow viewport where the others gathered, Halima and Ekon were deeply engaged in a conversation with Huck, Ariadne, and Hemant. A rogue beam of sunlight bathed the pod's newest arrivals in a heroic glow.

"Samson, Hera," said Halima, kissing each of us on the cheeks. "Thank you for joining us. Please, have a seat."

We gathered and sat around a large conference table in the middle of the bridge. Around us, the chatter dropped noticeably as the engineers listened on intently, hoping to catch every detail of the likely historic moment. Halima made no effort to redirect their attention. If anything, letting hope bloom among the pods was probably one of the best outcomes of Memo's mission to date. It had been a long time since humanity had a reason to be optimistic.

"Welcome everyone—" Halima began before Ekon's knuckle cracking interrupted her.

She silenced him with a glare. He flashed an apologetic grin across his dark, skin-tagged face.

"You know why you're here. As promised, Ekon and I will do everything in our power to make sure that Prime Minister Leal's mission is a success."

Guilherme Leal, or Memo as Huck called him, was the new leader of Pod Horizonte, having replaced its previous minister shortly after Huck's Release Day. The mission to destroy the Hive with a nuclear weapon had been a cooperative effort between him and a technician named Dieter from the infamous Pod Kano, who we assumed dead.

My eyes passed over the young faces positioned around the table, beholding them together for the first time since I'd flown their battered bodies in. Under Huck's dark straight hair was a handsome face, scarred by more violence than anyone his age should've seen. His hazel eyes glowed with hidden strength. Ariadne carried the same silent fortitude, despite the fingers missing on her dominant hand. She was a pretty young woman, her green eyes and subtly-curly hair would attract others in droves if her intensity didn't run them off. Hemant's stocky frame was a stark contrast against his companions. His short-cropped hair and clean-shaven face gave him a militaristic vibe. In addition to brimming with integrity, his rich brown face held something else. Concern maybe. It dawned on me that between these three flowed a special energy, resounding with resilience and bravery. A wave of peace washed over me. In that brief moment, I knew that they would turn the tide of the war and that I would be the one who carried them into battle.

"You all know Samson and Hera, of course," said Halima. "They are here because—

"I want to fly you to the Australian Territory!" I said, jumping up and spooking a few of the eavesdropping engineers. "To the Hive, I mean."

Ekon cackled to himself as Huck and his friends cheered, Halima and Hera each arched an eyebrow at me.

"Oh, Sorry," I said, awkwardly retaking my seat.

"Your enthusiasm is understandable, Samson. I'm feeling a bit of it myself. It would seem to be contagious," said Halima, letting out a deep chuckle, revealing the origin of the deep laugh lines in her freckled cheeks. "Each of you has already journeyed further than most. When compared to a rolling convoy, I can only imagine how much faster and safer air transport must seem. It's important to remind you the level of danger will not be any less. Perhaps even greater. Their observation network is down, but the Arthropods have never ceased to adapt. Their goal of planetary domination is no different because of one amputated limb. The Queens still consider you a threat and will operate accordingly. We've discussed your departure and believe an ambush is undeniable.

"This brings me to the much harder point to make. As you three are aware, Release Day is an important tradition that has been tainted by many of the pods. It serves a purpose in the war, giving our youth a chance to go where they are needed most. It transforms abstraction into reality, bringing their training full circle. Unlike Kano or Horizonte, many survive our release and go on to become successful citizens at other pods. Release Day is an important duty and part of our residents' service to humanity. And yes, crudely put, it maintains population levels.

"You have received the best treatment our pod has to offer during your stay, but don't forget that we are dying just as surely as the other pods. Our resources are dwindling no less than Horizonte's or Kano's. Humanity is on the verge of collapse if your mission proves unsuccessful.

"It is with that understanding, I would like to make some additional requests. Ekon and I would like to bump up our next Release Day to the day of your departure. Given the almost certain ambush, I'd like to open the gates and flood the field with vehicles and candidates alike. This would distract any attackers and give Samson the much-needed opportunity to get you safely airborne."

A look of shock passed across the three faces opposite me. Halima never took death lightly. If this was her decision, she would have labored over it for the duration of our guests' recovery. With everything we had thundering out of the pod, maybe the inverts would leave the plane alone long enough for takeoff.

"Ekon senses your uncertainty, young ones," said the deputy prime minister, fingering one of his dreadlocks. "This is what the candidates have trained for. They are willing to lay down their lives to ensure the survival of the human race. Right now, you are the greatest chance we hold. Perhaps it would be best if you told them that, *hmm?*"

"I'm not sure what you are asking," said Huck, still bewildered.

"Perhaps we will gather the upcoming cohorts?" said Ekon. "You could address them yourself. It will be a moment they will remember forever."

I heard Huck swallow from across the table.

"She's right," said Ariadne. "What we saw in Horizonte was a needless slaughter. This is purposeful. We are at war, so the loss of life is inevitable. We just have to make it count."

"I agree," Hemant said, snapping out of his concentrated gaze at the marred table's surface. "Before our Release Day, all I wanted to do was punch an invert in the face. We'll be giving these candidates a chance to do exactly that. It *will* be a slaughter. Of that, there's no doubt in my mind. The difference is they will die honorably on the battlefield instead of from something stupid like malnutrition or entertainment. We *have* to take back the planet. As reluctant as I am to be considered a hero, right now, we're the best choice."

Hemant stood. "I'll do whatever it takes," he said, driving his finger into the table. "Not for humanity, not for me, but for my brother. So he can enjoy the life humans were meant to live on the surface."

"I'll talk to them," said Huck, standing. "At least I can say I've stood in their boots."

Ariadne stood, followed not only by me but by every person in the room. I swirled to take in the moment as the engineers held out their hands in salute.

"For All," I said, adding my hand in salute.

"For All," the room boomed.

CHAPTER 7: HUCK

My mind spun as I shuffled away from the conference table. *No matter what we do or how far we go, it's like we can't ever escape Release Day.* I shook my head in disbelief. *At least this time it has a purpose.* It would take time to organize our departure and adjust the new time scale for the pod's release. I shivered as familiar icy chills dripped down my vertebrae. Even with Lafet's honorable intentions, the event would never sit comfortably with me. All these innocent teens… giving their lives for us. *Who are we to deserve them?* The daze continued well until I reached the bridge's meager break area. I grabbed a reusable tin cup and filled it with over-heated coffee from the carafe.

"What the hell are we doing, man?" I asked Hemant as he joined me with a cup of his own.

"Our duty, Huck," he said, his face wrenching in displeasure at the burnt coffee's taste. "We have a lot of people counting on us."

I stared at the twinkling red light on the front of the pot's hot plate, with each pulse, I thought about another life that would blink out with our desperate flight from the city.

"How am I going to talk to candidates knowing they are marching to their deaths?"

"Truthfully. You're going to tell them what they are fighting for, what's at stake, and you're going to be honest with them. You're not Carvalho, sending them into an orchestrated slaughter."

Ariadne parted with Hera and joined us, excited by the prospect of the mediocre coffee. As she stepped into the depressingly-beige room, Hemant nodded in greeting before offering her a cup of what passed on the bridge for coffee.

"Hera's going to help me assemble an expanded medical kit for the trip," she said quickly, sitting on a small metal table jutting out from the wall. "Since we're flying, I'm not limited to what I can carry on my back. We'll try to include something for every scenario. I'm also going to meet with Liesel's counselor and glean everything I can to help with symptoms of the Shock, for her or anyone else. Hera said the plane's ready, as is the convoy that aided us when we landed."

"God. It's crazy to think we can travel all the way to the Hive sitting," said Hemant. "I doubt it'll be easy, what with the fuel stops and all, but it'll be a heck of a lot easier than hitchhiking with another batch of transporters. I wouldn't mind another Mueller, but I sure as hell don't want another Yanus."

"That's the truth," added Ariadne, face reddening at the thought of the vile transporter who'd plagued us halfway across the last continent. After a pause, she continued, "Hera said depending on the conditions, we could be in the Australian Territory within a week of our departure."

"Jesus," I said. "It took us months to get this far. Too bad we couldn't have had a plane from the get-go."

"Well, as far as I know, we have the only one," said Ariadne.

"And to think people used to travel on these things every day," Hemant said, shaking his head. "Life must have been something different back then. Computers, planes—"

"Safety," I added.

Hemant smirked. "Well I've got a fair amount to do," he said, dumping his cup into the nearby sink. "None of which includes finishing this crappy coffee. I'll share the news with Arjun, then I think I'm due for some sparring with Omar."

"I guess I need to write a speech," I said.

●●●●●●●●●

In an effort to procrastinate the speech-writing, I made my way down to the arena where Liesel was training. She disliked me watching her, but I loved clinging to the shadows to see how rapidly she was progressing. Given the fact most of her life had been spent wielding nothing but garden implements, her newfound skills with weaponry were that much more impressive. Down in the sand, she was practicing with her regular trainer, a hard-ass named Gempo. Several of us had offered to train Liesel, but she was adamant about training with a stranger, unrestricted by the judgment of her friends.

To burn off anxious energy, I had taken the stairs down into the mid-levels of the pod where her training was conducted. They were poorly lit, their once crisp edges now crumbling, but they were a great way to burn off steam. On a landing between flights, I caught a glimpse of Mathias with another resident. The stranger's cloak matched the pod's rust-red walls, giving his head the appearance of floating. Like so many others, the stranger was a full head and shoulders taller than my sly, blond-bearded friend. Unconcerned with how he spent his personal time, I dismissed the interaction. Just before I turned, something passed between their hands, glimmering. *Whatever it is, I'm sure it's fine. Mathias wouldn't do anything without good reason.* I peeled my eyes away from the encounter and scampered down the steps before I was noticed. On the surface, trust was what kept us alive.

Word of our departure and bumped-up Release Day had

spread faster than an outbreak of mouth spots. Passing candidates who recognized me offered salutes, cheers, or even patted me on the back. I was cordial but uncomfortable with the attention. Each smiling face was a battered, bleeding corpse, waiting to be scavenged by the inverts. Aside from their distaste for plants, the inverts weren't picky about their food. They would kill and devour any human within reach, even cannibalizing their own, leaving the battlefield with only equipment, stains, and haunting memories. From the plane's vantage of relative safety, I would be torn between observing their sacrifice and protecting my mind. Watching scores of innocent people die at the appendages of the inverts would do no favors for our morale, which was equally as important as our physique. With a nod, I graciously pulled away from the well-wishers, sullenly making my way to the arena.

Before I reached the training area, I could already hear Gempo's condescending taunts echoing well out into the nearby districts. Deep in thought, I nearly walked right to the balcony's edge over the sandy arena. I slunk back to a crisscrossed steel pillar and watched closely. Reminiscent of my own final exam in Pod Horizonte, in the pit was a mechanical abomination flailing around. The "Arthropod" hung from a series of cables, its movements orchestrated by a series of small electric motors. Her trainer yelled his normal insults, but something tonight felt different. Liesel was sweating profusely, not entirely from exertion. Her actions were fearful and haphazard. Her weak slashes and pitiful stabs with the long-handled blade fell fruitlessly on the canvas-covered frame. Gempo wasn't tolerating any of it.

"Stop! Stop!" he yelled up to the young candidate pulling the control levers. "*Sailan,* Liesel. What the hell is going on? You are a ship lost at sea. Your stance, awful! Your blows, laughable! Your concentration, absent! If this is how you perform under stress, you won't have to worry about the Shock again."

Tears started rolling down Liesel's cheeks. It took everything in me not to risk the long jump down and give Gempo a piece of my mind. She collapsed into the sand in a pile.

"I can't do this! It was fine before… before…!" she said, on the verge of hyperventilation. "I'm going to have to use this thing… on *real* creatures." She threw the pole sword aside. "Do you know what happened the last time I was around one?"

"No, but I have a feeling you are going to tell me," Gempo said, rolling his eyes.

"I froze! I would've been eaten alive if the plane crew hadn't intervened. I'm scared to death that none of this will matter if I freeze again."

"That's because it won't," said the trainer calmly. "You aren't ready. My students have trained their entire lives. I've crammed your training into three measly months. Three months! You've been a quick study, but you are still a disaster with your *guandao*. But can you survive? Yes."

Liesel's head sprung up at the unexpected response. I took a step forward myself.

"You have an anger in you. An anger directed at yourself. Channel that anger, but redirect it at them. You are only as weak as you think you are!" he said, pushing on her forehead with a thin, sinewy finger. "Again!" He yelled at the lever master, then turned to Liesel. "Get out of the sand and attack!"

With newfound intensity, Liesel bounded up and recommenced her routine. Initially, her movements were rough, but she found momentum and focus. I watched, mouth agape, as she laid waste to her rusty enemy without taking so much as a scratch from the iron beast. She'd chosen her weapon for its length, the bladed pole conveniently keeping enemies out of striking distance. As she progressed through the series of moves, her artistry with the weapon emerged. When relaxed, her deadly grace with the broad blade filled me with much-needed confidence. She would've despised me forever for it, but if I'd felt her to be a liability, I would've had no choice but to leave her behind in Baghdad. I walked away breathing easier knowing that wasn't a decision I had to make.

"Better. Better," Gempo said, voice trailing off. "Again! This time in half-light."

•••••••••

On the way back to the apartments, I picked up some spiced wedges from the local food district. With all the anxiety from the upcoming speech and imminent exit, I could barely choke them down and ultimately offered them to a forlorn beggar on the way up. When I arrived at our rooms, I couldn't help but give Mathias the side-eye. Nothing seemed out of place, but I couldn't set my suspicion completely aside. The strange man had been an unusual addition to our team, escaping with Hemant from the drug-enforced servitude of Zabu's Muskrats where they'd hit it off. He earned my trust and proven his worth time and again, but that didn't make it any easier to completely dismiss what I'd seen.

With reluctance, I holed myself up in my bedroom for several hours until I had completed my woefully inadequate speech. When I finally emerged late that afternoon, my eyes were heavy and my body was exhausted from the frustration. I plopped down on the common room's bench seat and laid back, letting my body sink into the soft curves of its unevenly-deteriorating foam. The conversations around me ebbed and flowed, lulling me into a doze. It was there I remained until Ekon came to call. When I sat up, Liesel was curled up next to me, her beautiful golden curls draped across my shoulder. She smelled faintly floral, her hair still damp from a recent shower.

"Young ones!" he said. "How do we find yourselves on this wonderful evening?"

That was Ekon, always the optimist. I sat up, attempting to rub the weariness from my eyes.

"Good, all things considered," answered Omar. "Just ticking off the boxes."

"Please let Ekon know if anything is needed for your departure. We will give you every chance at success, but do not worry. The universe will take care of its own!"

"How do we know that the universe's own isn't the Arthropods?" asked Krista.

"Ekon has pondered this interesting thought much, wise Krista. They are living creatures just as we are. Ekon believes it is a matter of selfishness. They are not happy with what the universe has provided them, so they take what isn't theirs. The universe has bestowed on us this beautiful planet for our use. I find it hard to believe she would simply take it away. Ekon also cannot abide cannibalism among intelligent species."

"I never thought about it like that," said Hemant. "I don't guess I ever thought there was anything other than them watching my back. True or not, I kind of dig the idea of being favored by the universe."

"Worry less about truth and more about being, young Hemant," said Ekon, tapping his temple. "For whatever reason, the universe has chosen you to act in her stead. She will not turn her back on you. Now, enough philosophy. We are going to test the engines on the *Sekhmet* and Hera would like you to join us for the procedure. It will begin at ten-hundred hours in the staging area."

"That sounds really cool," I said. "It'd be nice to appreciate mankind's engineering in a non-life-threatening setting."

"It is truly awe-inspiring," said Ekon. "The vibrations are so strong, you can feel the connection to our ancestors who built it.

Assuming the test goes well, which it will because Hera's involved, it will mark the last major test before your departure."

"When do we leave?" asked Liesel, wrapping her cool hand around mine.

"In three mornings."

CHAPTER 8: KOLYA

"**A**ndrei?" I yelled. "Where's that damn boy? Andrei?"

I winced as the loud clang of metal vessels falling resounded through the lab. I looked up to find Andrei stumbling over a toppled shelf.

"I'm sorry, sir. It's just all the stuff on the floor. Sometimes I get—"

"Stow it, Andrei," I said, irritated by his clumsiness. "Don't tell me you can't avoid a few inconveniently-placed stacks. I need your help in the vault."

Andrei made a show of looking at the numerous piles dotting the cracked tile floor.

"Of course, sir," he said. "If you'll give me your list, I'll have the items arranged for your arrival."

"No," I said, shaking my head. "This is… different. I need to do private research. I'm concerned for the pod's welfare and I don't wish to raise alarms unnecessarily. You know how rumors can be, even among the supposedly unflappable vault clerks."

"I understand," said Andrei, with a look that told me he didn't.

It was no matter. The boy was as dumb as a pill bug—or

rather—polie, to use the slang of the surface. It'd been several months since Arjun's arrival and the time was at hand for their departure. I'd put off meddling with the warhead long enough, but time was of the essence. If we were going to make peace with the Arthro— with the *inverts*, the weapon needed to be out of commission. I didn't want Arjun's ham-headed brother to get any heroic ideas before the real work, the art of negotiation, was completed. But how to get a message to the Queens that I was an ambassador for peace…?

"Find a time when the vault will be uninhabited by any of its patrons. And I want time to work, so say… a several-hour window, *ponimayesh?*"

Andrei nodded so vigorously, his red curls bounced back and forth.

"Here's the tricky part: I need you to occupy the clerk. I can't have her interfering with my research. You see, I don't want anyone to feel at fault when I locate this problem. If I can fix it, everyone can save face and no one will be the wiser."

"Makes sense, sir," he said. "How do you propose I distract the clerk for several hours?"

"Don't act denser than you already are, Andrei. It's no secret how you provide for your sister."

The boy gasped.

"No one will say a word, boy. I'm just asking you to do what you already are. I'll provide triple your standard fee and *you* provide the service."

"Sir, I appreciate your offer, but the clerk, she's so…"

"Old? Why yes, she is, but the way she devours you with her eyes hasn't escaped me. You are the embodiment of youth. Just as your other clients want to forget their troubles for a few meager moments, she wants to forget what she's lost—her youth."

"But sir…"

"You'll do it, boy, and that's an order! You'll be pleasing both of us."

"Yes, Researcher Kolya," he said, anger burning behind his eyes.

"That's my boy," I said, cupping his soft cheek into my hand.

•••••••••

Andrei and I leisurely made our way up to the vault, where I hung back on the catwalk, people-watching to give him the necessary time to seduce the clerk.

"I'm not worried, Sveta. He's an obedient boy," I muttered. "He'll provide me with the time I need to disable the weapon."

While engineering had never been my primary area of expertise, I was quite skilled at it. I'd apprenticed in Munich before my Release Day building and maintaining medical devices. The hospital-grade equipment we'd been developing would have been commonplace in the early 1950s. Ironically, now it was outdated and cutting-edge at the same time. The inverts' electromagnetic curtain had thrust humanity back into the Industrial Age, but Arjun had given us a stepping stone back to our previous potential with his inspired spore-based destruction of the aerial network.

"A genius, that Arjun," I whispered, slowly opening the vault hatch, checking for signs of movement.

The coast was clear. *I'll give it to the boy, he's good at what he does.* With the clerk busy reliving her past in the circulation desk closet, I set about diffusing the bomb. I ran my hand along the meter-long aluminum tube that had been so finely crafted to hold the nuclear device within. According to Arjun, Dieter and his lab mates had risked their lives to secretly develop the weapon under Zabu's tyrannical reign. Two, and quite likely all three, of its developers, were deceased.

"Zabu has severe control issues, Sveta," I whispered. "Such a shame that the men's effort will be wasted."

I loosened the timer plate with my screwdriver, careful not to inadvertently pull apart the bundled wires inside. Instead of the color-coded rainbow I'd expected, there was only a nest of black wires.

"Damn them and their lack of colored wires. Why can't those miscreants follow a standard protocol?"

I laid the panel gently on the cart, and opened a second panel in the housing, revealing the radioactive material shrouded within its explosive sphere of hexagonal-shaped charges.

"Only one of the charges needs to fail to prevent the explosion from going nuclear, my dear. I'll pull several of the wires on the far side, just to be sure. Unless someone removes the core, no one will ever know it's been sabotaged."

I felt around the hidden side of the sphere, the decay of the enriched uranium within warming my hand.

"Not to worry, Sveta. It's harmless enough," I said as I plucked three of the wires from the charges. "There. They must've simply rattled loose during transit. Arjun did say it was a rough passage."

I opened the third panel and removed the wires from the chemical dispersal charges as well. I reassembled the bomb and flicked off the lights, just as I heard the clerk's giggle over the unlatching closet door.

"Oh, Researcher Kolya, my apologies," she said, fixing her disheveled hair and pulling her gray vest taut. "If I'd known you were here, I would have been of assistance."

I glanced over her shoulder at Andrei, still in the shadow of the door. His wide pupils were filled with a mix of self-loathing and barely-bridled fury.

"Quit fiddling around, Andrei," I said, clandestinely easing the screwdriver into my far pocket. "There's work to be done."

I watched as he vanished out of the main hatch of the vault.

"Youth," I said, shaking my head. "So temperamental."

"And vigorous," added the aging clerk.

When I shot her a glare, the flush of her face vanished as she lowered her eyes to the desk.

"Will you be needing anything else, Researcher Kolya?"

"No, thank you. I believe I'm finished for the day. I took the liberty of accessing the documents myself. They are all back in their proper place."

Without waiting for a response, I left the vault and caught up with my assistant on the catwalk, who turned to face me.

"Don't you ever make me do something like that again!" he said, his finger in my face, more hurt than angry. "I do what I have to do to get by, but I'm selective! That woman's proclivities… they weren't right! She did things to me. Things I will *never* forgive you for."

"Me?" I asked, meekly.

"I'll be your lab assistant as long as you'll have me, but you don't ever command my body again, do you understand?"

"Andrei, Andrei, Andrei," I said, splaying my hands. "You are in a very favorable position within the pod. People clamor to work at my side. You forget your place. You *will* report to my lab first thing in the morning and do *anything* I ask. That or I'll have your sister transferred to a lower-level pleasure district. If you thought the clerk had unusual fetishes…"

"You wouldn't," he said, fear etched on his face. "I mean… you can't."

"I can and I will. In my lab tomorrow, Andrei."

I strode away without so much as a backward glance. My intentions set, I took the sketchier set of stairs down to my lab. Without difficulty, I located a prominent whoremonger, dressed conspicuously despite his nefarious occupation. A beacon of ill-repute. *The taint of sin is heavy, Sveta, even in our home.* After assurances that I wasn't there for myself, I divulged the location and qualities of Andrei's sister, all the while filling his purse with points. She was becoming far too much of a distraction for my simple-minded assistant.

•••••••••

The next morning, I sat patiently in my lab for over an hour, drumming my fingers on the black-topped table, with no sign of Andrei.

"I've played my card, Sveta. I'll have to come up with something else to keep the boy in line."

A knock at the door caught me off-guard as an officer entered.

"Researcher Kolya?" she asked, looking bored.

"Yes," I said, curious.

"I'm sorry to tell you this, but your research assistant…" she began, flipping through her notes. "Your research assistant, Andrei, and his sister were found dead this morning by their neighbor. It appears related to human trafficking, but we can't be certain. Quite sad, really. You'll be pleased to know that he died trying to protect his sister. Rest assured, their deaths are being investigated. The suspect will be prosecuted to the full extent of pod code."

"Thank you," I said to the officer, enjoying her pleasant movements as she exited the lab.

"Pity," I muttered. "Now I'll have to train a new assistant."

I sat down at my desk, annoyed by the inconvenience. I suppose I could bring Arjun in to help. Better than an assistant, he would make one hell of a partner. Surely Andrei's death wouldn't lead back to me. Like lightning, an idea flashed through my skull. Or…

"It's decided, Sveta. We're leaving," I said, slamming my notes closed. "In three days. I don't care what you think. It's time. We're boarding the plane with or without Lafet's permission. Arjun needs me. If for nothing else, more stimulating conversation than those other ingrates can provide. They don't appreciate him as they should. And his brother…. Not only do they not look alike, but their IQs also couldn't be more different. Somehow, they've got it in their heads that they are related, but I'm more related to Arjun than that oaf."

When I returned from a quick trip to the supply depot, I could barely contain my excitement, anxious to pack for the upcoming trip. On the bed, I laid my shashka, an antique compass from my first excursion (which I was hoping would work properly now), and the fresh jumpsuits and armor I'd just acquired.

"I got the tightest set I could fit in," I told her. "I only steal what I need. Well, or things that the owners aren't appreciating sufficiently. It's an odd size. I'm sure they would've thrown it away eventually."

I threw a wad of relatively clean undergarments in the rucksack, panning the room for anything else I should pack.

"We're going to fly there anyway. Direct combat will be unlikely. Especially with Hera maintaining the plane. Speaking of being under-appreciated, I could show Hera what real care looks like. And don't act all sore, Sveta. You know you're the one I'm coming home to every day."

I added a handful of ration bars, maps, notes—anything I couldn't part with.

"I know it'll be heavy, but I'll be on a plane. I know you care about me, but I'll be fine. If worse comes to worst, I'll ditch the heavier stuff, alright?"

I felt a slight tremble in the walls, very unusual given the depth of my accommodations.

"What the hell was that?"

A second tremble followed as fine dust drifted down from the ceiling.

"That's not good."

CHAPTER 9: ARIADNE

When Ekon had mentioned just how soon we would be leaving, my feet rooted to the pitted concrete floor as if I'd been part of the pod since its inception. *Can we really be leaving?* Our three months of respite were over. Between packing gear, polishing the plan, and giving speeches, the remaining days would be nothing but chaos. I forced my feet to move, one reluctant step at a time towards my dorm. When I reached the common room, I paused by Arjun, who was scribbling furiously in a notebook. It was when he was in deep concentration he shared the most similarities with his brother. The pair had radically different abilities and physiques, but they were most certainly twins.

"Arjun?" I said, careful not to startle him.

"Yes?" he said looking up, eyes reddened from countless hours of writing in fine print.

"What are you doing?"

"If I'm going to leave, Kolya should have ample records of everything we've learned outside the pod. I've told him everything verbally, but he needs a reference. I don't believe his memory is as sharp as it once was, or as he purports it to be. Ciro and my findings cannot perish with me," he said, momentarily growing distant. "I may not have the fighting prowess of my brother, nor do I have the courage of Omar, but I do have this." Arjun held up the tabulated notebook. "*This* is my contribution to the world. I want to leave an extensive record at each pod we stop at."

"As much as I like your idea, I hope nothing happens to you," I said, rubbing his back. "Don't forget to get some rest, okay?"

Arjun nodded absentmindedly before reimmersing himself in his work. His burns were healing well, but it still pained me every time I laid eyes on them. Leaving his side, I questioned my contribution as I strode to my room in search of solitude. I was only mildly surprised to find Remi undressed in my bed, the thin comforter leaving little to the imagination. As our friendship had progressed, her interest in me had been quite clear.

"Hey stranger," she said, propping up on her elbow. Her dark hair tumbled across the pillows like waves at dusk. "Take a load off. You look like you need to relax."

I approached the bed and sat on the edge, where Remi was patting suggestively. She sat up, letting the sheet slink down, and started massaging my tense shoulders. I shrugged her attempts at relaxation off.

"Ariadne, you are wound as tight as a reactor tech," she said. "Let me help. Just a shoulder rub, I promise."

"Just a shoulder rub?" I asked, cocking an eyebrow.

"I figured it was worth a shot, but I can tell you have eyes for someone else," she said, sighing. Her deep red lips stood out against her pale face. She was beautiful in a handsome way. "You're in love."

"What are you talking about?" I asked as she resumed the massage.

"God, I hope you're not this dense on the battlefield," she said, moving to face me.

"You've got some kind of crush on that boy. Either you're not being honest with me or you're not being honest with yourself. Which is it?"

"Even if I did like him, it doesn't matter. He's with Liesel."

"God, and oblivious too. Don't you see the way he looks at you? He's with Liesel *because* he's not with you."

"But they seem so… in love," I said, splaying my arms in frustration.

"Liesel's in love," said Remi, throwing a baggy, holed sweater over her shoulders. "Huck clearly enjoys her company, but honestly, I'm starting to think he's as thick as you are in matters of love."

"Thanks," I said, rolling my eyes.

Remi leaned in and kissed me on the forehead.

"Even in as short of a time as I've known you, I care about you, Ariadne. You are a good friend and I'm glad to be fighting alongside you. But a good friend wants what's best for you, and in your case, that's Huck. I hope you let him in soon. You've seen it out there. You can't take anything for granted."

"What am I supposed to do? Go in there and tell Huck I'm madly in love with him and that he should break it off with Liesel?"

Remi shrugged. "I'm just saying there will be a point when you two see reality and I hope you embrace it. I wouldn't mind being around a single Liesel, she's a freaking goddess."

I laughed and rolled my eyes again.

"There's the Ariadne I like."

I hugged Remi and thanked her. She got dressed and after one last offer to stay, vanished into the corridor. I stripped off my jumpsuit and threw the covers over my head, wanting to absorb every last moment of privacy and solitude the pod had to offer.

●●●●●●●●●

The next morning I slept far later than I'd intended. I threw on a jumpsuit and rushed my way to the common room, anxious to plan the next few days in detail with my companions. Everyone was already up and around, making me the last to join the impromptu meeting.

"I know we were supposed to allot duties and such before we head up for Hera's gig, but I can't work on an empty stomach," said Mathias, cleaning his fingernails with his dagger. "I don't know about you lot, but I could go for some Wuhanian food."

I was about to protest, but not against the murmurs of assent coming from every direction. *Who was I to arrive late and then expect everyone to skip breakfast?* I sighed and stood as the eight of us made our way to the nearest food district. When we arrived at the restaurant, the owner was just opening the roll-up door. Excited by the prospect of a large group's ration points first thing in the morning, he drew the chain as fast as the door's wheels would allow. He quickly ushered us in and yelled for the half-alert chefs in the rear of the establishment to fire up the grills. Forgoing my usual coffee given the occasion, I ordered some steaming oolong to accompany the meal.

Our gracious server's enthusiasm only compounded when he realized who we were. We wanted for nothing throughout the course of the meal. The flavorful food was delightful and the companionship was even better. Any concerns and anxieties fled like mice before a cat, allowing us an uninterrupted reprieve, even if only for a moment. With the meal concluding, I had the waiter bring us a round of rice wine. Once I had the tray in front of me, I saw that all of the tiny ceramic cups bore their own distinct cracks and chips. Each was functional, but each was damaged. The wood tray had a vacant indentation—an incomplete set. Lip quivering, I took a cup and raised my little ceramic cup, proclaiming, "To Mei." Everyone raised their tiny cups, responding in kind.

With our bellies full and a warm glow in our cheeks, we headed upwards to the staging area for Hera's demonstration. Mathias wasn't the only one down in spirit. The toast had reopened fresh wounds. Each of us was still grieving the loss of Mei. Remi's words echoed in my head. Just like Mei, I could lose Huck in an instant. I watched as he and Liesel walked down the hall, messing with each other playfully as they went. *Who am I to interrupt his happiness?* I'd spurned his advances and he did the only natural thing—he found happiness somewhere else. Remi's words repeated in my head. *Maybe what's best for him* is *Liesel.*

When we entered the staging area, the cavernous space was filled with busy technicians, running from machine to machine, gearing up for the display. We approached the elevated perimeter where we found Halima and Ekon waiting next to the railing with Samson, who was jumping anxiously from foot to foot. I hadn't seen him this excited in as long as I'd known him. For a middle-aged man with an emerging gut to match, he was nimble on his feet. His walnut skin was complemented by his beige flight suit and gilet, which I now realized he wore all the time.

"Hey guys," said Samson, a friendly smile shining through his thick, dark beard. "With you here, I guess we're ready to get started. Hera's been ready since oh-four-hundred. If it was up to her, she would've started the damn thing before any of us got up here. I'll let her know that you're around."

He bounded down the flight of stairs leading to the floor level to commence the engine-start procedures. After being greeted with the standard cheek kisses from Halima and Ekon, they addressed us.

"We're prepared for your departure the day after tomorrow," the prime minister began, tucking a stray lock back into her head covering. "Everything is fueled, loaded, and charged. The bulk of your equipment is ready, save for a few of your personal effects and the weapon. We'll wait until right before takeoff to load that for safety reasons."

"I understand," said Huck. "Thank you for everything you've done, Halima. Your generosity has been tremendous. If we fail, it won't be any fault of Pod Baghdad's."

"Hush with that nonsense, Huck," she said, slapping his chest. "You've already accomplished more than anyone in decades. You'll do everything you set out to do, of that I have no doubt. And when you're done, I expect you all to come back to our beautiful city for a banquet in your honor and I won't take no for an answer."

"Yes, ma'am," said Huck, enthusiastically as I stifled a giggle.

Below, someone shouted something indiscernible to the deputy minister.

"What joy! They are ready to begin," announced Ekon through his wonky-toothed grin.

"Even I get a little nervous for this," said Halima, stretching out the fabric of her crimson hijab to fan herself. "At my age, I can never tell if it's hot flashes or job stress. Ekon, not a word."

An engineer approached Halima. With a nod, she granted her approval for the test to begin. The air filled with the whine of hydraulics echoing off the distant walls as air vents in the ceiling cracked open. A rain of dust twinkled as it fell through the shafts of lights onto the people and equipment tens of meters below. From our vantage point, I could identify Hera doing her last-minute visual checks of the twin engines, never completely satisfied.

Finally, the anticipated moment arrived. Everyone in the space quieted as Hera's lone voice rose above the rest.

"Clear prop!" she yelled, gesturing the commands. "Fire engine one!"

Making an asthmatic cough, the propeller of engine one began to twitch, then spin. Moments later, the blades whirled to life under the power of their engine, roaring so loudly that I had to cover my ears. Ekon had been correct, the vibrations within the enclosed space were so intense that I felt as though my skeleton would shake apart. I watched as Hera yelled, motioning to start the second engine, but her voice was lost in the noise. With the second engine purring smoothly, cheers and clapping rose from the spectators, loud enough to be heard even over the engines. Hera gave the signal for engine cutoff and we watched as each of the props jerked to a stop. Halima turned to us with a grin.

"Well that was a resounding success," she said as the ceiling imploded.

•••••••••

I sputtered as I sat up, my ears ringing. Somehow, I was on the ground—my entire body throbbing with a dull ache. I leaned over and coughed dust out of my mouth as I cracked open my eyes. Sights and sounds were a blur. As workers sprinted past, I tried to suss out what had happened. I craned my neck to check the pod's ceiling. A massive chunk of the metal and concrete was missing, having fallen down and crushed half of the convoy underneath. Through the gaping hole where the metal's jagged edges curled in like a foil lid, clouds of flying Arthropods flocked towards the pod, their charge led by pill bug-carrying powder moths. I cursed as I stood, ignoring the sharp pain in my knee. Polies were how Huck had said Pod Bogotá had been destroyed! The dusters could carry the damn things like bombs. I darted to Krista's side and helped her stand the moment I saw she was uninjured. Huck and the others were coming out of the momentary shock a hair slower than I had.

"Help me!" someone yelled.

The familiar voice slowly pierced my mental fog, bringing me to full awareness. I turned to find Hemant screaming and beckoning others to join him at a pile of debris. On hearing his pleas, we ran towards him and Ekon. I didn't know what was happening until I glanced down. Under a fallen support beam, concrete still clung to its anchors, was Prime Minister Lafet. Halima was conscious, but even a casual observer could see her injuries were grave.

"No!" I screamed. "Don't lift it! It may be all that's keeping her alive."

"Are you crazy?" Hemant yelled.

"If you remove it, she could bleed out!"

Hemant rubbed his forehead and looked at Arjun, who nodded in confirmation as a second, distant explosion sounded.

"Damn these stupid bugs!" he screamed, kicking at nothing.

A flash caught my eye. I looked and saw Halima weakly waving me to her side and ran to her, kneeling to be close to her face to hear her weak voice over the fracas.

"Go," she said breathlessly through the pain. "Plane… loaded. Ekon… bomb. Save us. Save *all* of us."

I looked at her for confirmation. The look I saw in her deep brown eyes was one of resilience, not defeat. With a final squeeze of my hand, she slipped away.

CHAPTER 10: HEMANT

Halima's lifeless frame lay on the ground, twisted and bent as the wreckage around her. I was completely immobilized by the sight of her. She'd been such a strong force in our lives since our arrival and, just like that, she was gone.

"Come on!" yelled Huck. "You heard Ariadne. We've got to go! Ekon, can you take us to the vault? Ekon!"

Ekon stood, frozen like a stone as the chaos swirled around us like a hurricane.

"Ekon? Sir?" I asked, putting my hand on his shoulder. "Can you take us to the vault?"

He took a moment to focus on me, his trademark optimism replaced by the thick trance of the Shock. He nodded.

"Omar, Krista, run to our rooms. Grab whatever you can carry and get it up here," yelled Huck. "Any hiccups, make for the plane. Ariadne, Liesel, see what you can do for the injured. Mathias, Arjun, see if you can help Hera and Samson while Hemant, Ekon, and I get the bomb. Clear?"

All heads nodded as we ran our separate ways. Ekon, in a daze, nearly had to be dragged to maintain the upbeat pace. As we sprinted through the passageways, flickering power impeded our progress. *This is bad.* More than one corridor was submerged in complete darkness, leaving us to feel our way through as dust alighted atop our heads. Each impact reverberated throughout the pod, signifying another hole in the superstructure. We had to get out before the inverts invaded the city. Likely, all quarter-million of the pod's inhabitants would die in the slaughter. *Jesus!*

"We've got to move, Huck," I yelled as we ran through throngs of fearful residents shoving their way up. "How the hell are we going to have time to load this *and* get out of here?"

His only response was to further prod Ekon. People now crowded the halls from one wall to the other, slowing us to a crawl. In an effort to avoid the masses, Ekon had enough presence of mind to lead us through a maintenance tunnel illuminated by the pale glow of emergency lights. As we moved through the shoulder-width space, all I could think about was how little it would take to trap us inside. Sweat started to bead on my forehead as my panic rose. Just when I thought I couldn't go any further, we emerged, all of us sighing with relief. We were only doors away from the Nucleus vault. Ekon entered his code and punch card, but the electronic lock merely beeped angrily.

"It's gone into lockdown," said Ekon, his optimism replaced by depression. "Ekon is sorry. Not even Ekon can override it alone."

"Let me," I said, grabbing a nearby fire extinguisher.

I wasn't about to let a measly bundle of circuits bring our mission to a grinding halt. I positioned myself to slam the tank down on the lock when a heaving voice bellowed, "No!"

I turned to see Arjun's friend Kolya, red-faced and gasping. Sweat saturated his yellowing clothes and his greasy hair and wispy beard were a mangled mass. Even having just entered the area, his stench was almost unbearable.

"I knew I'd… find you here," he said between gulps. "Good

thing. This oaf… was about to lock you out… permanently."

"Who the hell are you calling an oaf, Kolya?" I yelled. "It's not like I know how to hack the damn thing."

"Well, it's obvious… which of you got the brains in the family."

"Well at least I can run up a flight of stairs you—"

"Shut up!" yelled Huck.

"Gentlemen, please," said Ekon, speaking normally for the first time since Halima's death. "We must work together to get you back on your path. Allow him to work, if you please."

I glared at Kolya as he brushed past me to the wall-mounted console and began removing the faceplate with tools drawn from a small leather pouch at his waist. As he removed parts, he delicately placed each piece in an imaginary grid on the ground.

"You are aware that the pod is coming down around us, right?" I asked, unable to help myself.

Kolya muttered something in a foreign language and continued his work, in no more hurry than before. He'd slung down his tool bag. The more I examined it, the more I realized it wasn't a tool bag. He'd packed for an excursion.

"Going somewhere, Kolya?" I asked, prodding Huck with my elbow.

"Yes, if you must know," he said, his accent thickening with his discomfort. "I am accompanying Arjun to the Hive. I made the decision before the dusters began dropping their bombs."

"Your decision," I said, scoffing. "Huck was the one put in charge. I don't recall you ever asking for permission."

"I can't abandon the only other sound mind on the planet to be alone with you buffoons," he said as the security bars released their hold on the door with a loud clank.

"First an oaf, now a buffoon," I said to Huck. "You're *not* coming. There's barely enough room on the plane for us as it is."

Kolya ignored me, sweeping the vault door open and moving

towards a second hatch inside. *An inner vault.* With the second entrance open, Dieter's weapon laid exactly as I remembered it, though perhaps with a few more smudges on its white casing. I ran up to the weapon, forgetting all about the conflict, and began hoisting it onto my shoulders. Kolya was frozen, staring at shelves heavy with ancient volumes. We were surrounded by what must have been a hundred real books.

"God, this thing is heavier than I remember," I said, adjusting the carrying straps.

"Gentlemen, Kolya will go with you. Ekon wills it," said Ekon, raising his hand to silence me before I could speak. "Today will be a grave day for humanity. Earth will likely lose another tenth of its number. Researcher Kolya is one of the sharpest minds and his company will greatly benefit you. Allow him to join you and let Ekon carry one less burden into the future."

"Then he will come with us," said Huck.

Ekon nodded, then turned to remain in the vault.

"You need to leave, Ekon," I said.

"No. The universe will take care of Ekon as she always has. We will see each other again. Now, fly!"

The three of us took off in a dead run, my adrenaline-fueled strength helping me power down the corridors with the cumbersome device nearly as fast as I could without it. As we raced down the hallways, Kolya slung his pack forward to stuff in some of the ancient tomes. I rolled my eyes. I couldn't decide if he'd grabbed them out of thievery or preservation. After squeezing once again through the claustrophobia-inducing, labyrinthine maintenance tunnel, we again found ourselves virtually trapped between compressed bodies. People shoved and prodded as the fear brought out their most primitive survival instincts.

"We're never going to get through!" I said as another explosion rocked the pod, followed by fading screams and wrenching metal.

I looked at Huck wide-eyed.

"That sounded like—" I began.

"—a catwalk," Huck finished.

An older gentleman in the crowd turned towards me with a look of recognition. He said something to the man next to him who nodded.

"Hey!" he yelled. "It's them! The heroes! They've got the device! Let them through!"

"And why should I?" yelled another.

"Because they may not save us, Simon, but maybe they can save everyone else."

There was murmuring as the crowd slowly parted, giving us a clear path to the stairs, finding space where there didn't seem to be any. As we climbed, we were met with understanding faces filled with sadness, fear, resolve, and hope. Many people patted and touched us as we passed. We move as quickly as space would allow. I blinked away tears as I passed child after child, the people's sacrifices shaking me to my core. *I swear I won't let you down.*

Omar and Krista crowded us as we stepped off of the landing into the staging area.

"Where have you been?!" Omar yelled over the cacophony. "We were about to start a search. Samson's got the plane ready for takeoff."

"Things took longer than expected," I said, wiping my tears with my sleeve. "Help me get this thing on the plane."

Stunned, I stepped into the debris-laden area. The source of the noise was the roar of the plane's engines mixed with the gunfire from the few functioning vehicles. Another hole had been blown through the ceiling above, shrapnel having destroyed more of the convoy below, leaving us with only a handful of the expected protection. Workers were furiously scrambling to remove the last of the wreckage from the plane's path and working vehicles.

"What are you gawking at?!" yelled Hera, cursing to herself. "Get your asses on board!"

I craned my neck to see what Hera was alarmed about. Attempting to get through the holes were clusters of inverts, held only at bay by the unrelenting gunfire.

"Oh, crap!" said Huck.

The six of us took off towards the plane under the cover fire. Omar helped me sling the bulky weapon off of my back and into the fuselage already crammed with bodies. Hera slammed the door behind us. Having been unconscious for the last flight, I hadn't realized just how cramped the plane's relatively tiny cabin was.

"Everyone accounted for?" she asked.

I took a mental roll, but Huck beat me to the response.

"We're all here, plus one," he said, nodding at Kolya.

"Good," said Hera, winking. "We can die together."

"Not exactly optimism, huh?" said Mathias.

"Strap in," yelled Samson. "It's going to be a bumpy ride."

The loud groan of the pod's doors surmounted the ambient noise of the unsuspected battlefield as they parted for our exit. I was supremely grateful they still functioned despite the copious damage the pod had already taken. I threw myself into the woven canvas frame that constituted a seat and buckled in, donning a headset. At the rate the trucks were firing, they'd be out of ammo long before we topped the incline. If the inverts had any understanding of our plan, they'd be inundating the runway. I reached for Arjun's hand and squeezed. *How in the world are we going to get out of this alive?*

Vibrations increased throughout the *Sekhmet* as her radial engines revved harder, signaling our ascent up the ramp. With a more effective firing angle, Rico and Remi opened up with the plane's turrets.

"Cease fire!" immediately yelled Hera over the intercom. "Save it for when we're airborne."

I fell sideways into Mathias as the plane trundled up the slope to the exit, the ramp now far from smooth and littered with debris. Placing my hand over the microphone so as not to disturb Samson's concentration, I yelled to Arjun.

"What took them so long to attack?" I yelled over the noise.

"What do you mean?" he replied.

"Once they figured out how to destroy the pods, why didn't they wipe us out?"

"You don't get it, do you?" asked Kolya, whose broad shoulders were pinned between Krista and Liesel, much to their disappointment.

"Apparently not. Enlighten me."

"We're their food."

The realization jolted through me like electricity. What predator could ask for a better food source than seemingly automated dispensers conveniently located around the planet? *Holy crap.*

"It's a head trip," he said, bearing his yellow teeth. "Good to know your little light comes on."

"Wait," said Mathias. "You're saying they haven't destroyed us because we're critical to their survival?"

"Bingo," said Kolya.

"They eliminated Baghdad because its threat is greater than its reward," said Arjun, eyes widening. "It's punishment for harboring us."

"Exactly, my little friend," said Kolya. "Take it as a compliment. They really don't like your friends."

I spared a glance at Liesel who appeared on the verge of a relapse at the revelation. Even more emotionally sound, I felt a familiar icy sensation climbing my spine knowing that we were nothing more than livestock to them."

I took a deep breath, feeling the slightest hint of relief when the plane breached the surface and the cabin brightened. Then

Samson's voice broke the static.

"My God in heaven," he muttered.

CHAPTER 11: SAMSON

As the plane's upturned nose crested the top of the incline and settled on the pod's exterior, the insanity of our plight became obvious. The ground became an undulating blanket of Arthropods, all converging on our position and masking the runway. Our armed escorts emerged behind us and let loose with everything they had, desperately attempting to clear a way for us to taxi.

"They're all gonna die," I said, turning to my wife.

Hera blinked away tears as she returned her attention to the controls. With the escort no longer focused on anything but our advance, the deluge of Arthropods held back from the opening were now flooding into the pod. The guns ripping apart the enemy's chitinous exoskeletons did little to slow them, but littered the ground with corpses and covered the cockpit windows with their effluence.

"I can barely see!" I yelled.

"That's why we trained for instruments only," she said. "You can do this. Just get us off the ground."

I clumsily weaved the tail-dragger left and right, struggling to dodge the slew of parts that covered huge swathes of the taxiway.

I cringed when I heard the angry scream of a propeller ripping through an invert's carapace.

"I can't dodge them all! I'll tear up the plane trying!"

The radio! I furiously grabbed the mic, fumbling in the process and nearly dropping it.

"I need any available vehicle to clear our way. Plow right through them!"

Through the fuselage, I heard the roar of an engine and saw one of the cargo haulers speed up to get out ahead of the plane's nose. Traveling at its maximum speed, it blew through the inverts blocking the way, its low-slung heavy-gauge steel bumper blasting them apart, splashing their dark hemolymph asunder. I pushed the throttle forward until the front of the truck disappeared under the plane's nose, which I could barely see through the darkening windshield.

"We don't have enough airspeed!" yelled Hera, as a multipede's two halves spun out of our way.

"I don't know what to do!" I yelled.

"Push them!" she yelled, forcing the throttles to the firewall.

I felt a thump as the belly of the fuselage made contact with the ribbed canvas top of the cargo hauler. We began moving along the jarring terrain at an alarming speed. I thought briefly that the plane would shake itself apart. *Thank the universe for safety wire!* It took everything in me not to cringe or turn away from the carnage. The runway was a sea of writhing creatures. Our escort plowed through them as our propellers sliced through their remnants. It would be a miracle if we were airworthy by the time we reached our minimum takeoff speed.

"We're there!" I yelled in elation.

"Don't get excited yet," Hera said, unusually calm. "The tail can't lift. We're going to have to do a three-point takeoff."

Dammit! It's always something. I watched the needle on the airspeed indicator climb, eyes constantly flashing between my blurred view and gauges. Finally, we hit the necessary speed for a three-pointer.

"Now!" I yelled.

Hera and I each grabbed the yoke, pulling it toward us as hard as possible while applying the steady pressure necessary to maintain control. I heard the ripping of fabric as we tore free from the hauler below. *We're airborne!* Cheers rose from our passengers who could probably see better than I could at this point. Nausea began to rise but I suppressed it. I was determined to get us to safety before I let my stomach take control. I hit the lever to raise the gear only to have it whiningly object almost immediately.

"There's something caught in the gear."

"I'm sure. We should land soon and check the plane for damage. There might be something more life-threatening than the pitot tube we just ripped off."

I looked down at my airspeed indicator which showed nothing. At least with my flight time, I already had a feel for cruising speed. Takeoff and landing speeds would prove to be more of a challenge.

"Incoming," Rico said through the headset.

"I see them," said Remi.

The port and starboard guns opened fire, speaking in a language the Arthropods would undoubtedly understand. I opened my ventilation window and checked our six. A cloud of inverts was pursuing us as we climbed.

"Climb faster…" said Rico, dragging out the words.

"What's the matter, pretty boy, can't handle the heat?" said Remi, laughing.

"I'd prefer not to blow my load in the first few minutes."

"That's not what Phillipe said."

I stopped listening as their conversation devolved into increasingly vulgar stabs. It was good to have the kids back bickering again, if only for the sense of normalcy. I slid my hand over Hera's as we climbed out of reach of the low-altitude threats. Before adjusting our course to the southeast, I swung back over Pod Baghdad. Gasps filled the headset channel. Below, the pod looked like one of the disturbed fire-ant nests we periodically cleared out of the arena sand. Thousands of inverts poured in from the landscape, filling the pod. My vision blurred as I began to weep. There would be nothing left alive. Hundreds of thousands, slaughtered in a matter of minutes. Adults and children alike. The bloody things didn't discriminate. I looked back at the passengers. This mission *had* to be worth it.

"It's a shame you had to strip out the napalm tanks," I said, wiping my eye on the sleeve of my flight suit. I'd love nothing more than to fly back down and barbecue their asses."

"We didn't have any left anyway," she said, crying, her usual composure long since vanished. "All of our friends, our home—gone."

I pulled her into a hug, an easy thing to do in the cramped cockpit.

"I have you, *mon nounours*," I said in a terrible imitation of her accent.

She laughed before turning her head up to kiss my cheek.

"Now, how are we going to land with these nasty windows?" I asked.

•••••••••

About three hours' flight southeast of what used to be Pod Baghdad, (I cringed thinking of its desolate, bloody shell) we landed at the first safe pump house that dotted our way to Pod Bhopal. The original plan had been to make one overnight fuel stop halfway to our destination, but with Hera's insistence to inspect the plane and our collective desire to grieve, no one protested. It was a little upside to the day, but I was using a fraction of the airsick bags I had on my maiden flight. *Maybe one day, I won't need them at all.*

I had to scour the topographical map before finding a wide enough swath of flat land to put down on with our limited visibility. The target pump house lay at the foot of a mountain range innocuously marked as Granite Peaks. On the first pass, the arid plain appeared remarkably smooth and uninteresting—a perfect spot for a safe landing. Hera and I had done our best to wipe the viscous hemolymph from the vent windows. However, with our limited reach and how quickly it had dried, it was a futile gesture. I swung the plane around and lowered the flaps and gear for landing, wiping the sweat from my brow when the indicators lit affirmative.

Pulling the throttle back, the cumbersome giant drifted lazily to the ground. We landed smoothly, idling over to the pump house. The small trapezoidal structure lay at the edge of a long-abandoned town, nestled on a gradual slope rising to the distant snow-capped peaks.

"I hope the other pump houses are this easy to access," I said to Hera, already unstrapping from the copilot chair.

"Me too," she said, sighing. "None of the pump houses were built in consideration for aircraft. We'll have no choice but to rely on the topography. This flight will be over before it begins if we can't refuel. It's not like we can harvest natural gas on our own."

"We'll make it," I said, putting my hand on her shoulder. "We'll max out our tanks. If worse comes to worst, I think we could make it from here to Bhopal on the one fueling, though we'd probably glide in."

"No. We really need another stop, if only for a chance to stretch our legs. I would imagine it's feeling pretty claustrophobic back there."

As if to punctuate her sentence, the aft door flew open and our passengers hastily bailed out.

"Guess it's time for us to go too," I said.

I followed Hera outside, stretching as my boots crunched on the hard-packed ground. As Hera darted off to pull a wok-sized piece of multipede from the landing strut I examined the empty surroundings. The abrasive desert wind whipped across my face, making me feel as raw on the outside as in. The barren landscape was serene after our nightmarish morning. Huck and Hemant were already stretching a tarp they'd found to give us some respite from the incessant sun. The temperature was pleasant enough, but without the shade, we'd burn quickly.

"Lucky thirteen," I muttered.

"I'm sorry?" asked Mathias, squinting as he looked up.

"Sorry. I was talking to myself. I said 'lucky thirteen.' Ironic how few of us survived Baghdad's destruction."

"*Hmph.* I doubt we're the only ones. There were all kinds of little hideaways throughout the city. Eventually, the inverts will lose interest and leave. Maybe the ones left can eke out a living in the shell of the pod. You never know. I mean, don't forget about the survivors on the surface."

"That's just a myth," I said. "The only ones out here are the crazies."

"It's not a myth," said Hemant, approaching. "They're real. They saved me when I jacked up my leg when I got lost back in the Latin Territory. They nursed me back to health. There *are* good people out here, aside from the Demented."

"I wish they'd nurse *me* back to health," said Mathias.

"Shut up, man," said Hemant through gritted teeth. "I told you that in confidence."

Mathias held up his hands in defeat, but his grin never vanished. I couldn't help but wonder at the cause of their banter. Judging by the flush of Hemant's cheeks, I guessed a little romance must have been involved.

"How long are we staying here?" asked Hemant, happy to change the subject.

"I hadn't really thought about it. We mainly stopped to inspect the airframe and refuel while we're at it, but with what happened today, I'm open to alternatives."

"Could we stay the night?" asked Liesel, her soft eyes pleading with me to say yes.

"Any reason we shouldn't make camp, Hera?" I yelled.

"Not that I'm aware of," she responded from the opposite side of the fuselage.

"Huck?"

"It's fine by me as long as we post guards," he said. "I think we'd see anything coming a ways off given how flat it is."

"Then it's settled. Everyone spend the day resting and grieving as you see fit. I don't see any signs of life, which is in part a relief but also means rations for dinner. If you want to explore the ruins, go in a group. I don't suppose anyone would be willing to climb on the nose and clean the windows?"

"I'll do it," said Arjun.

"But what if you fall?" asked Kolya. "A broken leg could spell death on the surface."

"I'm more worried about a broken head, myself," said Hemant.

"Both of you, relax. I'll be cautious. This has to be done," said Arjun, running inside to grab some rags.

"You've got a hell of a brother, Hemant," I said.

"Thanks. I live for him."

"I thought Pod Horizonte separated siblings from their families at birth," said Hera, wiping grease from her fingertips. "It was the pitot tube, by the way. I think everything is good, but I'm going to do a more thorough inspection since we're staying the night."

"They do—did," answered Hemant. "I doubt they do anymore. When I met Arjun, it was one of those things. I just knew."

"As did I," said Arjun as he climbed onto the wing.

"That's fascinating," said Hera. "Love is something no enemy can take from us."

As everyone went their separate ways, I meandered around the plane, thinking about what my wife had said. I ducked under the belly of the aircraft to inspect the missing pitot tube and damage to the props when Mathias caught my eye. On the opposite side of the aircraft from the makeshift shelter, he was fiddling with a strange apparatus. It took me a moment to figure out what it was. *A Dust inhaler!*

CHAPTER 12: HUCK

"Everyone ready?" shouted Samson from the cockpit.

"Think so," I responded.

With the push of a few buttons, the twin engines began to spin. As much appreciation as I had for the technology, it would always be eerie seeing the blades spin so fast and yet so close to the fuselage. Despite the warmth of the morning sun, our overnight stay had been downright frigid. Liesel had curled up next to me for warmth, kissing and twining my arms around her as we drifted off to sleep. After the day's uninteresting explorations, we were beat. What little remained of the town's structures had succumbed to the harsh environment, long since picked over by the transporters who ran the route between Baghdad and Bhopal. I couldn't fathom how they crossed the oceans of sand. Even from the air, the sweeping dunes flowed endlessly from horizon to horizon.

Our only excitement in the abandoned city had come when we'd stumbled upon a solitary pede scrounging for food. Once we'd brought it to the brink of death, Liesel dealt the final blow, officially christening her weapon. She was the only person I'd known who cried the first time she killed an Arthropod. In many ways, her innocence was admirable. Unlike us, she'd been raised by someone with a motherly instinct. Greenskeeper Miranda had taught her to value nature and protect life when every influence around her suggested otherwise. Somehow, she had maintained a level of purity in an otherwise filthy world. Miranda had proven to be an invaluable friend to us. Her involvement with Pod Kano's Resistance had led to our escape—and had cost her her life.

My stomach churned as the wheels smoothly lifted from the ground. Liesel squeezed my arm a little tighter as the plane began to climb. Flying was a strange, unfamiliar sensation. I wondered if humans were even meant to fly, not having evolved wings like the Arthropods. Historically, humanity had always fought its nature. Even now, faced with extinction, many refused to give up. Our inherent stubbornness would keep us fighting.

Given the *Sekhmet's* bulk, it amazed me that the behemoth could get off of the ground. It didn't seem possible, but somehow it worked. I'm sure Zeke could've explained the principles involved. He had always geeked out over the math and physics of engineering. *It sucks having to watch your friends die.* I looked across the way at Krista, who had her arms wrapped around Omar. After Zeke's death, she'd found comfort with him. It had been a quick transition, but on the surface, life moved fast. I couldn't bring myself to hold any ill feelings toward her over it.

Given the vast distances of our journey, it was nice to be eating up the kilometers from the relative comfort of an aircraft. The roaring noises, wildly-oscillating temperatures, and substantial vibrations were almost just as intolerable as many of Yanus' ground vehicles, but it was faster. Much, much faster. The idea that we'd arrive at Pod Bhopal within three days of leaving Baghdad was a notion of insanity compared to the sluggish nature of our previous travels with the transporters.

My gaze lingered on each person in the cabin, wondering

who would still be alive when we saw our mission through. It was a thought never far from my mind. I couldn't stand the idea of losing anyone else. I wasn't particularly fond of Kolya, but I didn't want anything bad to happen to him either. He'd spent most of the evening complaining and muttering to himself, finally shutting up when Hera had grown so tired of it, she threatened to stake him to the ground and leave him behind. In the baking, poorly ventilated fuselage, his lack of hygiene was proving to be unbearable. I kept reminding myself that at some point, he would be valuable.

Before long, I gave in to the boredom and drifted off to sleep. I awoke with a sharp prodding to my ribs by Omar, nodding towards the window. On the ground below, there was a mountain range pushing up from the otherwise uniform desert and on the far side—a luscious carpet of green. We were finally leaving the desert. I grinned at Omar before waking Liesel and showing her the same. With the sight of the verdant landscape, everyone buzzed. I threw on my headset, which I'd slipped off to rest.

"Tell me we're going to have some shade tonight," I said.

"Better," said Hera. "We're going to the beach."

I didn't need the headset to hear the cheers over the engines.

"I didn't realize there was a beach between us and Bhopal," said Remi.

"There's not… exactly," said Hera. "The transporters can't drive straight through the mountains, so they take a southern approach to the City of Lights. It's on the coast. They refuel there before trading the Eurasian deserts for the Asian tropics."

"Why the City of Lights?" asked Krista. "People don't still live there, do they?"

"No," said Hera. "No one's lived there for centuries. The names on the transporters' maps stem from bygone ages, their origins lost to time."

I looked out the dusty window again towards where I could barely make out a distant cityscape, all but swallowed by the Earth. With the ocean twinkling in the sun behind, it was almost as though the tall ruins twinkled in the waning light. Perhaps its name was well-deserved.

"Any ideas about the invert population in the City of Lights?" asked Hemant.

"I believe I can answer that," said Kolya. "I've gotten back multiple reports that the larger cities are rife with them. Too many hiding spots. I think it would be best to avoid the area entirely."

"It's not that I don't trust you Kolya, but we are limited in choices," said Hera. "We've already committed to this location. We'll just have to be careful."

"And I've committed to living," said Kolya. "Perhaps Arjun and I will sleep on the plane. I'm sure we're smart enough to figure out how to fly it if the need arises."

I could almost hear Hera's eyes rolling.

"You will *not* touch the controls of this plane, Kolya, without my or Samson's express permission. Do I make myself clear?"

Kolya gave a reluctant grunt of assent.

"The pump house was built at an old air base on the outskirts of the city, which, fingers crossed, will be a decent place to put down," said Samson. "We'll be a short walk from the beach, but if the danger is minimal, I think we could all benefit from a dip."

"What about food?" asked Krista. "Can we hunt?"

"The old city is on the leading edge of the green belt," said Samson. "I can't promise anything, but there may be local wildlife if the Arthropods haven't eaten it all."

········

The landing wasn't bad, aside from almost rattling the teeth from my skull. We piled out the second the door was open, anxious to take in the fresh, salty air. Being the last in line for the door, I overheard Hera and Samson arguing.

"I'm telling you, Sam, number one didn't sound right," she said.

"Granted, I'm still getting used to piloting, but it sounded fine," he said. "All the readouts were in order."

"I may be tired, but I know my plane. Gauges don't tell you everything."

"Check it thoroughly. Rip off the cowlings. Pull the plugs if you need to, but keep the engine together. If we need a quick getaway, I don't want her pistons lying in the dirt."

"The problems may be deeper than that," said Hera.

"Let's pray that they aren't," said Samson. "I doubt we'd have what we need for a repair like that anyway."

I heard them rising and realized I was alone in the plane eavesdropping and scrambled out before they saw me. I couldn't imagine anything worse than falling from the sky. I watched my friends palling around with each other and decided not to share what I'd overheard. No need in making anyone else as uneasy as I was.

"This doesn't look like the beach," said Omar.

"It's roughly a kilometer to the south," said Hera, stepping out of the plane. "I saw it coming in, thanks to Arjun's window cleaning."

Arjun cracked a small smile.

"I'm itching to hunt," said Krista, surprising us.

"I think you've been spending too much time with Omar," said Hemant, laughing.

"I like it," she said. "It makes me feel independent."

"Are you opposed to company, Lady Independence?" asked Ariadne.

"Of course not," she said, rolling her eyes.

"Could I come too?" asked Liesel.

A brief hesitation flash across their faces before they agreed. Liesel needed to learn to survive. She couldn't spend all of her time depending on us. I remembered a time before Zeke's death when Krista was much the same way. She'd left the pod riding on Ariadne's coattails. It was only with her boyfriend's death that she truly faced the reality of living on the surface. Because of Krista and Omar's previous banished status, they'd been unable to enter Pod Kano with us, which turned out to be an unexpected benefit for her. During their time outside, she'd learned to master the hunt under Omar's tutelage.

Between the fingers Ariadne had lost in our fight against the giant spine back and the hand Krista had lost when we were ambushed outside of the caves, they could use someone with all of her digits. Though Liesel wasn't without her own wounds. Hers were just less superficial. As they departed, Remi ran out to join them.

"It feels weird having the girls go hunt while we lounge around on the beach," I said, sitting down with the others in the shade of the wing.

"No guilt here," said Omar, propping up his feet on a crate he'd pulled from the fuselage. "It's what they wanted to do."

"We can all go to the beach later," said Hemant. "I don't want them too far away from us after what Kolya said."

"The oaf uses his brain," said Kolya. "I like this."

"Shut up, man. Just because my brother likes you doesn't mean I won't pummel your ass."

"Just like someone with more strength than sense, always resorting to violence."

Hemant looked ready to tear Kolya limb from limb before Arjun diffused some of the tension.

"Kolya?" asked Arjun.

"Yes, my friend?"

"What are the dangers you mentioned in the city?"

"Well, you must parse through the vulgarity and fantastical language of the transporters, but underneath, I believe is truth. They describe flying bugs like I've never heard of in this region. Large bugs that shoot like rockets through the sky. They are said to nest in the tall buildings."

"No bugs can fly that fast," said Rico, squatting on a small metal barrel. "I've seen a lot of the inverts' flight abilities, nothing like you describe. Chompers can't fly in a straight line. Dusters are slow as a matriarch. And hooks are quick, but only for short distances. Plus, they can't fly very high."

"I think the transporters are right," I said. "You guys remember what happened to Yanus? Those weren't hook beetles."

"I forgot about that," said Hemant. "It feels like eons ago."

"Arjun told me about this Yanus," said Kolya. "He couldn't tell me much of his death. Please, share."

The researcher's eyes glowed with curiosity. The scientist in him was practically drooling for new information.

"I can't tell you much," I said. "One minute he was there, the next, there was a bloody smear on the ground where he'd been. All we could hear were his screams as his predators disappeared into the distance. They were dark and shiny. That's all I could tell."

"Fascinating!" said Kolya.

"Yanus was a pompous ass," said Hemant. "But he was a human. I don't find any human's death 'fascinating.'"

"Forgive me," said Kolya. "I sometimes get carried away. Arjun's journal was the most exciting information I'd received in years. It's part of the reason I came. I was stagnating in the lab, eating the falling crumbs when I wanted to dine on the meal. I can't ever replace Arjun's friend Ciro, but I will be his colleague as we make new discoveries."

"I'm a hell of a shot, but I've never had to shoot at anything faster than our plane," said Rico, brushing his dirty-blond hair out of his ruggedly-handsome face. "We didn't get a lot of target practice back in the pod. It wasn't just because of the noise. When the city is running out of source material for basic needs, any administrator worth their salt isn't going to waste ammunition on training."

"Your target practice is the world," said Hera, dripping with sweat as she climbed into the shade with us, sitting cross-legged. She grabbed a towel and began drying off the nape of her neck. "Good thing you and Remi are quick learners."

"We're talking about a new invert," said Rico. "One that's crazy fast and may fly higher than the others."

"Let's hope we don't run into them," said Hera, her accent deepening with her concern. "We're only about 1,000 kilometers out of Bhopal. With any luck, we'll be there after lunch tomorrow."

"Help!" screamed Liesel, sprinting towards us—alone. "Help!"

We flew out from under the wing to see what was the matter.

"It took her! Something took her!" she screamed through her sobs.

I wrapped my arms around her in an attempt to calm her.

"Who?" I asked. "Where are the others?"

"They're tracking her," she said.

"Who, Liesel?!"

"Ariadne!"

My heart stopped beating.

CHAPTER 13: KOLYA

"I told you so," I said. "I knew the City of Lights would be a dangerous place. We shouldn't have touched down here."

"Shut up, Kolya," said Hemant. "That's not helpful."

Another mess one of these foolish children had gotten us into. If Ariadne was dumb enough to get dragged off by this new threat, the smartest thing to do would be to leave her behind. I was looking forward to a hot lunch after days of rations.

"I know, Sveta," I mumbled. "It's not worth the fight. We'll go after her because their leader's in love with the girl, despite what he keeps telling himself. At least we'll get to study something different."

It'd been decades since I'd been on the surface. In many ways, it was as unchanged as it had been. It was I who'd changed. I was far older now, having spent more time reading than fighting in decades of late. Flying was a new luxury. I'd arrived at Pod Baghdad well before the discovery of the plane in Pyramid City. I found it fascinating to watch its restoration. Like many others, I'd made numerous trips to the upper levels to watch the ongoing repairs. The first time the engines roared, I almost did a pirouette.

"Arjun, Kolya, stay here with Samson and Hera," said Huck, his composure fraying like an old rug. "The rest of you, gear up. We've got a mountain to climb."

I found my way into the fuselage, looking for something to use as a fan while we waited for the away team's return. The heat of the humid coastal climate was something awful. While digging through the supplies, I saw Mathias through the porthole on the far side of the plane. He was shoving his things into his rucksack when something shiny caught my eye.

"Christ," I muttered. "Where on Earth did he get those?"

If another plane existed, Mathias had enough diamonds to buy it. I would recognize them even in their roughest forms. I watched as he carefully folded the sparkling rocks back into some parchment and tucked them into his rucksack. He walked around the plane, dropping his bag almost at my feet as he went to Huck's impromptu planning huddle.

I sat on the folding step ladder into the fuselage, eyeing the pack next to me. Making sure no one was looking, I discreetly unclasped the buckle and folded the top back. There in the side was the pouch.

"They're beautiful, aren't they, Sveta?" I said, parting the frail paper with my fingers.

I slid the pouch out of his pack, burying it deep in my pocket.

"Of course, he'll notice. But what do you suggest?"

Listening to my intuition, I dug a little deeper into the pack. *A Dust inhaler!* My, my, our little friend Mathias was a closet addict. Fate couldn't have dealt me a better hand.

"It's genius," I muttered, seeing the plan unfold in my mind's eye.

Reaching into my jumpsuit pocket, I pulled out the vial of eight venom that I rubbed on my shashka's blade to increase its lethality. I'd always been fond of using the inverts' adaptations against them. Popping open the inhaler, I let a single drop of the yellowish fluid drip into the device before replacing it in the pack.

"Substance abuse can be terrible for one's health, don't you think?"

•••••••

"Why'd you take this apart now?" Samson asked Hera as they walked out of hearing distance.

They'd been at it for the last two hours. Hera wanted to take apart more of the plane than Samson or I was comfortable with. I felt like a battle-fresh candidate sitting here on my laurels, waiting patiently for something to come pick us off. Arjun had been pacing ceaselessly since we'd heard the news of the girl. If we had to wait too much longer, I would start pushing to cut our losses and leave before we all died.

"Sit, little buddy," I said.

"I can't. What if they need my assistance?" said Arjun.

"They have no way to contact you. Wearing yourself out will be useless to all of us."

"I suppose you're correct," he said, plopping down on the crate next to me.

"Though a bit pig-headed, your brother is a fine fighter and will return the others to us safely."

Though likely without the little obnoxious runt if fortune favored me.

I placed my hand on Arjun's shoulder. "The inverts make formidable opponents, but you have to respect their methods and skill."

Arjun shook his head. "While I appreciate their tenacity, I can't admire any creature that's killed so many of my companions."

"Try thinking about it from a different perspective. You struggled with infestations of cockroaches and rats in Horizonte, yes?"

"Of course. I imagine that they plague every pod," said Arjun.

"What's your point?"

"Imagine that you were tasked with their eradication, hmm?" I said. "What would you do?"

"I would isolate a chemical compound to neutralize them and use it until they were no longer a threat."

"Don't you see, dear boy? It's the same! They are eradicating us, the difference is that they are also using us as a food supply. If you can apply your cold logic to the roaches then you can do the same for the Arthropods."

"But… but it's different."

"How? Pray tell," I asked.

"We are sentient beings and they are killing us," said the boy.

"Are cockroaches not sentient beings? Yet you hold them in equal disregard."

"I… I suppose."

"Look at these invaders through this new lens. They are simple beings, yes, but they have demonstrated notable intelligence. I've read your work, you are familiar with my hypothesis of the Queens."

I watched him nod.

"They are like us in more ways than most would care to admit. Like us, they consume all available resources, primarily focusing on food and procreation. The pods are dying, Arjun. You *must* see it."

"Of course I do. But what good is admiration?

"Not so much admiration as mutual respect. What if…" I said, pulling him closer. "What if we could communicate with them? Perhaps make peace with them?"

"How would that be possible? They attack the moment they see us. I've seen a little of their communication, but we couldn't decode their language without a lifetime of study and countless audio samples. I haven't seen a mag-tape recorder since we left Horizonte."

"I don't believe we can communicate with the drones, Arjun."

Arjun looked southeast towards the Hive, squinting his eyes as though he could see it in the distance.

"Yes, Arjun. The Hive."

"But… how?"

"We continue our trek, just as before. But instead of blowing it apart first and digging through the rubble after, we should seek an audience with the Queens. In addition to peace, imagine what we could learn from them about the galaxy. There's no telling what all is out there. Our forefathers barely ventured out of our solar system. We could barely get a foothold on another heavenly body."

"My previous question remains."

"We send a message to the Hive."

"How could we possibly communicate with the Hive? Even *if* we had a method, we're territories away."

"I have an idea. It would take samples of our urine and a captive powder moth."

"You want to use human pheromones," said Arjun, resting his hand over his mouth as he did when deep in thought. "I think I see where you're going with this. It's plausible, but the others will never agree with this idea."

"They don't have to know," I said. " We must be mindful should the opportunity arise. And worry not, my boy. There's nothing to lose. If we fail, then the status quo remains and we continue as planned."

"If my companions find out, I fear that they would never respect me as they did before."

I grabbed the boy by the shoulders and stared him in the face, which made him even more uncomfortable.

"Arjun. You are the most intelligent person in this group by leagues. Who are they to question the wisdom of your decisions?"

"I have no doubt you are correct, but they trust me. That's not a matter of intellect."

"Trust. Like they trusted you to go save Ariadne? That's just it. They don't trust you. I've been with you for mere months and from what I've already seen, your brother takes every opportunity to leave you on the sidelines."

"That's because he cares about my safety."

"No. It's because he doesn't trust that you're capable."

His two-tone face darkened as my words hit home.

Bingo, Sveta.

"Help me send the message."

"I will."

CHAPTER 14: ARIADNE

Where am I? It was pitch black. Not the type of dark where you hold your hand in front of your face and can see the outline. This was utter and complete darkness. My head was pounding like the Demented were drumming inside my skull. My mind was fuzzy. I looked left and right, my neck sluggish in its response. Not even a pinprick of light.

What happened? I retraced my memories trying to recall how I got here, wherever here was. The last thing I remembered was going for a hunt with Mei and—wait, that's not right. *Mei's dead.* I remembered her lifeless face staring back at me before we left the Saharan Territory. I had gone hunting with Krista, Liesel, and Remi. We'd found a trail. There was shouting, then nothing.

I gotta get out of here. I moved my fingers to feel the ground, but they wouldn't even twitch. My heart rate skyrocketed as I began to hyperventilate. *Calm down, Ariadne. Panicking won't help you. Think.* I could almost hear Grace's silky voice in my head. The Misfits boat pilot had helped several of us work through the trauma we had endured at the hands of the twisted humans known as the Demented. I tried to move my fingers again. I felt the subtlest of movements. *There's hope.* I kept trying until I could open and close my hand. I must have been hurt badly. In attempting to move my hand, I realized that the rest of me was also paralyzed. It was a strange realization. I had all of my feeling, but none of my mobility.

I started on the opposite hand when my concentration was interrupted by a disconcerting sound. It sounded like a toddler smacking when their mouth was dry. Whatever it was, it was alive and close by. I tried to work faster, but with little gain. Whatever invisible web froze me into place was taking time to unravel. With my hands functional, I moved up to my arms. The smacking grew louder, closer. *What* is *that?* I moved to my other arm. With uncoordinated movements, I could control my arms to the shoulders. I felt the ground around me. It felt like dried dirt, but ridged and smooth as though sculpted. It reminded me of cave grub tracks, but this construction was tubular and, from the curvature, maybe a meter in diameter.

I started working my abs trying to free up my torso when I heard crumbling not too far past my feet. Again, panic surged as Grace's imagined voice kept me sane. Something had joined me in the small chamber. I curled my shoulders into a weak sit-up as the smacking turned to intense chewing. There was something different this time. Something below my feet was moving—writhing—as muffled squeals echoed through the small chamber. *It's eating!* I hurriedly started working my legs, disregarding the messages from my imaginary Grace.

"Ow!" I yelped.

I sighed with relief when I realized the sudden twinge hadn't been a bite. When I moved my hips, my thigh wrenched with stabbing pain. Maybe I'd fallen into this mess. An injured leg would make any escape difficult. Working through the pain I got the leg moving, then switched to the opposite side. The squeals turned into a shrill, animalistic cry, full of pain. *Something was being eaten alive!*

If there was a worse way to die—unable to move and able to feel everything—I didn't know it. It'd be my death if I didn't get my ass in gear. The cries ceased when I was midway through freeing my remaining leg. In the darkness, something shuffled towards me, brushing my leg. I felt it begin to gnaw on my boot and reached for my dagger only to find it missing.

"Nod doday, bith!" I yelled, tongue uncooperative.

I began kicking at whatever creature was attempting to dine on me in the obscurity. The log-sized invert was stout, taking blow after blow as I sandwiched it repeatedly between my boot and the chamber's smooth wall. With a final, hardy blow, the creature's exterior membrane gave away as I splattered its innards everywhere, including all over me. The warm, foul-smelling ichor made me gag as it ran gray-green over my hands. *Wait, I can see!* I looked up and saw where my boot had knocked a hole in the tunnel. I kicked again, flinging my good leg toward the cracked wall in an effort to break out. It was like busting concrete, but when I finally had a hole large enough for my torso, I dragged myself across its jagged edges and out into the blinding sunlight.

"Where the hell…?" I said, surveying my surroundings once my eyes had adjusted.

I was in a shallow ravine full of boulders, having emerged from a sausage-shaped tube of earth, cleverly camouflaged to look like the surrounding igneous rock. I struggled in my weakened state to get to the top of the chasm to find myself standing just shy of the mountain's peak.

"Holy hell," I said, looking down the slope of the mountain.

If my predicament hadn't been so terrifying, the awe-inspiring view would have been one of a lifetime. In the distance, the sun was rapidly disappearing into the distant ocean. For that brief moment, I could forget about my troubles. Thankfully, I'd seen the City of Lights from the plane and knew my destination lay a handful of kilometers southeast from the base of the range. It was a day's walk at most.

"Now to get down," I said, my enunciation slowly returning.

The mountain had a deceivingly smooth grade down, but I knew from Professor Lucas' classes that loose rock had ended many candidates' lives. Say all you want about Pod Horizonte's corrupt administration, but our teachers and trainers (save for a few sadistic ones) cared about us and our survival. It'd been Professor Lucas who'd represented me before the tribunal when I pummeled my cheating boyfriend. Until it was expunged, Krista's banishment had been a result of her carrying my sentence. It took me a long time to realize just how loyal of a friend she was.

I eyed the slope. It would be impossible to make it down by nightfall with an injured leg, much less back to camp. With any luck, the others were looking for me, but would they know where to search?

"Better go as far as I can before dark," I said, hoping my own words would provide me with more motivation.

I was about to set out when a thump come from the sausage. *What if one of the others is inside?!* I kicked myself for not having thought about it earlier. I grabbed the largest boulder I could hold. With its sharp edges cutting into my fingers, I beat a rift down the length of the tube. With its interior bathed in light, there were multiple yellow, tear-drop-shaped larvae of something nefarious. Each in its own distinct chamber, and each with one or two of its own paralyzed snacks—none of which were my friends. In anger, I dispatched each larva and its prey, all of which would grow up to be human-eating Arthropods.

I collapsed into the grit, sobbing. I'd burned my daylight on the task and was about to be forced to bed down next to a nest of who-knows-what and try to rest with hunger pangs, a throbbing leg, and a headache to rule them all. Curling into the gap where the tubular nest merged into the ground, I lay there freezing and sobbing quietly until I fell asleep.

Thump.

I woke with a start. It was dark, but unlike inside the nest, I could faintly see under the light of the moon. There was something much larger than the larvae walking around. As its legs passed by my hiding spot, the appendages shimmered with a pale metallic blue in the starlight. Without risking exposure, I could do little more than hold my breath, hoping the invert wouldn't detect me. After a brief patrol, the creature parked itself on the far side of the nest and trumpeted a mournful fanfare.

Within moments, the sound of a second creature landing followed. *A mating pair?* As fascinating as that would be to Arjun, I feared I wouldn't be alive long enough to tell him, especially since I'd just killed their offspring. I curled myself tight and prepared for a long, long night.

The minutes ticked as slowly as they did when Trainer Lourenço made us run his interminable laps. I was grateful for the endurance his sadism imparted to us, though none of our training covered half the inverts we'd come across since we'd left the pod. As the pair slept, my only indication of time was watching the stars move across the purple-hued sky through my narrow view of the wide expanse. Finally, the sky's tone began to change, signaling the sun's rise and the end of my luck. With daylight, the creatures would go to work repairing the damaged nest and, in doing so, discover me weaponless.

In truth, I knew nothing of my foes, only having seen them from a distance. I could only assume I was unconscious during the flight to my present location. I smirked. Since coming to the Eurasian Territory, I think I'd spent more time aloft than grounded. The creatures began to stir and I reached for the only weapon I could find—a good-sized rock. Lying just out of my reach, I had to rotate it with the tips of my fingers through the gritty earth until it came into my grasp. With it safely tucked into my chest, I waited. *How was I going to stand up to my foes with a damn rock?*

I listened as one of the creatures departed. *This is my chance!* After some convincing and deep breathing, I flung myself from the crevice and stood.

Crap.

Standing patiently on the other side of the oblong nest was the Arthropod in question, staring as though it had been patiently waiting for me to emerge from hiding. The bluish-black invert stood taller than me, its sleek wings swept back along its narrow body. Its compound eyes stared down its aquiline beak, daring me to move. I let my arm with the stone slowly creep back. In response, I watched, terrified, as the female mimicked my speed as she lowered a glistening stinger from her abdomen. I swallowed, taking in the creature's obvious intelligence. I was dead.

Thump.

I glanced to my left. The male had returned. Under any other circumstances, the size difference would have been almost comical. The female was easily three times the size of the male. I prayed the male was harmless, like their similar, native counterparts. The thought was irrelevant as the male made a display of dismissing himself from the conflict. This battle would be female to female.

I paced slowly to my right as the hawk-faced invert matched me move for move. *What am I doing?* I wondered how long I could delay the fight before she attacked. If their ground speed was anything like the air, I wouldn't register my death just like I hadn't my capture. The difference was now the mother was pissed, knowing I'd killed her young. Even with her intelligence, she wouldn't appreciate the act being self-defense.

As I paced, I saw the glint of metal in a crag next to a desiccated skeleton. *A spear!* Judging by the bandoleers, it was a transporter long since dead. The rusted weapon might as well have been on the next peak over given my enemy's seemingly preternatural intuition. I was about to make a desperate dive when I heard a rock slide. For an instant, my foe was distracted and I dove, landing on the pile of bones, but with my hand successfully wrapped around the spear. The female wasted no time jumping on top of the crag, which sides protected me. I watched in terror as she foisted her stinger toward me, the girth of her abdomen preventing it from reaching. The brittle volcanic rock blocking her was crumbling and my would-be weapon was stuck in the transporter's bandoleer.

"Come on!" I screamed in frustration.

Confused, I heard what sounded like more screams. At first, I thought it was my own pleas echoing down the ravine, but when my attacker broke off the assault, I realized with excitement that it was the others! With her gone, I wrenched the spear free as I stood. I watched elation pass over the faces of my rescuers before I singularly focused on the invert.

"She's mine!" I stated.

I ran towards her, spear elevated, watching as she moved into the perfect position to counter my frontal attack. She opened her beak, letting loose an air-rending screech, and I hurled my hidden stone with all the strength I could muster down her gullet. Her cleverness disappeared as she bucked wildly, attempting to dislodge the rock. Taking advantage of her weakened state, I climbed a tall boulder. When she came around, I thrust my spear into the top of her abdomen where her heart chambers were located.

In the throes of death, everyone had to dodge the stinger and spray as she flung her body erratically. The male, no longer encumbered by his self-imposed rules of warfare, flew in to attack. With a light blow from Hemant's war hammer, the male was dispatched as the female's movements subsided and she crumbled to the ground. I held my hand out to Hemant for his hammer, which he reluctantly offered. The heavy weapon took my full strength to lift over my head but came down onto the female's head far easier as it turned my foe's once sharp mind into goo.

"Thanks for the distraction," I said, wiping the fluid off of my face and feeling like a badass.

CHAPTER 15: HEMANT

I stood there, mouth agape, as Ariadne dropped my hammer back into my awaiting hands. We had scaled the mountain just in time to give her the advantage over the creepy, streamlined invert, and she had kicked its ass.

"Are you okay?!" Huck asked, running to her side and tightly embracing her. "I was so worried about you."

"I'm fine, Huck," she said, as Liesel turned away, feigning an inspection of the creature's corpse.

"Looks like you didn't need much rescuing," said Omar, slinging his unused naginata onto his back. "Nice move with the rock."

"These things, these… mud raptors, are crazy smart. Well, at least the females are," said Ariadne, pointing. "If you hadn't distracted her, I don't think I'd be alive right now."

"How'd you get the limp?" I asked.

"I think that's where I got stung. The bitch paralyzed me! When I came to, I was in that thing," she said, gesturing to the long earthen tube. "There was a larva inside trying to eat me alive."

"Ugh," I said, shuddering. "How'd you get out."

"I literally wiggled one appendage at a time until I got them all working, then I smashed that little turd against the side of the nest. Incidentally, that's how I broke out. I hid until dawn and you saw how that ended," said Ariadne, pausing. "Thanks for coming for me."

"We would never consider not," said Huck.

"What happened?" asked Ariadne, looking towards Remi and Krista. "I don't remember anything between us going hunting and waking up here."

"It happened so fast," said Remi, on the verge of tears. "There was a buzzing, and the next thing we knew, you weren't next to us."

"By the time we located you in the sky, you were already a distant speck," said Krista, handing Ariadne her bow. "We never heard you scream. It must have injected you with the paralytic as soon as it picked you up."

"Thank the universe I can't remember," said Ariadne. "I've already had enough of the Shock for one lifetime."

"We'll have to constantly surveil the skies if we're going to have silent, high-speed attacks coming from up there," said Omar, pointing. "At least with the hooks we see them coming."

"How'd you find me?" asked Ariadne. "I thought for sure I would have to find my own way back."

"We saw which way the… uh… mud raptor took you," said Liesel. "That's where we started. When we got close to the base of the mountain, we saw the male coming and going."

"If you recall, that lazy-ass Kolya said that they like to roost high, so the mountain was an obvious choice," added Mathias.

"Well, I've had enough of mountains for the moment. I'm about as fond of heights as I am open water," I said. "Anyone else ready to head down?"

"Don't be a wimp, Hemant," said Mathias, dropping to a seat on the cliff edge, making me nearly break out in a cold sweat.

In addition to leaving the high perch, I was eager to be reunited with my brother. Ariadne was more than enthusiastic to leave the nest. She dismissed our offers of help and we began our descent. Like the hike up, the majority of the challenges came from all the loose rock which threatened our ankles with every step. By the time we stopped for lunch on a small shelf, we were only halfway down the slope, our progress notably slowed by Ariadne's injury. At this rate, the others would come looking for us soon.

"At least it's bloody beautiful up here," I said, observing the horizon. "Even the dead city has a certain serenity to it."

"Uh-oh," said Mathias. "Hemant's getting all contemplative again."

"What?" I asked. "We're on an insane, suicidal mission. I can't stop and appreciate life every now and then?"

"He's spot on," said Remi. "Appreciate it while you got it."

"I tried," said Mathias, sulking off.

Dammit. We'd all lost people we cared about, but like Krista when she'd lost Zeke, Mathias was going to take time to get over the loss of Mei. It was interesting how people could be so varied in their responses to trauma and grief. It'd take lifetimes to unpack the human mind. After what Ariadne had said about the female, Arjun's theories were proving more correct on a daily basis. Humans had vastly underestimated the intelligence of these beings. I feared that once we reached the Hive, their level of orchestrated battle tactics may prove to be impenetrable. We *had* to end their cycle of reproduction.

Not all inverts were born in the Hive, but it was their primary source of reproduction. Scientists like Kolya and Dieter estimated that over three-quarters of the aliens originated from there. Arjun had his own pet theories. He wondered if all the inverts had originally been produced there, but the species that had since evolved could breed anywhere. I shuddered at the thought. Since humans no longer had the technology to detect them, I wondered if they still received reinforcements from wherever their home might be. In reality, we still knew so little about them.

Regardless of where the inverts chose to lay their nasty eggs, the Hive's existence kept the conflict unwinnable, constantly resupplying the inverts at a rate far beyond what we could kill. It was only limited access to resources (resources being us) that kept their population in check. With a death blow to their citadel, humanity would finally have the opportunity to end their occupation of Earth. It was a day I hoped Arjun and I would see together.

Packing up after our brief respite, Huck called for the others who'd wandered off for a moment alone—a rare commodity when traveling with a group. When Mathias didn't return, I offered to retrieve him from his solitude. I climbed over the ridge where he'd vanished. There he was, sitting on a rock, appreciating the view as I had been.

"Nice view, huh?" I said. "Hey, I'm sorry about what happened. I'm sure Remi didn't mean anything by it. If you need anything, I'm here, okay?"

There was no response.

"Okay?" I repeated.

Nothing. I walked around to face him. Under his golden hair, his pupils were the size of saucers. In his lap was a Dust inhaler.

"Mathias!" I yelled, grabbing his shoulders. "What have you done?!"

I expected him to jump up and berate me or defend his actions, but instead, his body toppled over onto the ground.

"Ariadne!" I screamed. "Help!"

Ariadne hobbled over the hill as fast as she could manage.

"Oh God," she said as the others topped the hill. "What happened?"

I pointed at the inhaler. "He must've overdosed."

"Dammit," she said, running her fingers through her hair in

frustration. "Why couldn't he stay clean? I don't have what we need for this!"

"God, I hate this stuff," I said, picking up the inhaler and chunking it as far down the mountainside as I could.

"We might have needed that to bring him down safely."

"Crap! I'm sorry. What can I do?"

"You're stronger than me. Start chest compressions. Do you remember how to do that?"

"I think so," I said, rolling Mathias onto his back and beginning to pump his chest. "Do I need to breathe into his mouth?"

"It's not worth the additional risk," she said examining our companion. "If any of you pray, now's a good time to do it."

Eying the yellow foam on his mouth, I pumped and pumped, willing life to return to Mathias' body, alternating pumps and breaths. Several seconds, minutes, hours had passed when I felt Ariadne's hands pulling mine away from my friend's chest.

"No!" I said, crawling back to his side and continuing the life-saving movements.

"Hemant, you have to stop!" said Huck, his voice cracking. "He's gone."

"No," I said, pushing him away. "He can't die from a stupid powder! He's survived hundreds of inverts. He can't die from a damn powder!"

I felt Omar's bear-like arms wrap around me, restraining me.

"No!" I yelled, vision blurred by tears. "Not like this! Not like this!"

I collapsed on the ground, sharp gravel biting into my knees through the jumpsuit. I covered my eyes with my hands and put my face into the dirt.

"Why, Mathias? Why? You were my friend!" I yelled, sobbing uncontrollably. Anything you needed, I would have done to help you!"

I felt a tender hand on my shoulder and looked up to see Remi.

"He died in battle," she said. "Don't ever think otherwise. His enemy was only visible to him."

I nodded and turned away, wanting only solitude like that which I hoped Mathias had found. The one person I wanted most was Arjun, who'd remained at the plane with the others.

I lifted my head. "I want to go home," I said, sobbing.

"Home?" asked Remi.

"Wherever my brother is," I said.

"We can do that," she said.

"Huck, can we build a cairn like we did for Kurt?"

"Of course, brother," he said, gripping my bicep.

After an hour or so, we'd erected a small stone cairn over Mathias' body, whom we'd laid grasping his mace. Liesel had thoughtfully braided his long hair and beard, giving him a dwarven appearance in death. Mathias had been an incredible friend when I needed one most. We'd faced breaking addiction together, though it hadn't completely released its vicious hold on my friend. The monument would protect his body in the traditions of the Misfits, who refused to subject themselves, even when fallen, to underground rest. Like Kurt, I would carry the loss of Mathias for the rest of my life. It wasn't enough that the inverts killed my friends, but that the effects of their deaths took others as well. Every day, I was given further cause to stop at nothing short of their complete eradication.

With the observance completed, we continued the trek downward as the sun fell low in the sky. At the current rate, we'd reach ground level at dusk. By my estimation, we'd be about halfway back in the morning when we'd run into Arjun, Kolya, and Rico. I doubt Hera would venture far from the *Sekhmet* and Samson wouldn't venture far from Hera. I couldn't blame him. The second you weren't paying attention, things you love were ripped away from you.

Initially, the surface had seemed dangerous, but survivable. It occurred to me only now that surviving wasn't simply staying alive, but the ability to live. Remi matched her pace with mine as we made our way down a small valley.

"If you need me, I'm here," she said.

I nodded and she continued talking.

"I've experienced things I won't ever forget. Things few can relate to. It's why I take comfort in death. It's the only given in life. Ironic isn't it?"

I smirked. "I suppose it is."

"Take my advice: Whatever you do, don't let the past rule you. It *will* consume you. I've seen it happen to far too many people. People like Mathias."

"Don't you talk about him like he was weak!" I said, putting my finger in her face.

"I'm not," she said calmly, gently pulling my finger down. "He was ferociously strong, but his demons were stronger. You must keep your feelings in check. If not, they will invade your thoughts until they control you. You can't let that happen."

She clasped my hand in both of hers long enough for her warmth to seep in before turning to face the trail ahead. She was mistaken about me. I wasn't dealing with depression. I was dealing with fury. The inverts had taken and taken. I had full intention of returning the favor tenfold.

When we emerged from the valley, fate gave me a chance to exact my vengeance on an ambush four bone arachnids had set up. Thinking us easy prey, they had awaited our exit from the mountains. Fighting as a unit, all four of the eights were down in a matter of minutes. I delivered the final blow, crushing an eight's skull with my hammer. Once wasn't enough. I hit it again, spraying myself with its syrupy, black hemolymph. Again, I raised my hammer and dropped it on the invert's carapace. And again. And again until I felt the familiar hug of Omar's arms. His screaming was only a whisper in my ear.

"It's gone, Hemant! It's gone."

"*Aaaggghhh,*" I screamed, falling to my knees. "I hate the bloody bastards!"

Remi was at my side in an instant.

"I know you do," she said, cradling my head. "But if hate consumes you, they'll win."

They'll win. Her words carried a weight they hadn't before. *They will never win.* I nodded to Omar that I was okay and he backed away. I stood and faced Remi.

"They will never win. Not on my watch," I said through ragged breaths, tapping my temple. "Not in here or out here."

"There he is," said Huck. "Now, let's get the hell out of here before these things attract more inverts."

CHAPTER 16: SAMSON

"**W**here are they?" asked Arjun, pacing back and forth so furiously that he'd worn a track into the dusty earth. "They should've been back by now. I'm going to look for them."

"Like hell, you are, little buddy," said Kolya, fiddling with his mangy beard that cluttered his face. "As I said the last time, we'll go at first light. In the dark, we're nothing more than a liability."

"Speaking of which, I need everyone in their bivvies, now," said Hera. "The last thing we need is more unwanted attention."

I gave her a quick peck on the cheek before we prepped the camp for the night. The sky had become a sea of purple, bringing with it a chill that stabbed right through my layers of clothing. I looked back up towards the mountain, hoping in the rapidly diminishing light I could see any sign of the others. I sighed, seeing not even a hint of life. *If it's not one thing, it's another.* I didn't see how our having an early bedtime was going to speed up their return.

I set up my bivvy next to my wife's and tucked in for the night. The airplane's cabin offered more safety, but with great discomfort. Between its steep incline and poking metal rivets, I favored the hard-packed ground. In addition to masking our heat signatures, the insulated bivvies kept us comfortable enough for a decent night's sleep during the cool desert nights. The cramped one-person tents had been a godsend since their development by Pod Wuhan's engineers. They'd proven their worth time and time again, making overnighting on the hostile surface possible. It was a shame that the material didn't breathe, otherwise it'd make a great jumpsuit.

After watching Hera crawl into her cocoon, I shuffled into mine. I had always been a little on the husky side, something the designers at Wuhan hadn't accounted for. I'd always felt like a Monterrey-style burrito inside the narrow tent. I wondered how unusually tall people faired, unable to simply stick their feet out. The bivvy was only effective when sealed. Dismissing the thought, I zipped up the opening. Before I drifted off to sleep, I pleaded with the universe to deliver Huck and the others back to safety.

"Sam!"

The grogginess instantly vanished upon hearing my wife's fearful voice. I tumbled out of my bivvy as quickly as I could manage, almost tearing the thing apart in the process. The camp was encircled by multipedes. I grabbed my star mace and stood back to back with Hera, Rico, Arjun, and Kolya as the creatures churned around us.

"What are they doing?" I asked. "Why aren't they attacking?"

The pedes were thundering like a wagon train of old around our encampment, barely visible under the light of the moon. Their movement made it difficult to count, but it looked like four—no five—of the spiny beasts. Thankfully, they hadn't attacked the aircraft. With their bulbous armored segments, they could beat the thin sheet metal into smithereens without a second thought.

"They're waiting on something," said Arjun.

"I don't want to know what," said Hera.

"I'll jump into the plane and light them up," said Rico, making a move for the hatch.

"Don't be a fool!" snapped Kolya, drawing a sinister, lightly curved sword. "You could turn five into fifty. We shall do this the old-fashioned way."

No sooner had Kolya finished speaking than the pedes ceased their relentless march. A disconcerting silence descended on the camp. Directly in front of us, they peeled apart, allowing a formidable shadow to enter. *I must be dreaming.*

"I don't like this," I said. "Should we attack?"

"Wait," said Arjun. "This doesn't feel like aggression."

"They're inverts, Arjun," said Rico through clenched teeth. "All they do is aggression."

"Just wait," he said. "Please. If anything changes, I'll dispatch them myself."

Ahead emerged a sight surely few humans had ever seen and lived to tell. I shivered as I reached down to grab Hera's free hand, which was as icy cold as my own. Coming towards us from the distant forest was a giant colorless worm-like creature, clear as glass and covered in fine transparent hairs. Even more bizarre, the moist creature rested on a litter of pill bugs to avoid contact with the desiccated terrain.

"What in the fresh hell…?" Rico murmured.

Carried by its entourage, the strange fuzzy creature was brought forward until it rested meters from us. When the litter stopped, the night became as silent as death.

"Arjun?" I whispered.

There was no response. I glanced over at Arjun, whose normally rigid face was crimson with anger. He was visibly shaking.

"I believe they would like to communicate," said Kolya, barely restraining his excitement.

The glassy worm erected slowly, flattening its body until its belly was nearly a meter in width. It took everything in me not to view the new Arthropod as a threat, not knowing if it was about to ingest us whole or not. My mace suddenly seemed insufficient against such a gelatinous body. A phosphorescent twinkling bloomed within the creature's slimy chest. I watched, mesmerized, as the invert twinkled with light.

A dozen light-blue dots appeared. *Is that supposed to be us? If so, their numbers are off.* The dots gathered into a bundle and soared over a giant light-green dot—*Earth. It* was *us.* The dots came down next to a triangular shape composed of innumerable pink dots.

"Is that the Hive?" Hera whispered.

The scene vanished. *Damn. We interrupted it.* No sooner than I had the thought, the lights reappeared. This time, the rudimentary Earth reappeared with larger blue dots scattered over its surface.

"The pods," Rico whispered.

Thousands of pink dots flooded the sky, moving toward a pod. The blue dot winked out. The planet rotated to another, and the image repeated. Then another. Arjun screamed, grabbed Kolya's sword, and leapt forward, slicing the razor-jawed head off the worm. I stood in shock as the invert's corpse flung back and forth, spewing warm, colorless goo everywhere.

"Don't let it spray you!" yelled Arjun. "It's toxic!"

I avoided the spray like it was sulfuric acid. The pill bugs scattered, spurring me into action. There was a shriek from the multipedes as their bystanding ended and they jolted towards us.

"What the hell, Arjun?!" yelled Rico, grasping his short-handled war axe tightly.

"Why?" said Kolya, befuddled.

Arjun tossed Kolya's sword back to him and whipped out his razor net. With his angry outburst, Arjun had ended any chances of a parley. It wasn't like him to lose his cool, especially when there were others' lives at stake. As the pedes converged on our position, I felt woefully undermanned. *How are the five of us going to hold off so many?* As the first pede charged, I saw the glimmer of dawn and realized we likely wouldn't make it to sunrise.

Unlike me, Hera didn't linger. Using her spear, she vaulted into the fray, slamming its razor edge deep into the gap between the pede's segments. Using the weapon like a lever, she flipped the unwieldy creature on its side. As if orchestrated, Rico took advantage of the opening. He sliced open the invert's weak underbelly, spilling its fetid entrails over the ground. With a single contraction, the creature was still.

I tore my attention away from the disgusting scene to see a pede barreling towards me at full tilt. I rotated out of its way in the nick of time and slammed my mace down on its passing carapace, shattering the segment. In a fit of rage, it flailed its uncooperative, spiked body desperately trying to impale me. After successfully dodging the first two sweeps, the third sent me careening to the ground, bruised but intact and mercifully unpeirced.

Kolya was instantly at my side, hacking deep gouges into the creature, but none of his blows were slicing deep enough to slay the beast. It was Arjun with a flip of his closed razor net on the creature's head that disoriented it enough for Rico to decapitate it. The remaining three multipedes surrounded us, brandishing their spikes and taunting us forward as their jaws gnashed with hunger.

"Not today! You won't be eating this for breakfast," I yelled.

In actuality, I had no idea how I was going to prevent it. We were completely encompassed. The inverts had learned from the first two deaths and weren't giving us any wiggle room. As the first sliver of sun appeared above the horizon, I worried that it was for the last time. I smiled at Hera, whose face was speckled with the grime of battle. She flashed a smile before staring down our enemy in defiance. Neither of us was going to face them lying down. At least the polies had fled, their explosive nature posing as much of a danger to their kindred as to us.

"They're back!" Rico yelled in my ear. "Woo!"

Catching a multipede off-guard, Hemant burst forward, bringing his massive war hammer down, obliterating its brain, and covering the ground with chitin. The pede next to it began to sprout arrows as Ariadne filled its eyes, sinking each shaft in to its fletching. Liesel and Krista attempted to take the last one together, each landing unsuccessful blows. The creature instantly encircled them, its tight wrap exposing the weak joints between its segments. With one fluid move, Huck sliced upward through the pede, cutting it in half. The beast flailed in a mad rage but surrounded by weapons, its end was quick.

"Man, I'm glad you showed up when you did," I said to Hemant. "I wasn't sure how much longer we could've held them."

"About damn time," Rico said to Remi. "Where's the runt?"

All traces of the victory buzz vanished on the faces of the arrivals.

"Where's Mathias?" asked Rico again.

Hemant simply shook his head.

"Aw, damn," said Rico. "I was just beginning to like the guy."

"What happened?" I asked, already suspecting his addiction was to blame.

Ariadne quickly explained what happened on the mountain. She told us how Hemant and Mathias had been forced to take the drug in Pod Kano during their tenure in Zabu's corrupt militia, the Muskrats. After becoming dependent, Ariadne had saved their lives as they suffered the ill effects of the withdrawal. With Mathias, there had been suspected depression, further agitated by the loss of his friend—Mei. The pull of addiction had proven too powerful. With currency to spend, it was all too easy to fall back into his old trappings in Pod Baghdad. Not even the best-run cities could be free of their vices.

"I'm so sorry, Hemant," I said, knowing the two were close.

I watched as he went to his brother for comfort. Arjun seemed unusually cold towards his twin, despite the wave of emotions that Hemant was dealing with. It was a little strange given their normal camaraderie. I'd never understood Arjun's complicated emotions, so it was easy to dismiss his lack of reaction.

As much as a slow morning would've been in order after the chaos we'd endured, we were anxious to get off the ground and distance ourselves from the heaps of dead Arthropods. It would only be a matter of hours, if not minutes, before their corpses attracted other hungry inverts anxious for an easy meal. We cleaned ourselves of the viscera as quickly as possible and after stowing our gear, climbed high into the sky.

"Next stop—Pod Bhopal," I shouted.

CHAPTER 17: HUCK

As the *Sekhmet* lifted off above the City of Lights, our climb attracted a swarm of hooks. Rico and Remi had become quite adept at shooting them down and easily kept them at bay until we reached an altitude that they couldn't. I watched the coastal city grow smaller and smaller as we flew inland to Bhopal, feeling a slight disappointment that we hadn't been able to swim or explore. Between almost losing Ariadne to the mud raptors and the multipedes' ambush of the camp, I was happy to be escaping with our lives.

I turned back from the window and caught Liesel staring. I returned the smile, but I couldn't help but think how she wasn't the one. She was kind and beautiful, but she wasn't Ariadne, which left the relationship feeling woefully one-sided. I didn't know how I would break the news to her without breaking her heart.

The plane eventually settled into its chilly cruising altitude, which was a far departure from the heat of the desert far below. Feeling the pull of drowsiness, I pulled the mashi-repelling blanket from my pack that I'd kept from our travels with Taha and wrapped it around me. Of all the Arthropods we had to contend with in the new territory, at least it wasn't those little buggers. The only thing scarier than a big invert was a nearly invisible one that flew at bullet velocities. After all the mountain climbing and overnight hustle to reach the camp, I was beat. I pushed the haunting memories of the mashi from my mind, wadding the rough fabric against the fuselage's superstructure, and dozed off. Any rest was plagued with interruptions and turbulence, but it was better than nothing. I finally abandoned all efforts to sleep when a loud discussion broke out between Rico and Hemant.

"What do you mean, he violently attacked it?" asked Hemant.

"The thing was trying to communicate with us and Arjun just lost it," said Rico. "I didn't think he'd ever lose his cool, especially not around something new."

"That explains why he wouldn't talk to me," said Hemant. "What was it? We were too busy trying to get off the ground for me to check it out."

I sat up, equally interested in the conversation.

"Morning, Sleeping Beauty," said Omar.

"Hey," I said, my voice cracking with dehydration.

Rico handed me his canteen and I took a swig of the tepid, yet refreshing, water before handing it back to him.

"It looked like a slug had sex with a caterpillar," said Rico. "The fuzzy thing was translucent until it started the light show. It basically showed us that if we go to the Hive, they're going to destroy all of our cities. I was thinking, 'Hell, all the more reason to go! We just have to exterminate them before they do us.' That's when your brother struck."

"It sounds out of character for him," I said.

"I believe I can shed some light on the situation," said Kolya, groggily turning towards us.

"Please do," said Hemant.

"Rico failed to notice the copious amounts of slime that accompanied the glass worm's arrival," he said, his nappy hair matted against the side of his head.

Slime! That's when the realization hit me. "It's what killed Ciro!"

It must have been the same species that killed Arjun's partner during our trek across the Saharan Territory. The two had been deeply in love, united by a common fascination with nature, both native and invasive. Both scientists at heart, Earth's surface was a place of wonder and discovery for the pair. Two of these "glass worms" had snuck into our camp one night, dissolving the transporter guards down to the bone and suffocating Ciro inside his bivvy, leaving a shiny trail as their calling card.

"It's the same type of invert that killed his lover," said Omar, clarifying for Rico who still looked perplexed.

"Oh," said Rico. "That I understand. Love brings out the intensity in all of us. Apparently, Arjun's no different."

"Intense rage, you mean," said Hemant. "All we know is loss. And based on what you're telling me if we don't succeed in this mission, we stand to lose everything."

"We have to see this through," said Liesel, who'd been listening intently since her eyes had opened minutes before. "We're all dead if something doesn't change anyway. Their message only changes the timescale."

"You notice that Samson never even questioned our continuation when he took off," I said, smiling. "I think we're all—"

"Incoming!" yelled Samson, rousing everyone still asleep.

Rico bolted towards his turret across from Remi who was already scanning the skies.

"There!" she shouted. "Eleven o'clock. More raptors!"

Damn. I'd been hoping we were safe at high altitudes. Unlike the other species, the raptors could match the flight capabilities of history's jets. *Sekhmet,* a prop plane, couldn't hold a candle to their maneuverability or speed. I slammed on a headset for hearing protection as Remi released her first few rounds.

"I can't keep them in my reticle!" she yelled. "They're too fast."

"I can't see them at all," yelled Rico.

Remi popped off more rounds and swore.

"They just dodged my bullets!" she screamed, perplexed. "Hot damn!"

Sekhmet shuddered as an impact rattled her airframe.

"Status report," said Hera over the headset.

"Nothing back here that I can tell," responded Rico.

"The elevator controls are sluggish," said Samson. "That's not good."

"They're coming around!" yelled Rico. "Raptors at five o'clock."

Stereo gunfire echoed through the cabin as the two gunners desperately tried to defend the plane. Another impact shook the aircraft, causing Liesel to squeeze me even tighter. Instantly, the plane began to list into a banking turn as Samson released a slew of expletives. His and Hera's hands danced over the controls, doing everything they could to right the plane. Unbalanced as it was, they managed to keep the plane on course by overcompensating with one of the engines.

"We can't handle another pass like that," yelled Samson. "Take. Them. Out."

"Roger," said Rico.

Both guns began to unload toward the creatures.

"Dodge this!" yelled Remi, slinging her turret hard against its mountings.

I heard the death shriek of one of the raptors.

"I got it! I got it!" she yelled.

"There's still one left!" yelled Rico.

I watched as he took careful aim at the remaining incoming raptor. With battle-hardened intensity, he stared down the barrel and waited for the right moment before firing. Anxiety plumed in my chest, thinking he'd never fire, but then the creature blew into halves.

"Got it!" he yelled, jumping up.

A cheer erupted from the passengers as the creature's inertia carried it into the belly of the plane, its wing leaving a gaping diagonal tear. One minute, Rico was there, the next, he'd been replaced by a fine cloud of crimson mist. I was frozen in shock.

"Rico!" screamed Remi, who'd narrowly dodged the same fate.

The number one engine began to shudder.

"It can't handle the excess load!" yelled Hera. "Pull back the throttle! I knew something was wrong!"

The engine sputtered to a halt as Hera struggled to restart it. With the damaged controls and the loss of an engine, the plane tilted downwards into a corkscrew as my weight seemed to compound. *I thought I'd die against an Arthropod, not in a plane crash!* I stared across the aisle at Ariadne, whose green eyes met mine. As Liesel gripped me around the waist tightly, eyes clamped shut, Ariadne mouthed to me, "I'm sorry." I nodded, my eyes starting to burn.

"I love you," I mouthed.

A smile slowly crossed her face, but before she could respond, she slipped away into unconsciousness. I felt the familiar warmth of tears running down my cheeks. The plane's speed steadily increased as we hurtled toward the ground in a flat spin. I caught Kolya crossing himself out of the corner of my eye. Everyone was coming to terms with our upcoming demise. My eyes didn't leave Ariadne's peaceful face until the blood rushed from my head and everything went black.

••••••••

A crack of thunder jarred me awake. *I'm not dead,* I thought as I pried my eyes open. When I took in my surroundings, I wondered if death would've been preferable. My head throbbed as though my brain was too big for my skull. My body racked with so much pain every muscle must have been bruised. Across from me were no longer the faces of Omar and Ariadne, but an open vista of a rocky bank in the midst of a wild jungle. The gray clouds that stretched above threatened a downpour at any moment. I'd somehow survived the crash, still strapped into my seat, but the plane had been rent in two. I reached down to unbuckle and found an unconscious Liesel still gripping my torso. I gently jostled her awake.

"Liesel?" I asked. "Are you okay?"

At first, I was greeted with a moan. Her eyes slowly fluttered open. When she saw where we were, her attention rushed back as she began to panic.

"Hey, hey. You're alive. Take a deep breath."

She regained control of herself and deliberately took several slow deep breaths.

"Is anything hurt?"

"Everything," she said, bringing her hand to her head. "Especially my leg."

I looked down at her jumpsuit, but couldn't see anything. I unbuckled and knelt down. From the seat, a support pole had dislodged and pierced the back of her calf. The bleeding had already stopped, but I knew with the pole's removal, it would begin again in earnest.

"You've got some metal stuck in your leg. Sit still until I figure something out, okay?"

Liesel nodded. I scanned the area for anything I could use as a bandage. Thankfully, my pack had been so tightly wedged between the seats, it had stayed with us. It had some medical supplies, but Ariadne carried the majority of the medications. I looked over the rest of the plane's cross-section and saw Remi, lying unconscious against the bulkhead.

"Remi!" I said, excitedly running over to her.

My heart sank when I saw her face. Her head had been pounded against the airframe during the crash. The left side of her skull was completely caved in.

"Dammit!" I screamed, collapsing to my knees, crying. "I can't take this anymore! I'm so sick of this crap!"

I picked up a rock and hurled it angrily into the jungle, throwing one after another.

"I hate you! I hate all of you!"

"Huck, you're scaring me!" yelled Liesel, pulling me out of my tantrum. "What's going on?!"

"I'm sorry," I said, tears flooding down my cheeks. "I'm so sick of everyone dying."

"What is it? I can't see."

"Remi's gone. She's dead! And worse, I don't know if any of the others survived. We may be the only ones."

"You can't think like that. We survived. That means the others might have too."

I nodded and wiped my face on my dirty sleeve, examining the torn hull of the plane around us.

"What do we do?" she asked.

"I don't know," I said. "First thing's first, let's get you out of there."

I shuffled through my bag until I found an adequate bandage. I knelt down next to Liesel and looked at the pipe. It had snapped off cleanly, so I was hoping there wouldn't be loose pieces in the wound.

"This is going to hurt like hell," I said, handing her a torn strap. "You might want to bite down on this. Ready?"

She nodded, fearfully, putting the thick fabric in between her teeth.

I gently, but steadily, pulled her leg off of the metal tube, trying to ignore her muffled screams. With the foreign material removed, the wound began pouring blood. I applied a styptic pack and wrapped it quickly to discourage more bleeding.

"It's over," I said.

Liesel let the strap fall from her mouth, wincing in deep pain.

"If this were any other circumstances, I'd say stay off your leg for a week or two," I said. "We're going to have to get moving. I'm guessing we've been unconscious for a few hours. It's a wonder the inverts haven't found us yet."

"Are we going to search for the others?"

I thought for a moment as I examined the fuselage.

"Of course," I said, dropping my head. "It'll have to be on our way to the pod. The plane must have broken apart in the air, otherwise, they'd be close by. There's no way of knowing how far or in what direction they are. With your injury, we can't linger."

"What if they come looking for us?"

"I'll leave a note, just in case, but they'll likely come to the same conclusion if they can't easily find us—they'll head to Pod Bhopal. If there's any luck in the universe left, we'll meet them along the way."

"So we're giving up on them? she said.

"Of course, we aren't. We'll spiral out from the crash site a little way out, but then we have to head towards the pod. We're no good to anyone dead. If by chance we get to Bhopal and they're not there, we'll get help and come back."

"How far are we from the pod?"

"I haven't the foggiest idea, but I know which direction to go," I said. "After I bury Remi, we'll go as far as we can before it gets dark."

Before Liesel could respond, an all-too-familiar, bone-shaking roar erupted from the jungle.

"Time to go!" I said.

CHAPTER 18: KOYLA

I awoke with a bright light shining into my eyes.

"What happened?" I asked, feeling the sore lump on the back of my head.

"We crashed," said Ariadne, checking my pupils. "Are you injured?"

The girl's bedside manner left something to be desired. As I flexed my muscles and tested my joints, I couldn't help but notice she was barely keeping her composure, unsuccessfully hiding her abject fear behind those jade-green eyes. *She's so weak, Sveta.*

"I don't believe so. How's Arjun?"

"I'm fine, Kolya," he said, walking up. "Ariadne woke me just before you. I will be uncomfortable for several days, but I am not seriously injured."

"Thank God," I said. "Help an old man up, would you?"

Arjun tugged my arm, helping me climb out of the reclined position the crash had left me in. When I first saw what was left of the plane, I practically fell to my knees.

"Astounding!" I said.

"That we survived?" asked Ariadne. "Absolutely. Now, if you're alright, I'm going to go check on the others."

I nodded.

"We must have… yes," I said, pointing towards the wing. "We must have spun like a seed pod drifting through the air. And the trees, they acted like a net, cushioning our descent."

"It's extraordinarily unlikely but obviously possible," said Arjun.

"Yes," I said, patting him on the back. "I must offer my thanks to the heavens. Excuse me."

"What an interesting turn of events, my dear," I said, standing from my prayers and crossing myself. "Thank heaven that I survived. Our work is not yet complete."

The near-death experience confirmed that I was on the right path. I *would* make peace with the inverts. I picked up my bag, which had survived like the others, jammed into the rigid compartments under the mesh seats of the vintage craft. I dusted it off angrily. There was still no sign of my prized shashka, the sword that had seen me through my first release.

"Minister Lafet must be looking down at you with such scorn," I said to Samson, who was staring at the plane uncomprehendingly.

"What's your problem, man?" said the burly man, giving me a two-handed shove in the chest. "We're alive, aren't we? Why'd you even come on this mission if you're going to complain the whole bloody time? You knew it wasn't going to be a stroll around the central shaft."

"I'm upset because I have to walk the rest of the way to Bhopal because of your incompetence. I've already spent enough time in the company of Arthropods."

"Oh, *you* could've handled the plane better? I don't recall *you* having any pilot training. Oh, wait, you're smart enough to figure it out yourself if some dumb cowboy like me can fly it, is that right?"

"Sam!" said Hera forcefully.

"What?" he snapped.

"Let it go," she said, glaring at him.

I stood there, staring at the miserable excuse for a pilot. He didn't deserve the woman at his side—engineer and pilot. The man couldn't even retain his lunch in the air.

"If you two are done bickering, I could use some help collecting supplies from the crash site. Our gear is… everywhere," said Ariadne. "We need to get out of here as quickly as possible. Stay close."

"It's getting late. I think a wiser idea would be to stay the night," said Arjun.

"But the noise from the crash…" said Hera.

"If the Arthropods were going to attack us, they would have already," he said. "Staying here offers Huck the best chance of locating us."

"Do you agree, Kolya?" asked Hera. "If we're going to risk it, I'd prefer a concurring opinion."

"I do," I said. "The boy is the wisest among you. I would heed his judgment if mine is unavailable."

Ariadne rolled her eyes. "We'll camp here for the night. As long as we have daylight, there's plenty to be done. We'll need food and water. At first light, we'll search for the others."

Ariadne dealt out duties and everyone went to work. I continued scouring the grounds for salvageable materials. The ground was littered with debris from the crash, but very little of it was undamaged. The majority of what had survived the crash was in the sealed compartments built into the fuselage. I was about to give up any hope of finding my sword when Arjun yelled for me. He was running towards me, excitedly, with my shashka in hand.

"I found it, Kolya!" he said.

"Thank you, my friend!" I said, embracing him. "It would have been intolerable to fight with a foreign weapon, much less this measly dagger.

Once everyone was content that we'd found everything of use, we relaxed a moment. Feeling the call of nature, I wandered off into the nearby copse of trees, cutting my way through the waist-high ferns that blocked every god-forsaken step. I felt a tickle and plucked off the tick crawling up my sweaty neck. I'd forgotten what a hellish place the surface could be even without the Arthropods. Making sure all traces of adrenaline from the crash were gone, I pulled out the small flask I had allotted for my urine specimen and made the deposit.

All human urine contained pheromones, which were imperceptible to humans. Perhaps it was an unnecessary trait that we'd evolved past over the millennia. The Arthropods, however, were adapted to be highly sensitive to chemical signals, using them for communication and identification. If I was going to arrive safely at the Hive, I was counting on my urine acting as a white flag for clear passage.

I began the short walk back to camp when I ran into Hemant on his way to relieve himself. *How fortuitous.*

"Good evening," I said, catching him off-guard. "I know we haven't always seen eye to eye, but if I may be so bold... I believe you are risking Arjun's life more each day you allow him to accompany us."

"Can we talk about this later?" he asked, dismissively. "I really need to pee."

"Why not now? This is the best time for a private conversation," I said, gesturing toward the empty forest.

"Fine," he said, turning his back. "Why should I leave Arjun behind now after he's come all this way? He wants to be here."

"Let's not pretend we are fools. We both know no one is coming back from the Hive," I said. "Do you really want his death on your conscience?"

Hemant sighed. "I can't say I haven't thought about it. Arjun has become an adept warrior. His skills are nearly as sharp as his mind."

"But we are talking about the Hive, my friend. It is, as they used to say, a whole 'nother ball game."

Hemant chortled at the outdated phrase I'd borrowed from my newfound collection of archaic books from the vault.

"He'd never forgive me if I left him behind. He's just as devoted to this mission as I am. Of course, I don't want him to die, but if he's willing to give his life for a cause, who am I to stop him?"

"You are his brother. His twin. He will listen to you," I said, as Hemant finished and made his way over to me. "The world can't afford to lose his intelligence. If you insist he remains in Bhopal, he will do it begrudgingly, but you would be saving his life."

"I can't. We've always assumed I'm the older one, but I can't boss him around like that. Besides, Bhopal is home to the Special Forces. It's nothing like the research-focused Baghdad where he'd planned to stay before all this," Hemant said, gesturing towards the jungle. "It would be nothing more than captivity for him."

"He's your brother, my friend. I trust you will make the right decision when the time comes."

I walked away, leaving him alone with his thoughts.

"Oh, he'll try to make him stay, Sveta. I can feel it," I said to myself. "Arjun's festering anger will bubble over like a stew left too long on the eye, leaving us free to do the real work."

I arrived back at camp just as the hunting party returned with a bounty of small rodents, root vegetables, and handfuls of small, green nuts.

"What are those?" asked Omar. He was as thick as Hemant, but an excellent fighter with his double-bladed weapon.

"Flying squirrels," said Arjun. "I suppose that their small stature has helped them evade becoming prey to the Arthropods. We've also found yams and water chestnuts."

"It doesn't look like there's much meat on them," said Samson, extending the wing flap of one of the squirrels."

"Of course, that would come from the round-bellied man," I mumbled.

"What was that Kolya?" said Samson. "I didn't quite catch it."

Hera put her hand on his arm to calm him, her weakened state stealing his attention from my remark. She hadn't looked so good since the crash.

"It was nothing," I lied.

I needed to keep some semblance of peace until the time came to rid myself of their excess baggage. Surviving the journey to the Hive alone would be near impossible without help. To make first human contact with the Queens, I was willing to make some sacrifices. It was of paramount importance that Arjun and I sent our message as quickly as possible. It wouldn't do to be slaughtered on the Hive's doorstep.

I took a little walk around the encampment to help me think while Ariadne and Arjun prepared a mixed stew with a tiny fire. Like many Earth species, the Arthropods communicated through vibrations, movements, and pheromones. Short of the necessary time to parse out their vibrations and movements left only pheromones. Our message would be a crude one, but with any luck would not only inform the Queens of our intent to communicate but would specifically mark us as the ones who sent it.

"Kolya," said Arjun, catching up with me. "Would you mind if I joined you?"

"You are always welcome company, which is more than I can say of some of your friends."

"I wish you wouldn't be so hard on them. They're good people. I wouldn't be alive if not for them."

"You underestimate yourself, Arjun. Didn't *you* discover that no one survived Horizonte's Release Day in the mag-tape footage?"

"Yes, but—"

"Wasn't it *you* who devised that clever way to slay the Nightmare with Ariadne's arrow?"

"Well, me and—"

"And wasn't it *you* who figured out how to use the spores on the antenna bugs? Perhaps they wouldn't be alive without *you*."

Arjun stopped for a moment.

"You should be leading this mission, my little buddy. Not your love-struck, useless friend, Huck, and certainly not an anger-prone, hormonal child like Ariadne."

"Under their leadership, they've got us this far. Even Halima praised our progress," said Arjun, wrestling with his feelings. "Despite what you think, It's been a team effort."

"You'll see it for the truth eventually," I said. "Mark my words, they will try to push you out. Everyone in this group wants to be a hero, and the fewer people they have to share the limelight with, the better."

"I refuse to believe that will happen."

I shrugged, letting him think what he pleased.

"Have you come up with any ideas for methods to capture a powder moth?" he asked.

"No, I'm afraid I haven't," I said. "There are many uncertainties with this plan."

"Like what?"

"I'm not certain that the duster, as they call it, will return immediately to the Hive, nor am I sure that the chemical message will survive the transit."

"I think it will," said Arjun, receding into thought. "Arthropods are creatures deeply ingrained with habit. If something significantly deviates from the norm, I suspect that any involved Arthropods would withdraw and regroup. If they are all in service to their hierarchy like you propose, I think it will stop at nothing to update their leadership."

"Arjun, I didn't realize you could be such an optimist!" I said, laughing. "Now, judging by the faint smell on the air, dinner is done. Run along and get you some before greedy Samson takes it all."

Arjun smiled and disappeared between the erected rows of tents. I eventually made my way to the fire and had several helpings of the stew. The food during my first journey hadn't been anywhere near as tasty. Ariadne had a knack for understanding plants and their flavors. When combined with what she'd learned from her deceased friend Kurt, it made her a phenomenal chef. It would be a pity when we had to part ways. I was scraping the last of my stew from the crude bowl when Arjun sat down next to me, handing me his flask.

"I did what you asked," he whispered. "I relaxed before I captured it to ensure that I was in my calmest state."

"That's my boy," I said, patting his back. "I surmise that their scent receptors are extremely accurate. If we can convince their leaders that we don't fear them, they might allow us an audience."

"An audience with whom?" asked Omar, grabbing the flask out of my hand and taking a swig.

"Omar, that's—" Arjun started, before I calmed him with a hand.

"Gross, Kolya," said Omar, thrusting the container back in my hands. "Your hooch tastes like dog piss."

For the first time since I'd known him, Arjun laughed. It wasn't a raucous laugh, but rather almost more of a hiccup. Its origin must have been quite the surprise since everyone turned toward the unfamiliar sound. Within moments, everyone in the camp was laughing with him. Fortunately for us, no one was curious enough to ask what we were laughing about. Even I began chuckling to myself.

CHAPTER 19: ARIADNE

Out of the corner of my eye, I caught Kolya rising from his prayers. I had found his religious devotion unexpected. Deity or no, our survival had been nothing less than miraculous. It was unfortunate Kolya's beliefs didn't make him any less of an asshole. He'd barely been conscious before he was picking fights and laying blame for the crash.

No one had been conscious during the impact. Hera had managed to stay alert the longest as the intense forces had clawed the plane apart in midair. Every time I thought about the incident, my heart sank. Rico was gone and I didn't know if I'd ever see Huck, Liesel, or Remi alive again.

"I think we should head directly to Bhopal," said Hera as Samson gently lowered her onto one of the seats he'd dislodged from the plane. Hera winced at the pain, but continued, "I believe Huck and the others will do the same.

If they're alive, I thought. "If I knew they were fine, I'd agree. We don't know what shape they're in. They could be immobilized. Huck has some aid gear in his bag, but I have the majority of our medical supplies. We need to find them."

Hera took a deep breath. "What I remember is blurry. Their half of the plane was the first to detach from the rest. I… I can't be certain at what altitude the break occurred. They could be kilometers away and I can't begin to speculate direction."

Our own section had ripped in two as it broke through the dense tree canopy, snapping countless vines which now hung forlornly around the crash's clearing. Hera had sustained the most grievous injury of all, taking a piece of sheet metal to the abdomen. Gratefully, the shrapnel hadn't pierced any vital organs, but her travel would be an arduous affair. I'd tended to her as best as I could, leaving her to handle much of the ongoing treatment.

"We have no idea where they could be," said Omar. "I want to find them as bad as you do, but we need to be pragmatic."

"So we just abandon them?" asked Krista, face flushing. "Is that what you'd do if I was with them—be pragmatic?"

"It's not like that," he said. "Hera needs more help than we can give her in the field. We have no idea where the other part of the plane came down. God, we don't even know if they're alive. If they are, though, they're on their way to Bhopal."

"Right now, we need to salvage all we can and get some rest. We're no good to anyone unprepared and weary," said Hemant. "We'll look for them at first light."

We spent the remainder of daylight harvesting undamaged supplies and taking inventory of food. Thanks to Hera's navigational skills, we figured we were a little over a week's hike from Pod Bhopal and would need to ration accordingly. There wouldn't be any help coming either. In the chaos of the attack, no mayday signal was broadcast. The radio didn't survive the crash, having broken free from its housing, it smashed itself on the bulkhead.

The last two jungles we'd been in, one in the Latin Territory and one in the Saharan Territory, had both been from the relative comfort of vehicles on tried trails. Having crashed in the middle of nowhere meant hacking our way through the crowded forest floor with daggers, which were far from the appropriate tool for the job. After seeing the atrocities Zabu had committed with his token machete, I felt a mild relief at not having to handle one.

Jungles were still very much a wild ecosystem. The air was filled with the buzz of insects, the croak of amphibians, and the pitter-patter of off-and-on rain on broad leaves. In addition to the Arthropods, we would be facing dangerous native flora and fauna and hostile terrain, which could prove just as deadly. Teeming with life, there would be ample prey to hunt in the jungle. The trick was not becoming the prey.

"Hey," said Hemant, his steps softly crunching on the damp ground. "Everything's packed. I think we'll be ready to move out in the morning. Did you get all the meds?"

"Yeah," I said, brushing off my jumpsuit's trousers. "Most of it survived, thanks to the bin. I'm more worried about the bomb. I remember what Arjun said about radiation leakage when we crashed Yanus' carrier into the cave."

"I think we're in the clear. Arjun looked it over and turned it on. The display is all jacked up, but he doesn't *think* it's leaking."

"That's somewhat comforting. Frankly, I'm astounded that it survived the crash. It seems we are as favored by destiny as Kolya believes. I'm just glad it's not rigged to explode on impact," I said, smirking.

Hemant's face grew pale. "I hadn't thought about that."

"Best I can figure, the plane must have floated to the ground and the canopy acted as a rudimentary net. If it'd fallen any other way, we wouldn't be having this conversation."

"I think you're right," said Arjun. "Kolya and I came to a similar conclusion. We believe there's hope for the other party as well. Like us, they also had an intact wing. Kolya believes that the diety of his orthodox faith was watching over us."

"And what do you think, brother?" Hemant asked.

"Though I don't believe in destiny, our unexplainable success does give me pause."

"I don't care what it is, I'm glad we're alive," I said. "And I have to believe that Huck, Liesel, and Remi are too."

•••••••

"Time to move out," said Omar, singularly focused on the task ahead.

What little sleep I'd had was restless, continually waking with concern over Huck. I spent every alert moment questioning why we'd waited until morning to begin the search. Krista followed behind Omar, flashing me a brief, supportive smile. I made my way to Samson and we helped Hera to her feet.

"I can manage," she said.

"You of all people know you shouldn't," I said. "Samson, do *not* let her tough through this injury or she'll never make it to Bhopal."

Samson gulped. "I won't let that happen. This mission has already seen too much death."

"That's a little harsh, don't you think, Ariadne?" asked Hera.

"Not at all. I don't think you'll listen to anything less. In the short time I've known you, I've learned how fiercely strong and intelligent you are. I'd follow your leadership anywhere, but this is one time you have to listen to *me*. And my orders are to prioritize that injury."

"Yes, ma'am," said Hera, giving me a mock salute with a hint of newfound respect.

As a company, we parted the viney veil and pushed into the knee-high undergrowth, beginning our ever-expanding grid in search of the others. We took turns rotating to the front of the line, hacking our way through the ubiquitous vines and leafy plants. No matter the effort I took to avoid them, wet leaves were constantly smacking me in the face. Within the first half-hour, I'd soaked through my clothes, though whether from sweat or the humid environment was beyond me. Before long, a layer of spider webs covered me from head to toe. Mosquitos were out in force. *This is going to be a miserable week.*

After several hours of continuous uphill and downhill hiking was when we heard it—the roar. Louder than anything I'd ever heard even from a distance, it echoed through the vegetation-covered hills. I made eye contact with Hemant, then Omar.

"Is that was I think it was?" I said, my voice shaky.

"I'm not waiting around to find out," said Hemant. "Look, Huck's alive. I know it. Don't ask me how, but I do. And I guarantee that if he heard that, his ass is running to Bhopal with Liesel and Remi in tow."

I looked back towards the sound, the same direction we'd come from. We couldn't search with a spine back on our tale. None of us would survive. I was torn by indecision. I couldn't shake the image of Huck, lying somewhere in a pool of his own blood, unable to move and pleading for help.

"I hope to the universe you're right," I said, making one of the hardest decisions of my life.

"You two done?" said Omar, rolling his eyes.

"Sorry," I said sarcastically. "Kolya, help Samson. Omar, we're up front. Arjun, Krista—"

"On it," she said, giving Omar a dirty look. "We've got the rear."

"I'll have you know that I was—" began Kolya.

"Kolya, right now I don't give a rat's ass what you were. Help Hera and Sam keep up. I'm sure you were awesome, but that was decades ago."

Aggravation splashed across Kolya's face. For the first time since I met him, he'd been offended and not the other way around.

I didn't have time or desire to feel sorry for him. We had a super invert to outrun.

After a quick verification that Hemant's heavy load was stable, Omar and I began hacking through the brush with newfound voracity. Fortunately, the thick undergrowth was sporadic and we were able to make better time in the lighter-vegetated areas. After many more kilometers, we could hear the furious sounds of the spine back fading in the distance.

"You think we lost the Nightmare?" asked Krista.

"God, I hope so," I said. "I just hope it's not chasing Huck."

"I think it knows we're here," said Arjun.

"Now you're seeing things in the shadows, man," said Omar. "We took down their communication network. They're a bunch of disoriented drones now."

We'd taken out the antenna bugs that composed the aerial network that their hierarchy had used for global monitoring and communication. There was little reason to suggest they could still communicate on a planetary scale.

"Arjun is right," said Kolya. "That shiny back at camp represented us as twelve dots before Arjun laid waste to it."

"The shiny?" asked Omar.

"The glass worm," said Arjun. "It's what he's started calling it."

"What?" asked Kolya. "You guys coin silly names all the time."

"Twelve dots," I said, frustrated. "I don't understand. We were twelve people at the time."

"That's just it!" said Kolya. "They *knew* Mathias was gone before those of us at the camp did. They are still communicating somehow, even if it is far more limited than before. That glass worm was an emissary and since when are emissaries dispatched without approval from the higher-ups?"

"He makes a good point," said Hera, wincing, her arm wrapped around her husband's shoulder.

Sweat beaded heavily on Samson's brow from the added burden. We'd arrived in a clearing of sorts. An opening in the canopy allowed for a refreshing breeze to stir the thick air. The ground was still cluttered with waist-high plants, limiting our visibility. The sky was beginning to take on the colors indicative of sunset.

"We need to stop for the night," I said.

"That's not a good idea," said Omar.

"If we push Hera, we'll lose her."

"We don't know that. Hell, we don't know anything. We aren't even supposed to be here!"

"No, we aren't!" I said. "But we *are* here and we're damn well going to make the best of it. I'm not losing another person on my watch."

"Suit yourself, but Krista and I aren't sleeping where we can't see the ground," said Omar, picking up his pack and heading into the jungle.

Krista stared back and forth between Omar and me before rising to follow him.

"No," I said.

Omar turned around. "What did you say to me?"

"I said 'no.'"

Omar let his pack slide down his arm, thumbing his nose as he smirked.

"What are you going to do to stop me, princess," he said.

"You are part of this team and as much as I hate to admit it, we can't survive without your help. You're going to stay, and that's an order."

"I agreed to follow under Huck's leadership," he said. "But if you recall, he's not here right now. I'm doing what's best for me and Krista."

"God, you can be so selfish!"

"Look at you. You're forcing me to stay when you know damn

well that this place isn't safe," he said, closing the distance between us. "Who's being selfish now?"

Before I knew it, I saw red. The same vibrant red I'd seen when I discovered that my old boyfriend had slept with my best friend and roommate—Krista. It was an event that had almost got me banished from Pod Horizonte.

Omar was far larger and stronger than I was, but I was faster. Before I could think, I'd thrown a nose-crunching punch and the fight was on. Omar tackled me to the ground, delivering a painful blow to my side. I struggled to breathe but managed to flip my leg around his neck and fling him to the ground. As I rolled on top of him thinking I had the upper hand, he continued the roll, pushing me from behind until I landed chin-first into the dirt. It was only with the violent jolt through my jaw that the red dissipated and the screams of the bystanders pierced the veil of my anger. Omar's spittle landed in the dirt beside me.

"Don't you *ever* order me around like your minion again, *princess*," he said, the last word lingering like the bile in my throat.

I fought back the tears and the urge to disappear into the woods. The thought of facing the others felt nearly as daunting as leaving the pod on the morning of our Release Day.

"Help her up," said Hemant.

"You wanna take me on too?" asked Omar.

"Help her up," came a milder voice.

I realized it was Krista.

"You too?" asked Omar.

There was an uncomfortably long pause.

"Whatever," said Omar.

I heard the scuffle of his feet as he came to my side and hoisted me up with more force than was necessary. "You know I'm right," he whispered into my ear just before he released his grip so quickly, I almost fell back to the earth. I sheepishly turned to look at my companions. Instead of embarrassment or disgrace, I felt support. Omar collected his things and march off into the woods, giving no time for Krista to follow.

"He won't go far," said Hemant. "He'll never admit it, but he needs us as much as we need him."

"He's right, you know," said Krista. "He taught me a lot about survival while we were stuck outside of Pod Kano. Things I never recalled learning in class. Things I suppose he picked up from his father, I mean, Carvalho."

Omar had come from a loaded past. In Horizonte, children were separated from their parents for training, never again to be reunited. The wealthy often circumvented the protocol, often bestowing advantages to their children during training. This nepotism was exemplified in Omar—the prime minister's son. Omar had despised his father, even seeming unaffected when he learned of Carvalho's death. Due to the tumultuous nature of his relationships and highly punishing training, it was no wonder he could be hard to get along with. However, it had been me who'd thrown the first punch. If my close call with banishment had taught me anything, it was that I had deep-seated anger issues. What came next was one of the hardest things I'd done since leaving the pod.

"I'm sorry," I shouted at Omar.

I watched as his receding figure came to a halt and turned.

"What did you say?" he said, holding a hand to his ear.

"Don't be a dick," Krista yelled.

Omar began his deliberately slow walk back to where we stood. I watched, pained, as with each step his smirk grew. When he finally stood in from of me, his smile nearly crossed from ear to ear. It was a disconcerting sight with the blood draining down from his nose through his beard. *So much for "do no harm."*

"Did you want to tell me something, princess?" he said.

I swallowed my pride.

"I'm sorry," I choked out. "Would you help us find a safe place to set up camp?"

"Let me enjoy this for a moment," he said, putting his hands on his hips.

Before he could bask in the moment, Krista gave him a sucker punch to his unprepared abs.

"Jesus, Krista," he said, struggling for breath.

"You're being an asshole," she said.

"Fine," said Omar, grunting. "I'll help. By the way, that's a hell of a right hook, Ariadne."

"Call me princess again and I'll make sure your nose is never straight again," I said. "And I'm still the leader, but I'll listen to your advice."

"Deal," he said, shaking my hand and reminding me of all the bruises I'd be nursing.

At Omar's suggestion, we set up our camp a little way into the jungle on a hilltop which gave us a good vantage over the clearing below. I made an herbal poultice as the sky grew dark above, hoping that with the morning's arrival that my face wouldn't look like a balloon. Before I followed the others to bed, I silently pleaded with the stars above to return Huck to me safe and sound. I didn't want another moment to pass without him knowing the response I was unable to form on the plane as it fell from the sky.

CHAPTER 20: HEMANT

I sat on the ground, mindlessly chewing my measly breakfast next to my brother and his friend. Kolya's profuse sweating hadn't done his body odor any favors. None of us smelled like hibiscus, but it was as if the man's stench emanated from within his bones. After missing the opportunity at the City of Lights, I was looking forward to when we could all take a dip.

The meager nourishment was a partial portion of our dry rations. Subsisting on a full portion of rations during a normal day's exertion was hard enough. I'd be trekking through the thick tropical rainforest with a heavy-ass bomb strapped to my back. At this rate, I'd be starving long before dinner. As unappetizing as the bars had become, resisting the urge to shovel the rest of the bar into my mouth was difficult. As a safety precaution, Prime Minister Lafet had ensured that the *Sekhmet* was stocked with enough emergency rations to last a whole crew weeks, but then again, she hadn't anticipated most of them raining down onto the jungle floor. *Huh, maybe we'll come across one or two.* Ariadne and Omar had agreed that hunting would be best limited to once daily. At dinner, we could take the time to slow cook our bounty, which posed the least threat.

This bar would be it until then.

Ariadne and Omar. Those two were something else. The tension between them had been building for a while. It started with little jabs and annoyed looks, but last night it had erupted into full-blown fisticuffs. I was glad it was over. Having let off the steam, maybe we could focus on the task at hand instead of these piddly dramatic spats. Omar looked relatively normal, save for his bloated nose. Ariadne, however, was a hot mess. Her face was purple and her tooth had a little chip after her faceplant. Another token to add to her missing fingers. By the end of this god-forsaken mission, none of us would look the same.

It prompted me to check on Arjun's facial scarring. I didn't care what he looked like, but it hurt to know I'd been powerless to save him from the flames. As it was, I'd forever walk with a slight limp in my leg and a nasty-ass scar on my shoulder. The cuts on Huck's face and chest had mostly healed, but he'd have incredible scars all over his body even if we headed home now. And Krista was flat-out missing a hand. She'd been one of the weakest in our entourage, but life on the surface had hardened her into one of our strongest members. Every one of us was worse for the wear, having each sustained serious injuries at one point or another during the mission.

My original plan before Memo's mission had fallen into our laps had been to drop off Arjun in Pod Baghdad where he could geek out with the other scientists. From there, I would solo to Pod Bhopal where I would train as a member of their elite fighters. So much had changed since then. Now, after a relatively brief stop in Bhopal, we were going to head southwest to Pod Bandung, then behind enemy lines, deep into the Australian Territory to the Hive.

The construction for Pod Wagga in the continent's southeast corner of the territory had begun at the same time as the other pods, but it had never seen completion. Too close to the site of the

Arthropod Landing in the Outback, I guessed. It was a miracle the others were finished in time with the rate the inverts multiplied and spread. Here we were centuries later, and if anything, humanity was in worse shape than ever.

I still didn't know how the hell we were going to pull this stunt off, but we'd made it this far. I was hopeful that I could convince Bhopal's notoriously hardcore trainers to teach me some new skills that I could put into practice on our mission's final leg.

"You going to eat that?" Kolya asked Arjun.

"Yes, he is," I said before Arjun could speak for himself.

Kolya shrugged. "I didn't want it to go to waste."

"I'm sure that's exactly what you were thinking," I said. "If you care for Arjun as much as you claim to, you'd be more interested in making sure that he eats. Eat your breakfast, Arjun."

"I'm not—"

"Eat."

Arjun reluctantly finished off the half-portion while Kolya looked on in disappointment.

"Look man," I said. "I'm hungry too, but I'm not about to take food from others. If you're so interested in proving how sharp you still are, help me find some berries or nuts while we're hiking."

"Even a weasel has the occasional good idea," he said.

I rolled my eyes, uninterested in engaging with his prodding. When he turned, I noticed a familiar shape on his back.

"Kolya, freeze," I said, standing.

"What is it?" he asked. "Are you pulling my leg?"

"What I wouldn't do for Ade's khopesh right now," I mumbled.

I pulled my dagger and, with a quick upward slice, removed the blood midge from Kolya's back. The football-sized invert fell with a liquidy plop to the ground. Before it could squeal, I plunged my blade into its thorax.

Kolya muttered something in a foreign language as he turned.

"I despise those little bastards. Was it just the one?"

"As far as I know," I said. "Hey, everyone! Midge check!"

Around the campsite, everyone stopped what they were doing to check each other over. Samson and Krista each had one as well. The seemingly harmless little boogers could stealthily bite and given enough time, could cause a dangerous amount of blood loss.

"Judging by the heft of that one, he enjoyed you for quite a while, Kolya. I'm surprised he could tolerate your flavor," I said, dishing out some of his own medicine.

"Take the other half of my rations, Kolya," said Arjun.

"No, Arjun," I said. "You need—"

I put my hand on his arm and he jerked away, surprising me. "Stop telling me what to do, Hemant. Kolya has more body mass than I do. If he's lost blood, he needs enough nourishment to generate more. I will be fine."

"Thank you, little buddy," said Kolya, biting into the bar with enthusiasm.

I stood there perplexed. In all my years around my brother, I'd only seen hostility from him a handful of times. Virtually none of it had ever been directed toward me.

"Are you guys about ready to go?" asked Omar with a look of annoyance.

"Actually, I need to go for my morning constitutional," said Kolya.

"Are you freaking kidding me?" asked Omar. "Tell me that you haven't been sitting around all morning and when we decide to move out, that's when you have to take a dump."

Kolya shrugged. "It's the call of nature, what can I say?"

Omar plopped down into the soft grass, making himself comfortable. We knew it'd be a while. As Kolya walked off into the woods, I was thinking, *If that Nightmare comes this way, I'm leaving your grouchy ass behind.*

One eternity later, Kolya came bustling back into the remnants of our camp, long since taken down, breathing hard.

"I… came… as fast… as I… could," he stammered. "There's something… out there."

"All the more reason to get moving," said Omar.

"We can discuss it on the trail," said Ariadne.

Kolya checked over his shoulder but seeing nothing, he picked up his gear and we made our way into the thicket. Once we were moving at a steady pace, Arjun could no longer contain his curiosity.

"What did you see?" he asked.

"Probably his shadow," joked Krista.

Mocking wouldn't help the matter, but I'd quickly tired of Kolya's tales. At first, they were far-fetched and amusing, but they'd become ridiculous and annoying. In addition to being sticky-fingered, he was also a pathological liar.

"I saw a powder moth," Kolya began, ignoring Krista's jibe.

"A duster?" asked Omar. "And it didn't poison you?"

"That's what was so strange. After I finished… doing my business, I rose to pull up my pants, and there it was, circling only meters above my head. It was barely further than from me to you now. And it was watching me."

"Watching *you?*" I asked.

The powder moths were perhaps the slowest breed of Arthropod, but it made them no less deadly. Their sporish poison drifted down from their wings, filling the lungs of their unsuspecting prey and rendering them lifeless. Their ability to carry the exploding pill bugs made them a docile, yet extremely lethal, opponent. The idea of a normally hostile invert deliberately choosing not to attack was unusual, though, after the light show, I was a little more open to the bizarre.

"Did you kill it?" asked Samson.

"Kill it?!" said Kolya, whining. "What was I going to do if it decided to dust me?"

"So you ran from it, but it didn't chase you?" asked Krista.

"Right," said Kolya. "It just watched me. I kept looking back at the duster with its fiendish blue eyes thinking I was mad."

"Now it's got blue eyes?" said Omar, already turning away. "We've got too far to go to investigate freak sightings."

Ariadne looked at me with resignation before turning back to help Omar cut through the vegetation blocking our path. I looked back at Kolya and Arjun and shrugged. If Arjun was offended, he hid as well as his other emotions.

"I believe you," I heard him whisper.

Kolya was a scientist and a renowned one at that. *Is a benign duster that unusual? Hell yeah. But maybe there's something to it. Maybe it's doing surveillance.* Then I remembered his story about choking the pede. Then there was the one about hitching a ride on a hook. I shook my head. *It's all bologna.*

We marched steadily through the steamy terrain for several hours, each lost in our own misery. I was tired, dirty, and irritated, wanting nothing more than to set up camp and sleep it off. Hera was getting worse by the minute, her wound constantly reopening. We couldn't afford to take our time. When we stopped for a break, Ariadne struggled to retain her composure when she saw the severity of Hera's injury. I put my hand on her shoulder hoping the gesture would give her a modicum of comfort.

"What if we make something to carry her?" I asked.

Ariadne nodded, her face etched with concern. With my back free of its payload, Krista and I fashioned two branches and one of our mashi blankets into a comfortable, yet ugly, stretcher. Offering Samson some much-needed relief, Kolya offered to split her weight with Krista. Hera groaned as we loaded her onto it.

"I hate to be a burden," she said, weakly.

"You've never been a burden," I said. "We wouldn't be alive if it wasn't for you. It's the least we can do to repay the favor."

Hera nodded and closed her eyes. She was in bad shape. We'd already lost Rico. Huck, Liesel, and Remi were big question marks. I couldn't bear to lose anyone else. I reached down to pick up the bomb when I heard a strange sucking sound.

"You guys hear that?" I asked.

Everyone paused to listen.

"What is that?" Ariadne asked.

"Let's be cautious," said Arjun.

"Yeah," said Omar. "It might be a friendly, blue-eyed duster."

"Knock it off," I whispered, making my way up a mulchy incline with my brother at my side.

When we crested the top of the hill, we saw it. Down at the base of the slope was the largest snake I'd ever seen. Scars ran up and down its lengthy, bulbous body, looking as though its organs wanted to burst through its skin. In its mouth was a twitching spring tongue, meaning we were near water, the toadies' native habitat.

"Has Earth's wildlife already adapted to eating inverts?" I whispered. "I thought you said that takes a ton of time."

"It does," said Arjun.

"Then what am I seeing?"

"Look at the damage on its body. I think it's a Demented snake."

"Are you freaking kidding me? A Demented snake?!"

"Think about it. Animals are just as desperate for sustenance as we are. The Arthropods eat most of the native wildlife's prey. What's left besides Arthropods? If he's that large, he's been eating them for a while. It's safe to assume that there are more like him out there."

The creepy reptile gave me the willies. I heard a *wump* as Kolya plopped down onto the forest floor next to me.

"How exciting," he whispered. "Earth will never be the same."

"That's not what I'd consider exciting," I said.

"Life wasn't meant to be a constant," said Kolya. "Always adapting. What are the Arthropods if not the 'fittest?'"

"I'll show them 'fittest,'" I said, pointing at Dieter's weapon.

Kolya looked pensive for a moment.

"We'll see," he said. "Arjun, do you think it's safe to eat?"

"Are you kidding?!" I asked.

"Relax, brother," he said. "No, Kolya. The corruption of a Demented's mind would be a natural expression of corruption on a cellular level. If we find something to eat, it'd be best if from now on, we checked it for any signs of the disease."

We made our way back down the hill and informed the others of our findings.

"See, now blue compound eyes don't seem so ridiculous after all," said Kolya.

"We'll see," said Ariadne. "Now, if we are near water, we need to resupply. We're not exactly on a normal transporter route, so we can kiss the fresh pump house water goodbye. We'll have to purify our own."

"Yum," I said. "Fish pee water. I can hardly wait."

"I think you mean toadie pee water," said Omar.

CHAPTER 21: SAMSON

We made our way down to the river through tall, reedy grass that clawed incessantly at our legs. I struggled under the added burden of my wife's makeshift litter. I'd relieved Krista the second I felt up to it, not wanting her to shoulder what I felt was my responsibility. The conversations ebbed and flowed around me, but all I could think of was how rapidly the situation was deteriorating. I was kicking myself for not listening to Hera's concerns about the engine. *If only I had listened, we wouldn't be in this mess.* If anything happened to her, I'd never forgive myself.

Reaching the river bank took far longer than expected. Movement through the densely-packed trees was hampered by pitfalls, vegetation, and the occasional Arthropod—none of them with blue eyes. It was mid-afternoon before we found the water, hearing its babbling well before we could lay eyes on it. Life hadn't exactly abounded since the inverts had moved in, but there was a noticeable uptick in the volume of native fauna near the water source. Cooler air surrounded the calm, green-hued river and gave us some reprieve from the oppressive jungle heat. Kolya and I gently lowered Hera to the ground as everyone collapsed from the day's hard trek. I crawled to her side, noticing the abrupt change in our movement had awoken her.

"Hey," I whispered.

"Hey, yourself," she said.

"How are you holding up?" I asked, fighting back tears.

"I'm doing okay," she lied.

I picked her cool hand up and gave it a squeeze.

"I should've listened to you," I said, feeling the first drops roll down my cheeks.

"*Shh*. You couldn't have known. It probably would've been fine if we hadn't had to push it."

I turned my head to wipe the tears on my sleeve and saw Ariadne approaching.

"But I should've trusted you."

Hera cupped her hand gently on my face before a fit of coughing racked her feeble body. I grabbed the cloth I'd been using to wipe my brow and, turning it to a fresh side, gently held it to her mouth. When the fit had passed, Ariadne knelt at her side. Once the coughing had subsided, I went to tuck it away and saw that it was speckled with blood. Without letting Hera see, I turned it toward Ariadne. The color fading from her face said far more than words. My tears poured forth as if trying to match the nearby current as I tried poorly to mask my distraught state.

"Why don't we stop here for the night?" asked Ariadne, placing her hand on my arm.

"Won't the spring tongues… bother us?" asked Hera, weakly.

"We'll set up a rotating watch," she said. "If they can't sneak up on us, they'll likely leave us alone. Do you need anything, Sam?"

I shook my head, wrapping my hand tightly around my wife's. I sat still as a stone as the shadows grew long, as the hunting party returned, as Hemant took the second watch. I was still in the same position when the sun's morning light breached the trees and shined onto Hera's still face, bathing her in radiance for one last time. I don't know how long I sat there before I felt Krista's gentle hand on my shoulder. I couldn't bring myself to face her as she nestled down beside me.

"I was with Zeke for only a moment compared to the lifetime you and Hera had together. It was enough to know I loved him though. I naively hoped we could build a life together after this was all over," she said, pausing to stare into the dirt. "For a long time, I hated everyone and everything on the surface. All it does is take and take. After a while, the truth hit me: We can't take a damn thing for granted—especially not as long as the Arthropods are around."

I finally looked at her. Her face shown with sympathy and wisdom beyond her years.

"I know you're older than me, but take my advice. If you let this gnaw at you, your survival will be irrelevant. You'll be as hollow and empty as Pod Wagga. I know that's not what Hera would want. It took me a long time to realize that it wasn't what Zeke would've wanted for me either."

"What can I do?" I asked. "We've been together so long, I don't even remember what life was like before her."

"You can live," she said pointedly. "And you can help us take back our planet from these selfish assholes."

She rose without another word, returning to Omar. I continued to stare at Hera's lifeless body, willing her chest to rise and fall, knowing well that it never would again. Grief washed over me in waves, pulling me further and further down. But letting it go so that I could swim to the surface felt like forgetting her. *Young or not, the girl's right.* They could take everything from me, but they couldn't take my will. For the first time, I saw our young companions not as lucky kids, but for the heroes they were. They'd experienced more war and loss than many of the oldest in our society, and yet here they were, not just alive, but thriving. I slowly rose to my feet, pausing to allow the circulation to resume. As the tingles spread, I realized that I had the attention of the rest of the encampment.

"We do this for Hera and Rico," I said as they looked on in solidarity.

Not having ever discussed our end-of-life plans, I'd been at a loss as to what Hera would prefer done to her body. Ariadne and her friends presented me with several options, but the one that resounded with me was cremation. I couldn't bear the thought of the nasty critters desecrating her corpse. When it came time to set the pyre aflame, I'd been reluctant to do it. Ariadne thoughtfully offered, but it was my place. I forced myself to place the torch Arjun had crafted into the dry kindling. Within moments, the collected wood was consumed by fire.

"Fly, my love," I said, watching the ashes drift up into the sky on plumes of dark smoke.

Once Hera's fire had burned down to embers, I reluctantly departed, heading down the river in search of a crossing point. For the next several klicks, I kept turning back to look over my shoulder as the smoke plume grew fainter and fainter. *I'll never be the same without her.* As we trekked underneath the blistering noon sun, Kolya and I struggled to keep up with our younger companions. Life in the pods had made the two of us soft. With the loss of Hera, motivation had become a constant battle. The scant sashimi lunch had been a nice reprieve from the dry rations. Having had little appetite, I hadn't eaten much and my energy was waning. At least the fish wouldn't constipate me as much as those bloody bars.

After some trial and error, I'd found a somewhat manageable routine. Every time I thought about Hera, I redirected the feelings of anger and grief and molded them into drive. It did little to alleviate the heartbreak, but it kept me going when I might have otherwise given up. The verdant area we hiked through was distractingly gorgeous. The river was flanked by low-hanging trees and animal trails made our passage downriver far easier than it had been prior.

It would've been an easy place to let my guard down had Arjun not warned us that the smoothed grass trails were indicative of the spring tongues. Omar and Ariadne deemed the risk was worth the progress we made not having to chop through every vine and bramble with our daggers, which made poor analogs for a machete.

"Look!" yelled Arjun, interrupting my thoughts.

With added enthusiasm, Kolya and I sped up to round the bend. The second I saw the clearing, my heart lightened. A grove of guava trees! As far as the eye could see. And they looked ripe.

"My God," I said.

It's amazing how quickly my mood improved with the prospect of fresh fruit. With no regard for safety, we spread hastily through the bushy trees in search of sweet treasure. I parked myself in front of a large tree and plucked one of the perfectly ripe green guavas off of the branch. Slicing it into quarters with my dagger, I bit into it. *God, was it good.* With the juices streaming through my beard and down my chin, I devoured the thing and reached for another. And another. As the mellow buzz from the sugar high took effect, I longed for nothing more than to share the moment with Hera. I sat in the grass, overcome with sudden anguish. *"You must keep going,"* her voice echoed in my head, giving me solace.

I reached up to grab another off a low-hanging branch when I was interrupted by a scream of terror. I grabbed my pack, which I'd let fall to the ground beside me, and sprinted toward the sound's origin. Kolya's body was stretched parallel to the ground amidst the branches of one of the fruit trees, fingers wrapped tightly around its trunk as the tree flexed under an invisible weight. Omar and Hemant were already diving in to help.

"Don't let it eat me!" he screamed. "It's got my legs!"

Kolya's face was beet red with panic, his eyes wide with the looming fear of death. With Hemant and Omar helping Kolya, I rounded the bush to identify the source of the attack. Just as Arjun had warned, there was a massive spring tongue. The toady's sticky tongue was tightly wound around each of Kolya's legs and its spikey-haired body was pulling with enough power that I could hear the protests of Kolya's joints. I darted forward to attack it, but with a flick of its tail-like abdomen, it sent me sprawling and my mace flying. I struggled to stand, desperately trying to regain the breath knocked from my lungs. Krista handed me my weapon and with a nod, we silently agreed to attack it together.

We rushed forward, but the creature was too fast. Before I could land a hit, it threw me back a second time. Krista jumped clear over its abdomen, dodging the blow, but was scratched up by the invert's spiny hair. As Kolya's helpless screams continued, she landed on the other side, recoiling from the pain. *Where the hell is Ariadne? We could use her arrows right now!* Arjun appeared from between the trees, his eyes widening when he beheld the spectacle. He fished something from his belt and flung the small package at the creature.

I instinctively covered my ears as a small explosion rocked the jungle. Arjun's little explosive device blew the toady apart, bathing the grove in its viscera. When I opened my eyes, its two halves sat smoldering on the ground. Kolya was carefully extracted from the tree as he whimpered his thanks to his rescuers and his God.

"What the hell was that thing?" I asked.

"Sticky bombs," said Arjun. "From an old friend. We need to leave. The other Arthropods will have heard that."

I stood, ineffectively trying to sling the spring tongue's innards from my jumpsuit. Kolya groaned, plainly sore from the ordeal. We were disgusting, and in the heat, the smell would be noxious if we didn't rinse off soon. I looked around but still didn't see Ariadne.

"Where's Ariadne?" I asked.

Panic donned on everyone's faces. Before we could begin

searching, a commotion came through the trees. As we all looked towards the noise, the trees parted, and through them came a small group of humans—with Ariadne as their hostage. I stared on in silence as she struggled fruitlessly against the clamp-like grip of a long-haired warrior.

Covered in natural fibers and armed with rudimentary weapons, the group appeared to be a hunting party. Two of their members darted forward and dragged the toady's corpse away, hurling it into the river. Arjun walked up to the warrior holding Ariadne and began speaking in United, all the while, not letting his razor net collapse. I wasn't sure why he bothered. These people looked like savages, probably Banished—those evicted from pod life. I was surprised when he elicited a response.

"You lead the enemy onto our land. You steal and damage our food," the warrior said with an unfamiliar accent. "We take the girl as payment."

"Like hell, you will," said Ariadne, struggling.

The man grinned. *Definitely Banished. Probably kicked out of Bhopal for sexual deviance.*

"Please understand," said Arjun. "We meant no harm. We were passing through and thought the trees were naturally occurring. I can leave you with gifts for compensation."

Arjun pulled out more of his sticky bombs. The man took the bundle from his hand as more warriors emerged from the trees, taking our weapons and tying our wrists with a coarse hemp rope. A bald, ebony-skinned woman addressed us.

"We will take you and your gifts to the Proctor," she said, scowling. "It is he who will decide your fate."

CHAPTER 22: HUCK

With Liesel's injury, we made painfully-slow progress across the rugged terrain. I crested the top of the hill, on the verge of passing out under my friend's dead weight. For the last few hours, she'd been unable to hold herself up and was growing weaker by the moment. I slowly lowered her down at the base of a tree, dropping her the last few centimeters by accident when my arms gave out. I muttered an apology, but she was unconscious. Maybe for the best. I crouched down at her side, checking her wounded leg. When I raised her pant leg, the noxious smell made me gag. *Gangrene.* I cleaned the wound as best as I could, stifling the vomit that lingered in my throat, and gently laid her down to rest.

The hilltop afforded us a view of the haze that clung to the treetops as the bright orange sun dipped low in the sky. I squinted in the distance, hoping to see any sign of Bhopal, knowing full well that I couldn't. I looked over at Liesel, who was already beginning to pale. *Best case scenario, she's going to lose her leg. Worse case…* Liesel wasn't going to live without immediate help. For the briefest moment, I considered giving her a merciful death. *What the hell are you thinking? That's* not *who you are.* If I was going to find help, I wasn't going to do it sitting here. I took a deep breath and decided I could make it further before nightfall. I couldn't see the pod, but I could make out a clearing in the forest below. With any luck, there would be something—anything—there I could use.

I struggled to lift Liesel's ragged body, almost dropping her again in the process. I began the careful descent down the rooty slope of the hill, doing my best not to lose my footing and subject my passenger to a lethal tumble. Once I arrived at the base, there was no way I could go further. I had exhausted my last reserves of energy. Frantically, I searched for any shelter we could take refuge in for the night. I was pushing forwards toward a large hollow tree when I heard a *whump*.

I dropped to the ground next to where I'd dropped Liesel, clutching my chest and struggling for breath. I lay on my back, the wind knocked clean from my lungs, my muscles so weak I could barely move. I watched as a furred figure loomed over me, his blunt club raised and ready to end my life.

"Stop," said a gruff voice. "What have you found for me, Gunther?"

"Not sure," said Gunther.

Another man entered my vision. His face was gnarled like an old tree, his fingers twisted and bent unnaturally.

"Take them to the healer," the man said.

"Now?" Gunther asked.

The older man gave him a look of reproach.

"I'll make Manu help," he said.

The first man gave a curt nod and walked away grumbling. *A healer.* Maybe Liesel could finally get the help she needed. Gunther, and presumably Manu, grabbed Liesel and took her away. I gave a moan in protest and received a swift kick in the side. Moments later, they returned for me. Hoisting me by my arms and legs, the fur-clad duo carried me through the tall wooden palisade surrounding their village.

From the glow of the fire in the center of their village, I could make out rudimentary thatch-roofed huts scattered throughout the enclosure, some larger than others. Villagers milled around, looking on as if strange visitors were nothing out of the ordinary. As each one passed, a vile odor followed in their wake. Others looked as though they were deliberately not making eye contact. *Where on the surface am I?*

The men took me inside a small hut and laid me on a wobbly table next to Liesel. Her normal glow was all but gone, replaced by an icky pallor. Her curly blond locks clung to her face with sweat as her body shivered, despite the room's warmth. Wood crackled in a stone fireplace, illuminating bundles of herbs and jars of dark liquid that lined the shelves of the single room. By healer, they'd meant something far different from a trained medic. I craned my head up, but it was immediately thrust back down to the table. Hard.

"Move and I kill you," said Gunther.

"Where—"

Gunther rapped the side of my head with his club. *Point taken.* By the time the white faded from my vision, a woman loomed over me, her face lit by a chamberstick resting on the table's uneven surface. She had a subtle beauty about her, further obscured by her tattooed face. Around her head, she wore an unusual animal-skin cowl, ornamented with small bones. *A freaking witch doctor!* I almost sat up again, but my head still throbbed from Gunther's last blow.

"What happened to your friend?" she said in a soothing voice as she lowered the hood.

I looked at Gunther who nodded, approving a response.

"She was stabbed in the leg," I said. "She may have gangrene."

"That has an easy solution," she said, calmly pulling out a serrated stone blade and smiling. "We amputate."

"What! No!" I said, sitting up, before being slammed back down into the table.

She let out a soft, musical chuckle.

"Relax," said the woman. "It may come to that, but it would not be my first choice."

"Okay…" I said, shaking off her sick attempt at humor.

"They call me Marie," she said, cutting away Liesel's trousers with a sharp metal knife. "I'm a healer. Despite the archaic tools, my family has been working in the medicinal arts for decades."

"Marie," I said, "Can you save her leg?"

The healer felt around Liesel's wound, inspecting it, and even smelling it. Even with the tender touch, fluid seeped from the gash. I turned my head to avoid getting sick.

"The infection is spreading, but I'll use what I have. I have powerful methods, but they come at a cost. Is this something you are willing to accept?

Liesel, my friend, lingered on the verge of death. If there was any chance she'd live, I wanted to take it. I nodded.

"I'll give her something that will put her into a healing sleep."

Marie poured a dark, shimmering liquid down Liesel's throat from a small wooden vial. She then went to work scraping the dead flesh from my companion's wound. The process and odor were so nauseating, I distracted myself by taking the time to carefully examine Marie's collection of plants and tools. Once the majority of the dead tissue had been removed, Marie applied maggots to the wound, as she explained, to eat the remaining dead material. It was revolting to watch, but a familiar survival technique taught to candidates.

"It's funny how insects can be both our best friends and worst enemies," I said.

"You assume that the Arthropods are our worst enemies," she said, looking into my eyes.

"Why wouldn't they be?" I said, sitting up slowly to avoid another knock from Gunther.

The guard took an angry step toward me.

"Leave us," she said to him.

With a scowl, he marched from the room.

"When you've spent your life on the surface, you realize our greatest enemy is your mind. Once it turns on you, all hope is lost."

"You're talking about the Demented, aren't you?"

For the first time, I noticed the lack of pod tattoos among the copious amounts of ink her body brandished.

"It matters not what you call them. Their minds are their enemies, making them our enemies," she said, her eyes falling. "It is said that a healer shouldn't kill. Those with corrupted minds aren't killed. They're freed."

"I don't understand. What could drive people to consume the Arthropods?"

"Hunger," she said. "You can't understand until you've felt it. It gnaws at your bones, consuming you from the inside. It brings the strongest of wills to their knees. When one is starving, one can't avoid eating the meat that is so prevalent, yet so dangerous. Every time food gets scarce—"

"Marie," said the gnarled man, shuffling in with Gunther in tow. "The young man has suffered enough without you burdening him with the worries of survival. Tend to the girl. I'll watch the boy."

"Yes, Proctor Evans," said Marie with a shallow curtsy.

"Come with me, boy," said Evans. "I'll show you the encampment."

I nodded, following him out of the circular opening of the cob structure. With a clearer head and a vertical stance, I could take in the little village for what it was. Inside the spiked perimeter fence were a number of odd dwellings, all built from the same style of construction as Marie's hut. Outside of each wooden door hung a lantern, giving the quaint village a cozy vibe. It was clear they'd been here a while, surviving undoubtedly like the others we'd found had. Though he didn't discuss it in detail, Hemant had appreciated his time with the survivors. I hoped that we'd just gotten off to a rough start.

"You're wondering how we survive," Evans asked. "You have a name, boy?"

"My name's Huck," I said.

"It's a pleasure to meet you, Huck. You may call me Proctor Evans. I'm the leader of our little settlement."

I glanced down at his arms, covered by long woolen sleeves. If he noticed, he didn't say anything. I couldn't help but wonder what markings he bore underneath the rough, brown wool.

"Take a look around, Huck. What do you see?"

"Houses, buildings, fence, trees—"

"Look deeper, Huck."

I looked around for something less obvious. Everywhere were people milling about, doing daily tasks like cleaning, gardening, building."

"A functioning society?"

"Exactly, my boy. A functional society. And do you know why it functions so well?"

I could sense where this was going.

"Good leadership?"

"I see why you've survived so long, Huck. I'm like you, a survivor. Gradually, I found others and took them under my wing. We built this place with our bare hands. Our bear hands, Huck. Thanks to Earth's gift, the neem tree, we've survived for decades. I'm not going to lie. We've had our trials, but each time, we've pulled through."

"That's quite admirable."

"Admirable," Evans chuckled. "It's survival, my boy. Speaking of which, we could use another pair of strong backs around here. What do you say, Huck?"

"As much as I appreciate the offer, I have to reach Bhopal and reunite with my friends. We got separated—"

"Your friends are dead, I assure you. It's a miracle you made it here. Out there not only lurks the Arthropods but the Great Beast as well."

"I refuse to believe they're dead. And if you're talking about a spine back—giant invert, sharp spines, stabby nose-thing—we've already killed one in our travels. We call it the Nightmare."

"Nightmare," Evans said, mulling it over. "I like that. Maybe there is more to you and your friends than meets the eye. Regardless, I would like you to stay, but I won't hold you against your will."

The roar of a bonfire caught my attention. As the fire blazed, Gunther stood back with a torch, smiling deviously. Each flame climbed higher than the fence as smoke drifted into the star-strewn sky.

"You can do that?" I asked.

"Absolutely. We've propagated the neem and planted grove after grove around our settlement. The only creature that could bother us is your Nightmare, but its territory generally runs further north. Only very recently has it begun to harass our territorial borders," he said, clapping his hands. "Now, enough talk. Let's eat."

I was starving. Gunther had taken my pack when he took me down, so I was dependent on their generosity until I located it. I hoped Liesel would recover quickly and whatever 'cost' was minimal. The idea of missing the others at Bhopal because I was held up here sent waves of anxiety through my stomach. Proctor Evans grabbed my shoulder and guided me to a hand-carved wooden chair by the fire.

"Everyone, this is Huck, our guest of honor. It is he who will be fed first."

I felt incredibly awkward but took the honor in stride. My appetite wasn't about to let me play coy, even with the unappetizing smell that lingered on the air. Within moments, the massive stew pot was steaming, its lid rattling as the hearty odors escaped. As promised, once the stew was served, I was given the first portion. I looked around for Marie, but couldn't find her among the sea of faces.

"Drink, Huck," said Evans, laughing. "You're holding up the others."

I took a deep draught of the rich broth. It had a far earthier taste than I'd expected and the meat had a fishy texture. I looked at the residents, who all seemed to be waiting for something.

"It's excellent," I said.

The group erupted in cheers and dug in as if I'd given the approval. Evans patted me on the back.

"I think you'll find that you like it here, Huck," he said before milling about to socialize with the others.

I drank more of the stew, returning for a second helping. With no one paying attention, I could give in to my ravenous hunger. The vegetables were fresh and delicious, no doubt harvested from the garden nearby. The meat was unusual, unlike anything I'd had on the surface, likely coming from the stables at the end of the compound. My food experience on the surface had been far from standard. So much of it had been eaten raw, cooked strangely, or region specific. All I cared about was that it was delicious and filling. I spent the evening chatting with other residents, finding that many were indeed descendants of survivors and Banished, most of their crimes, they happily confessed were theft born of necessity. Even out here, aggravated crimes weren't tolerated.

When I could squeeze out of the onslaught of questions, I made my way back to Marie's cabin to check on Liesel. I knocked but heard no response. I tried the handle and realized the door was locked from the inside. I jiggled the handle in frustration when the lock sprung open. I hesitantly cracked the door. The interior was dark, illuminated only by moonlight through small windows. I found Marie's half-burned tallow candle and used a homemade match to light it. When I turned, I found Marie bound and gagged, her eyes shouting a message of warning. Liesel lay where I'd left her, her top partially unzipped.

"Can't leave well enough alone," said Gunther from behind.

Whump. I expected the blow to render me unconscious, but nothing came. I open my eyes, which I'd cringed shut, and turned. Behind me, Gunther lay bleeding on the floor, Manu stood over him with a blunt wooden staff. Manu pointed at Marie, reminding me of her restraints. I dashed over and loosened the knotted hemp rope.

"What happened?" I asked as soon as her gag was free.

"Gunther," Marie said, spitting towards his unconscious frame, "He dropped me from behind like the coward he is. When I woke, he was about to take advantage of your friend. That's when you interrupted him."

"I thought Evans didn't allow conduct like that."

"Ha!" said Marie.

Manu let out a wispy chortle.

"Evans all but encourages it. He lets the strong take advantage of the weak. Believes it makes them stronger. If it wasn't for Manu here, I might have become someone's whore long ago."

"Thank you," I said to Manu, who replied with a subtle nod.

"If you're waiting for him to speak, it's going to be a while. Evans cut out his tongue."

"What?"

"If you believed Evans' story, you're not as bright as I'd hoped. Half of the trees that he 'planted' are slow growing. Either he's been here far longer than he claimed, or Manu's story is true."

"Manu's story? You just said he was mute."

"Mute and previously illiterate, but not stupid. When I came, he knew there was something different about me. He rightly figured a healer of my provenance was unlikely to be corrupt. It took a lot of frustrating hours, but I taught him to read and write. And he had one hell of a story. Evans arrived years ago with his crew of Banished, including Gunther. The group had been kicked out of Bhopal for horrendous crimes. They subjugated Manu's people, the survivors, and cut out Manu's tongue for spreading dissent. Only a fraction of his people are still alive."

"Why'd they leave Manu alive?" I asked.

"They used him as an example, making him do horrible things. They keep him on now as a kind of pet, but they've thankfully lost interest in him."

"Jesus Christ."

Manu tapped on the table.

"Time to go," said Marie. "We've got to escape."

"How the hell are we going to do that?" I asked. "Liesel's unconscious and the party out there is getting intense."

"We'll use the party as cover, they're getting intoxicated. Their judgment will be poor, but their aggressiveness is staggering."

"They're drunk?"

"Not exactly. You don't realize what you ate, do you?"

The question raised goosebumps on every square inch of my body.

"That's right. They didn't give you any of the dark stuff though, I can tell."

"You mean everyone here is Demented?!"

"Not yet," said Marie. "It doesn't happen overnight."

Manu banged his staff against the table.

"There are donkeys in the stables. While everyone's delirious, we can sneak out the west gate."

"Why haven't you escaped before now?"

"Because I'm a coward," she said, turning away from me. "But I refuse to let you and your friend get trapped in this snare."

Manu immediately lifted her chin to face him and shook his head from side to side. Then he pointed at her and flexed his arm, telling her that she was strong. He grabbed my hand and placed it into Marie's. He pointed to Liesel, then to himself, and pointed at the door.

"I think I get the message," I said.

While Manu draped Liesel over his shoulder, I stepped over Gunther. Marie yelped from behind me. Gunther had awoken and grabbed her ankle. In a blur of motion, she dropped to one knee and plunged a tiny blade into the side of his neck, spraying his blood all over the dirt floor. Within moments, his body went slack.

"That's been a long time coming," she said.

We rushed out the door and to the stables. With the donkeys loaded and softly braying, we guided them to the west gate where Manu easily dispatched the bored guards. When I took a final look back at the roaring fire, Evans stood there, staring straight at us, eyes burning as hot as the flames. Making no move to pursue us, we turned and stepped bravely out into the night.

CHAPTER 23: KOLYA

I suppose things had gone from worse to merely bad as opposed to the inverse. It'd take our present captivity over being a spring tongue's dinner any day of the week. My back and knees continued to throb as the strange warriors led us to their leader, a proctor, he called himself. I felt another jab in the ribs, prodding me forward.

"Surely you can move faster than that, old man," said my guard. "I don't want to stand downwind of you any longer than I have to."

I ignored the jibe and continued on. It was Samson's fault for getting us into this mess. I was a researcher, dammit. I didn't belong in the thickets of the surface. I longed for the comfort of a pod, at least for a few nights. I looked back at my guard. He looked ridiculous with his shorn head and solitary braid.

"What was I thinking, coming out here like this, Sveta?" I muttered.

"Have something to say, old man?"

"Stop patronizing me!" I yelled, turning to face him. "I'm one of the world's premier scientists. Do you have—"

I was on my back before I knew what had happened, my vision

blurring from the edges. A girl's lone face formed in the clouds above as my vision grew dark.

"Sveta…?"

"Researcher Kolya," asked the lab manager, a stern woman with tightly bound hair. "This is your new lab apprentice, Candidate Sveta. She's to study with you until her Release Day."

"Thank you," I said, kissing her hand. "It's a pleasure to meet you, my dear."

"You as well, Researcher Kolya," the young girl said. "It's truly an honor."

"The honor is mine. Please call me Kolya. My title sounds far too formal."

The girl nodded, shaking her short blond ponytail. Her blue eyes sparkled with a hunger for knowledge. I could tell instantly that she would make a fantastic apprentice.

"So, Sveta, what brings you to my lab in particular."

"I've read all of your work. I'm kind of an admirer. I'd like to study with you until my release, then I hope to return to your side after serving a year with the transporters."

I laughed deeply, adjusting the operating tools in my tray. Everything in my lab had to be meticulously organized or I couldn't concentrate on the work at hand. The research wing might be as old as the rest of the outdated pod, but that didn't mean we couldn't keep it tidy. The sterile surroundings of the lab's dissection room had never been very welcoming, but I found the cleanliness comforting.

"A rough choice of service for such a dainty little thing," I said, "We'll see how you do in the lab, but I can tell you hold promise."

I watched a smile cross her face, bringing out her little dimples.

"What are we going to do today?" she asked.

"Observe the room. You tell me."

"Well, the room has been prepared for an operation. Sterile tools are at the ready. Headsets are plugged in, indicating possible noise disruptions. There's no gurney, so I can't say with certainty what the subject will be."

"Good analysis, Sveta. You're on your way to being one of the few competent people in the pod."

With that, there was a knock as the lab door swung open.

"Researcher Kolya, the subject has arrived," said Martín, one of my assistants.

"Excellent. Bring it in."

As soon as the outer hatches opened, the muffled shrieks of the muzzled hook beetle permeated the lab, reverberating off the walls and stabbing my eardrums. I pointed to the headset. Sveta removed her hands from her ears just long enough to jerk them on.

"Much better," I said with the cries attenuated.

"That was… unpleasant," said Sveta through the static, which worsened with each movement of the cord. "So we have to be tethered to the walls throughout the operation?"

"For this, yes. It's not bad once you get used to it. Just try your best not to get tangled or drag the cords through the examination. Lab safety is of the utmost importance."

"Yes, sir."

We could still hear the piercing whine of the unwilling creature through the headset, but the set's over-ear design reduced it to a tolerable level.

"Pay careful attention today, Sveta. I will rely on you to document all you see for further investigation."

"Should I take notes on the hook now, sir?"

"Hook beetle, Sveta. I won't have any of that candidate jargon in the confines of my lab. Or if you prefer, *Megasoma uncinus*, its Latin binomial, though I tend to only use that in my formal papers. And no. Right now I need your assistance more than your personal account. Our conversation is being documented on mag recorders next door."

"Yes, sir. What will we be doing today?"

"I'm glad you asked," I said, smiling.

I enjoyed my precocious new charge and her initiative.

"Today we'll be performing a vivisection of the hook beetle to test my latest formulation of an anti-Arthropod spray. It has yet to be successful on a live subject, but works well in Petri dishes, albeit in controlled environments."

"A vivisection? You mean it will be alive when we cut into it?"

"Yes, but no worries. Their pain receptors operate differently from ours. Not to mention, they are quite limited intellectually. I doubt what we are doing even registers with the creature."

"Okay," said Sveta, doubt etched across her face.

In time she'd learn how truly stupid the creatures were. There was intelligence in their rankings, but it wasn't present in the lower levels. I suspected they had a hierarchy, but those ideas still needed more thought.

What does the spray do?"

"Wait and see, my dear," I said, hopeful that this would be the day it proved its effectiveness.

We approached the beetle, writhing on its back within its constraints on the polished stainless steel table. The table was one of the purest examples of untainted materials in the pod. As head of the department, I barely managed to keep hold of the invaluable antique much to the chagrin of the recycling administration. If the recyclers had their way, they would have stripped the lab of everything long ago if not for my adamant refusals. *How could they expect me to work with inferior tools? Bah.*

"Blunted bone saw, please," I said.

Sveta handed me the round-tipped instrument. The serrated blade was as sharp as the hook beetle's razor beak, but it lacked a point to avoid damaging any of the fragile internal organs of the creature.

"We'll start here," I said, pointing to the gap that ran the length of its belly. "After the sides, this narrow gap is the hook beetle's most vulnerable area. Cut anywhere else and you'll need a power saw."

I held the knife at an angle, just over the mucousy membrane that covered the creature's belly. Even with the blunt tip, the hair-thin joint was weak enough to pierce with the blade. When I'd located the exact spot, I shoved the tip in as our subject wrenched back and forth, straining the vice-like grip of the restraints.

"Are you sure it doesn't hurt?" Sveta asked as I sawed down the abdomen.

"Is that sympathy I detect from the budding scientist?"

Sveta bit her lip and said nothing else. Her young innocence was an interesting juxtaposition against the gruesome work in front of her. When I reached the end of the belly, the chitinous ribbed structure sprung open with a loud crack. The new apprentice jumped back, clinging to the wall in fear. I laughed as her eyes darted from the twisting hook beetle to me, her face pale.

"It's fine, my dear," I said through the headset. "It's a perfectly normal reaction to the incision. These chitinous plates provide protection for the underbelly. Without the flesh of the abdomen holding them together, they tend to spring apart violently."

"A warning would've been nice," she muttered.

I ignored the remark. She was young and would learn in due time. Should she survive the release, which I earnestly hoped she would, she would come back far more hardened than I could ever train her to be.

"What are we looking for?" she asked, slowly approaching the splayed subject.

"The Arthropod's heart chambers. Unfortunately for us, they lay buried deep within the abdomen. We have to dig."

"But the hook…the hook beetle is still alive. It looks like it's in agony."

"Put your concerns aside, Sveta. These creatures are as dumb as cinder blocks composing the walls. I assure you that these are just involuntary muscle spasms. Its instincts are trying to keep it alive. Its discomfort will end soon enough."

"Why do we need to keep it alive through this?" she asked. "Could we not drain its hemolymph and then do the study."

"You must learn to part with your empathy towards them, Sveta. These creatures kill us mercilessly by the thousands as the pods of the world hold their Release Days. Wait until you've seen your friends ripped apart and devoured as you are sprayed with their blood. When you return, I promise you won't be discomfited by any amount of suffering we inflict."

She nodded but appeared on the verge of fainting.

"Now," I said, reaching into the ubiquitous white filling surrounding the Arthropod's internal organs. "We find the heart!"

This was too much for my dear assistant. With my hand plunged deep into the gooey abdomen as I pushed aside brown organs and black hemolymph dripped onto the floor, she wretched into the nearest biohazard disposal bin.

"Some are too weak, I'm afraid," I muttered.

"I'm not weak, this just feels… wrong. Even for them."

"Stay or go," I said. "It's of no importance to me, but how did you think I completed all those papers of mine you cherish so? If you want to study the Arthropods, you must set your feelings aside. They are scum and you must treat them as such."

She wiped her mouth with her clean sleeve.

"Alright," she said, taking a big gulp and struggling to retain what was left of her stomach's contents. "I'll stay."

"Good. I've found the heart. Please, look."

She slowly approached the belly of the beast and looked down into what I'd revealed. Nestled deep within the fat and organs were the heart chambers. A long series of pods connected by a long tubule.

"Most people are only interested in the pheromone glands of the Arthropods, but their bodies have so much more to teach us. Grab that spray bottle off of the counter to your left."

Sveta complied, bringing the bottle to my side.

"You get to do the honors. While I keep the other organs clear, I want you to saturate the chambers with the spray. Don't worry about my hands. It's innocuous toward humans."

Sveta tentatively held the bottle aloft, then began spraying the fine mist on the length of heart chambers, saturating it from front to back.

"Now we watch," I said excitedly.

Right before our eyes, the hemolymph inside and outside of the chambers began to crystallize, freezing the muscles mid-contraction. The creature's cries became deafening, even through the headset. Writhing like a demon, it lifted itself off the gurney, slamming back down with enough force to crack the white tile floor below.

"It's working!" I shouted.

Again, Sveta had her back to the wall. Tears trailed down her cheeks. With one final arch of its back, the creature came back down and all sound and movement ceased.

"Thank God," I said, taking off my headset.

I took a clean rag and wiped the sweat from my head. I needed another shower. I felt disgusting. Sveta removed her headset as well and came to my side.

"So what was that?" she asked.

"That's a little something I developed to kill the Arthropods. It reacts with the chemicals in their hemolymph causing crystallization. You saw how quickly it arrests muscle movement and fluid flow."

"That's an incredible discovery. One that could save us."

"I agree, but it's far from perfect. This was the first time it worked on a live specimen. However, it's useless in the wild. It cannot be applied externally. So, until I find a way to successfully inject it into their hemolymph, it's of no practical benefit."

"Wow," she said. "While I am uncomfortable with your methods, your research is fascinating. I'd like to continue to help you."

"I would like that," I said. "You will need to firm up your constitution."

"I will try," she said. "Provided they don't change the end goal, I hope you will be open to suggestions on less… problematic methods of experimentation."

"Deal," I said, smiling.

"What's next on the agenda?"

"We must put the corpse in cold storage, where we will monitor how time affects the crystallization. The gurney is one of very few, not to mention, won't fit in the cold bays. We'll need to unstrap the creature and slide it in by hand."

"Yes, sir," Sveta said, revitalized, ironically, by the death of the beast.

Sveta began loosening the clasps on the right side of the metal gurney. I had just begun rinsing tools and loading them into the autoclave when I heard her scream. I spun on my heel just in time to see the invert cock back its free leg and send it careening towards Sveta's chest, impaling her against the wall.

"No!" I screamed as I looked on in abject horror, watching the wall crack in every direction from the epicenter of the destruction. "Sveta!'

I darted across the slick floor with no regard for my safety, twisting my ankle in the spilled hemolymph when I almost fell. I grabbed Sveta's hand and held it as the blood dribbled down her chin. She looked at me in sorrow as her neck went limp and her head sunk down to her chest.

I started sobbing. I should've never let my guard down. I thought for certain the creature had perished. I determined at that moment that I'd never be wrong again.

"I'm sorry, my dear Sveta," I whispered. "I will carry your spirit with me forever."

I heard movement behind me and recoiled when I felt a searing pain in my leg. I spun as I fell to the ground, clutching my injured leg. The invert had sliced my thigh open, leaving my femoral artery draining out onto the floor and mixing with the accumulated hemolymph. I stared into the invert's eye as it clouded with death, my head a mix of righteous anger and newfound understanding. *Well played.* I'd been an idiot and it would cost me my life and that of my apprentice. There was more to these vile creatures than met the eye.

"Researcher Kolya!" Martín screamed as everything faded to black.

"Kolya, can you hear me?" asked Ariadne, turning to the others. "He's awake."

"What happened?" I asked groggily, touching the sore spot near my temple.

"One of the guards knocked your ass out," said Hemant. "Best if you keep a lid on that 'premier scientist' thing."

"Uh, yes. I suppose so," I said with a grunt as I rose to one knee.

"Get moving, old man," said my guard impatiently. "Fall again, and I'll kill you."

With help, I stood and we continued our way toward the warrior village, albeit, now with an atom-splitting migraine.

CHAPTER 24: ARIADNE

Guided by our captors, we trudged along a nearly invisible path through the woods. I walked in stunned silence, fearful after the heavy blow Kolya had received. After a few kilometers of marching, we arrived at the party's fortified village. Arjun and I looked at each other, mouths agape, as we took in the sight. The wooden palisade was a sight to behold. Topping out at roughly six meters in height, each of the former tree trunks had been sharpened and charred, giving the wall a formidable appearance. After a shout from the guard, the hefty gate parted and we were allowed to enter.

My nose crinkled as I entered. A noxious smell similar to bad onions soaked in ammonia clung to the air like a wet blanket. The inhabitants made little attempt to mask the odor from going long periods of time without leaving the confines of the small village. There were enough occupants that the rather large enclosure felt crowded. Children were playing contentedly as they worked in various capacities related to farming or cleaning.

"What is this place?" I asked Arjun.

"I'm not sure. Survivors maybe?" he responded.

"Whatever it is, I don't care for it," said Omar.

"Great observation, Baker Street," said Hemant. "We're their prisoners."

"Shut up," said Omar. "I mean something's not right. I can smell it."

"I can smell it too," said Krista, "But I call it body odor."

As we neared the center of the village, an older man emerged from the central building, arms extended. His face was bumpy as an old piece of cypress and his thinning curly hair was gray as the overcast skies above.

"Welcome, friends, to Bastion," he said. "Let me introduce myself. I am Proctor Evans. Nila, Joso, release them. This is no way to treat our guests. My apologies. We are not in the habit of holding strangers against their will. You must be hungry. Please, sit by the fire. I will have something prepared for your arrival."

Nila cut the rope binding my hands, giving me some much-needed relief. I couldn't shake the feeling that the bald woman would've much rather buried her knife into my chest. I looked down at my forearms and I massaged my wrists. They were red and raw from the coarse hemp. As she cut everyone's bonds, each exposed wrist bore similar friction burns.

"Can I have my pack?" I asked Evans. "I'm a medic."

Evans looked at Nila and Joso and nodded.

"I must insist that we keep your weapons until your temperament is understood. If you are bandits, we can't have you parting our heads from our bodies while we sleep."

Joso leaned over and muttered in Evans' ear as Nila directed the warriors to return our packs. His long hair obscured his mouth, preventing me from reading his lips. There was some obvious dismay among them. They must have hoped to split up our belongings amongst themselves.

"You," Evans said, pointing at Hemant. "What is your name and what is this load you carry?"

That's all we need. Some backwoods miscreants taking possession of our bomb. All of a sudden, the contents of my rucksack seemed trivial by comparison.

"I'm Hemant," he said, standing tall. "It's a special weapon designed to exterminate the inverts. We've been tasked to take it to the Hive."

"The Hive. My, my, how interesting," said Evans, rubbing his chin. "We have a large invert here. Perhaps we could use this device to rid us of its presence."

Joso whispered in his ear again.

"It doesn't work?" Evans said, turning to Joso for confirmation.

"Proctor, if I may," said Arjun. "The device was damaged during our arrival. It is beyond all of our abilities to repair it, but I'm confident that the technicians at Pod Bhopal can fix it. However, its use on the local Arthropods, regardless of size, would be a waste of its capabilities."

"It's a weapon of vast power then," said Evans, taking a little too much interest.

"They're expecting us and the weapon in Bhopal," I said. "Our friends are already there waiting for us."

"Would this be a young man and woman wearing similar attire to you?"

"Yes!" I said with far too much enthusiasm.

"I'm sorry to be the one to tell you this, but they are dead," said Evans. "One of our hunting parties found them a few days ago. Or at least what was left of them."

The air vanished from my lungs as I collapsed to my knees, shaking my head. I felt Krista embrace me as she crouched next to me, whispering consolations into my ear.

"No. That can't be," I muttered. "He's lying. He has to be. Huck can't die."

"We have no reason to trust him, Ariadne," she said, voice

trembling. "We also have no reason to doubt him. He clearly saw them."

I shook my head, refusing to believe it, all the while unable to shake the grisly image of Huck and Liesel dismembered from my mind. I started to hyperventilate. Krista pulled me into a tight squeeze, all the while rubbing my back and crying with me.

"Were there others?" asked Samson. "Another woman. Dark hair. Slightly older."

Through the film of tears, I could see Evans shaking his head.

"I'm sorry, friend," he said. "There were only the two."

Out of nowhere, the women of the camp brought out steaming bowls of food, placing each one into our hands. A kindly older woman helped me to our feet. *Probably Remi too.* We'd grown quite close over our time in Baghdad, finding comfort in our late-night conversations. Her memory would always have a cherished place in my heart. As appetizing as the food smelled, I couldn't bear the thought of eating. Neither could anyone else, except Kolya and Omar, the latter of which noticed Krista glaring.

"What?" he said. "We have to keep our energy up."

"I can't believe you," said Krista.

"You should both try to choke some down. You never know when our circumstances might change."

"He's right," I forced out, allowing the warmth of the vessel to soothe my hands. "Huck…" I started sobbing. "Huck wouldn't want me to stop. He'd beg me to keep going."

I forced myself to drink some of the thick, brown broth. I couldn't bring myself to eat any of the white chunks of meat floating among the vegetables. Krista managed to drink some of hers as well, politely sipping so as not to offend our new hosts. Hemant and Arjun couldn't have looked more alike at the moment. They both stared into the fire, internal torment etched onto their faces. Samson came over and patted my back in a paternal gesture.

"I'm sorry, Ariadne. I know you two were close."

"Thanks, Sam," I said, wiping a tear with the back of my hand. "First Rico and Hera, now Liesel, possibly Remi, and… and Huck. I thought he would be with us to the end."

"Me too," he said. "I thought he'd outlive me for sure. I can't offer much, but let me know if you need anything, okay?"

I nodded and gave his hand a squeeze.

"I find it unlikely that you are in the mood to join our afternoon hunt," said Evans, rubbing his hands together. "Please make yourselves at home. We have a recent vacancy in one of our cabins. It's been prepared for your arrival. Tomorrow after our morning meal, we will discuss how you can repay our hospitality. We need to kill the Great Beast before it discovers our village. You will help us kill the Nightmare."

With a look of disdain splashed across her dark face, Nila escorted us to a poorly-lit cabin in the northwest corner of the village. Under different circumstances, I would have found the place fascinating. The walls were lined with the medicinal herbs and concoctions of a healer—like me. I collapsed onto one of the low, wooden-framed cots that the villagers had brought in and pulled one of the salves from my pack as Nila closed us in. I heard the clank of the key as it turned in the lock.

"Would anyone like something for your wrists?" I asked.

"You don't have to do this, Ariadne," said Hemant. "We're all adults. We can put it on ourselves."

I grabbed my burly friend by the arm and forcefully pulled him down to a squat in front of me and began rubbing the greenish paste onto his inflamed skin.

"Thank you," he said.

I smiled. I hated the speed of life on the surface. Its relentless pace gave no one the appropriate amount of time needed to grieve. I'd work through the loss of my friends when we were safely nestled away in Pod Bhopal. Until then, I would put all my focus on the task at hand. Right now, that was serving as team medic. Lastly, Kolya sat down in front of me. As I applied the salve to his wrists, he stared at me with a look of puzzlement. After a minute or two, I couldn't take it.

"What?!" I asked.

"None of you understand, do you?" he asked, rubbing his head where he'd been hit. "Not even the smart one."

"What are you going on about, old man?" asked Omar.

Kolya chuckled to himself and shook his head.

"What's wrong with you, man?" asked Hemant. "We just found out our best friends died and you're laughing. Show some freaking respect."

"That's just it. I don't believe that they are," said Kolya, still laughing. "Arjun, tell me the story of naming the spine back."

"Okay," he said, his eyes questioning. "Otto named it the Nightmare after we fought it in the Latin Territory."

Kolya splayed open his hands, waiting for us to figure it out.

"*We* named it!" said Hemant. "There's no way Evans would know!"

"Bingo," said Kolya.

"Then where's Huck?!" I asked.

"Ariadne, we still have to face the possibility that our friends are dead," said Samson. "I hate to say that, but Evans just conclusively proved we can't trust him. What's to say he didn't kill them afterward?"

"Not to be a pessimist, but he's right," said Omar.

"Ariadne," said Krista. "Do you still feel like Huck's alive?"

I paused for a moment, taking time to calm my chaotic emotions. "I do."

"That's good enough for me," said Krista.

"Me too," said Hemant. "So what do we do?"

"Evans wants us to help kill the Nightmare," said Ariadne. "We could ditch him in the woods."

"He's too smart for that," said Kolya. "When he looks at you, you can tell he's calculating. Whatever his game is, he's playing it several moves ahead of us."

"If we take down the beast, then we no longer have any value to Evans," said Omar. "That could be a risk in and of itself."

"Evans said that the beast hasn't been coming this far south," said Arjun. "That leads me to believe it's following us. For us to make it to Bhopal, it's in our best interest to kill it."

"I concur," said Kolya, giving a nearly imperceptible wink to Arjun.

"Then we kill it, but after it's killed enough of them that we can overpower them," I said. "We know how it works. If we can anticipate it well enough, we can outlast them."

"It's a big gamble, but it has potential," said Omar.

●●●●●●●●

With the sky still hued in the purples of dawn, we assembled around the smoldering remnants of the evening's bonfire. Evans addressed the hunting party. Unfortunately for us, there were enough of the local warriors that overpowering and escaping during the hunt wouldn't likely be an option.

"Have you encountered the Great Beast before?" asked Evans, knowing full well that we had.

"We have," said Arjun.

"And how did you defeat it?"

"After a trying battle, we altered an arrow and fired it through the creature's neck, bringing it to the ground. Then Omar finished the beast by decapitation."

"Tell him about the babies," said Kolya.

"Babies?" asked Evans.

"Yes," said Arjun. "Upon its death, its abdomen shook violently before exploding with numerous offspring, which disappeared into the surrounding woods."

"Interesting," Evans said, stroking the scruff of his chin. "Joso, have your men bring all the pitch they can carry. I don't want any more of those vile creatures roaming around."

Joso nodded as Nila grabbed Arjun.

"What are you doing?!" yelled Hemant.

"So you don't get any crazy ideas in your youthful heads, Arjun will be staying here with Nila," said Evans. "Have no fear. She will care for him well unless we fail to return."

I spared a glance at Omar. *So much for that idea.* Within moments, we were loaded down with the necessary supplies. Evans had our weapons returned, no longer worried about us being a threat to him or his warriors. We set out north from the encampment under the proctor's lead, walking in the opposite direction I wanted to. If Huck was alive, he was headed southwest toward Bhopal. After walking through the morning, Evans called for a stop and motioned Joso forward.

"What do you make of this?" he asked, pointing to a rock's surface.

Joso rubbed his finger through the familiar brown goo and held it to his nose. It was the same substance I remembered Otto harvesting to scare off the smaller Arthropods. That was before he realized it attracted other spine backs.

"It's the Great Beast's smear," he said. "It's fresh. We're close."

As if in answer, there was a thunderous roar in the distance. Regardless of the fact we knew what to expect, the sound still brought back hints of the Shock, something I'd learned that I'd never completely escape. I took a deep breath. I had to keep my head.

"Ready the ropes," said Evans. "The creature will come to us."

"What are we doing?" asked Hemant.

"Joso's men will hide ropes across this corridor between the trees. We're going to bait the Nightmare, encouraging it to charge. When that happens, it will be oblivious to everything else. During the charge, the men will tighten the ropes, tripping the Great Beast. Once on its belly, under Hemant's guard, Omar will repeat his famous stroke."

"Why do I have a feeling that we're the bait?" I muttered.

"Because you are expendable," said Joso, pulling his hair back into a bun.

"That's no way to treat our guests, Joso," said Evans. "It's because you have the most experience with the creature. Whatever you do, you mustn't flee. We will bring it down, but it must be singularly focused on you."

"I understand," I said. *It doesn't mean I have to like it though.*

Moments later, we were corralled at the end of the corridor—unsurprisingly—like bait. My hands grew numb as I waited anxiously. Time dragged by as the terrifying sounds of the Nightmare resounded through the trees, constantly growing closer. I nervously flexed my fingers around my bow, desperate to maintain the blood flow so my hands would be ready for the ensuing battle.

"Do you think it'll be alone?" asked Krista.

"I doubt it," said Samson. "Are they ever?"

"Is it just me, or are we taking on all of the risks here?" asked Kolya.

"That's exactly it," I said. "Evans was just being cordial. I think Joso stated their true feelings about us."

I heard the trees splinter before I saw them. From the woods flooded over a dozen Arthropods, none of which were our primary target, but all of which were concentrated on us. *Screw Evans' strategy, I'm keeping us alive.* As the first hook angled towards me, I rolled and fired an arrow into its head, slowing it enough for Krista to drive her katana deep into its side. Immediately, the air grew hazy.

"Dusters!" I screamed. "Masks up!"

I fumbled in my pack for one of the masks we'd stolen from the pheromone farm in Pod Kano. What'd been developed to produce the dangerous intoxicant would ironically be providing us with much-needed safety.

"What about them?" Krista yelled, pointing to the warriors. "They have to survive or Arjun's going to get it!"

I looked towards the warriors who had pulled a woven gray fabric from their cloaks and strapped it across their faces.

"I think they're fine," I said. "Look out!"

Krista dropped and rolled just as an eight's saw-like leg spun over her head.

"Thanks!" she yelled without slowing her attacks.

We continued fighting until we heard the trumpeting roar of the Nightmare. Exactly as planned, there was the spine back, rearing in all its glory at the far end of the corridor. That familiar rush of adrenaline shot down my back like ice as I beheld the rage behind the Nightmare's compound eyes. Every haunting memory of our previous battle returned. *This is for you, Leni.* Like Zeke used to warm up his shoes on the track, the beast clawed at the ground with its lanky legs, which were disproportionately skinny when compared to the creature's massive girth. With a final trumpet, it charged through the thickening air.

Evan's men had divided into six teams split among three thick ropes. *Three chances.* As the creature rumbled past, the first group jerked up their line far too late. The second rope only clipped its rear legs, barely slowing the beast's train-like momentum.

"Hold," I said, questioning the command myself as the last wave of warriors tightened their rope. "My God, I hope this works."

Wham! The creature plowed into the ground as our vision was completely obscured by the toxic sporish powder released by the powder moths.

"It's down!" Omar yelled. "I'm going in."

"Ready the pitch!" yelled Evans.

Moments later, triumphant cheers erupted from the warriors. The species we'd initially found so difficult to defeat had been easily thwarted by a homespun rope. Omar cleaved its head from its body with his dual-bladed naginata. *That's two, Omar. Impressive.*

We made our way through the lingering haze to where the creature lay. Its corpulent body was already blackened with the village's harvested pitch. Joso approached the creature with a flaming torch, hair sweaty and disheveled from battle. Before any offspring would have the chance to escape, he lit the carcass on fire. A wall of heat nearly knocked me on my buttocks as the fire roared to life.

"Look out!" screamed Hemant.

In a final spasm of its corpse, the creature's spikey body flung itself onto a dozen unsuspecting warriors. I turned, cringing at the screams of those still living as the fire consumed them. Without batting an eye at the unexpected loss of life, Evans approached me. With their greatest threat dead, the rest of the inverts vanished into the woods. Any stragglers had been quickly dispatched.

"We couldn't have done it without you," Evans said to Omar, patting him on the back.

I smirked. Apparently, the rest of us hadn't done anything. The reaction wasn't lost on Joso.

"You're welcome to be bait anytime," said the stout man.

"Back to camp, everyone," said Evans.

"Wait," said Arjun. "Where's Kolya?"

"I'm here," he said, emerging from the woods. "Forgive me. My bladder doesn't hold as much as it used to."

"Bloody coward," Hemant muttered under his breath, earning him a glare from the researcher. "What a surprise."

CHAPTER 25: HEMANT

When we marched triumphantly back into camp, the villagers left behind already had a feast prepared for our arrival. Unconcerned about food, I frantically searched for Arjun to verify his safety. When I saw Nila crossing camp, I approached her so fast, she drew her staff defensively.

"Where's my brother?" I said, huffing.

Using her staff, he gestured towards where Arjun was helping a woman carry a load of dried stalks away from one of the village gardens. I breathed a sigh of relief and ran to him, grabbing him by the shoulders.

"Are you okay?"

"Yes, of course," he said. "They aren't forcing me to work, I took this upon myself."

"Thank the universe," I said, leaning closer. "I don't trust these people."

"They haven't earned my trust either, however, they seem like honest, hard-working people. I volunteered to help with dinner, but they weren't inclined to allow it, so I'm helping in the gardens. Now, if you will allow me, these stalks are causing my arms to itch."

"Oh, sorry," I said, having forgotten about the bundles he held.

I watched as Arjun finished his work and joined us for dinner. Unsurprisingly, it was almost identical to the previous night's meal, though, after the harrowing hunt and knowledge that Huck might still be alive, I found the food to be far more appetizing. After I'd eaten several helpings, I asked Evans what the unfamiliar meat was.

"It's a local shellfish we harvest from the river," said Evans. "With our numbers, we couldn't survive on the crops we grow alone. So we supplement our food with the local fauna."

"I haven't seen many crustaceans in our travels," said Arjun. "I would be interested to learn more about potential food options. I would've been willing to help prepare this meal, but the cooks wouldn't allow it."

"That's because I gave them orders not to. With you being an outsider, letting you near the food didn't seem wise," said Evans. "It's of no importance. You'll learn more about us in time."

Arjun nodded but was obviously unsatisfied.

"Now, time for celebration," said Evans, doing his signature clap. "In thanks to our guests, they will drink first!"

The warriors grew visibly excited at the prospect of drinking. After the day I'd had, I wasn't opposed to the idea of a stiff drink. I wondered how village hooch compared to that of the pods. The children of the village brought out a huge iron pot and an unwieldy two-handled cup. They began ladling the pot's contents into the large cup as more wood was added to the fire. The sun had set and the sky was dotted with the first stars of twilight. The cool, evening air brushed over my arms and for a moment, I could almost forget about my troubles.

A hunched-over woman with gray hair peeking out from her headwrap brought the cup to Omar as the warriors began chanting. With a grin, Omar took the first draught. He hid it well but almost gagged. Laughing spread among the warriors.

"If you're going to be one of us, you have to learn how to drink!" said Nila, taking the cup and a heavy pull.

"Nila," Evans scolded. "Guests first."

Nila returned the cup to Omar who took a second drink. Still masking his issues with the taste, he managed to choke down the remainder of the cup to the pleasure of the warriors before handing the empty vessel back to the woman.

"What is it?" I whispered to Omar. "Hooch?"

"I don't know," said Omar, wiping the turbid liquid out of his beard. "It's thick and salty. Like drinking gravy. I never thought I'd miss the laborers' crappy hooch."

The woman brought the cup to me. I held my nose and drank several glugs of the vile liquid before I had to come up for air. Thankfully, the warriors seemed contented, so I passed it to Arjun to my right. When I thought it was safe to breathe through my nose, I did and was greeted with a metallic taste like nothing I'd encountered before.

"God, that's rough," I said.

After we each had choked down as much as we could tolerate, the cup started making its rounds through the warrior ranks. With no difficulty, they drank heavily as we looked on perplexed.

"Maybe it's an acquired taste," said Samson.

"I have no interest in acquiring this taste," said Kolya, smacking his lips.

"Anyone feel buzzed?" asked Omar. "I figured I'd be feeling something by now."

I took stock of my senses.

"Not really," I said. "Are we sure it had alcohol?"

"Do warriors drink anything without alcohol?" asked Krista, laughing.

I shrugged and realized that my shoulders felt strange. Not like when Mathias and I had been forced to use Dust. Instead of a feeling of pleasurable detachment and intense power, time seemed to slow as an intense hunger filled my belly.

"Anyone besides me want more dinner?" I asked.

"Definitely," said Ariadne. "I don't think this is alcohol, though. It reminds me of—"

"Pheromones," finished Krista. "Are we drinking pheromones?!"

"I… don't know," said Arjun. "I don't like this, Hemant."

"For once I can't help you," I said. "I think we have to ride whatever this is out."

"You think they'd get offended if I go throw it up?" asked Samson.

"I wouldn't," said Kolya with carefully measured words. "This seems to be an honor. I have no intention of being on their bad side."

As I scooped another helping of dinner into my bowl, the effects of the drink hit the other villagers. The warriors were yelling, jumping, and shoving each other in good-natured fun. As the evening wore on, I kept eating and eating until my stomach felt like it was going to burst. I wasn't the only one. Arjun, who'd always been a peckish eater, had downed enough of the stew I thought he'd double his weight.

As time passed, I became more and more energetic, unable to sit still. Against my better judgment, Omar and I joined the fray, eventually devolving into wrestling matches between their strongest warriors. Late into the evening, we departed from the raucous party and headed to our quiet little corner of the camp for a much-needed night's sleep.

••••••••

Something was tickling my forehead. I scrunched it up, hoping the sensation would go away so that I could go back to sleep.

Whatever it was continued its annoying distraction and I moved to brush it away, but my hand couldn't move. My eyes sprung open as my adrenaline spiked. *I'm not in bed.* I looked around and my heart leapt into my throat. Myself and my companions were all strung up on angled wooden frames situated around the village fire. New wood was being added to the ashes of the night's bonfire and was just beginning to catch.

"Wake up!" I yelled, realizing that I was the first awake.

I watched as my groggy companions came to.

"Arjun, you okay?"

"Mmmhmm," he mumbled, groggily.

"What in the fresh hell…?" asked Omar. "Wait! Where's Krista?"

"I'm here," said a voice behind me. "Ariadne and I are tied to a post behind you."

"Dammit," I said. "I knew this place was rotten."

"Rotten is such a harsh word, I think," said Evans, striding into the center of the frames where we all could see him.

"You lying sack of—" I began.

"Tsk. Tsk. Tsk. That's no way to speak to your host. And accusing me of lying?"

"You lied about Huck," I said. "Did you kill him? Did you?"

"I did not," said Evans. "What I said wasn't so much a lie as a prediction. He killed one of my prized soldiers and escaped with my healer, my slave, and two of my pack animals. His death is only a matter of what reaches him first, me or the creatures."

"If he killed your man, I'm sure he had a good reason," said Ariadne.

"That's of little importance now. You are his friends, so I will hold you accountable for his actions. It is from you I collect… compensation," said Evans, eyes glowing with malevolence.

"We're not your prisoners, cut us down and we'll leave you be,"

I said with all the courage I could muster.

"I think not," said Evans. "You see, we've endured a long period of deprivation. That is something I promised my followers they'd never have to tolerate under my leadership. When they swore their allegiance to me as their proctor, it was under the assumption that I would provide for them as a shepherd does for his flock."

"What are you talking about?" asked Ariadne. "What more do you need? You said you have enough food. Under the safety of the neem trees, you've carved out a perfect little existence here. We even brought down your most fearsome enemy."

Proctor Evans began rolling up his sleeves, revealing the markings of banishment. No one seemed surprised.

"Do you know why I was banished?"

No, but I have a feeling you're about to tell us.

"Hunger. Absolute hunger. Starvation so powerful it makes you hallucinate. What little I could steal was of such poor quality that I was still malnourished. I had a distended belly to show for it. One day after stealing a bundle of fruit, I was eating it in the abandoned apartment I called home. It was dark. The only light coming from the central shaft through a small window. The shopkeeper found me and nearly beat me to death, breaking many of my bones," said Evans, gesturing to his distorted face with his twisted fingers. "Then something clicked. Why should *I* die while others lived? Is this life not about survival of the fittest? Once I healed, I returned to the same shop and stole another basket of fruit, making sure to be seen. This time, when the shopkeeper arrived at my apartment, I was waiting for him. I split his head in two with a fire axe."

Ariadne sucked in her breath. *No wonder this guy was banished. He's a headcase.*

"I hadn't had meat in months. It was too well guarded and only found in the higher food districts. So I did what I must to survive. I ate the shopkeeper with his fruit and then threw his bones into the recycling chute."

"You're a monster," said Krista.

"No!" Evans said angrily, then calmed. "I'm an opportunist and a survivor."

"Apparently your pod didn't see it that way," said Samson.

"No. I suppose not," Evans said, chuckling. "I wasn't caught for several months. But during that time, I found out just what *anyone* will do to survive. You think me a monster, but we are all monsters given the right circumstances. I didn't stop at satisfying my own needs. I had a thriving butcher shop before it was all said and done. And don't tell me that the good people didn't know where my stores came from! It was only when some self-righteous customers reported me that my colleagues and I were banished! *They* are who disgust me!"

What had begun as a calm delivery had devolved into an angry monologue. Evans was insane with anger. He was so worked up that he was literally spitting his words.

"What. Are. You. Going. To. Do?" I asked through clenched teeth.

Evans took a deep breath and his hostility disappeared hauntingly fast.

"We can barely maintain enough livestock to produce our milk and wool," he said. "And we tire of the flesh of the inverts."

The realization of what we'd been eating hit me. *Shellfish my ass.* My mouth went dry at the thought.

"We crave real meat, the red meat of Earth. We are going to kill you. Some of you will be eaten fresh, others will be preserved for the upcoming months until another group passes our way."

Dear God! This isn't the first time he's done this, nor will it be the last. If we manage to escape, we can't leave this sicko alive.

Joso made a move towards Krista that Omar could see.

"Don't you dare touch her!" he shouted. "I won't let you eat her!"

"Eat her?" said Evans. "That would be such a waste. The two of them will be saved to satisfy our other hungers."

At that, Omar and I started thrashing at our ropes. I wasn't going to die without a fight, especially if someone was planning on eating me and my brother! Joso walked up to Omar and slammed his club into his skull, knocking him unconscious. I froze, staring at him. I was no good knocked out.

"Who first?" Nila asked, licking her dark lips.

"The chubby one," said Evans, pointing to Samson. "I like when my meat has a little marbling."

The bile rose in my throat as Nila approached Samson.

Ptooh. I looked toward the origin of the strange sound. It had come from my brother, who had spit dribbling down his chin. I looked down at the ground as one of Dieter's sticky bombs rolled to a stop between Evans' legs.

"What the—?"

Then with an ear-shattering explosion, everything above Evans' thighs vaporized.

CHAPTER 26: SAMSON

I hung limply, stretched across the wooden frame. I stared on, flabbergasted by the smoldering legs on the ground. As I came out of the daze, I realized that I was covered with fine bits of the proctor's bones and flesh. I shuddered and stared at Nila, still brandishing her knife, mere centimeters away from my throat. Since losing Hera, a small part of me was ready to die. I'd spent most of my life surrounded by the Kaaba faith, but the religion had never resounded with me. But I had to admit that the concept of an afterlife where I could spend eternity with my wife—now that was appealing.

When the shock of Proctor Evans' death finally lifted, Nila howled in anger and flew towards Arjun, forgetting all about her previous target. I listened as Hemant screamed, powerless to stop her. Just before she reached him, an arrow pierced her neck. The wound slowly bled, the red a stark contrast against her dark skin. After a few lingering steps, she collapsed, first to her knees, then fell face-first into the hard-packed earth.

I looked around frantically to ascertain the arrow's source but could identify nothing. Equally alarmed, the warriors began to scan the surrounding hills. A second arrow whistled through the air and Joso dropped, an arrow deeply embedded in his heart. As the warriors dove for cover, three more were killed by the hidden sniper.

"What's going on?" asked Kolya, his voice trembling.

"I have no idea," I said. "But they're killing our enemy, so I'm bloody thrilled."

"The arrow looks hand-crafted. It may be the Demented," said Omar. "I wouldn't get too excited."

"What the hell was that, Arjun?" Hemant said, laughing hysterically.

"I only pretended to drink and act intoxicated last night," he said. "Something about it didn't feel right."

"And you couldn't have shared that with us?" asked Omar.

"I was wrestling with my decision to abstain," he said. "When they came for us in the night, I feigned sleep, but I grabbed the only weapon I could, my single remaining sticky charge."

"And you had it in your mouth how long?" I asked.

"Long enough that the adhesive dissolved off," he said. "I believe I'd like to vomit once I'm cut down."

Hemant shook his head and laughed. "I love you, brother."

"Hey, the arrows have stopped," said Ariadne.

I looked around and saw the villagers hesitantly emerging from their hiding places. One approached me with a knife.

"Hey, wait! What are you doing?" I said. "Evans is dead. You don't have to do that."

The man reached up and cut my ties, releasing me. I dropped heavily to the ground, almost falling as my muscles woke, but the man held me upright.

"Evans does not speak for all of us," he said, hanging his head. "We suffered his leadership because we had little choice. If anyone deserves to die, it's us, for our cowardice as your lives and countless others were threatened."

"No, man," I said. "You only did what you were forced to do."

Tears welled up in his eyes. He moved through our ranks, cutting our bonds and helping each of us down. We heard a loud creak, and every head turned when the main gate swung open. My jaw dropped when I saw Huck and Liesel walk in accompanied by two strangers. With speed rivaling an eight, Ariadne shot toward Huck. The second she reached him, he lifted her high into the air. With her legs wrapped around him, she grabbed his face, pulling him close and kissing him with a passion that made time stand still. I was a mess of emotions. My heart burst for their newfound happiness, but the romantic scene made me long for Hera.

"Whoo!" yelled Omar, "About damn time!"

"Yeah!" yelled Hemant.

"That's my girl!" yelled Krista.

Liesel stood quietly to the side, looking on sadly. When the lingering kiss was finally over, Huck let Ariadne to the ground as we walked forward to join them.

"I thought you were dead," she said, crying tears of joy.

"I knew if we survived, you could have too," he said. "We were going to search for you, but the Nightmare ran us off. We figured we could rendezvous at Bhopal, but then we had our run-in with this place."

"What happened?" I asked.

"Long story," Huck replied. "I'll fill you in on the way to Bhopal."

"Huck, a moment?" said Liesel.

Everyone feigned disinterest, stepping back a few paces. I doubted I was the only one who couldn't turn my ears away from the conversation.

"I love you, Huck—"

"Liesel, I—"

"Let me go first, okay."

Huck nodded.

"I love you, but I've known since the beginning your heart belonged to Ariadne. Deep down, I knew there was no future for me and you. I'm hurt. I'd be lying if I said I wasn't, but what I want most is to see my friends happy," said Liesel, looking down at her feet. "Can we stay close?"

"Of course," said Huck. "You are an amazing person, Liesel. I hope you know that."

Liesel cracked a beautiful smile, but the hurt was still visible in her eyes. When she turned her attention back towards the rest of us, I tried unsuccessfully to look ignorant of their exchange.

"I'm glad you're back, man," said Hemant, "Don't take it personally if I don't kiss you, alright?"

"I'd take it personally if you did," said Huck, winking.

"I'm glad you're okay," I said.

"Hey, Samson," he said. "It's good to see you. Where's Hera?"

"She—" I began, but choked up before I could finish.

Huck understood. "God, I'm so sorry, Samson. She was one hell of a person. When we get a chance, we should do something for your crew. Remi didn't survive the crash either. I'm sorry."

I let the loss of Remi join the growing cloud of grief swirling in my chest. We'd expected it after Evans' failure to mention her when he spoke of the others. It didn't make it easier to hear the confirmation.

"I figured that was the case when she wasn't with you," I said, then changing the subject. "Who are your friends?"

"Guys, this is Manu. He helped save us from one of the more aggressive warriors," said Huck.

Manu gave a small bow.

"He's mute, but can communicate through other methods," said Huck, then gesturing towards a pale, tattooed woman with a bow and quiver. "This is the village healer, Marie. She saved Liesel's leg, which was in bad shape after the crash."

"The honor is mine," said Marie, as the villagers surrounded us.

"Where do we go from here?" asked the man who'd cut me down.

"If you'll allow me," said Marie, stepping on a nearby table as Manu steadied it. "People of Bastion, I remind you that we are no longer ensnared by the proctor's shadow. You are each your own person, capable of making your own decisions. You can choose to follow the detrimental path set forth by Evans, drinking the creatures' blood, or you can be free and live a good life that benefits all humans."

"But Evans said we can't survive without enough meat!" someone yelled.

"That's a lie," said Ariadne, stepping out from our ranks. "People can survive their entire lives without *any* meat. Meat is beneficial, but there are ample sources around, you need only know where to look. You *never* have to consider killing another human for it."

"Who's going to stay and teach us how to look?" asked the man. "You?"

Manu drummed on the table, making some gestures to Marie when she looked his way.

"Are you sure?" she asked.

Manu gave a clear nod.

"Manu will stay," said Marie. "He remembers the old ways, those from before Evans and his scourge. He's studied the healing arts under my tutelage. He will lead you beyond this period of darkness."

The villagers nodded with contentment. It was clear that they had many issues to work through, like a prisoner with a life sentence suddenly set free.

"Wait," said Hemant. "You said blood."

Marie nodded as she climbed down from the tabletop.

"You mean to say we drank blood? Their blood?" asked

Hemant, pointing out of the gate.

"Yes," she and Arjun said.

"I'm going to be sick," said Krista.

"Me too," said Hemant.

I felt queasy at the thought, but I knew the vile drink had long since passed out of my stomach.

"What about you?" I asked Marie.

"Huck has kindly allowed me to accompany you to the Hive," she said.

I gave a questioning look at Huck.

"How long have *you* been drinking the blood potion or whatever," asked Omar, intently curious. "How do we know you're not some Demented she-devil intent on murdering us in our sleep?"

"You don't," the cowled woman said, walking away.

• • • • • • • •

Breakfast the next morning was delightfully vegetarian. We'd spent the rest of the day sharing our accumulated knowledge with the villagers, who incidentally, flat-out refused to believe I'd ever been in the skies, much less piloting the airplane.

Marie offered to lead us to Pod Bhopal, though everyone was reticent to accept her guidance after her tenure with Evans. Hunting medicinal herbs had the side effect of her having intimate knowledge of the surrounding landscape halfway to our destination. By her optimistic reckoning, the pod was only five or so days out. Maybe it hadn't occurred to her that she was dragging along two out-of-shape older men and a girl with a freshly-injured leg. I looked down at my waistline. Since the crash, it'd gone down in size, but I was by no means fit. The unusual woman seemed trustworthy, but after all the legends and first-hand experiences I'd heard of the Demented, I wasn't sure how much to trust anyone who consumed their blood with any regularity.

I sat by the fire and listened as Marie and Arjun talked at length about the deleterious effects of the Arthropod hemolymph on the human body. With Manu's help, we discovered that it was only with the arrival of Evans and his ilk almost a decade ago that the residents had begun eating the previously forbidden meats. Evans had spread many lies about nutrition and survival to achieve his personal ends.

"Despite what he claimed, Evans sounded like he enjoyed being a cannibal," I said.

"I think so," said Marie. "He was twisted well before he took the first draught of their blood."

"So, am I going to become one of the Demented now?" asked Hemant.

Marie let out another of her musical laughs, making me silently question her sanity.

"That's unlikely," said Arjun. "It would seem that it is a cumulative process."

"Can you explain that?" Hemant asked.

"It has to do with how much you consume and with what frequency and duration," said Kolya. "Over time, it slowly alters your cellular function and impairs judgment."

"How long have the villagers been drinking the stuff?" asked Krista.

"Not as long as Evans and his minions," said Marie. "They were drinking it when they arrived. You saw how aggressive they'd become. That's why I targeted them first. I believe the others can halt the disease's progression in its tracks, provided they never consume it again."

"You never answered my question," said Omar. "How much have you been drinking?"

"Evans was quite convincing at first. He told me that the drink would unlock my understanding of life itself, a prospect that is very tempting as a healer. I drank a considerable amount as well as used it in my medicines and rituals. One day, something happened," said Marie, her face clouded with dark memories of the past. "Something sinister took over me. When I came to my senses, I'd done something awful. I knew it was because of the vile brew. I vowed never to touch it again."

"And you want to take this nut job with us?" Omar asked Huck.

"Do not call her that!" said Huck. "You saw what she did for us. She saved all of our necks."

"Marie, can you promise me that you'll never repeat this 'something awful?'" I asked.

"I cannot."

"Jesus!" said Omar, stomping around. "Are you going to take responsibility for her, Huck? Because I sure as hell ain't."

"I've seen nothing but good intent from her," Huck said, standing. "So, yes, I take responsibility for her and as your leader, this matter is closed."

"I hope for your sake you're right," said Omar, putting his finger in Huck's face.

"Me too," said Krista.

Huck returned to his seat next to Ariadne.

"I love that you never stop seeing the good in people," she said, taking Huck's hand.

"Not Zabu," said Huck. "That guy was an asshole."

I chuckled to myself. It felt good to laugh. Being surrounded by the energy and drama of youth as one significantly older had its challenges, but they made me feel young at heart. I looked at Kolya wondering if he felt the same, but I didn't see him. He was probably making his last-minute preparations for the next leg of our journey.

CHAPTER 27: HUCK

We returned the donkeys to the stable, feeling that they would prove far more useful to the village's inhabitants than to us. On foot, we headed out into the jungle, leaving Bastion behind among a wake of mixed feelings. The settlement saved our lives and introduced us to new friends. It had also been a place of horrific suffering and agony, not only for us but for anyone who'd been unfortunate enough to fall into Evans' trap.

Just outside the village's eastern walls, we were finally able to cross the river on a bridge originally built by Manu's people. With renewed vigor, we trudged along under Marie's guidance, hoping to make good time to Pod Bhopal, the next stop on our journey.

"This was your original plan, right Hemant?" I asked. "How's it feel?"

"Yeah," he said. "Though how the hell I thought I'd ever make it this far on my own is beyond me. I can't count how many times I would've died if not for someone's help."

"It's been quite the journey."

"Why Bhopal?" asked Kolya.

"I was young and hot-headed," Hemant said, looking back

to check on Arjun. "Even though it was only months ago, it feels like a lifetime. All I wanted to do was punch an alien in the face, you know? I guess I thought I could rid the Earth of them single-handedly."

Kolya let out a deep belly laugh.

"If only it were so easy," he said. "You were quite the fool."

"I still hope to learn from Bhopal's elites," said Hemant, glaring. "They have a reputation for being the best in the world. I'm not joining them as I'd originally planned, but I want to train with them while we recuperate."

"You think they'll let you?" I asked.

"I should think so," said Omar. "We've crossed nearly half the world to get here. If we don't have what it takes, I don't know who would."

"I just hope it's nothing like Kano," said Ariadne, shuddering. "Like Zabu."

"I can't go back to that," said Liesel, using the blunt end of her guandao as a walking stick to help her over the rough terrain.

"It can't be like that," said Hemant. "Even the last communiques Pod Horizonte received from them indicated that they were still regularly dispatching troops to the Hive."

"Not that any of them were returning," added Samson.

"Don't forget that Memo's idea was that we would be successful *because* we were such a small force," I said. "He believed we could infiltrate the Hive. We should too."

"With a super weapon that doesn't work," said Omar.

"There's that," I said. "Arjun thinks they can fix it at Bhopal. I have to believe him."

"I'm carrying the thing there, regardless," said Hemant. "Even if we get there and they can't fix it, I'm not giving up. I'm doing something. Anything to rid the world of these nasties. If I have to march—"

"Quiet!" said Marie in a forced whisper.

I froze, taking in the sounds of the jungle. I heard the movement of distant water, the chirping of bugs, and… there it was. I felt a pit open in my stomach. It was that recognizable gnawing sound the inverts made when eating. Judging by the cracking of an exoskeleton, they were consuming one of their own.

Whatever it was, the sounds emanated from just over the rise. Marie motioned for me to join her, crawling up the subtle slope, careful not to slip in the accumulated detritus that was so common on the forest floor. I slowly peered over the edge with her, quietly parting a plant's fronds. Finding the source of the noise was simple. There, across a small creek, was a horde of hook beetles, devouring a decomposing multipede. As the vinegary odor entered my nostrils, it felt as though the smell withered my delicate nasal hairs.

"That thing's been dead for a while," I muttered under my breath. "Go around?"

Marie nodded. We began to make our way back down when I heard a loud crunch. Every head spun towards Samson, who'd stood on a downed tree, thinking it was sturdier than it looked.

"Sorry," he mouthed, cringing.

It was too late. I could hear the hooks skittering up the incline. *Dammit.* I turned just as the first one crested the hill. I pulled the dao from my shoulder and readied myself for the enemies charging toward us. Flying inverts typically had the advantage, but with the canopy above, their wings were practically useless and the lumbering hooks were slow on the ground.

When the first was meters away, I spun to the side and brought my sword down like a clever, which bounced harmlessly off of the beast's hardened chitin with a ping. Its beak plowed into the dirt, disoriented by the blow, giving me time to spin the blade and plunge it deep into its weak side. As I removed my blade, another hook beetle blew past, charging at defenseless Samson, whose leg was still stuck in the rotting log. I sliced at its side and sheered off half of its spindly legs, making the creature an easy kill. Inertia carried it forward with enough momentum to frighten Sam, who jerked away in an attempt to escape. I heard the loud crack from paces away as his knee wrenched apart. I cringed as he began screaming. He'd have to wait.

I turned to identify the next enemy but was pleased to find only one remaining. The girls had made quick work of the others. Brandishing his heavy war hammer, Hemant swung the weapon like a baseball bat, cracking the hook's exoskeleton and sending it soaring toward a tree, where it landed with a loud crash.

"I don't know my own strength!" he said, invigorated.

Samson screamed again as Ariadne ran to his side.

"How bad is it?" I asked.

Ariadne looked at me with a vacant expression. *Oh, that bad.* I followed Samson's writhing frame to his knee, bent at an inhuman angle. His leg, partially embedded in the rotten trunk, had held fast as he fell, ripping his joint apart. His face was white and beaded with sweat.

"His bellowing is going to attract every invert for kilometers," said Krista, looking around nervously.

"Can you give him anything?" I asked. "We need time to build a litter."

"I got something," said Omar, who pulled a morphine syrette from his pack and jammed it in Sam's neck, silencing him."

"Who the hell is the medic here, Omar?" said Ariadne, indignant.

"He was going to give us away," he said.

"I thought the Arthropods couldn't hear," said Liesel.

"Well that was probably enough vibration to get their attention," said Kolya.

"He's fine," said Omar. "Look."

"Hera…" said Samson blissfully.

He lay there, mesmerized by the sky, no longer preoccupied with anything other than the memory of his wife.

"How are we going to get him out of here?" I asked, running my hand through my hair in frustration. "He can't walk. He's high as the catwalks."

A thunderous crack permeated the woods. I swung my attention toward the sound. The rotting tree that Hemant had knocked the hook into was breaking along its weakened base and toppling over.

"Move!" I yelled.

We dodged the falling trunk, fanning out of its way in every direction. The tree landed with a boom that echoed through the forest. When I turned, I saw with dismay where it had fallen. Its wide trunk lay atop of Samson's body, leaving only his twitching hand visible.

"Oh, no!" said Krista.

I gasped, frozen in disbelief. *Not Samson, the kindest of us all.* A chorus of snapping filled the air and I felt a tug on my shoulder. *The whole bloody jungle's collapsing!* My first thought was the Arthropods had heard the tree fall, but then I realized it was something far more alarming. *The vines!* The vines from the fallen tree were pulling down the other trees like dominoes.

"Run!" shouted Marie.

We struggled to follow her lead as she darted through the woods with cat-like precision, keeping us just ahead of the life-ending clubs as they swung down from the sky. Omar and I grabbed Liesel, wrapping our arms around her back and thrusting her injured frame forward. I refused to lose another person to the tree fall. The jungle was tumbling down around us as we dodged branches and leapt logs while struggling through the thick brush. I risked a glance over Liesel's shoulder and saw the collapse was right on our heels.

"We're not going to make it!" I shouted, breathless.

"Hang on!" yelled Marie. "We're almost there!"

Not to Bhopal! What the hell is she talking about?

Seconds later, I saw broken ground ahead, signaling a ravine. With a leap, Marie disappeared over the edge. *Here goes nothing!* The three of us jumped feet-first over the edge into the unknown crevice.

At the bottom, we became a painful knot of limbs as each subsequent group landed uncomfortably on top of us. As the forest's trees fell over the ravine, they plunged us into darkness. Soil and bark sprinkled down on our heads as the crackling faded into the distance.

"Everyone accounted for?" asked Ariadne.

Everyone sounded off, including Marie.

"I can't believe he's gone," I said, coughing, after an uncomfortable silence. "He was the best of us."

"Not a single one of them is still alive," said Hemant. "The crew of the *Sekhmet*, I mean."

"We owe them our lives," said Krista, standing. "We'd all be dead in the desert if they hadn't found us."

I stood, brushing myself off. With my eyes adjusting, I could barely discern the shapes of the others by the scant light filtering into the trench.

"Now what?" asked Omar.

"We find a way out," said Marie, pushing past him.

I pulled a flare from my bag and ignited it. We walked south, watching our step as we traversed the uneven ground. At least it wasn't raining. In a steeply eroded ravine like this one, heavy rainfall could drown us all. After what felt like an hour of walking, I was caked with sweat and grime. The ditch had turned into a cave, yet we pressed on.

"Should we try the other way?" asked Omar. "What if there's no way out?"

"Or worse," said Krista.

"This place is familiar to me," said Marie. "I recommend that you trust my judgment."

"Like you trust your judgment?" said Omar.

There was a blur of motion and Omar froze, a wicked knife lingering at his throat.

"If I wanted to kill you, I would've done so already," she said. "We need each other to survive. Trust me or walk away."

After being with Omar so long, I could detect when he was afraid, as he was now.

"I'll do it your way," he said, eyes darting to me.

She hid the knife as quickly as she'd brandished it and resumed her point position.

"That was awkward," I mumbled to Hemant.

"You're telling me," he said. "I never saw her move. Remind me not to get on her bad side."

"She saved Liesel's life," I said. "I trust her."

"At least one of us does," he said.

I was surprised that not even Hemant held Marie in high regard. I could sense the good in her, but it seemed to be lost on everyone else. I dropped back to where Liesel was falling behind.

"Do you need any help?" I asked.

"No. Thanks though," she said. "Don't feel like you have to take care of me anymore. I can manage. It's weird. Every minute that goes by, I swear I feel stronger."

"I know. Since we left Kano, you've been growing steadily stronger. I'm not back here because I don't think you can do it. I'm here because you're injured and this is what friends do."

"I'm sorry, Huck. I'm feeling a little on edge too," she said. "Thanks for offering, but I really am fine. Almost normal."

I recalled what Marie had said about the cost of Liesel's treatment, wondering what the side effects of her rapid improvement would be.

"It's normal to be on edge. We just watched our friend die and ran from the tree equivalent of a landslide. I'm a little shaken up too."

"It's not just that," she said. "This place… It doesn't feel right."

"What do you mean?" I asked.

"I feel like we're being watched. And it may be my mind playing tricks on me, but I swear I heard someone talking behind me."

I froze in my tracks. Hemant noticed.

"What is it, man?" he asked.

"Mantis wraiths."

"Are you sure?" asked Kolya. "Arjun told me about your run-in with the creatures. How would you know?"

"Liesel said she heard talking behind us," I whispered as the others gathered. "Do you remember the sounds?"

"What did they sound like?" asked Kolya.

A loud chittering echoed from down the cavern.

"Like that," I said.

CHAPTER 28: KOLYA

"I got this," said Liesel, her eyes going cold and dark. "Watch the other direction."

"Liesel, wait!" Huck said. "Are you crazy?!"

"They need to meet the new me," she said, backing away into the darkness with a devious smile.

"I'll go with her," said Marie, vanishing into the shadows behind her.

"What do we do, Huck?" Ariadne asked.

Huck stood there under the orange light of my flare, looking as perplexed as I was about the girl's newfound bravery. After a split-second, he collected himself. For a moment, it looked as though the boy was hiding something.

"Hold like she asked," he said. "She's been well trained and Marie has her back. Ariadne, you, Omar, and Krista make sure nothing gets past them. Kolya, you and Arjun stand between us with the light. Hemant, and I will watch the front."

"I can't believe he's letting that witch lead us, Arjun," I grumbled, once the others were out of earshot. "You saw her collections of potions and herbs. A dark shadow follows her. She's a danger to us."

The sorceress had led us down some god-forsaken subterranean tunnel. If she didn't kill us, she would get us killed. I let my hand fall to the pommel of my sword. The second I saw a move against us, she'd taste my poisoned blade. Her kind, pursuers of the dark arts, couldn't be trusted. I flinched as some sparks from my flare fell down on my unprotected skin.

"I'm sorry my brother called you a coward after we fought the spine back," said Arjun, keeping a cautious eye on the tunnel at my back. I waved off the slight.

"I'm not bothered by the criticism of limited minds," I said. "I'll be the judge of my actions, which were a far cry from cowardly, mind you. What concerns me more is your brother's desire to drive us apart."

"Drive us apart? He cares deeply about me. I know he's not fond of you, but he has no reason to separate us. Intellectually speaking, we are an invaluable component of this mission."

"He's scared by what he does not understand. Together, we are a force to be reckoned with. He's afraid that with our wit, we will no longer need his muscle."

"You're being paranoid, Kolya."

"I'm not," I said, halting in the tunnel and leaning in close to his face. "Mark my words. Your brother will find some way to tear us apart. When he does, he will reveal how little he truly cares about you."

"You're mistaken about him," he said, masking his doubt. "Back there in the woods, you weren't just urinating, were you?"

"Ha!" I said, sarcastically. "Is that doubt I detect, my young friend?"

"Not at all," said Arjun, my attempts at humor escaping him. "I suspect that you had ulterior motives."

"Aside from the blind spot toward humor and your brother, nothing escapes your clever mind, does it? What I said was true.

Being older has diminished my bladder capacity, but no. I wasn't off peeing in the woods. I sent our message, Arjun!"

Arjun looked dismayed, having been left out of the momentous affair.

"I would've liked for us to do it together, but the opportunity presented itself and I had to take advantage of it, then and there," I said.

"What opportunity?" asked Arjun.

"You and your friends were so focused on being bait, none of you took the time to observe our surroundings. Judging by the looks of things, the warriors from Bastion had set up that site to ambush their 'Great Beast' long before we came along. It was far too well organized. They just needed bait and we fit perfectly into their plan. I suspect that had Huck and Liesel not escaped, they would've served the same purpose."

"That would explain why the creature's take-down went so smoothly," said Arjun. "They were more prepared than they'd let on."

"Exactly. Evans was a tormented man, but he was profoundly intelligent," I said. "While Ariadne was calling for us to hold, I noticed what looked like large woven baskets suspended in the canopy. They were traps, Arjun! That's why we weren't overrun with the smaller Arthropods before the attack."

"And you suspect if not for the basket traps, we wouldn't have survived long enough to be bait."

"Correct. That's when I snuck away. I wanted to see what bounty the traps held within. That's when I saw it."

"A powder moth?"

"Not just a powder moth, Arjun, but *the* powder moth! The one with the blue eyes! The traps were obviously not designed to capture the dusters, but it was a fortuitous circumstance. Destiny weaves as destiny will! An invert must've triggered the trap just as my little observer flew below the canopy and was caught in its snare."

"Tell me about them," Arjun said, hungry for knowledge. "I've only ever seen them from a distance or their bodies mauled on the ground."

"With its wings pinned, it couldn't fan the dust. Though given its past reluctance to poison me, I'm not sure it would have anyway. So while I was grateful for the mask, it was unnecessary. Their powder is expelled from cup-like depressions under their wings. Without dissection, I can't say for certain how it's generated. They have thin flaps that cover the depressions, so they have control over when they use it. Care for some raisins? The villagers… gave me some."

Arjun nodded, holding out his hand for some of the dried fruit. He meticulously examined each one as he ate them.

"I have to admit, the creature was almost cute once I was close enough to admire it. Its opalescent blue compound eyes give it quite the adorable look," I said through a mouthful of food. "Knowing their dust is harmless on the skin, I saw no harm in feeling its fuzzy coat. It was quite soft. Aside from their deadly powder, they seem like they could make a great pet."

"We've run into docile Arthropods before, like the wake striders. They posed no threat to us and only warned the others when they felt threatened. Though, admittedly, they never picked up exploding pill bugs and threw them at us."

"This is the fundamental problem with mixing emotions and science. Just because nature has created something plush doesn't mean it's friendly. When I looked at the creature, I could almost sense intelligence there. I made the mistake of underestimating them before, I will not do so again."

"What happened?" asked Arjun.

"Perhaps another time, my young friend."

"And the urine?"

"Yes, of course. With the creature trapped, I poured my specimen on one side of its abdomen and yours on the opposite, careful not to spill any of it into its dust pouches. I suspect that the water content of our urine has likely already evaporated, but with any luck, the scent of our pheromones will cling to the creature's hair."

"And you released it from the snare?"

"Yes, but not before speaking to it."

"Did it give you any indication that it understood?"

"I have no way of knowing," I said, shaking my head. "With simple words and hand gestures, I asked it to carry our message to its home. I tried to communicate that you and I are ambassadors for our species wishing to travel to the Hive and negotiate for peace. I asked for safe harbor for the two of us."

"What about my brother? My friends? Don't they deserve safe harbor?"

"I want no harm to come to them, but we cannot protect them as long as they seek a violent solution. The Arthropod Queens must believe that at least the two of us come in peace."

Arjun nodded, withdrawing into his mind.

"After that," I continued, "I flipped over the basket and it lept off the ground in a blur of brown and blue. It whirled around me once before climbing up through the trees above and into the sky. Regretfully, I have no way of knowing if it heeded my instructions. Once it was out of sight, I returned to you."

"You left me alone," said Arjun. "I would've liked to come with you."

"I wasn't worried about you, my friend," I said. "You are a survivor. Think of how long you lasted without me at your side. I left you because your friends do their best to ignore me. They'd never miss me. You, however… they would've noticed your absence."

"So what do you think about our new witch friend?" I asked.

"I don't know," said Arjun. "Huck trusts her. In general, he's been a good leader. I believe that her guidance could make the rest of the trip to Bhopal significantly easier."

"On the surface, perhaps, but how do we know what she's doing behind our backs?"

"Kolya, we're attempting to communicate with the Queens without our companions' knowledge," Arjun said, dropping his voice into a whisper. "How are we any different?"

"But we *are* different. What we're doing is in the best interest of all humanity."

"Then perhaps we need to trust Marie as my companions trust me."

"For one who's made a pact with evil, there can be no trust," I said.

CHAPTER 29: ARIADNE

Standing at the rear of our group next to Krista, I avoided the light of Kolya's flare, allowing my eyes to adjust to the surrounding darkness. I chuckled. *It's not like I'll be able to see them anyway.* The invisible inverts could kill quickly and silently, only shedding their cloak after death. I focused my attention on the sounds drifting through the moist air that blew through the cavern, watching for the slightest shimmer against the rocky, root-strewn walls that contained us. From the dark tunnel behind us, I heard a scuffle. The icy screeches of wraiths echoed out from the black, followed shortly by their death rattles. I had confidence in Liesel but feared Marie's return would bring devastating news. Finally, I saw a glimmer in the obscurity and drew my bow.

"It is only us," said Marie, emerging first from the shadows.

Marie was as clean as the day we'd met, the only visible hemolymph dripping from her glinting blade. Liesel was covered from head to toe in the dripping black fluid. Seeing no sign of human blood on her, I ran to greet her.

"God, I'm glad you're alive," I said. "What were you thinking?"

"I wasn't," Liesel said. "Something overcame me. It was like a calm fury. Trainer Gempo's training kicked in and, man, did it feel good to kill those bastards."

"Liesel's a freaking badass!" Krista said, laughing.

"What happened?" asked Huck, drawn by our conversation. "Did you get them all?"

"We believe so. It was mostly your friend," said Marie with a subtle grin. "She's quite formidable with her blade. I see she knows the Dance."

"The Dance?" I asked.

"This Trainer Gempo, he's a warrior of great renowned, correct?" asked Marie.

Liesel shrugged.

"Her moves were as fluid as the water," said Marie. "She knew precisely where and how to strike her opponents. It was as if she knew where they were going to be before they did. The Dance is a skill that, before today, I thought only existed in legends."

"I'm impressed," said Omar. "Who's this Gempo guy?"

"My trainer in Baghdad," said Liesel. "He was constantly ragging me about my technique. Nothing was ever good enough for him."

"I think he'd be proud," I said.

"That still doesn't explain how she fought these mantis wraiths," said Kolya. "I distinctly remember Arjun telling me that they were invisible. How did you fight these cloaked beings in the darkness?"

"Gempo made me train in the darkened arena every morning," said Liesel. "He'd move from sandbag to sandbag, taunting me, constantly repeating, 'Listen. Don't listen.' It didn't make sense until just now."

"Well, whatever it was worked," said Hemant. "I'm impressed."

Liesel looked sheepish.

"As fascinating as this conversation is," said Marie, "we need to reach the surface by nightfall."

"Agreed," said Hemant.

Slowing for nothing, we marched through the remaining tunnels until we reached the exit at dusk. After Marie had scouted ahead, we set up camp in a small rocky cove in the failing light. Formed by ancient river currents, the slate alcove and overhang made the perfect little defensible position for the night. Huck parked his bivvy next to mine and sat down next to me.

"I'm sorry," I said.

"For what?" Huck asked.

"For taking so long to come around. I was doing everything I could to push you away when all I really wanted to do was bring you close."

Huck embraced me, kissing me on the forehead.

"I haven't exactly been a charming prince."

I craned my head up, kissing his lips and drinking in his piney smell.

"Stay with me tonight," I said, looking into his hazel eyes.

"I'd love nothing more."

As we ate, I couldn't take my eyes off Huck, nor he, mine. With everyone retiring for the night, Huck joined me in my cramped little tent, no longer denying our desire to be with each other. For over an hour, we lay there, silently kissing, wrapped up in the comfort of each other's arms as our tongues and hands explored. With each blissful moment, my heart grew more and more full, until it felt as though it would burst. Reluctantly, I pulled back from his lips.

"What is it?" he whispered.

"I want to be with you," I said.

"You are," he said, kissing along my collarbone.

"I mean, I want to be *with* you."

"Oh," he said, with a nervous grin.

I felt him tense slightly. The moment's bliss wavered.

"If you don't—"

"No, I do," he said, taking my hand and kissing my fingers. "I love you. It's just… I've never…"

"I love you too," I said, smiling. "If you do other things as well as kiss, you'll be fine."

Huck's smile deepened as his cheeks turned a rosy pink.

"Is it your first time too?" he asked, curiously.

I nodded sheepishly. Despite my past romances, I'd always resisted the beckoning call of hormones. At that moment, I couldn't have been more grateful. The first person I'd completely share myself with would be the love of my life.

Huck gently kissed my mouth and my cheek, then he slowly moved down the side of my neck, filling me with tingles. With one hand cupped behind my head, his other drew my jumpsuit zipper down until I felt the snap of it disengaging from the other side.

"Is it okay if I see you this time?" he asked.

I giggled, thinking back to the incident in the medical truck.

"I wouldn't have let you get this far if it wasn't," I said.

•••••••

When we woke the next morning, I couldn't stop smiling. With every glance at Huck, I felt the warmth return to my cheeks as I tried not to giggle like a little girl. I'd felt love before, but nothing like the invigorating feeling currently pulsing through my veins.

We climbed out of the bivvy and joined the others who were awake. When Hemant pressed a cup of his cold-brewed coffee into my hands with a wide grin, I realized we were the worst-kept secret in the camp. My flush changed from amorous to embarrassment—not shame so much as exposure. I half expected Omar and Hemant to start cheering for Huck, but everyone seemed pleased that the inevitable had finally happened. Huck sat next to me, bringing me a bowl of freshly cut fruit.

"Thank you," I said, making no attempt to hide my smile.

"No matter what happens on the rest of our journey, I'll never forget last night," he said, taking my hand in a gentle squeeze.

I squeezed it back, happier than I'd ever been. After breakfast, once we could finally let go of each other, Huck positioned himself at the center of the group.

"Can I get your attention?" he asked.

"You've had it all morning, man," said Hemant, as he and a few others chuckled.

"Yeah, okay," he said, turning a bashful red. "For real though. I hate to bring down the mood, but we should do something for the crew of the *Sekhmet*. Samson, Hera, Remi, Rico, and even Ahmad, though we never knew him, saved our lives in the desert that day. They didn't do it just because Ekon asked. They did it because they truly believed in what we were doing. They believed in it so much, they flew thousands of kilometers to rescue us. Now, every last one of them has given their lives for the cause. For us. We owe it to them to honor their memories. I would like to do something more permanent when the war is over. For now, I think we should build a monument to the four of them."

"We've already been here too long," said Marie. "Lingering would be unwise."

"I agree with the witch," said Kolya.

"I'm not a witch," said Marie. "If I was, I would have turned you into the toad you are, then eaten you."

Kolya pursed his lips together and didn't utter another sound. I was beginning to think he was superstitious enough to actually believe her. Funny how he had crossed continents fighting invasive aliens, but the imagined threat of witchcraft halted him in his tracks.

"Enough, you two," said Huck. "Marie, though I agree, this isn't negotiable. You don't have to help, but would you mind keeping guard."

"For you? Of course."

Under normal circumstances, I would have been reluctant to trust our new friend, but Huck implicitly did. I trusted Huck with my life and my heart, so as a result, I trusted Marie. She stalked off to keep an eye on the perimeter, moving silently through the brush with feline agility as Huck divvied out tasks. I doubted there was anyone she couldn't get the drop on if the mood fancied her. Their last whiff in this world would be of lavender as they collapsed, their life force pumping out onto Earth's unforgiving surface.

"Ariadne, would you like to build Remi's cairn? I'd like to help you if you're willing."

"I'd like that very much," I said, taking his hand.

He led me to the bank of the slow-moving creek, not far from where we'd established camp. Each of us gathered handfuls of the layered gray stones that had been smoothed by years of the water's erosion. In reverent lines, each group made repeated trips to the bank, toting back our rocky bounty, one armload at a time. When we finally had enough, Huck and I began placing our rocks into a monolith, positioned to withstand the elements for the decades to come.

Once all the pillars were completed, Huck pulled out his sketchbook. I recognized its haphazard construction from the myriad loose leaves he'd scrounged back in Pod Horizonte that composed it. Like everything else in the pods, paper was a hot commodity. Many of his best illustrations had lists and tallies on their backsides from their previous lives. What was once someone else's trash, Huck had turned into treasures. Everyone gathered to see where this was going. We didn't have time for him to sketch something. We'd already lost hours of daylight to the monuments.

"I've been working on these for a while," Huck said, sensing everyone's concern.

The papers crinkled as Huck opened his book. The smell of dampness and mildew filled my nostrils with the turn of each page, the signature odors reminding me of Horizonte. He carefully drew out five leaves of paper, each with a remarkable likeness to one of the members of the *Sekhmet's* crew. Only one I failed to recognize.

"This was Ahmad, or at least as best as I recall him. I only saw him for a few moments before he was killed by a suicidal hook."

"They're beautiful, Huck," said Liesel.

"Quite extraordinary," said Arjun. "I believe they would've liked them."

"They're amazing," said Krista. "I need you to do one of Zeke for me."

"I would be honored," he replied. "Since we couldn't give any of them a proper burial, I'd like to include these in the cairns. If everyone approves, of course."

"You never had to ask," said Omar, as the others nodded in consent.

With the monuments completed, we loaded up and set off once again behind Marie, who assured us that we were only days away from the pod. I held hands with Huck as we trekked through the reddish-green shrubs that shrouded so much of the ground, slapping our legs with their broad leaves as we walked. I longed for a hot shower, a warm meal, and a good night's sleep. What I wanted most, I already had.

CHAPTER 30: HEMANT

About damn time. I shook my head, chuckling. I was beginning to wonder if those two would ever get together. As observant as the two could be, they were thick-headed when it came to how they felt about each other. Even being days away from Pod Bhopal, seeing them as a couple lightened everyone's mood. Liesel handled the change with grace but was changing in other ways. The once soft edges of her personality were now sharp, her trepidation replaced by tenacity. What she'd done in the cave was impressive by any standard. There were candidates who'd trained their entire lives who couldn't take down a wraith. Gempo must've been one hell of a trainer or Liesel one hell of an apprentice. Though I'd never known the man, I hoped he was still alive somewhere. When the final battle came, we'd need as many warriors like him as we could muster.

Just as Marie had said, after several days of travel we could make out Old Bhopal in the distance. As night fell, we set up camp in a copse of trees looking out over the sloping landscape. Below laid what was left of the long-abandoned city, few remaining structures still towered above the lush green carpet that had swallowed it. *Somewhere down there is Pod Bhopal.* I put my arm around Huck and Ariadne as we took in the view of the ghost town. Directly ahead lay a vast lake. Crumbling concrete piers reached out, only to be swallowed by the murky depths, each hearkening back to an age past. If my eyes weren't playing tricks on me in the waning light, I could just make out the transporters' access road.

"We made it," I said, grinning.

"I wouldn't say that until we're safely inside the pod," Huck said, smiling. "We still have several kilometers to go. There's no telling what all is hiding in there."

"I feel unstoppable," said Ariadne. "I was tired, but I feel like I could make it to the pod tonight."

"I know what we can do with your excess energy," said Huck.

"And that's my cue to leave," I said, laughing.

I went and draped my arm over Arjun's shoulders, favoring the leg that I had injured in a multipede attack the day prior.

"We're here, man!" I said.

"Good," he replied.

"Good? It's great, Arjun! Think about how close we are to our goal."

"To your goal, yes."

"What do you mean, Arjun?" I said, sitting down. "How is this not our goal?"

"May I remind you that it was your goal to train at Bhopal, not mine."

"I'm not talking about Bhopal. I'm talking about how close we are to the Hive."

"Oh," he said.

"What's the matter with you, man?"

"Have you ever considered that I might have different goals from you?"

"Arjun, I… I mean… I guess not," I said, at a loss for words. "I thought we were together on this. On Memo's mission to destroy the Hive."

"The bomb no longer functions, Hemant. We need to consider the possibility that the scientists at Bhopal can't fix it. The pod is primarily composed of warriors."

"What happened to your optimism, Arjun?" I said, my irritation increasing. "I've lugged this heavy-ass monstrosity thousands of kilometers and now you're losing hope? And what do you mean, mostly warriors? What are you saying?"

"Kolya is concerned that they may have let their knowledge lapse. He said that—"

"Warriors are a bunch of idiots. No, I get it. I'm sick of hearing Kolya's crap. The man is an immoral leech who thinks nothing of people different from him."

"Don't say that. His research has helped us survive this far—"

"His research? That's rich," I said, my voice rising. I felt Huck's hand slide around my arm in an effort to restrain the upcoming outburst. "I seem to remember our fighting being what's helped us survive. That was something we did well before he decided to tag along. The man's almost as bad as Yanus, disappearing whenever danger is around. The man's a bloody coward, Arjun!"

"Take it back!" yelled Arjun.

I was taken aback by the so rarely-seen fury bubbling out of my brother. I could count on one hand the number of times in his life that he'd been this emotional.

"Arjun, I—"

"I know what you think, Hemant. How is what you're saying any different from that which you accuse Kolya? You consider those without brawn equally as worthless."

"You don't know what you're talking about, Arjun," I said, tearing up. "I never could've gotten this far without you. We're a team. We've always been there for each other. I may be a big dumb oaf; but I'm your brother, and I care about you."

"A brother would care about my friend," said Arjun.

"You know what? You're right," I said. "I don't like Kolya. I've got a limited amount of things I can care about. That's you, these friends, and getting these damn inverts off my planet."

Arjun's anger began to subside.

"Have you considered that there might be another way?" he asked, sighing.

"Another way to what?" I asked.

"Another way forward."

"What are you suggesting, Arjun?" asked Huck, who'd been reluctant to join the conversation until now.

"That perhaps we could—"

"She's a witch! She's a witch!" screamed Kolya, bounding towards us from the tree line. "Don't let her touch you! I knew it! I told you!"

I turned to see Marie gliding from the woods, serene as ever. Kolya brandished his shashka and faced her, quivering.

"You keep him around for humor, no?" she said.

"The least you could do is explain why Kolya thinks that," said Omar.

Huck glared at him, but Omar merely shrugged.

"Of course," said Marie, placating him. "I chose to make a request of the benevolent Earth spirits while the moon is full."

"You see, admitted witchcraft!" Kolya said, eyes wide and pointing.

"I fail to see how it's any different from your gods," said Marie.

"God! Not gods! There is only one, true God!"

"Fool. There are many gods. Your religion has only blinded you to others. The faith I choose to practice is my own and no business of yours."

"Marie," said Ariadne. "May I ask what your request was?"

"For you, I will answer. I believe the spirits desire for us to regain control of our planet. I regularly ask them for wisdom and guidance in regard to our goal."

"And do they answer?" asked Kolya, eyes bursting with anger.

"Sometimes I hear their voices on the wind—"

Kolya burst forward, sword swinging, irate over her communion with the spirits. Their duet became a blur of motion. Kolya screamed and fell to the ground, writhing in agony and bleeding through a dozen shallow cuts. Marie stood unfazed with only the slightest cut marring her appearance.

"He'll live," she said. "I hope he learned his lesson."

"I'm sorry, Marie," said Huck, pushing by Arjun to reach Kolya. "Are you okay?"

"Yes," she said. "They're only scratches. They'll be healed by—"

Marie's last word caught in her throat as she stopped breathing.

"Ariadne, do something!" Huck yelled.

Running over, she cradled Marie as her body slumped to the ground, spasming violently as a yellowish foam appeared at her normally crimson lips, now as pale as her skin. A thought tickled the back of my mind, but I couldn't place it.

"I don't know what's wrong!" Ariadne screamed.

Kolya started laughing. I darted to him, grabbing him up by his collar.

"What did you do, you bastard?"

"I sent the witch to join her precious spirits," he said, spitting.

"You bastard!" I said, punching him in the face. "How can we stop it?"

"You can't!" Kolya laughed, his teeth outlined in blood. "It's eight venom. She'll be dead in moments."

I punched him again and again. Arjun grabbed my arm to stop me. I slung him off, accidentally breaking his nose in the process.

"God, Arjun! I'm sorry!"

My brother looked at me with a hurt that stung far worse than an eight's sting.

An eight's sting! "That's it!" I yelled. "Ariadne, give her some of my blood!"

"If I do that, it could kill her!" she yelled.

"She's going to die anyway," said Omar.

"Try it," said Huck.

Ariadne nodded. "Get my bag."

The night stretched on eternally before dawn finally reared its head. Ariadne spent the entire time micro-dosing Marie with my blood, which was not only compatible but carried the antibodies necessary for Marie's recovery.

All was far from right with the world. Huck and Omar had tied Kolya to a tree until we could figure out what to do with him. Arjun was no longer speaking to me, leaving me hollow as an empty shell. I looked over at the unkempt man, squirming against his restraints as they reddened his skin. I hated that despicable man for the wedge he'd driven between me and my twin. More than once, the thought had crossed my mind to dispatch him then and there. What stayed my hand was the fact that if I killed him, I'd be no better than he was.

We remained at the overlook for two additional days while Marie recovered. By the third day, we had to move her, regardless of her condition. Like they did with everything else, the inverts ruined our spot, harrying us down the slope to the lake. With our enemies slain, we could take in the body of water that spread off into the horizon before us. From a distance, it had appeared large, but surmountable. Up close, it seemed to go on forever.

"Did I ever tell you I'm not fond of water?" I asked Huck.

"Maybe once or twice," he said, smirking.

His usual upbeat attitude had been a casualty of the last few days. He and Ariadne both had dark shadows under their eyes from long nights taking care of Marie, who was finally back on her feet, albeit, still weak.

"Any ideas on getting across, Arjun?" I asked.

Arjun looked at me blankly before walking to Kolya and offering him a drink. The man drank deeply from the flask, water splashing down his face and beard as his hands were bound behind him. It already hurt to see Arjun's face mottled by burns, but now he also brandished a dark, swollen nose from my inadvertent punch. In the past, I'd found time to be more effective than words with my brother. I hoped he'd come around soon.

Since we'd left camp, we confiscated Kolya's venom and kept him restrained at all times. When searching his rucksack for his venom, I'd found a number of our belongings, all of which were forgotten when I'd discovered Mathias' pouch of rough diamonds. With Huck's blessing, Omar and I interrogated him. In the end, the most I could get out of him was that he'd found the diamonds stashed on the plane before the crash and pocketed them. I smelled a lie, not trusting him in the slightest. That's when it hit me. *The yellow foam!* Marie and Mathias had both foamed at the mouth. If not for the fact Mathias had obviously overdosed, I would've suspected Kolya of murder. He was clearly capable of it. Arjun's proximity was all that kept me from further brutalizing the man.

I stood at the lake's edge, staring out over the water and questioning who I'd become. Huck joined me in the clearing and I shared my findings. Disintegrating stone pavilions mounded in vines and moss made the area feel haunting. I could almost see through the years of growth back to when children ran happily in the park, their parents following closely behind.

"I trust that man now less than ever," I said.

"Do you have any proof that he hurt Mathias?"

I shook my head. "If there was any, I threw it off of the cliff."

"We can at least keep a close eye on him," he said.

I couldn't bear the thought of my brother spending any more time with the questionable man.

"You want to go into the city and find a way across or go the long way around?" I asked. "I'd normally be in favor of the walk, but I think I can stomach a boat ride to shave another day or two off this nonsense."

"I'm sorry, Hemant," said Huck. "Zeke wasn't my brother, but I loved him like one. Not a day goes by where it doesn't hurt. I know Arjun's not dead, I'm just saying I can't imagine what you are going through."

"It's frustrating because he's right there," I said, pointing at him as he knelt by the water. "It doesn't matter what I say to him. He's as silent as Manu and always tending to Kolya."

"It's not just you. He's not talking to any of us."

"That bastard has wormed his way into Arjun's mind and turned him against us. Did you hear what he was saying about there being another way? What other way could there possibly be? Coexistence? Surely not."

"I don't know, Hemant, but I'm with you. If the last four hundred years have taught us anything, it's that it's either us or them. We've got no choice but to get the bomb fixed and get on with the mission."

"We need to rest too," said Ariadne, walking up. "As team medic, that's not a request. We're worthless if we're not ready. Maybe that'll give us time to train with their elite soldiers. Anything we could learn from them would be beneficial on the last leg of our journey."

"I thought you said rest," said Huck, arching an eyebrow.

"We'd still be sleeping in beds and eating proper meals," said Ariadne. "The real rest won't come until this stupid war is over."

If I may interrupt," said Marie, striding towards us with Omar and Krista. "I used your brother's binoculars. Down the shore appears to be a dock with a vessel attached."

"A vessel? Here?" asked Huck.

"Could it be the transporters?" asked Ariadne.

"If these guys are as hardcore as their reputation leads me to believe, they probably train in the old city," I said. "Everyone in their program has earned citizenship. After what we've endured on the surface, what use could an arena really be?"

"Fair point," said Huck. "Hopefully they won't mind if we borrow their boat."

"Huck, what are we going to do about Kolya?" asked Ariadne.

"I've been thinking a lot about that," I said before Huck could respond. "Let me be the one to break the news to Arjun, but I think in light of recent events, I think it's best to leave Kolya and my brother here. He should be well cared for. As for Kolya, I think we should turn him over to the Bhopal's Tribunal Council for attempted murder."

"He's still a 'premier scientist,'" said Omar, using air quotes. "I doubt they'd do more than give him a slap on the wrist."

"He tried to kill you, Marie," I said. "I can't just let him skate by, further corrupting my brother's mind. I want him out of Arjun's life for good."

Marie put her hand on my forearm.

"Have no fear," she said. "His time will come."

Despite the heat, I felt a chill as her words rolled across my mind. For someone who'd been helpful and kind, the woman could be bloody terrifying.

"I'd like to join you in this pod," said Marie. "I've never set foot in a living city."

"You think they'll let her in?" asked Ariadne.

"I don't see why not," said Krista. "She's the toughest one of us all."

"Then let's go," Huck shouted. "To the boat!"

"Wait," said Marie. "I wanted to thank you all for saving my life. Your healing abilities surpass my own. I wouldn't be alive without your intervention."

Ariadne blushed. "I'm not as advanced as you think, I just had a lot of training and adequate gear. It's not the same as centuries of wisdom and decades of experience."

"Thank you, nonetheless," she said.

As the others sauntered off, I happened to look up into the sky. There, a hundred meters or so high flew a duster. A surge of panic rose in my chest until I realized it wasn't attacking. I watched it circle languidly above us. When it came around, I gasped. Even from a distance, I could make out its deep blue eyes.

CHAPTER 31: FEN

My arms burned with the familiar warmth of my morning routine. I liked the pain. Pain meant strength, and strength meant power. As a woman in ranks upon ranks of men, that couldn't be understated. Next to me, sweat dripped from Mego's brow onto the already damp mat below. Our trainers made things as authentic as possible, keeping the practice zones as muggy as the oppressive heat of the surface above. Our training was nearing its end. My unit, Sigma Squad, was on the cusp of graduating from Pod Bhopal's Special Forces Training Camp in a matter of weeks.

"198, 199, 200," Mego said, letting out a contented sigh.

He rocked back into a squat before standing, waving his tired arms forwards and back. Slipping on his jumpsuit top, he flipped his dark, shoulder-length hair out of the collar's way before tying it back in a small bun.

"How many more you got?" he asked, flashing me a handsome smile.

"It's not a competition," I reminded him again.

"Not to you, it's not," said Mego.

Not that macho crap again.

"200," I said, sitting back, my short braid unraveled from the workout. "I'm just as powerful as all the guys here. It's too bad they won't be convinced until I lead my unit out of this place in formation."

Mego rolled his deep brown eyes. Even when he was annoying, I could get lost in those South Asian features of his.

"Fen, you are and have always been a badass. Anyone who can make it here from Pod Wuhan has more than proven their merit. Remind me how many of you made it here?"

"Fourteen," I said begrudgingly.

"*Fourteen* out of *125* who set out," he said gesturing towards the rest of our platoon. "Look around. Everyone's earned their place here."

"Fine, I concede. Now, can we go get some breakfast before we hit the track?"

"Yeah, I'm freaking starving. Vita-shake at Jaxx's?"

"You read my mind."

We jogged down a few levels to where our favorite little spot was. The more structured training would begin mid-morning, so it was important to have our warm-up, calisthenics, and meal finished before then. It was nice to be responsible for our own routine. Trainers knew when someone was slacking. With the threat of being dropped from the competitive program and demoted to laborer, slacking wasn't a huge issue. Save for the occasional bad egg, everyone wanted to be here. You didn't subject yourself to the arduous trek to Bhopal to have your ass handed to you on a daily basis unless you were focused on the end goal. Graduates were the world's most highly-trained soldiers, training in advanced combat arts to rid the world of the Arthropod invaders. Sigma Squad's Release Day (our second one) was growing perilously close. I was nervous but prepared. Plus, I had Mego at my side.

As we rounded the central shaft to the restaurant, I couldn't help but admire his physique. All the extensive working out just served to make him hotter. I wasn't complaining about his added endurance either. Being a member of the voluntary corp meant that we were treated like adults, even though the majority of us were still under twenty-one. They figured if we were sharp enough to survive the surface, we could handle our own affairs.

Our friendship had started innocently enough. There weren't separate gendered dorms for the trainees. With far fewer women than men joining the program, dorm assignments were mixed. I'd been assigned to Mego's room and we'd become fast friends. It was only in the last few months that our feelings had become more romantic in nature. Trainers warned against relationships in the field, but neither of us wanted to deny how we felt about each other. I was of the mind with something to protect, I would fight even harder.

We arrived at Jaxx's and slid into the booth next to two of our squad mates, Roque and TomTom. TomTom had traveled with Mego from Pod Bandung. The two were often confused for each other. Each of them had the same long hair, muscular build, and similar complexions. Though they were friends, they were quite different. For one, TomTom was possibly the gayest guy in the pod. And two, he rocked a little goatee. I launched myself into the opposite booth, purposefully slamming into Roque.

"*Oof!*" he said, shoving me back. "That would have gotten old a long time ago, but I like the idea of you throwing yourself at me."

A smile split his soft face from ear to ear. Over our time together, I'd grown close to the short guy. Against his fair skin, his blue eyes almost twinkled under the pendant light hanging above the table. I could see why TomTom was so attracted to him. He wasn't particularly muscular or intimidating, but he could keep up with everything the trainers threw at us. His shy personality and subtle sense of humor made him quite endearing.

"Watch your mouth," I said, laughing. "TomTom might get jealous."

"Not on your life," said TomTom, reaching across the dingy table to grab Roque's hand. "I trust him with all my life."

TomTom was a big softy, a touch more feminine than many of the few women in the forces, but just as formidable on the battlefield as anyone else. He and his twin daggers had a reputation for sneaking up on unsuspecting inverts and having them lying in the dirt before they realized he was there. Mego claimed that TomTom had made his passage to Bhopal significantly easier. While some had called my movements beautiful, they felt clumsy next to TomTom's stealth.

We each ordered our usual shake. It was a relatively light meal but had enough nutrients to get me through the day's training to when I could eat real food. It only took one bad experience to learn that heavy training on a full belly was miserable. I slurped mine down the second it was out, letting out a belch when I was done.

"We'll get you pod-trained eventually," said TomTom.

"Never," I said. "I prefer to keep my animalistic edge."

"As long as you don't keep your animal stench," said Mego, pinching his nose. "You're not getting anything tonight unless you shower first."

"Ooh," said Roque.

I smiled. I loved these guys.

"So do you believe any of this nonsense floating around about 'Memo's Misfits?'" asked TomTom. "Gah, what a stupid name."

"I don't know," I said, shrugging. "I mean, the rumors sound legit. Memo is what people call Minister Leal, Pod Horizonte's leader. It makes sense that he'd dispatch a special team."

"But Horizonte is known for, what, recycling? That's not exactly special forces material," said Mego, climbing onto the table. "Fear us, inverts! Or we'll turn you into meat patties!"

"Get down! You'll get us kicked out again," said TomTom laughing as Mego climbed back down to his seat. "The invert's antenna bug network *is* down, that's a certainty you can see from the skylights. Now whether they did it as the rumor states is another thing."

"I find the hardest thing to believe is that the same group has made it through so many pods and continued. Who does that?"

"I mean, I did," said Roque. "I stopped at Baghdad on my way from Munich. Choosing to leave again was a tough decision, but I was dead set on being a Clunkie."

"True, I suppose," I said. "You think they're really headed here?"

"We'll certainly find out," said Mego. "You think they'll arrive in an actual airplane?"

"Forgive the pun, but I think that's a flight of fancy," I said. "This is how rumors turn into legends. There's no telling how much truth there is to their story. It's not like Madan has been forthcoming about it."

"The prime minister has his own agenda to contend with," said Roque. "He wants *his* recruits to save the world, not some backwoods recyclers from the Latin Territory."

We laughed until we heard the gong piped through the pod's speaker system, signaling the next training session.

"All good things must come to an end," said TomTom, scooting out of the booth after me.

•••••••

Tired and sore after another day of training, Mego and I headed for the showers, which like the dorms, were mixed. Coming from a pod where everything was rigorously gendered had been an adjustment, but now it felt old hat. We stripped, showered, and dressed in the crowded locker room. There were always furtive glances around the room, but rarely did anyone behave inappropriately. The benefit of everyone being highly trained soldiers was that no one messed with others, lest they have their face pulverized.

With freshly cleaned bodies, we picked up some food on the way back to the dorm, ravishing it once we arrived. Bhopal's cuisine wasn't bad if you were in training. It was a far cry better than the nutritionally-lacking food of Wuhan. You could eat your fill and still feel hungry. Ironically, the first time I felt contently full was on the surface. A belly full of fresh fish and fruit will do that to you. I felt as though I could've run to Bhopal on my first sugar high. Pod Bhopal strived to be elitist in every way, and that extended to the food. It prioritized nutrition, specifically for the special forces, knowing we couldn't build the necessary physique without proper intake. They just turned a blind eye to the other residents who didn't have it quite as good.

We'd opted for Bandung-inspired food. With some effort, I coerced Mego into some satay from an upscale restaurant a few levels up. Ironically, he wasn't a huge fan of his home pod's cuisine. The perfectly seasoned meat was worth the extra ration points. I wanted to eat all that I could before I was out fending for myself again on the invert-infested surface. It wasn't like I could take livestock with me. I threw the last skewer on the plate to return to the restaurant and jumped into Mego's lap, kissing all over his face.

"But I still have chicken in my teeth," he complained.

"Do I look like I care?" I said, kissing him again.

Before he knew it, I had his jumpsuit top thrown on the floor and was kissing down his neck as he groaned pleasantly. Mego pulled the zipper down on my top, exposing the athletic support underneath and kissing the soft skin just above my breasts.

"Floor or bed?" I asked.

It was his turn to say, "Do I look like I care?"

I pushed him down onto the built-in sofa and started to remove my pants when there was a knock at the door.

"Are you freaking kidding me?" I mumbled.

I rolled off of Mego and tugged my zipper up with a jerk, blowing the loose strand of black hair out of my face.

"If that's TomTom, tell him to go walk the surface," he said.

I hit the button on the panel and listened to the hatch's mechanism click uselessly. *Dammit. That's the third time this week.* I gave the hatch an encouraging bump with my palm and it reluctantly opened.

"Dude, I—" I started before looking up and saluting. "Oh! Captain Diaz. Come in."

I suddenly realized I wasn't anywhere near appropriately dressed for an officer's visit. I tried to surreptitiously zip my top as she acknowledged Mego's presence. Her guard detail closed the hatch behind me. I hid my snicker when they had trouble getting it to function properly.

"I apologize for—"

She held up her hand, the stern expression on her pale face freezing me in my tracks.

"This is an unannounced visit during your free time, Lieutenant," she said. "I'm not preoccupied about how I'm received. How much are you aware of this group, Memo's Misfits?"

"Very little," I said. "I'm not sure how much is willful speculation versus actual truth."

Diaz invited herself to have a seat on the sofa and suddenly I was glad she hadn't arrived five minutes later. I watched her as she analyzed the tiny dorm's state of cleanliness, but neglected to comment. Every hair on Diaz's head was always in its proper place under her gray officer's cap, even after guiding us on a 20-kilometer run. We didn't keep the place sparkling, but at least it didn't look like some of the younger guy's cesspools down the hall.

"Put aside everything you've heard for the moment. What I'm about to tell you has been verified, ironically thanks to what this group has done to bring down the Arthropod's communication network. These 'misfits,'" she said with disdain, "have come from Pod Horizonte."

"It is true," muttered Mego.

He shut up when Diaz narrowed her eyes at him.

"Their merit is of little importance to me and to Prime Minister Madan. They will be allowed to join our ranks should they prove worthy. That's not in dispute. However, we cannot let the atomic weapon they carry fall into enemy appendages because of this group's lack of training. It's unbelievable that they have successfully brought it as far as they have."

"So we're going to take it from them?" I asked.

"We're going to *requisition* it," she corrected. "If they care to join our battalion on its march to destroy the Hive, then that's their prerogative."

"We're going to the Hive?!" I asked.

"Those will be your orders, yes," said Diaz, ignoring my outburst.

"Yes!" I said, then corrected myself, "Yes, Captain."

"If I may ask, how do we fit in?" I asked.

"I'm restructuring your squad to include them," she said. "I understand there are six of them. You may keep three other recruits of your choice. You will be responsible for seeing them successfully through training."

Inside, I was screaming.

"Permission to speak freely, Captain?" I asked.

"Permission denied. It is what it is, soldier. May I remind you that you are under orders? Enjoy your evening."

God, the Hive. Clunkies were always sent to wherever the need was greatest, but the Hive is where we all dreamed of going. I waited until Diaz had left the dorm to vent.

"Woohoo!" yelled Mego as he picked me up and spun me around. "The Hive. I never thought we'd actually be going there."

I gave him a sharp punch to the abs, knocking the wind out of his lungs.

"After all we've done, now we have to babysit some greenies. And just before we leave too! We were ready for the trials. This'll set us back months."

"Sorry," he groaned. "I'm too excited to worry about them. They made it this far. They can't be that bad."

"I hope you're right," I said.

"I'm always right," he said, smiling, as he tugged my pants' zipper back down.

CHAPTER 32: HUCK

We approached the outskirts of the city, the trees thinning around us, guiding our way to the single intact pier where the identified boat rested. Even maintained, the pier's aging concrete edges were disintegrating. Cracks formed across its wide span, kinking the large-diameter pipes running the length of its construction.

"It looks almost long enough that we could walk to the other side," said Liesel.

Omar lifted Arjun's binoculars to his eyes, scanning the horizon for active threats before checking the length of the pier.

"The boat's there like Marie said. Looks seaworthy, but it's hard to tell with the distorted perspective. Maybe a few hundred meters out."

"Why in the world is it so long?" asked Krista.

I waited for Arjun or Kolya to chime in with their usual knowledge, but there was only silence, save for the pleasant cool wind whipping off of the water.

"I'm sure it had some alternate use. With all the pipes, maybe they pumped their drinking water in from the lake," I said, facing the intact skyscraper at my back. "Man. I don't know if it's because we're closer to the Hive, but I keep thinking more and more about what the surface might be like when humans return."

"I know the feeling," said Ariadne. "It's too bad they couldn't simply peel off the vines, patch up the concrete, and replace a few windows."

Liesel let a melodious laugh escape. It was the first time I'd heard the heart-warming sound since we'd broken off our relationship.

"If only it were that easy," I said. "I bet it will all have to be torn down. I'm a little scared to stand here. The foundation is probably so bad, it could topple at any moment."

"Unlikely," said Arjun.

When everyone turned, he pursed his lips as though he regretted speaking. I hated seeing my friends down, but I found the frigid feelings between the brothers especially discomfiting. With our arrival at Bhopal, a false sense of invincibility and excitement bloomed within me. However, the strained emotions among our members reminded me just how much stress burdened our already-heavy shoulders.

"I have an idea," I said with a smug grin.

"I'm scared," said Krista, a smile creeping across her face.

"Last one to the top is a polie," I said, sprinting off towards the looming abandoned tower.

"Huck!" Ariadne yelled, voice fading. "Don't be stupid!"

"Not if I get there first," Hemant said, shoving my shoulder.

"Losers," Omar said, shaking his head as he pulled ahead of both of us.

"Hell, no!" Hemant said, glancing at me. "I'm not about to let the upper beat us."

I chuckled at the reference to Omar's former social status, pouring on as much speed as I could muster just in time to see Marie glide past the three of us like we were standing still.

"Good God," I said as we ran into the building's ground floor.

Marie and Omar had already bolted up the stairs, but I had to stop for a quick breather. The empty lobby was littered with ornate, broken blue and white tiles and the tattered remains of a once-colorful decomposing rug.

"This place must have been… quite the sight… back in the day," I said between gulps of air.

"Damn, she's fast," said Hemant. "But at least I can beat you!"

Hemant took off up the stairs, laughing. The race had seemed like a good idea at the time, but we were wearing each other out needlessly. Not to mention the huge unnecessary risk I was taking exposing us to dark floors and blind corners for a bit of fun. *Too late now.*

"So stupid," I said, shaking my head. "I'm a terrible leader."

Still gripped by the moment, the drive to win overcame my sense of logic. I rounded the next flight and jumped over where Hemant had fallen on a mangled steel door marked with beautifully swirled writing with the word "EXIT" written in United beneath.

"Slowpoke!" I yelled, darting up the next flight.

On the uppermost floor, I had to climb over a mountain of rubble blocking the staircase's exit. I rolled over its summit and down onto the landing. A cloud of dust plumed into the air as I came to a stop on my buttocks. I stared up into the faces of the victors, Omar and Marie. Hemant climbed down from the pile more gracefully, huffing and puffing as Marie offered me a hand.

"Guess you're the polie," said Marie, the corner of her mouth turning up.

Her sly smile gave the mysterious woman an even more menacing edge as she lifted me with ease to my feet. I rested my hands on my hips, in a vain attempt to look as though I wasn't winded, and wandered to the edge. With cautious steps, I walked through the strong gusts swirling in through the wide opening to the floor's edge. Omar jokingly shoved me from behind, spiking my adrenaline.

"Dude!" I said.

"Relax," he said, chortling. "I had a grip on you the whole time."

"What a view," said Hemant, looking out over the ruined cityscape. "Look, you can see it."

I followed Hemant's finger to a rise across the lake where the pod's white circular surface stood out in stark contrast to the verdant surroundings. Unlike the previous pods we'd visited, Pod Bhopal looked as new as I imagined it had on the day it was finished. Nearby trees were neatly cleared away, giving the pod a manicured appearance.

"What do you make of that?" I asked, mouth agape. "It's so…"

"Clean," said Omar.

"If they run their pod like a well-oiled machine, it makes sense that it'd look like one too," said Hemant. "Maintenance to a pod's exterior is just… unheard of."

"It appears that they do many things outside of the pod," said Marie, peering down the building's sheer side, "like capturing your friends."

My stomach lurched up into my throat. I turned on my heels and sprinted back the way we came, forgetting all about my weariness. When we reached the bottom, a squad was waiting for us. A monstrous man wrapped his bulbous hands around my neck like a vice and lifted me off the ground. I stared into the dark eyes embedded in his walnut face.

"Are you sure this scrawny thing is their leader," he asked.

"That's what the smelly one said, Ondo," said one of the soldiers.

"What's your name, boy?" said Ondo.

"Huck," I eked out, struggling for breath and grabbing at his sausage-size fingers.

"A weak name for a weak boy," he said, dropping me to my knees.

I gasped for air. Soldiers, presumably Bhopal's elites, held each of my companions captive. A wave of guilt washed over me. My stupid attempt to boost morale had led to the squad getting the drop on us. *That silly urge almost got your friends killed.* I stood, slowly.

"I don't recall giving you permission to stand, *boy,*" he said, shoving his war hammer's blunt shaft into my stomach.

Ariadne whimpered. It took several seconds before I could breathe properly again.

"Sounds like Huck has an admirer," said Ondo, stepping over the rubble to Ariadne. He lifted her chin to meet her eye-to-eye. "What do you want with this weakling? Come spend some time with Ondo, he'll change your mind."

"Never," she said, shaking off his touch.

"Your loss," he said, shrugging. "Be on your way then. I expect you to be out of the vicinity of Pod Bhopal by the end of the day."

"But we're headed to Bhopal," I said, my voice cracking.

Ondo began laughing hysterically, his squad mates joining in. When he finally caught his breath, he spoke.

"You? Headed *to* Bhopal?"

I nodded.

"You do realize that Bhopal is home to the Clunkies, the most badass, sons-of-bitches killers in the world, not a place for training would-be matriarchs, right?"

Scattered laughs broke out from the cluster of bodies surrounding us.

"If you're so hardcore, how come you're hanging so close to home, harassing us instead of heading to the Hive?" asked Omar.

"Someone's a smart ass," said Ondo, leaning into Omar's face. "I'm *here* because I follow orders, boy. My orders are to protect the perimeter from not only the inverts but kiss-ass Clunkie wannabes. Now tell me, why the hell should I let your pathetic little band into my pod?"

"Because if you don't, I'll sever your head from your body and force-feed it to your men," said Marie in a sensual voice, making her even more terrifying.

Ondo looked a little rattled but hid it well.

"And how exactly would you do that, freak?" he said, eying her up and down.

"The man holding me—he's unconscious," she said as her guard dropped to the ground.

There was a blur of the red and black fabric of Marie's clothing. When the motion stopped, she held her wavy knife at Ondo's thick neck, drawing a hint of blood. Her legs wrapped around him from behind, holding her high enough to reach the giant's throat.

"Alright, alright," he said in a whisper. "You've proven your point. I'll let you in—but only you!"

Marie tightened the knife.

"Okay, okay!" he said. "Your friends too!"

Marie dropped to the crumbled cement and with a flourish, sheathed her knife.

"You sure you don't want to hang out with Ondo?" he said, voice shaking.

Marie hissed and Ondo's dark skin paled.

"Who the hell are you guys anyway?"

"We're from Pod Horizonte," I said. "We're headed to the Hive."

Murmurs of shock and awe floated up from Ondo's troops, completely reversing the dynamic.

"Ho-ly crap. You're Memo's Misfits!" Ondo said with amazement. "I'm sorry. I had no idea. Look, no hard feelings, alright? Guys, let them go."

I let out a sigh of relief when my friends were released. The Clunkies didn't appear all that different from us. Maybe a little older. Maybe a little harder. Then again, the last time I looked in a mirror,

I almost hadn't recognized myself. Extra body fat had vanished, replaced by muscle. My once soft skin had toughened, carrying with it a plethora of scars. I'd given up fighting the constant growth of stubble. I kept my beard trimmed short, leaving enough length to hide my facial scarring. Arjun was the only member of the entire group who went through the trouble of shaving.

"Cut his bonds," said Ondo, pointing at Kolya.

"No!" I said, drawing attention. "He's our prisoner."

"You guys are getting more interesting by the minute," said Ondo, inspecting our captive. "Who are you?"

"I'm Researcher Kolya of Pod Baghdad! I'm the world's most renowned—"

"Seems like you should've gagged him too," interrupted Ondo.

Everyone began snickering as Kolya's face turned beet red.

"Minister Madan will hear about this!" Kolya spat.

"Oh, I'm counting on it," said Hemant, patting the man condescendingly on the shoulder. "I'm recommending you be tried for attempted murder."

Kolya's face transitioned from red to purple as he started muttering angrily in a creole of Russian and United. From the parts I could decipher, he slandered our lineage in a most abhorrent manner.

"Hemant, Kolya was under the impression—" began Arjun, but Hemant held up his hand.

"We will discuss this later, brother."

Ondo's crew looked on uncomfortably.

"Okay, then," said Ondo. "Who's ready to see the pod?"

I looked at Ariadne and grinned. "Let's go!"

Ondo led us across the crumpled asphalt that had once composed a busy thoroughfare and towards the awaiting dock. I kept turning back to gawk at the forlorn buildings. This was one of the larger cities I'd come across. I struggled to fathom what life must have looked like so many years ago.

"It's a head trip, isn't it?" asked Ondo, reading my mind.

I nodded.

"Want to know something crazy?" he said, not waiting for an answer. "People used to wake up and walk to work. Maybe take a train or bike. However they did it, they did it without fear. Aside from birds and rodents, the cities didn't even have wildlife to speak of. No real enemies aside from themselves. Hell, they didn't even carry weapons!"

"Unless they were a Sikh," said a member of Ondo's horde.

I turned to see a short, yet intimidating, freckle-faced girl. Her striking red hair hung down in double braids, draped on either side of the recurve bow sticking out above her head.

"Yes, unless they were a Sikh, Trivia," said Ondo, rolling his eyes. "She's full of useless information, thus her nickname. Though if you ever need to know anything about the past, she's the man, *err,* the woman."

I laughed, looking back at Arjun. "We have one of those too. He's working through some stuff, so he hasn't been himself lately."

"The surface will do that to you," said Ondo, stepping onto the dock. "Fair warning: This platform isn't as stout as it used to be. Everyone in break-step so we're not all marching with the same rhythm. Unless you want to go for a swim, that is."

Aside from the flex of the supports as we headed to the barge docked at the far end, the crossing was unexciting. I stepped over a rusty piece of upturned rebar and came to a stop in front of the shallow-draft vessel.

"It reminds me of Mueller's barge back across the ocean," said Ariadne.

"Yeah, but the Misfit's barge didn't have a roof like this one," said Krista, flexing a sharp edge of the metal painted to look like water from above.

"Don't get too excited," said Trivia. "The roof's got so many holes in it, it may as well not be there. It is only there to protect us from the mud raptors."

"Mud raptors?" said Ariadne, eyebrows raised.

"What?" she asked. "It sounds a lot better than jet bugs. That's what we used to call them. I know you've had some run-ins with the boogers."

"I just… I'm surprised you know the term," said Ariadne.

"You guys really don't get it, do you?" Trivia said, shaking her head. "You guys are famous, like worldwide. You're Memo's Misfits! Since the aerial network collapsed, everyone's talking again—and they're talking about you!"

CHAPTER 33: KOLYA

"Famous my ass," I mumbled, stepping onto the barge. "At least they got the misfits part correct."

The small boat rocked with the scuffling of so many bodies, further agitating my already annoyed gut. I squinted as the sunlight shot through one of the many rusted holes in the corrugated roof and into my eyes. Omar forcefully led me to the rear of the vessel and thrust me down on an unforgiving metal bench.

"That's a good boy," he said. "Stay there and I won't knock you upside the head."

I spit on his boots.

"Disgusting," he said, wiping the spittle on my pant leg. "What happened to you, man?"

I turned away to look out over the sparkling water that reminded me of my travels so many years ago. *I crossed a land bridge near one lake that was so large, you would've thought it was an ocean, Sveta.*

"Whatever, man," Omar said, tiring of waiting for an answer that would never come. He sulked off, returning to his pathetic, crippled girlfriend.

The giant named Ondo pushed the barge away from the moorings. His crew split in two, grabbing long poles from racks on each side of the roof. With the padded end held aloft, the aluminum poles were lowered into the water until they reached the lake's shallow bottom. The pushers then nestled the pads against their shoulders, shoving the boat along. Each pusher walked the length of the boat, thrusting it forward before pulling the pole out of the water and returning to the bow to repeat the process. The crew moved with the precision of experience. I snickered to myself at the thought of Huck and his friends trying to operate the poles without their expertise.

"What a novel way to cross a lake," said Krista.

"It's silent," said Ondo. "Natural gas makes for a quiet engine, but it's nothing like poling the thing across. Of course, the technique doesn't work in deep water. It's also painfully slow."

"I'm not in a hurry," said Liesel. "Being out on the water is quite pleasant."

"That's because we haven't been noticed yet," said Ondo.

"Noticed by what?" I said.

"Raptors, man," said the giant. "They live in the towers deeper in the city. Lucky for you, that stunt your friends pulled in the skyscraper went unnoticed. You're lucky. We keep that particular tower clear because of its proximity to the dock. I can't believe you guys made it all this way doing stupid crap like that."

Stupid crap like that was why Arjun and I should be on our own. If only he would see reason. I remembered Ariadne's story of her capture by the mud-sculpting inverts on the mountain. I would only wish such an agonizing death on my worst enemies—or perhaps practitioners of the dark arts. After seeing first-hand what the creatures could do to an aircraft with their razor-sharp wings, the barge's thin roof brought me no comfort. *Pity the girl didn't perish like the drug-addled runt, my dear. At least the knowledge we gained from the girl's abduction was valuable.*

Arjun made a move to join me but was halted by his abhorrent brother.

"Arjun, will you just listen to me?" he pleaded.

Arjun paused and gave him far more attention than the oaf warranted. Hemant made no effort to conceal the conversation from my ears.

"He's not good for you. He may be smart. Hell, he may even care about you, but he's not your brother and I sure as hell don't trust him," he said, giving me the side-eye. "I think you should stay away from him, okay?"

Arjun stood there for several moments pondering his response.

"I believe I will hold my own council on who I interact with, *brother*," said Arjun, heading towards me.

The oaf looked deflated as his brother took a seat. *What do you know, Sveta? He feels.*

"How are you holding up, little buddy?" I asked.

"In all honesty, I'm not sure what to think," he said. "I'm torn between my loyalty to you as a friend, to Hemant as my brother, and my dedication to our original mission."

"Your assignment was to end the war and return humanity from the surface, was it not? We would be following the spirit of the mission, only adapting its execution. Remember that loyalty is earned not through blood, but through actions. I've heard the way Omar talks about his father. Do you see him pining away because of their biological relationship?"

"I don't."

"The surface has changed your brother. For the worse, I think. He fears what he cannot control. That includes you."

"How is that different from your fear of Marie?" asked Arjun. "She's a healer that has beliefs in the older ways, like you. She has yet to pose a threat to any of us."

"Not like me!" I said. "I believe in the one true God. If he represents light, she worships the darkness he shines against. I know it's hard for such a logical mind to understand, but I live by faith. She's consumed the blood of the beasts, Arjun. I've studied ancient texts for longer than you've been alive. Witches were fearsome beings, loathed by believers of all faiths. Each aspect on its own is enough of a threat, but when you combine the two, you get… *her*. Think what you wish, but she *will* turn on your friends. What I did was to protect you. I will not lose another apprentice!"

"Apprentice, Kolya?"

"Yes," I said. "I hope you don't mind. I've been considering you my apprentice for some time now. I am, as they say, 'old guard,' and I do not offer apprenticeships lightly. Your intellect is quite possibly the highest I've ever seen. I would love nothing more than to impart everything I know to you."

"I… I don't know what to say."

"Say you're honored, my boy," I said, laughing.

"I'm honored," he said, looking down at my bindings. "How are you going to mentor me if we're separated?"

"Perhaps we won't be."

"What are you saying?"

"Your brother has made it clear to me that he has every intention of leaving you at Bhopal, even urging me to help convince you."

Arjun shook his head. "He wouldn't do that. He knows how much this mission means to me. Bhopal holds nothing for me. Maybe Baghdad, but—"

"From his point of view, you are little more than a burden. A distraction. He doesn't trust that you can take care of yourself, nor can he control you. You will always dwell in his shadow, Arjun unless you choose to step out from under it. Perhaps it is a blessing. If I'm imprisoned here, at least I will have good company," I said, chuckling.

Not that I have any intention of being a prisoner—here or elsewhere, Sveta.

"We've been spotted!" yelled Trivia, trading a pushing pole for her bow.

Arjun jumped up to see what had grabbed everyone's attention.

"What is it, my boy?

"Raptors. A cloud of them coming this way," he said, turning to his brother. "Hemant, we should cut Kolya's bonds. We would benefit from his blade."

"The envenomed one? No way in hell," he said, shaking his head.

The buzzing grew louder in my ears as the air vibrated with their fury. The raptors had closed the distance with dramatic speed and began dive-bombing the slow-moving barge. The pushers now wielded their weapons, defending the boat against the flying inverts.

"How do you target them?" yelled Ariadne. "I'm burning through my arrows and not hitting a damn thing!"

"Wait for the dive," yelled Ondo. "When they're right in front of you, you can't miss and they can't dodge."

Ariadne tracked one of the attackers with the broad-headed tip of her arrow, following it as it dove towards the vessel's port side. Just as the giant had instructed, she loosed an arrow which sank deep between the compound eyes of the creature. There was no time to celebrate. The invert's inertia carried it directly toward her. With astounding reflexes, she rolled out of its way just as it impacted the decking. The thick-headed Clunkie behind her wasn't so fortunate. Carried forward by its momentum, the raptor's dead weight plowed through him, ripping him in two as both vanished in an eruption of water. I turned back just in time to dodge a severed raptor head flying past me.

"Arjun!" I yelled, "I'm not going to survive tied up like this!"

"Hemant," he yelled. "We have to untie Kolya."

"I said *no*, Arjun! I don't trust him!"

"I do!" replied Arjun.

"I don't care!" yelled Hemant.

Time stalled around the twins as the battle raged on. Judging by the look that crossed the oaf's face, he knew what an egregious error he'd just committed. With three poorly chosen words, he'd firmly driven the wedge between himself and his brother. *Checkmate, Sveta.* Arjun silently turned his back on his brother and helped guide me under the seat to safety.

"I don't know that I can forgive him for this," he whispered, tears masking the anger in his eyes.

"I don't know that you should," I said, choosing my words carefully.

From my position of relative safety, I watch as the Clunkies and Misfits fended off the attacking inverts. Rust from the roof rained down as the raptors tried to claw their way through it. Mercifully, it held. Following Ondo's targeting strategy, enough of the raptors were killed to drive away the rest.

"They're leaving!" shouted a tall Clunkie. "Good riddance you stupid f—"

The soldier's face froze and then he disappeared. Wasting not a second, Trivia rolled to the starboard side where the boy had been standing and loosed an arrow. I followed its course to where a raptor held the boy in its clutches. The arrow hit its mark, going directly into the boy's eye, depriving the raptor of its live prey.

"Why'd you do that?!" yelled Liesel. "We could've saved him!"

Trivia shook her head. "I've seen a raptor nest. If I'm taken by one, I'd expect you to do the same for me."

I hobbled back into my seat once I was sure the threat had passed. The pushers returned to their positions and guided the boat the remainder of the distance to shore. Ondo ordered half the Clunkies out first to clear the area before letting the new arrivals disembark.

"I'd like to see how far they'd get without Arjun's help, Sveta," I muttered.

One of the Clunkies jerked me up so fast it made me light-headed, prodding me forward with his weapon.

"I can guide myself, thank you!" I said.

"I imagine you do a lot of things yourself," he said, snickering.

Miserable bastard. I felt the push of his mace in the small of my back as I was escorted to the pod. The surrounding manicured grove was reminiscent of parks that only existed in the archives. I closed my eyes. The fresh smell lingering on the wind made me wish that I could remain among the trees forever. For a moment, I could almost forget my troubles. When we reached the entrance, the pod's age was obvious, but as we'd noticed from a distance, the place was extremely well-kept. The special forces weren't ones to laze around.

Ondo guided us to a small, recessed entrance near the large main gates. He motioned for Huck to follow as the rest of us looked on from the top of the short staircase. The giant pushed a red button on a panel and we waited. I was checking out the boxy camera mounted above the door when the speaker cracked to life.

"What is it, Ondo?" the staticky voice asked. "You're not due back for hours. You know if I let you before your designated time Madan will have my ass."

"Stow it, Breaker," he said. "You'll open it when you see who I've got with me."

"Who the hell is he and why should I risk cleaning latrines for him."

"Breaker, it's them, man. It's Memo's Misfits."

There was a drawn-out silence from the radio.

"You sure?" Breaker whispered.

"Pretty damn sure," he said, his eyes darting towards Marie.

"Jesus. I can't believe they're really here."

"Really here and still waiting for you to open the door, man."

"I'm sorry, Ondo. I can't break protocol. The times are randomized for a reason."

Ondo knuckled his forehead.

"I'm sorry, Huck. We're going to have to find somewhere to lay low until he can open the door."

"What if we make it worth his while," said Omar. "Hemant, do you still have the things?"

"If Breaker accepts a bribe, his punishment would be worse than cleaning a few toilets," said Ondo.

"Wait, wait," said Breaker, who'd apparently never stopped listening. "Ondo, what are they offering?"

"You know what you're doing, man?" he asked.

"I do," said Breaker. "I'll do anything for my sister."

"What's he talking about?" asked Huck.

"People who can't hack it in the program… They find them positions elsewhere."

"Ondo, don't. Please," said the disembodied voice.

"He has a right to know. This could affect him too," Ondo said to Breaker. "Look, Huck. Sylvia was forced into a life of servitude to the soldiers. You can imagine what that means. Breaker's been trying to put together enough to get her out."

"Jesus," said Ariadne. "Of course, we'll help. How much does he need?"

"To risk letting you in?" asked Breaker. "Three months' ration points or equivalent."

"No," said Ariadne. "How much to get her out, period?"

"I… I don't know what to say," said the staticky voice.

"You could start by telling us how much," said Hemant.

"Um… Two years worth. Then I could pay for a new placement."

"Deal," said Huck.

There was a hiss as the steel hatch's lock disengaged and air exchanged. A skinny kid with dark skin and glasses emerged, squinting in the sunlight. Hemant approached the guy, who I could only assume was Breaker and pulled something shiny from his pocket.

"Those are mine!" I said. "You have no right!"

"They were never yours, nor is half the stuff in your pack," said Hemant.

The oaf dumped a handful of my rough diamonds into Breaker's hands, nearly bringing the kid to his knees with gratitude. Having my gems thrown away had the polar opposite effect on me.

Mark my words, Sveta. They will pay for what they've done to us.

CHAPTER 34: ARIADNE

"I don't know how to thank you guys for this," Breaker said, hunched over, almost in reverence.

We piled in through the narrow door before Ondo swung it shut behind us. Breaker pulled himself together enough to hit the controls, sealing us in. Hemant took a few steps into the pod and froze, taking a deep breath.

"You okay?" I asked.

"Yeah," he said, tearing up. "I've worked so hard to get here. I mean, this is where I planned to go. It's where Arjun and my ancestors are from. It feels like a big deal."

"It is, Hemant," I said, smiling. "I'm proud of you."

"Breaker, get those stones somewhere safe!" said Ondo. "It won't do you any good if they get confiscated."

"Don't tell a soul where they came from," added Omar. "If what you say is true, we'll probably have people grabbing at our jumpsuits as it is."

Breaker went off to stash the stones and quickly returned.

"I'll tell everyone I let you in because of who you are," said Breaker. "I've never been so happy at the prospect of cleaning a bunch of nasty-ass toilets."

"If you need any additional help with your sister, let us know," said Ariadne. "We have zero tolerance for slavery—regardless of what anyone calls it."

"Thank you…" Breaker began.

"Ariadne," she said, before introducing the others.

"I'm good with tech, so everyone calls me Breaker."

"Does everyone go by a nickname?" asked Liesel.

"Not everyone," said Breaker. "Just the ones who have some notable characteristics. You've met Trivia. Ondo goes by his birth name because he hates—"

"I will kill you where you stand," Ondo interrupted.

"Breaker!" said a uniformed man, entering the vestibule. "Who the hell gave you permission to open my door?"

"How does he do that?" Breaker and Ondo said in unison.

"Sir, it's them, sir. It's Memo's Misfits."

"I don't care if the bloody UTE president descends from his reclusive holy cloud in Munich and graces us with his presence, you don't touch that bloody button until my preordained time…"

I listened as the dressing-down continued to grow increasingly vulgar as time wore on. It finally ended with Breaker being offered the expected choice between latrine duty or lashes, of which he chose the obvious. After dismissing Ondo and his crew for debriefing, Madan dropped his angry demeanor and turned to us with a smile that didn't reach his eyes.

"Excuse the unpleasantness," he said with a strict demeanor. "I won't tolerate insubordination, even for those with a reputation such as yours. They both knew better. I'm Prime Minister Arnav Madan. You will address me as General Madan."

Out of the corner of my eye, I saw the normally fearless Ondo cower slightly under the prime minister's gaze. I wasn't sure what to expect when we arrived, but Arnav Madan wasn't it. He had short, white hair though didn't look over fifty. His fair skin had been prematurely aged by extended time in the sun—unusual for someone of his status. As we introduced ourselves, I could tell that under his jumpsuit (another unexpected choice for someone in administration), he retained a soldier's physique.

"The inflated tales of your heroic adventures have preceded you," continued Madan. "I've had enough contact with Ministers Okoro and Leal to get something closer to the real picture. Leal will be thrilled to hear you're alive and well."

"Ekon's alive?" I asked, looking at Huck and grinning.

"Alive and weird as ever. Few survived the attack. They're living in the shell of Baghdad. I'm not going to lie. It's rough over there, but they're surviving," he said, gesturing towards Kolya. "Now, who's this gentleman? You didn't introduce him."

"I am Researcher Kolya. I'll have you know that I'm a premier—"

"Asshole," coughed Krista, causing Kolya to fume.

"Minister Madan, this man is our prisoner," said Huck. "He began our journey from Baghdad as part of our team. We've been holding him since he tried to murder our companion, Marie."

"Murder, eh?" he asked Kolya. "What do you have to say for yourself?"

"I was protecting them from the darkness in her," he said, pointing at Marie, who remained stoic as ever. "She's the embodiment of evil."

"Uh-huh," said Madan, turning to Huck. "What kept you from meting out battlefield justice?"

"Sir?" he asked.

"When you're in the field, the commanding officer has the right to be judge and jury."

"That never occurred to me," said Huck. "The man is quite unpleasant to be around, but he actually is a valued scientist. I wanted him to have a fair trial before your Tribunal Council."

"Very admirable," said Madan, escorting us into the staging area.

I was awestruck by the stark differences between the past pods we'd visited and Bhopal. The place was freshly painted and immaculate. Unlike the other pods, there was no sign of nature's encroachment. It still bore the settling cracks and crumbled corners, but they'd made every effort to keep the pod well-maintained and spotless. In the middle of the wide floor was a fleet of transporters, loaded for bear. Two men stood by the lead vehicle, engaged in a heated discussion over pod cuisine.

Madan continued, "The Tribunal Council is far too busy—"

"But he tried to kill her!" said Liesel.

"I don't care for being interrupted," said the minister, silencing her. "In my pod, I'm the supreme leader and you will respect me as such. Understood?"

Liesel nodded.

"As I was saying, the Tribunal Council is far too busy to deal with such a petty matter, but I have a solution."

"Brick. Ian. Get over here." yelled Madan, pulling the men out of their discussion.

The pair joined us. Brick lived up to his name. His shoulders were nearly as wide as I was tall. He looked as though he could snap a multipede in half without sweating through his bandanna. Ian was rail-thin, but menacing with a scar over his left eye. A crossbow peaked over his shoulder.

"Captain Brick, this is Kolya," said the minister. "As of this moment, he's banished. Lug him out of here with you. If he causes any trouble, you know what to do."

I gasped, getting the trio's attention.

"In these parts, we don't dick around with punishment," said Brick. "If he pulls his weight, he can ride with me as long as he pleases, but from this moment on, he's not welcome in any pod. Ian will make sure he gets the mark."

"Go to hell, the lot of you," Kolya said through his teeth, spitting at our feet. Only Arjun received anything other than an evil eye.

"Saddle up," said Brick.

"Wait. They're leaving now?" asked Huck.

"Yep," said Madan as Ian sliced Kolya's bonds and led him into the personnel carrier. "Finished loading this morning."

"That's it then?" asked Arjun. "No trial?"

"No trial," said the minister before yelling, "Gates clear?"

"Gates clear," a worker responded.

"Open the gates," he yelled, heading towards the control room.

I flinched as the gates began parting. I'd never be comfortable with that sound as long as I lived. One after one, the vehicles' engines cranked up. The natural gas created a soft purr compared to the roar of the plane. I felt my eyes water as I thought of Remi and the others who'd gotten us this far.

Not wasting any time, the first vehicle charged up the ramp. One after another, each truck peeled out until only the personnel carrier with Kolya remained. Arjun took a few tentative steps forward as it started to roll. Time stood still as the realization of what was about to happen hit me. I looked on in horror as Arjun glanced back at his brother, face scarred from burns and soul broken from perceived betrayal. His gaze flicked back to the carrier, then back to Hemant, before he took off in a sprint towards the vehicle's open hatch.

"Noooo!" Hemant screamed as he watched his twin disappear into the back of the vehicle.

Hemant shirked off his heavy load and shot forward, chasing after him, but Huck was faster. Before I could think, Huck was struggling to retain him from behind as Hemant thrashed against his weaker frame.

"Let me go!" he screamed.

"I can't!" Huck yelled. "He'll hate you!"

"I don't care!" he screamed. "I'll never forgive myself if something happens to him!"

"He's made his choice! You have to let him go!"

"No! Huck, let me go!" Hemant screamed, collapsing to the ground in a deluge of tears.

Krista's hand slid into mine as I realized I was sobbing with him. Hemant's heart was being ripped asunder while I looked on powerless. The last image I had of Arjun was him standing with that sick sack of crap as the gates nestled back into each other, sealing us in.

With one final forlorn cry, Hemant stood. He wiped the tears and snot from his face and turned his anger on Huck with a shove to the chest.

"Why the hell did you hold me back?! I could've stopped him!" he said pointing towards the impassable gates.

"Hemant, I—"

"Get a hold of yourself, soldier!" said a wiry uniformed woman, approaching us.

Hemant still had so much to say but buttoned his lips. Her short hair and stern face meant all business. I caught myself standing more rigid, instantly fearing the riding crop she toted under her arm.

"Here I was thinking you were one of the only two of your unit fit for this place," she said, looking from Hemant to Omar. "Your brother chose his path. If he's capable, Captain Brick and the others will take care of him. I'm Captain Diaz, your superior officer. I'd take you down to the courses and test your mettle right now, but the minister insists that you get some R&R."

"Our superior officer?" asked Huck.

"What did you think this was?" she asked, daring him to answer.

Huck didn't take the bait. Two uniformed officers came and claimed Dieter's weapon, which Hemant had left lying on the floor.

"By entering Pod Bhopal, you've submitted yourself and the weapon to Prime Minister Madan's authority, and by proxy—mine. You will be rigorously trained. Should you fail or elect to discontinue, we will place you in a supportive role befitting of your skills." she said, turning towards two others. "This is Lieutenant Fen and Cadet Mego of Sigma Squad. Fen will be your squad leader and answers to me. You will follow her instructions as if I'd delivered them myself. They will show you to your dorms. Your training will begin the day after tomorrow."

"We didn't come here to join your ranks," Huck said cautiously. "We're on a mission from Prime Minister Leal to the Hive."

"Minister Madan and I are fully aware of your mission. If you can keep up with our extensive training regimen, we may allow you to accompany our next battalion and the weapon to the Hive."

·········

After more explanations and introductions, Mego and Fen escorted us to our dorms, but I didn't pay attention to a word they'd said. All I could think of was Diaz's words, "…we may allow you to accompany our next battalion…" The premise behind our entire mission had been to travel to the Hive in the smallest possible group to limit the odds of detection. Even doing so, the Arthropods had done all they could to destroy us, somehow knowing the threat we posed.

We were only different from all the previous missions in two ways: we had a chemo-nuclear weapon and we had remained a small, covert team—though not always for reasons we liked. It's hard for a group to grow when your members keep being killed.

I didn't know exactly what our newfound squad leader thought of us, but she seemed irritated by our arrival. No one, save for Marie, said a word from the Nucleus to the dorms. After showing us our rooms, Fen and Mego left us alone for the evening to recuperate. Unlike the previous two pods, the common room at the end of the corridor was buzzing with the activity of cadets. The last thing any of us wanted to do at the moment was socialize. If we were famous, I was thankful news of our arrival hadn't spread yet.

We all squeezed into one of the tiny two-person dorms. Having spent so long in such close proximity, none of us were ready to part from each other's company. The spartan room had a living area with a sofa, a small table, and a shelf. Stretching off from the living area were two bedrooms, a half-bathroom, and a kitchenette.

"What are we doing?" said Huck, hair sticking in all directions from running his fingers through it in frustration. "We came all this way only to have Arjun and the bomb ripped right out of our hands."

I glanced at Hemant. He sat, staring at the wall, looking like he was ready to pull the legs off of an eight.

"I have to go get him," he mumbled.

"You can't," I said. "Arjun chose to leave, even if it was a result of that bastard's mind games. You have to let him figure things out on his own."

"Hemant," said Omar. "You've dreamed of training with the elites here. Diaz said he'd be in good hands. I don't like her, but I think she's being straight with us. Let's train our asses off—all of us. When the transporters return, we'll find a way to get out of here and head to Bandung together, okay?"

Hemant's intense focus on the wall never wavered.

"There's one problem," Liesel said softly, getting everyone's attention. "Arjun and Kolya aren't coming back to Bhopal."

CHAPTER 35: HEMANT

"**Y**ou want to run that by me again?" I asked, facing Liesel.

"They're not coming back," she repeated.

"What do you mean, 'they're not coming back?'" asked Huck. "How do you know?"

Liesel squirmed under the pressure. "I overheard them talking in the tunnels just before we ran into the wraiths. I meant to say something, but I didn't know how… or if I should."

Liesel hung her head.

"It's alright, Liesel," said Ariadne, taking her hand.

"What did you overhear?" I asked, scooting to the edge of my seat.

"They had some plan. I couldn't hear everything, but they sent some sort of message to the Hive. They're planning to negotiate for peace."

I was flummoxed. I jumped up and grabbed my pack and hammer, which cadets were permitted to carry within the pod.

"Where the hell do you think you're going?" said Omar, blocking my way to the exit.

"If I leave now, I can catch up with them."

"Like hell, you can," he said. "They've got quite a lead on us, not to mention vehicles."

"Diaz made it clear we can't leave, Hemant. Especially not with our weapon," said Huck. "We'd be risking everything. We can't accomplish this mission if we're banished, imprisoned, or demoted."

"You have no right to tell me what I'm risking, Huck!" I said, nose to nose with him. "I'd die for Arjun. *You* were the one who held me back!"

I felt the gentle tug of Ariadne's hand on my arm. "He did the right thing, Hemant. I would've done the same."

I shrugged off her arm.

"*But…* that was before we knew where they were going," she added.

"What are you saying?" I asked.

Ariadne looked at Huck with a sly grin.

"Damn," said Omar, falling back into the sofa's cushions, "Just when I thought I'd get a decent night's sleep."

"What's the plan?" said Krista.

"Wing it like we always do," said Huck. "If we're going to get out of here, we need to learn more about this place."

"Just like old times," I said, sighing.

"We're at a serious disadvantage," said Ariadne. "We don't know this administration, nor do we have any allies. This won't be like escaping Kano. These guys are far more organized."

"What about Ondo and Trivia?" said Liesel. "They seemed nice enough."

"We have to be very careful who we talk to," Huck said. "Anyone who helps us would be risking insubordination charges, maybe even be labeled as traitors."

"There's another issue," said Ariadne. "We don't know how our popularity will affect us. Everyone could know who we are by morning."

"She's correct," said Marie. "We are no longer shrouded by the veil of anonymity."

"We have to play nice like we're really committed to training," said Huck. "That'll benefit us in more ways than one. We make allies, find transportation, steal the bomb, and get the hell out of here."

"When I woke up this morning, I sure didn't think I'd be planning an escape from a military pod," said Krista. "But I'm in."

"Madan was planning on defying all this mission stood for anyways," said Omar. "I didn't drag my ass from Horizonte to have another prick in a uniform tell me what to do."

"Life's certainly never boring with you guys," said Liesel.

"It's too claustrophobic for me underground. I wish to return to the surface," said Marie. "But when the time comes, it will be me who opens Kolya's throat."

"Not if I get to him first," I said.

"No one's killing Kolya, alright?!" said Huck. "I hate the bastard too, but sentencing him to death is a little harsh."

"I wasn't asking permission," Marie said straight-faced. "The time will come when I watch his blood pool at my feet."

The unusual, tattooed woman was stone-cold. Death at her hands sounded far more insidious than anything I could devise. I shuddered. At least everyone was in agreement about leaving.

"Thank you. All of you," I said. "Let's not spend a second longer in here than we have to. I've got a twin brother to catch."

•••••••••

"You're him, right?" the short-haired guy in the next shower over asked, scrubbing his underarms.

I looked around, but he couldn't have been speaking to anyone else. I'd woken up early after a piss-poor night's sleep and come down to the communal showers in search of some relaxation. God, a hot shower felt good. Last night had been the first night I'd spent away from my brother since I'd stayed with the survivors what felt like ages ago.

"Yeah, I guess," I said.

"Roque," he said, offering a soapy hand over the chest-high wall. "We're in the same squad."

"Hemant," I said, shaking his hand. "How is it we've already been assigned? We just got here yesterday."

"They've known you're coming for a while. Mego said unless you guys were dragged in unconscious, you'd be in our unit."

I nodded. It wouldn't have been the first time we'd arrived at a pod that way. I hoped rumors of my breakdown hadn't circulated. Life in the high-pressure atmosphere was already going to be challenging enough. Not to mention, hiding our forthcoming escape.

"There you are!" said another guy, bursting into the showers. "I was hoping to catch you all lathered up. Need any help?"

An Asian guy jumped into Roque's stall and planted a kiss on his cheek.

"Good to meet you," I said, fumbling with the soapy knob in my haste to escape the affectionate display.

"Sorry," said Roque, playfully pushing his friend away. "TomTom didn't mean to make you uncomfortable. He never stops goofing around."

I still wasn't used to romance between men, much less publicly. I didn't care one way or the other, but it wasn't something I'd grown up around. Discovering my brother kissing Ciro had come as quite a surprise, though not to anyone else. I couldn't believe I'd known my brother as long as I had and was oblivious to the fact he was gay. I'd grown to love Ciro like a brother before he was killed by some mysterious invert. Without either of them around, life somehow felt… emptier.

"It's okay. I've finished anyway," I said, still keeping my eyes low. "It was a pleasure to meet you both."

I grabbed my things and headed back to the dorm.

"Hey," said Huck, loitering outside my dorm. "I was hoping I could talk to you."

"Sure," I nodded. "Come on in."

"Um… don't people typically get dressed *before* they leave the showers?"

I looked down and realized I was dripping on the tile floor and couldn't help but laugh. I told Huck what had unfolded in the showers and had to listen to his snickering as I threw on some clothes.

I was the only one of us staying alone. It hadn't even been a choice. Everyone was happy to give me some space and though I profoundly missed my brother, I appreciated the time alone with my thoughts.

"I wanted to apologize for what went down yesterday," he said. "I still don't know if I made the best decision, but I'm your friend, through and through. You know I'd do anything for Arjun too."

"I know," I said. "We're good."

"Thanks, man. That means a lot," Huck said.

The tender-hearted moment was interrupted by a knock at the hatch. I opened it, expecting to find Ariadne, but was greeted by the squad leader who'd escorted us down the day before. Over her shoulder, I saw Mego and the rest of our group.

"Morning," she said.

"Good morning," Huck and I replied in unison.

"Good morning, Lieutenant," she corrected. "Tack that, el-tee, or sir onto the end of your responses."

"Yes, sir," said Huck. "How may we help you, Lieutenant?"

"Since administration doesn't seem to think I have anything better to do, I've been ordered to show you around," she said. "I'm hoping you slept off your stupor from last night. I don't want to have to repeat myself."

"We're ready and willing, sir," I said.

"Good," said Mego. "Let's get you guys looking like cadets."

•••••••••

"Damn," I said, admiring my new jumpsuit in the mirror. "I could get used to this."

We were in one of the upper-level market districts, being outfitted for apparel. Unlike the off-white jumpsuit and red armband combo I'd worn in Horizonte, I found the cadet's dark gray jumpsuit and light gray piping to be rather dashing by comparison. The material was far from new, likely scavenged from the damaged suits of past cadets. The talented tailors of Pod Bhopal had made every effort to put together decent, albeit piecemeal, outfits for the cadets.

Before the fitting, our lieutenant had taken us to a restaurant called Jaxx's. There we ate a breakfast that rivaled Zabu's welcome feast back before we'd fallen from his favor. Despite essentially being held against our will, cadets, and elites—those who'd completed training—were treated equally well. Our squad mates seemed nice enough, but anyone with a few brain cells could tell the lieutenant was peeved at the upheaval our arrival had caused for her.

After a visit to the level's barber, I was starting to feel like a civilized human again. Omar being Omar had once again buzzed his head. Unlike Omar, who was relishing his beard, I was happy to be clean-shaven. Huck still preferred some stubble to mask his scars. He and I had gotten similar haircuts, longer on top, and short on the sides. If I felt relief, I couldn't imagine how the girls must have felt after chopping off most of their length. Krista had her hair cut quite short and braided tightly against her scalp. Liesel's curls now dangled just above her shoulders. Ariadne's hung just below her ears—a look Huck couldn't get enough of. With hair trimmed, bodies clean, and jumpsuits changed, we all looked a little different.

Only Marie remained unchanged, refusing all services and garb. Being so far underground made her deeply uncomfortable. She seemed constantly alert and suspicious, far more unnerved than I'd seen her. Not only was I in a hurry to return to the surface for Arjun, but I also didn't want Marie to snap. None of us were confident in her mental fortitude, nor did I want to push it. Who knows what havoc that sludge had reeked on her system? No one seemed to mind that she was a survivor. At first, residents constantly approached her with curiosity but were quickly driven off by her snarl. Lately, no one had bothered her.

When Roque and TomTom joined us for the fitting, I introduced them to the others, trying my best not to look bashful.

"You clean up nicely," said TomTom, checking me out.

Roque jabbed his elbow into TomTom's ribs.

"Just admiring," he said, smiling at his partner. "You know where my loyalties lie."

"TomTom's right, Hemant," said Huck. "You do look snazzy."

"You're not so bad, yourself," I said. "Um… where's Omar?"

"I'm here," said Omar, strutting uncomfortably out of the dressing room in a jumpsuit several sizes too small for his muscular frame.

I laughed so hard that I was crying.

"Did they leave your suit in the dryer too long, man?" I eked out between chuckles.

"His ego is having trouble fitting in the suit," said Ariadne, struggling to catch her breath.

"No, he ate too much for breakfast," said Huck, turning red.

"Whatever," said Omar. "You guys suck. I'll see if I can find a proper suit while you guys pull yourselves together."

"How did that happen?" I asked once the hysterics had wound down.

"I may have changed the size on his request slip this morning," said Krista, bringing on another bout of laughter. "I couldn't resist."

It was good to see everyone in a good mood. With all the danger on the surface, it was nice to blow off some steam. I wished Arjun could be with me to enjoy it. Even though it was of his own making, I tried not to dwell on the guilt I felt knowing he hadn't had any respite. I wanted to grab Kolya by the neck and beat him senselessly for turning my brother against me. He was my only-known blood relation. I wished he would've shared his ideas with me. Whether I would've agreed or not, I would have listened. Arjun was a font of insights. Maybe there was some merit to their idea, something I was missing. Why did he have to confide in that bastard?

"I have to ask," said Ariadne, once Omar was properly dressed. "What's the training like here, Lieutenant?"

"Relentless," said Fen, partially lifting her shirt. "You don't get abs like these sitting on your ass. That's for sure. You guys better be up to it."

"You get the mornings to do your own thing," said Roque. "Most people do stretches, yoga, warm-ups, that type of thing. You'd be a fool to chill out during that time. Once the gong rings… it's on."

"The trainers here like to run you ragged," said Mego. "Every day, we go home worn out. Some days, I'm not even up for making out."

Fen grabbed a cushion from the outfitter's seating area and slung it at him.

"It's different from the candidate training," said TomTom. "Laps have been replaced by obstacle courses, weight lifting by strength relays, sparring by war games, and mechanical inverts by real ones."

I glanced at Ariadne, thinking back to when our sadistic trainers had decided to let several cohorts battle a live invert. Huck's cohort had luckily escaped that one. In a way, I was grateful for the practice. It might have been part of the reason I was still alive.

"What about the sorties to the surface?" asked Huck. "Are those part of training, El-Tee?

"Everything is part of training," said Fen. "Once a squad proves itself competent, the trainers will start tasking the squads with surface missions."

"How long does that take, Lieutenant?" asked Krista.

Fen shrugged. "Some of the trainers are hard-asses. If they see potential, it could be a few weeks. If they don't—months. You guys sure as hell better not slow us down. You've already put us behind schedule. We were ready to face the trials before you came along and we were reorganized."

"Sorry about that, sir. This wasn't exactly our plan either," I said, before catching myself. "We don't want to wait months. We're in a hurry to annihilate these bastards."

"That's the only attitude I expect from you," she said, then pointing at Ariadne and Krista. "Trainers don't like cripples. I'm not thrilled about your injuries either. It's just another thing to slow us down. The trainers will do their best to make life difficult for you, so you'll have your work cut out for you."

"Great," said Ariadne. "I get to prove my worth—again."

"Welcome to modern womanhood," said Fen.

"Normally, squads have six months to prove themselves. After that, they are looking at reassignment," said Roque. "However, the next battalion is leaving sooner than that, so that's our deadline."

No pressure. Each of us had more to lose than we cared to admit. I would do everything I could to see each of my companions through this ordeal. Hopefully, we'd all be better for it, but it was going to be tough.

"When will we be cleared to leave, El-Tee?" asked Huck. "I mean, for the Hive."

"Just as soon as we can pass the Drome."

CHAPTER 36: FEN

The next morning, when I returned to our dorm after a scalding-hot shower, Mego pressed a steaming mug of fresh coffee into my awaiting hands. I let the warmth pass through the worn ceramic mug into my hands as I breathed in the deeply pleasant aroma. It was my single moment of peace before the day's demands raised their wearying heads. I curled up on the fraying, stained sofa that, like the mug, had seen so many cadets before me. With my feet tucked underneath my body, I watched as Mego read the third part of the current serial being passed around. Usually, the tattered booklets were nothing but smut, but this one was a thriller he couldn't put down. Judging by the look of things, he'd finish it today, then have to anxiously wait for the next installment to be circulated.

I was grateful for the quality coffee after the late night. We'd stayed out to take the new cadets by the Drome. When they found out that it was the largest obstacle standing between them and the next phase of their mission, they were itching to see it. Officially, no one was allowed in, but leave it to bored, highly-trained soldiers to find a way to sneak in. Despite the trainers' desires, it was the worst-kept secret of the pod—but that made it no less intimidating. Their reactions were still fresh on my mind.

"What in the universe is that monstrosity?" asked Hemant.

The four of us had led the newbies through the maintenance tunnels to where they dead-ended, just above the Drome. After silently lowering the grate down to the floor, we quietly piled out and made our way to the railing overlooking the mismatched, multi-story obstacle course.

"That, my friend, is the Drome," said Roque.

"What is it?" asked Krista. "It looks like a rubbish heap."

Mego started chuckling, but I didn't think it was any laughing matter. The Drome was what stood between me and leading my squad into the annals of history. It was already enough that I had to start over again, nearly from scratch. Diaz must want me to fail. Why else would she restructure my squad? The practice was unheard of save for serious injury or misconduct.

"The Drome is one of the most diabolical obstacle courses that man has conceived," I said. "It's designed to make sure that anyone who leaves Pod Bhopal can handle the pressure of being a Clunkie."

A hiss of steam escaped from the bowels of the edifice as it voiced its agreement.

"They had to demo through the floors of several districts to make enough room for it," said Mego. "And it still keeps growing."

"Do we just run through it?" asked Liesel, a worried look on her face.

"That's one way to put it," said TomTom. "The rules are straightforward. Your squad has to reach the exit to pass. You're only allowed the loss of one member."

"How many chances do you get, El-Tee?" asked Huck.

"One," I said.

"You're kidding. Right, Lieutenant?" said Omar, turning to face me.

I shook my head.

"So you've never done it before, Lieutenant?" asked Ariadne.

"No," I said. "Squad leaders decide when their team's ready. It's as much of a test of our leadership as it is for our squad's abilities."

"And if we fail, we face reassignment?" asked Huck.

"Yeah," said Mego, nodding. "If the trainers see a lot of potential in you, you might be one of the lucky few reassigned to another squad, but most are immediately placed in supplementary roles."

"What's inside?" asked Omar, crouching down for a better view.

"Clunkies, the nickname for the elites who've survived it, are forbidden to talk about it. So naturally, they do, especially once they get a few drinks in them," said Roque. "They like to scare the mess out of newbies like you. Supposedly it's full of traps, pitfalls, and—"

"A thousand sharp, pointy things that can kill you," interrupted TomTom. "Plus, when you finally reach the bottom, your team—or what's left of it—has to face live inverts."

"Joy," said Hemant. "Is it timed?"

"It doesn't have to be," said Marie, pointing at several contraptions connected to the looming, crimson structure. Large clusters of rail-mounted bars waited patiently to penetrate the metal-clad exterior and block off the sections behind.

"It took me several trips up here to notice that," I said. "You're quite observant."

Marie gave a slight nod in thanks.

"I don't see it," said Liesel.

"They seal off sections as you pass through the course," said Ariadne. "Either you stay ahead, or you're trapped behind."

"Exactly," I said.

"It gets even more sinister than you think," said Mego.

"I'm not sure how that's possible," said Hemant.

"The course is human-operated by the most sadistic squad in Bhopal," said TomTom. "Xavier and his Tau goons love nothing more than to see how many recruits they can kill or maim during a run."

"Jesus," said Huck. "I knew it would be hardcore, but this is not what I expected."

"Madan takes training extraordinarily seriously," I said. "He's a good leader but has zero tolerance for weakness. He devised the original Drome thirty years ago and it's been tacked onto ever since, becoming more and more vicious."

"You think we can pry tips out of Ondo and Trivia?" Huck asked Ariadne. "If they've been doing sorties. They've passed it, right?"

"It's one thing to scare recruits," I said, "But another to share insights and strategies. We could all be penalized for cheating and those are consequences you really don't want."

"I guess we have no choice but to get our asses in shape," said Omar.

With my coffee finished and feeling a little more alert, Mego and I went to meet Huck and the others. As expected, they were up and ready when we arrived.

"What first?" asked Huck as we entered Sigma Squad's training arena.

"Lieutenant," I reminded him. "First, I'll lead a series of stretches. Everyone pick a spot."

We scattered around the rubber-coated floor, pocked from years of use. I started the routine with everyone in a prone position. *How is it that rubber never loses its smell?* I transitioned into the first pose. The new cadets might be pretty fit, but they were sorely lacking in flexibility. I made a mental note to work on that.

"Don't force it, Omar," I said. "You pull something, you'll only slow us down."

"As if they weren't already," Mego muttered.

Judging by the look on Ariadne's face, she'd heard the remark. Maybe it'd help them stay motivated. I *was* going with the next battalion to the Hive and wasn't about to let some hot shots keep me from doing so. With the yoga complete, we moved on to the track. I rolled my eyes as the newbies tried to hide their soreness. *God, we have a long way to go.*

"We'll be doing a five-k at a comfortable pace," I said. "Remember, our mornings are a warm-up for the harder stuff. We stay together, no lollygagging."

"A five-kilometer warm-up?" Krista mouthed to Ariadne.

"Yes," I said. "If that's going to be too much for you, I could go ahead and put you in for reassignment. Maybe you'd get a nice, cushy gig in the sewage tunnels."

She lowered her head in defeat.

"If that's all the whining, let's get started," I said, leaping onto the track.

Twelve laps later, half of us were barely breathing hard, but the rest looked like they could faint.

"You guys aren't living up to your reputation," said Mego. "I thought you'd be... I don't know... less weak."

"Look, man," said Hemant. "We've traveled thousands of kilometers and survived countless invert attacks. The fact that we get a little winded when we run isn't a big deal."

"Isn't a big deal?!" I yelled, coming to a halt. "I'm trying to turn you into elites! If you thought you were going to meander to the Hive, then you should've kept walking. We would've walked right by your rotting carcasses when our battalion marched. I had a squad of trained cadets, ready to take on the Drome, but then you waltz in and Diaz sees fit to stick you with me! I'm not in the habit of babysitting or defying orders, so you get your crap together or I will personally push you into the nearest recycler. Clear?"

"Yes, sir," he said, eyes forward.

"That goes for all of you. Hit the gym, eat a light breakfast, and reassemble in the Platoon III arena when you hear the gong. And be ready to have your asses handed to you."

I finished my normal round of push-ups far faster than normal, channeling my anger into every thrust off the mat.

"What were they thinking this was, coming in here like that?" I asked.

"Cut them some slack, Fen," said Roque. "If half of what they say about them is true, I'm glad to have them in our squad, even if it does suck to lose the others."

"Cut them some slack? You saw them in there. They couldn't even run a few kilometers without looking like they were going to pass out. Diaz is going to tear them to shreds and then take it out on me. I've worked too hard to be dragged back down into the mire."

I felt my eyes begin to burn. My mother back in Wuhan had been a birther—a woman predisposed to having valued reproductive qualities. Birthers were treated more like factories than people. I'd die before I'd be consigned to something like that. She'd never minded, humbly accepting her lot in life, but I held enough resentment for the both of us. I was anxious to see the Arthropods off this planet so humans could choose their own destinies, not have one forced upon them. I sat back on my haunches as Mego clasped my hand.

"I have to believe there's something to them," he said. "They've come this far, with a weapon unseen since before the pods. Hell, they took down the damn aerials! Imagine what they could do if they were in as good a shape as us. Sigma will be unstoppable."

"I suppose, but this is crunch time if we want to make the next flotilla," I said, sighing. "I don't know if I can get them ready in time. And who the hell ever heard of a squad of eleven?"

"Diaz doesn't seem to count Marie since she's an outsider," said TomTom. "Fen, you do realize Diaz didn't place them under your command to punish you, right? She gave them to you because you're the best damn lieutenant these miscreants have ever seen. I don't mind spending extra time with them to get them up and running."

"Same," said Roque and Mego simultaneously.

I felt my cheeks warm.

"Thanks, guys."

After a brief meditation and breakfast shake, I felt rejuvenated as the anticipated gong summoned the various squads to our platoon's arena. Diaz was already on the podium, waiting. As the five squads formed up, I caught Xavier's sinister gaze. His foreboding grin set me on edge. The leader of Tau Squad was all too eager to hurt anyone who got in his way and trained his Clunkie minions to follow in his footsteps.

The man's spiky hair served as a perfect reflection of his barbed personality. The tattoos lining the sides of his head illustrated his prowess as a warrior but failed to warn of his prowess as an asshole. The man and his numerous piercings icked me out, but I refused to let him notice. My squad's lives would be in his dastardly hands come time for the Drome. He would stop at nothing to bring me to my knees. For whatever reason, he found the thought of a woman's success repulsive. The fact that he'd been the first squad leader of the current battalion to pass the Drome had only inflated an already bursting-at-the-seems ego. When tasked with operating the Drome, he took to the responsibility like a deity on judgment day.

"Attention!" said Diaz.

The sound of more than fifty boots slamming together echoed through the chamber.

"The day of the battalion's departure grows closer. In two months' time, all squads that have passed the final trials will depart Pod Bhopal for the Hive," said Diaz, staring at me through the excitement as though I was the only one in the room. "We will face our enemy with a new weapon—a weapon brought to us by the newest cadets of Sigma Squad."

Every head in the room swiveled to inspect my new recruits. Xavier's eyes never left mine. He was drawn to fresh meat like a multipede to a green candidate. My new teammates seemed strangely bothered by the recognition. Most of the cadets viewed them as heroes. Even though I viewed them as a liability, I couldn't figure out why they would be annoyed by the attention. I thought back to what Diaz had said. I couldn't believe I only had two months to prepare seven new members.

"I'm pleased to bring you great news," Diaz said, rigid as ever. "Our battalion will be led by none other than your prime minister, General Arnav Madan."

Pride swelled in my chest as cheers erupted around me. It was one thing to be yet another battalion marching off to the Hive, but to warrant the general himself leading the charge. *There* is *something different about this mission.* It was never far from my mind that not a single battalion had ever returned from the Hive. Between Madan's leadership, the downed antenna-bug network, and the new weapon, we couldn't fail.

CHAPTER 37: HUCK

I'd never been so sore in my life. Ever. I hurt in places I didn't know could hurt. The discomfort was rivaled not by my candidate training, but by the first day of forced labor working the vats in Kano's Dust facility. *Speaking of which, I wonder how Midge is doing.* I waddled into our dorm and slowly lowered myself onto the sofa next to an equally uncomfortable Ariadne.

"And to think we have to repeat this tomorrow," I said, grunting.

"I know," said Ariadne. "I'm too exhausted to think about moving again."

I laughed, feeling a deep cramp in my abs.

"Don't say anything funny, okay?" I asked, making us laugh all the more.

There was a knock on the door. I assumed it was Hemant, but was surprised when Roque and TomTom stuck their heads in.

"You guys busy?" Roque asked.

"Only if whining counts as busy," I said.

"I figured you guys would be feeling it," Roque said, chuckling. "TomTom and I made you dinner."

"I… I don't know what to say," I said.

"Thank you would suffice," said TomTom, smiling. "You guys pulled your weight out there today. We appreciated that. I don't know what we'd do if you guys had been a bunch of slackers."

"Thank you, TomTom," said Ariadne. "For the food and the encouragement."

"You're welcome, but don't expect this every night. I like cooking, but not that much," said TomTom.

"Can I ask you guys a question?" asked Roque.

I shrugged.

"When Diaz mentioned you guys in her address, you looked like you'd just watched a friend fall down the shaft. What's the deal?"

I paused, looking at Ariadne, who gave an imperceptible shrug.

"Everything they're planning is wrong," I said.

"What do you mean?" asked TomTom, confused. "Madan is leading the battalion himself. You know, he's the only prime minister in the world to work his way up to the top from being a laborer? How much more support do you need?"

"It's not that. I'm sure Madan is a great leader and I feel honored, but none of this is what Memo wanted."

"Memo, meaning Prime Minister Leal?"

"Yeah. His entire plan was centered around us being a small, imperceptible task force, sneaking the weapon into Hive," I said. "Big groups have always been overrun and wiped out. Covert groups lacked a nuclear device. Even back before the pods, the bombing campaigns couldn't penetrate their extensive subterranean networks."

"You don't understand, Huck. With each missing battalion, Madan analyzes what went wrong and adjusts it for the next mission. That's why he keeps adding onto the Drome," said Roque. "He's so determined that this battalion will succeed, he's leading the charge."

"He's not disputing that," said Ariadne. "Nor are we ungrateful for the training and hospitality. It's just that we had a mission, and Madan's plans go blatantly against the spirit of it."

"I'm sorry, guys," said Roque. "Even if I agreed with you, Madan is more stubborn than a den matriarch. You'll never get him to change his mind. It's part of what makes him so resilient. Take it from me, if he's leading the mission, we'll be a force to be reckoned with."

I nodded, thanking them for the food once more as they left.

"I don't know how the hell we're going to sneak out of here."

●●●●●●●●

The first two weeks of training were a blur. We'd spend the morning warming up, followed by a truly relentless training regimen. If the human body was capable of it, we did it. Diaz was determined that every soldier's body be in its peak condition. Ariadne and I often arrived back at our dorms so tired that we slept until it was time to repeat the routine. As much as we were excited to be with each other, there was little time or energy left for intimacy.

Unlike the learning methods as a candidate, everything in Bhopal was taught through application. Nothing theoretical here. How do you pace yourself on a non-stop, thirty-kilometer run through the forest? Have Tau Squad chase you through a simulated forest until you figure it out. What order do you take on an ambush of mixed Arthropod and Demented enemies? Rho Squad operates lethal mechanical inverts while Phi Squad tries to fill you full of arrows. How do you escape from a mud raptor nest when you're paralyzed? Trainers inject you with a numbing agent and force you to escape a clay tomb before you suffocate. Having survived the actual ordeal, Ariadne had the role of administering oxygen to the cadets who passed out. I had a newfound respect for her after I watched so many of Platoon III's cadets fail the Tomb. With no training and having suffered from the Shock, she was still able to save herself from certain, agonizing death.

Like the Tomb, the tasks were not only physically demanding but equally mental. Nor were they without loss. We were unusual with our squad of eleven, but many of the others had less than the prerequisite ten due to unfortuitous circumstances. An unavoidable fact of the intense training was that sometimes cadets died. And when someone didn't have the physical or mental fortitude, Diaz immediately dispatched them for reassignment. Like Madan, she had no tolerance for weakness, citing that outside of the pod, it would cost the lives of the "more worthy" soldiers.

Marie proved to be an incredible asset to Sigma Squad. Nothing that Diaz could throw at her would slow her down. She was the embodiment of lethality, fortitude, and finesse. I was supremely grateful that she was on our side. As the days wore on, Lieutenant Fen's original distaste for us waned as she saw our dedication and resilience. Outside of training, she even allowed us to drop her formal address.

One evening after training, Sigma was dining at Jaxx's, Fen's preferred hangout. The place's food was in the style of Pod Pittsburgh, where I had been destined before Memo's surprise mission. The food was fine, but I wasn't a huge fan of a philly— greasy, cheesy meat crammed into stale bread—the house specialty. I ignored the glares from its loyal clientèle when I ordered their mediocre pizza. I didn't care because tonight we were celebrating. It was the first day that none of us were sore!

"It's a milestone!" said Roque, raising his third or fourth mash beer high into the air and splashing some of the mug's contents on the table.

Xavier plucked the beer out of his hand and took a deep draught.

"What the hell, man?" said Mego. "Don't you have minions to antagonize?"

"No," he said, sitting on the back of the booth. "I delegate that sort of stuff. What are we celebrating?"

"None of your business, asshole," said Fen.

"*Mmm,* feisty. I like it."

Mego jumped up and squared off with Xavier.

"Let it go, Mego," said TomTom. "He's not worth it."

"What are you going to do, Wee-go," said Xavier. "Or are you going to let this femme fight your battles for you?"

Hemant wiped his mouth, slowly rising to meet Xavier face-to-face.

"What did you call him?" Hemant asked.

Xavier poured Roque's beer over Hemant's head. "A. Femme."

I put my hand on Hemant's forearm, a silent warning to guard his actions.

"Apologize to him," Hemant said, frothy beer dripping off of his lower lip.

The entire restaurant went silent. Everyone faced the spectacle, anxious to see what would transpire. I had the distinct impression that Xavier's misdeeds were well-known throughout the pod. Judging by the looks, I don't think the residents were used to him being challenged. Diaz might value his sadism, but his individualistic approach couldn't be beneficial to any team dynamic. Hemant was not one to back down when a friend was insulted, especially when the remark hit so close to home.

"I don't think I will," he said. "No, I know I won't."

There was a blur of motion as Hemant shattered a wooden chair over Xavier's back. Before the spikey-haired menace could react, Hemant jerked him up off of the floor and prostrated on the bar.

"Apologize," Hemant commanded, the front of Xavier's jumpsuit wadded tightly within Hemant's large fist.

Xavier muttered an insincere, half-assed apology.

Hemant released his grip as Xavier rolled off the bar, collapsing to the floor. Defeated, he stood and disappeared into the sea of bodies churning outside the establishment.

"Thank you," said TomTom.

"Anytime," said Hemant, throwing a handful of ration points on the bar. "Sorry about the mess."

As Hemant sat, Fen beamed, visibly proud of her new squad mates.

"You just royally pissed off the most sadistic person in the pod," Fen said. "You know there will be hell to pay come the Drome."

"I'm counting on it," said Hemant.

•••••••

I wasn't surprised when Roque and TomTom dropped by for another visit that evening.

"Hey, Huck. I'm not interrupting anything, am I?" asked Roque.

"No," I said, gazing at Ariadne. "We were just talking."

"Okay," he said, looking awkward. "Could you ask the others to join us?"

"Sure," I said.

Within moments, nine members of Sigma squad were crammed into the minuscule space. Only Fen and Mego had been left out.

"I... um—" began Roque.

"Spit it out, babe," said TomTom.

"I really appreciate what you did for TomTom back there, Hemant. It's um... got me thinking. I remembered what you said about your mission, and well... We'd like to help you."

"Help us *how*, Roque?" asked Ariadne, probing.

"I want to help you guys continue your mission—the way Minister Leal intended."

It took a moment for what Roque was offering to sink in. He was not only risking his skin but all of Sigma's. If we were caught, it would mean the end of our mission and, quite possibly, life sentences for all of us doing who-knows-what.

"I mean… That's incredible, Roque. Thank you," I said. "What did you have in mind?"

"So there's this place where Roque and I used to sneak off to before we were roommates. You know when we wanted some privacy," said TomTom, anxiously twisting the tuft of hair under his lower lip. "Bhopal has never been the most welcoming place to guys like us."

"It's some sort of abandoned garage or something. There's a bunch of derelict quads in there, the type that transporters use," said Roque. "They're in bad shape—dry-rotted tires, oil leaks, mouse-eaten wires—but they've been forgotten."

"And most importantly, there's an exterior door," said TomTom. "I'm sure it's locked though."

The gears in my mind began turning. If we could get the quads fixed, we might be able to sneak out right under Madan's nose. I hadn't known Roque and TomTom long, but I already knew them to be loyal comrades and fierce warriors. I'd welcome their companionship.

"What about Fen and Mego?" asked Liesel. "We can't just leave them behind to face punishment on our behalf."

"We won't. I think it's best if we do this on our own, giving them deniability," said TomTom. "When we're ready, I think I can convince them to come with us."

"If we do this, Madan will be livid," said Omar. 'I'm pretty sure nothing happens without his consent."

"You're spot on," said Roque. "We can't afford to get caught. Reassignment isn't all that bad unless you get one of the undesirable subservient positions, like Breaker's sister. I heard that you guys helped get her out. But if we piss off Madan, there's no telling what horrid tasks he'd find for us. And there will be no one to help us then."

Ariadne shivered at the thought. A searing anger rose from my chest to my face. Bhopal might be immeasurably better than Kano, but it hid its dark underbelly well. If humanity wanted a future, it needed to move past all forms of slavery.

"You mentioned Breaker," said Liesel. "Could he fix the quads?"

"Breaker?" asked TomTom. "He can fix anything if he has the parts. Do you guys have anything of value? Quality parts are hard to come by."

I looked at Ariadne.

"We have a few rough diamonds left, but we used most of them to free Breaker's sister," she said.

"Where the hell did you guys get diamonds?" asked Roque.

"Long story," I said. "Would anyone trade ration points?"

"Unlikely," said TomTom. "They need something more real."

"Let this *Breaker* examine the quads," said Marie. "If he will make a list of what he needs, I will see to it."

"Okay," said Roque, drawing out the word. "This pod's still a big unfamiliar place. Are you sure?"

"I wouldn't have offered if I wasn't," she said.

"Great," said Roque, slapping his hands together. "Ariadne, could you meet Breaker and me at our market district after training?"

"Sure, but why me? Huck knows more about engineering than I do."

"Breaker is notoriously… cantankerous. You having freed his sister, I think, will help ensure his cooperation."

CHAPTER 38: KOLYA

A week after leaving Pod Bhopal, we arrived at the outskirts of an ancient city on the territory's coast. From the rise, we could look out over the pristine waters of the Indian Ocean. As predicted, the Arthropods hadn't interfered with our journey. Reason or no, the Sea Dogs had grown jumpier by the day, constantly living under the fear of a massive ambush. I looked down and smiled at my companion—grateful he'd seen the light and joined me—thinking back to our last moments in the pod.

"That's my boy!" I said to Arjun as he jumped into the carrier.

Without a word, he grabbed the handgrip running along the inside of the carrier's roof, looking back forlornly at his friends. I squeezed his shoulder, turning to face him. When I looked back towards the others, Huck was restraining Hemant as he screamed and thrashed against him. As the hatch latched into place with a thud, a wry smile cut across my face. Arjun was crucial to brokering peace with the Arthropods. His intelligence had been wasted dicking around with those pals of his. Under my tutelage, he could finally spread his wings and be the fiercely insightful individual I knew him to be.

"You made the right decision," I said, sitting on the unforgiving metal bench running the length of the carrier and packed with grisly-faced transporters. I rubbed my wrist where the restraints had chaffed.

"I suppose we're letting anyone into our ranks now," growled Ian, his wiry frame jostling from side to side as the vehicle lurched through the first rough terrain.

"You won't be saying that when you realize how much of an asset we are," I said.

"Intelligence doesn't equate to survival," he said, sticking a toothpick into the corner of his mouth. "If either of you becomes a liability, I'll put you down myself."

"You, my friend, don't exactly look like the epitome of strength," I said.

"Don't worry your nasty little head about such things. I've got ten years of surface time, so I'm as snug as a cave grub up here. When you've got half that, talk to me about strength."

Not exactly a ray of sunshine, eh Sveta? I looked at Arjun, whose gaze was frozen on the heavily-scrubbed floorboards shining between the worn black boots of the other transporters. I imagined that Arjun would be second-guessing himself for days if I didn't intervene.

"Arjun?" I said.

"Yes," he said, slowly turning towards me.

"Let him go. If you don't sever the connection, you'll rot away."

"He's my twin brother. I can't just let him go."

"You can. And you will. If you have the opportunity to reunite with him when this is all over, then it is as destiny intended it. If not… You *must* let go."

He nodded silently, returning his attention to the floor.

"What's that thing?" asked one of the men through his jungle of a beard, kicking at Arjun's weapon resting on the floor.

"It's a razor net," said Arjun, his focus not leaving the scuffed diamond plate.

"What's it do?" he asked.

Arjun raised his head slightly but avoided the man's eyes.

"It operates like a lasso. I can keep the weighted net closed and use it like a flail, or I can open it and scissor everything it closes around."

"When we make camp, I would very much like to see you demonstrate this."

We rode for hours, making awkward small talk with the toughened transporters that composed the Sea Dogs. The tight-knit group had spent a lifetime facing the dangers of the surface together, making us strangers in a new land. It was clear that they didn't anticipate us being around long enough to bother getting to know us. Under their protection, I would have the necessary time that I needed to reacquaint myself with my blade. With any luck, maybe they'd forget about marking me as Banished.

The Arthropods did little to impede our progress, so little that the seasoned Sea Dogs grew uneasy. That evening in camp, I listened as a restless soldier went on and on, unnerved by the lack of confrontations on the normally-hostile southeastern route. "Something's not right," he repeated. I planned for us to secure passage to Pod Bandung once we reached the port city. With us no longer in their company, the wanton violence that they were accustomed to would undoubtedly follow.

"Our message must've gotten through, Arjun," I said, pulling him out of earshot.

"It would seem so," said Arjun, slinging out his bivvy and letting it float down until it settled on the leaf-strewn ground.

The first drops of rain landed loudly with a pop on the broad leaves of the jungle plants surrounding the campsite.

"If it's not one thing, it's another," I said, tucking my bag into my tent where it would stay dry.

We made our way closer to the clearing, where Brick had built a small fire recessed into the ground. The Sea Dogs' cook, William, had a hearty stew of root vegetables and Ian's wild-caught game bubbling within the hour. William, not Will as I quickly discovered, was one of the few clean-shaven transporters. The wizened man was borderline obsessive when it came to his personal cleaning and grooming, befitting qualities of a chef. His food, though delectable, couldn't take the transporter's mind off the inverts' disconcerting absence.

"I don't like this," Ian said between bites of stew. "We've been together for years, Brick. I've never had an entire day without an attack. Not one damn day."

"I know," Brick said, spitting a string of tobacco onto the damp earth.

"Something's been changing for a while now," said William. "You can feel it on the wind."

"William, you've been saying something was changing for the last eight years," said Ian, letting out the dry, hacking laugh of a lifelong smoker. "Eventually, you're bound to be right."

I surveyed the sky from the tarp we'd draped off one of the vehicles, wondering if the blue-eyed duster still lingered over us. *It's out there somewhere, Sveta. Watching us. Protecting us. It's the only explanation as to why we're still safe.*

"We were under constant attack," said Arjun, drawing attention.

He'd said hardly a word since we'd left the pod, limiting his communication to gestures with anyone but me. I placed my hand on his knee, silently urging him not to reveal too much to our newfound comrades.

"Explain," said Brick.

"My friends and I were on our way to destroy the Hive," said Arjun. "The Arthropods were constantly at our heels or setting up an ambush. They knew we were coming for them."

"Wait. That was you guys?!" asked Brick, slapping his knee. "Hot damn!"

"Forgive Brick, Arjun. His enthusiasm sometimes overwhelms his common sense," said Ian, turning to his leader. "If it's so awesome, why didn't he stay with his little friends?"

"Because they had no vision of the future," I said.

"Sounds like they had plenty of it," said William, tilting back his wide-brimmed hat. "I mean, they brought down the inverts' spy drones. If it wasn't for the dern rainclouds, we'd be seeing more stars than ever, thanks to them."

"They couldn't see past the eradication," I clarified.

"See," Brick said, holding out his callused hand towards me in validation. "You have to have a plan for what comes after."

"Spare us your thoughtful analysis, Brick," said Ian. "Thinking is not one of your strengths."

"He's correct," said Arjun. "The future of humanity must be extensively planned if we want to regain our former glory. However, the point I was making is that the Arthropods no longer see us as a threat."

"Don't see us as a threat, my ass," said Brick, standing. "I'll show them a threat!"

"Sit down, Brick," said Ian. "We all know you're good with a weapon. It's why we tolerate you as our leader. What's your point, young man?"

My hand tightened on Arjun's leg.

"I believe the threat rides with my friends and their super weapon, which we no longer carry," said Arjun. "With the Arthropods' focus so heavily directed towards them, our travels should be significantly easier. With less time spent fighting, Kolya and I should have more time to focus on our data collection."

"Superweapon… Interesting," said Ian.

"Data collection," said Brick. "Now that sounds like the way of the future."

"Universe save us," said Ian, rolling his eyes.

With the vast ocean momentarily out of sight, Arjun and I stepped down the ramp of the cargo hauler. After having arrived at the crumbling city's edge, Brick ordered us to march alongside the vehicles through the dilapidated buildings and mounds of rubble. It took us from sun-up to sundown to make our way through the ruins of Masula Port. Between the overgrowth and collapse, the abandoned city was a haven for would-be hiding spots. Like the previous days, it was as if the inverts had all but abandoned the planet.

Once we'd cleared the city, we reluctantly climbed back into the stifling vehicles, thankful for the disconcerting, but delightful, reprieve from the oppressive heat. I could smell the salty air of the ocean long before I could see it again. It'd been years since I'd seen such a vast, saltwater expanse. With the threat of danger so minimal, we'd opened every measure of ventilation the vehicles had. The vent slats did nothing to alleviate the copious humidity thick on the tropical air, but the views from the decimated coastal highway were something to be admired. The inviting sand and scalable mountains had me wishing that I could spend the afternoon roaming the area, studying all the flora and fauna I could find with my new apprentice, Arjun.

"Did I ever tell you about our last trip overseas?" asked Arjun.

"Only about Huck's parasites and you nearly drowning. Why do you ask?"

"I was thinking about the boat's sergeant-at-arms, Kebe. He was also Captain Lolade's first mate," Arjun said, beginning to sniffle. "He taught me and Ciro a plethora of maritime facts—knowledge that was helpful on more than one occasion. Do you know much about the ocean?"

"I know precious little of the oceans, it pains me to say," I said. "I learned only about the seas and rivers I'd encounter on my initial journey and what little was known of their inhabitants. This will be my first ocean experience."

"It was my understanding that the creatures disliked large bodies of water, but on our Release Day, we clearly saw evidence to the contrary."

"Like what?"

"The spring tongues, for example. They thrive in the water, though they are amphibious Arthropods. Then there are the wake striders that live predominantly on the water."

"Without breaking the water's surface tension," I added. "Barely a water creature."

"But we've discovered so much new information since leaving the pod. New species. New behaviors. We've even found evidence of further adaptations," said Arjun, growing animated. "Earth is over seventy percent water, Kolya. I find it unlikely that a species adapting so rapidly to our native conditions doesn't have a presence in our oceans."

"There are stories," said William, so softly I thought he was talking to himself. "Some of the men talk of distant shadows, lurking in the water. Shadows as large as the duners themselves."

"You can't trust a word from these superstitious numskulls," said Ian, earning a few scowls.

Ian's prowess with the crossbow was all that kept the abrasive man in the good graces of the other transporters. Arjun had told me of Huck's difficulties with the unforgiving weapon before he'd given it up in favor of a more refined weapon—a type of sword called a dao. Though I hadn't had a chance to witness Ian in action, it was rumored that the sharpshooter never needed a second shot.

"It's true," interjected Putri, a muscular woman with a sneer that could curl paint. "I've heard the sounds, laying in my berth at night. Felt like ice in my bones. Not something I'm likely to forget."

"Those were the complaints of your lover, Putri!" said Yuze, a burly man covered in self-administered tattoos. "Likely lamenting how ugly you are."

The carrier roared with guffaws and slurs as Putri turned purple beneath her scraggly short-cropped hair. When the laughter didn't immediately die down, she leapt from her seat and threw Yuze against the wall, delivering blow after blow into his unprotected abs.

"Enough," yelled Ian, stopping her in mid-blow. "Brick will have my head if you rupture someone else's spleen. You can't fight your way out of every sad truth of your life, Putri."

The burly woman gave him an obscene gesture before letting Yuze slump to the floor. Once she'd regained her composure, I leaned in.

"Tell me. What did you hear?" I whispered.

"A wail, like a tortured soul," she said, placing her hand over her heart and revealing the raised hair dotting her arms. "Shook my core, it did."

"Resonance," said Arjun, eyes widening. "Did no one else hear it?"

"The men feel immune on the boat. Nights are filled with gambling, drinking, and cursing. I can't abide that vile hooch or their atrocious behavior, so I spend much of my time in my berth..." she leaned in close, "reading."

"Hmm," I said, leaning back. "And you're sure it wasn't a whale?"

"What's a whale?" she asked.

I looked at Arjun, who shrugged. *Maybe there* is *something out there.*

"Besides you, how many of the transporters take the boat to Pod Bandung?" asked Arjun.

"All of us," said Putri, surprised by the question. "We've been operating one of Bandung's underwater boats for years."

"I thought most transporter groups specialized in land or water," said Arjun. "This is the first I've heard of a group doing both."

"Normally that's the case," said William. "We took over the route because there weren't enough volunteers. That's what tends to happen when the last boat vanishes with its entire crew."

CHAPTER 39: ARIADNE

I found myself leaning against the railing of the central shaft in the wee hours of the morning, watching the market district vendors arrange their wares for the day's hustle. I admired the fortitude of the shopkeepers, coming in day after day to conduct their minimally profitable, but essential, businesses. Perhaps there was a zen to the monotony or a pleasure in serving others. Without a doubt, the slow lifestyle was preferable after the chaos they'd experienced earning their citizenship.

For a brief moment, I allowed myself to imagine a day when I might settle down when my only worries would be something far more benign than the task that lay ahead. I pushed the thought out of my mind. As enjoyable as it was, I couldn't dream of the future until I'd resolved the issues of the present. After the destruction of Pod Baghdad, we could stop at nothing until the creatures' reign on Earth was over.

My thoughts drifted to Arjun, wondering where he was and what diabolical ideas that snake Kolya was hissing into his ear. *Negotiation with the Queens? "Pffft*, Not likely," I said to myself. I feared that at the first whisper of a challenge, the objectionable man would abandon

Arjun, running away like the coward he was. Hemant had placed his brother's care above all else, only to have Kolya twist Arjun's mind into perceiving that protection as distrust. It may have been wrong, but I *wanted* Marie to catch Kolya. More than stealing Arjun from us, he threatened our mission. If he found a way to communicate with the inverts, he would trade our secrets the second it gave him an advantage.

It was one thing to traverse Earth's hostile surface, but going behind enemy lines to the Hive? That was going to be inconceivably tough. No longer having Arjun's invaluable wisdom to guide us made me question if the journey was even possible. *Man, I miss Ciro. He would've known what to do.* We could always count on him to bridge the gap between Arjun and us in ways not even Hemant could. Like so many others, Ciro had been taken too early. When Roque and Breaker approached, I couldn't help but wonder if one of them would be next.

"Hey," said Roque, yawning. "Sorry. I'm not much of a morning person. You ready?"

I nodded.

"You remember Breaker, of course," he said.

"I do," I said. "How's your sister?"

"She's great, thanks to you," he said, beaming. "She'll never have to debase herself again."

"If I had the power, no one would ever have to participate in that type of work against their will," I said, my head drooping. "So many of the things we've seen in the pods sicken me. At times I wonder if humanity's worth saving."

"It is," said Roque. "For every act of evil seen, ten times as many acts of good go unnoticed."

"You'd make a good guru," I said, looking up at him and smiling. "I wish I had your sense of optimism."

"I don't think about it as optimism so much as examining our reality holistically."

"Either way, it's a refreshing view of the world," I said, hoping one day Roque and Ekon would get the chance to meet.

"Guys, we're going to draw attention," said Breaker, hopping from one foot to the other. "Can we get a move on?"

"And then there's Breaker's pessimism," said Roque, grinning. "Come on."

Roque led us down a corridor between the market stalls and into a dimly lit maintenance stairway. Breaker had been right. I was attracting looks. Word had spread about our arrival and people were noticing. I scrunched down my neck, futilely using the jumpsuit collar to hide my face. Most of the bulbs illuminating the passage had long burned out, being replaced just often enough to keep the flights from being submerged in total darkness.

"Fair warning: I know we just talked about the good, but hidden places like these are where the bad tends to thrive," said Roque. "Don't make eye contact. Don't talk. Just follow."

I found Roque's comment to be a little unnerving, but tagged along anyway, not seeing any alternative. As we climbed, I couldn't help but notice the copious amounts of graffiti plastering the dingy walls. A fair amount was poking fun at the prime minister's rigidity, but one particular work stuck with me. In large block letters against a background of writhing inverts were the words, "Our time is over." I bit my lip, feet glued to the ground at the mural's base. Roque doubled back to pull me ahead.

"Come on," he said. "Don't dwell on it."

Humankind still fought against the threat, but short of a miracle, it was a losing battle and everyone knew it. I couldn't help but think that if our last-ditch effort failed, our time *would* be over. We continued the upward journey, squeezing between dealers and addicts alike and past sex workers plying their trade, whether voluntarily or not I avoided thinking about. Finally, we arrived at a landing that looked minimally different from all the others. Roque moved a rack of old clothing aside, revealing a small hatch nestled in the wall.

"Here it is," said Roque, kicking at the entrance with his foot. "It's a little cramped."

I almost missed it at first glance. The metal door was covered in the same grime patina as the surrounding walls, making its burnished handle its only distinguishable feature. When there were no passersby to observe our entrance, Roque cracked the door.

"Through there?" said Breaker. "I thought you said we were going to a large hidden room?"

"I did. We just have to take a maintenance tunnel to get there. Its actual entrance is inaccessible to cadets."

"I don't do tight spaces," said Breaker, turning to leave. "I'm out."

"Breaker," I said, tugging on his top. "We can't do this without you. We need your help."

"This isn't what I signed up for, Ariadne. Look, I appreciate all you've done for Sylvia, but I can't go in there."

"What if you closed your eyes and I guided you through?" I said.

Breaker muttered something under his breath.

"I'm sorry, what was that?" I asked.

Breaker walked really close to me and repeated, "Would you hold my hand?"

I paused. "Umm… Sure."

It hadn't crossed my mind that not just a cadet, but a graduate of Bhopal's elite program, could be claustrophobic. I nodded to Roque, who opened the hatch and climbed in. Foreign particles rained down onto my neck and into my jumpsuit as I ducked through. *So much for my shower.* Cramped was right. The whole journey would be on hands and knees, surrounded on four sides by metal conduits and exposed wires. The shaft hummed with electric current and hydraulic flow.

"I can't hold your hand like this," I whispered, "but you can hold on to my ankle. Probably better anyway. Roque won't notice, though I'd hurt him if he said anything."

Breaker nodded in thanks, genuinely fearful of the tight confines, poorly lit by the twinkling of periodically-placed instrument panels. As Breaker took my ankle, it occurred to me that bravery wasn't always what we expected. As we crawled forward, I made sure to let him know of every upcoming turn or change in inclination. It took several lengthy minutes to reach our destination. By the time we crawled out of the maintenance duct, greasy dust and sweat caked our skin. The room was lit by natural light filtering in from the portholes above. *The surface.* The space was barely tall enough to stand and dark even with the sun's rays streaming in. Occupied spider webs clung to the corners, giving the place an anything-but-romantic vibe. I wasn't sure what Roque and TomTom had seen in the place.

"Well that sucked more than I recall," said Roque, dusting himself off as best as he could.

"How in the world did you find this place?" I asked.

"Desperate times call for desperate measures," said Roque, winking. "Some of our friends found it a while back when they were exploring. When TomTom and I wanted an escape before we lived together, we'd come here."

"This place smells like rat piss," said Breaker. "Remind me why I'm doing this, Roque."

"Because you owe Ariadne a favor," he said.

"No," I said. "You owe me nothing, Breaker. You're here because we can't continue our mission as intended without you. And I know you have a good heart, otherwise, you'd have never come this far."

"I suppose," said Breaker. "So, tell me what I'm looking at."

"Okay," said Roque, jerking off the cover of one of the quads and filling the air with dust.

"Bad idea," I said, coughing.

"Right," said Roque. "I'll just leave the rest on for now."

"Good thinking," said Breaker, rolling his eyes.

"I have your word what's said in the room stays between us, alright?" asked Roque.

Breaker nodded.

"Ariadne and her friends need to escape the pod, and they need to do it on these quads."

"Wow. You see the condition of this thing, right?" said Breaker, crouching next to the exposed vehicle. "Mice have eaten through every hose and wire and made nests in every hollow. I bet every gasket on this thing is trash. Not to mention, it's humid as hell in here. I bet these things are so rusty, their blocks are frozen in place."

"Are they fixable or not?" asked Roque.

"With enough time, parts, and points, anything is fixable," said Breaker, shrugging. "It's going to take weeks just to figure out what all needs to be done. Complete tear-downs. How are you planning to get these things out of this room?"

"There's a ramp and a door over here, next to the fueling station," said Roque, tugging at the pump's dry-rotted hose, which crumbled in his hands. "Well, we're going to need one of these too."

"God, how old is this place?" I asked.

"Judging by the quads?" said Breaker. "I'd say this place hasn't seen action for the last twenty years at least."

"How soon can you get us a parts list?" I asked.

"I don't know. A few months maybe," said Breaker.

"We need it in weeks, not months," I said.

Breaker let out a deep sigh. "I might be able to do it if I live up here. The things I do for you guys…," he said, shaking his head. "Roque, I want this place cleaned. And cleaned well. I'm not lifting a finger until there's not a web in sight or the faintest hint of rat feces."

"Deal," said Roque, grinning.

"I'll need some sort of workbench with a vice, a bright-ass lamp with magnification, all my tools, and a cot."

"Anything else?" asked Roque.

"Delivered meals. I'll work round the clock when I'm not on duty, but I want to be pampered while I do it."

"Whatever it takes, man," he said.

"What about the tunnel?" I asked. "Will you be okay?"

Breaker took a deep breath, running a grungy hand over his face. "It wasn't as bad as I thought. I think I can brave it now and then after what you did for us."

•••••••

That evening after training and dinner, there was a newfound energy in our steps as we headed up to the quad room to clean. I had enlisted everyone's help, smuggling as many bin liners as I could without being noticed.

Emerging in the damp room, Liesel shuddered at the smell.

"You could've warned us, Ariadne," said Krista, nasal from holding her nose. "I could've worn my mask."

"It was suspicious enough with this many of us traveling together," I said. "Add masks to the mix and I'm pretty everyone would've been interested in our activities."

"I suppose," she said, pulling her jumpsuit top up over her nose.

"Where do we start?" asked Omar, still processing the massive workload that lay ahead.

"There are eight quads in the room," said Huck. "Why doesn't everyone take one and the area around it? Whoever's left can lug trash."

"Good enough for me," TomTom said, shrugging.

Omar slowly drew the cover off of his quad after the warning I'd offered from Roque's experience. He whistled.

"This sucker has seen better days," he said. "Looks solid though. If the thing was built to survive the elements, surely it could handle a few rodents."

"You don't think there are any left in here, do you?" asked Hemant.

"Dude," said Huck. "Are you afraid of rats?"

"Not afraid, Huck," he said. "I just don't like being in a confined space with them."

"So… afraid?" said Krista.

"No, I—" Hemant began, but it was a losing battle.

The laughter made the work less tedious. We loved Hemant and his little eccentricities. As if we weren't filthy enough after the passage, the work left us a wreck. My hair was disheveled and interspersed with cobwebs, my nose felt like I'd never get the rat smell out, my fingers were encrusted with God-knows-what, and my jumpsuit belonged in the trash. Even Marie, who worked tirelessly without complaint, was strung with debris. The place was clean. Far from immaculate, but clean. I was sure that once disassembled, the quads would reveal myriad more hidden treasures. Breaker had a decent working environment, though I would never be in a hurry to stay overnight after what I'd seen.

"Remember that corner?" TomTom asked Roque.

"How could I forget," he said, smiling from ear to ear. "That was where we first—"

"I think we've done enough damage for one day," interrupted Omar. "How are we supposed to get these bulky bags back through the tunnel?"

"That's the best news," said Roque, elbowing a console in the wall. "We don't have to."

I watched as a nearly invisible recycling chute opened on the wall.

"Smooth, man," said TomTom.

"I thought so too," said Roque, laughing. "Though it was fifty-fifty if it still worked or not."

"We still need to meet Breaker's other demands, but I think the place looks good, said Huck. "Anything else?"

"Only that Breaker's got his work cut out for him," I said.

CHAPTER 40: HEMANT

"Hemant, you're up," shouted Diaz.

It was a ten-on-one day, or as the squads called it, a "tenner." Bhopal had proved to be exactly as rigorous as I expected. I hadn't known beforehand what fiendishly clever training exercises they'd come up with, but a tenner was one of them. It wasn't a question of if you survived—but how long. I took my first tentative steps into Bhopal's simulated forest. The purpose-built arena was two levels tall, complete with tree analogs, rope vines, woven shrubs, rubber dirt, and countless hiding spaces.

As much as my concentration needed to be in the moment, I couldn't help but be distracted by everything going on. It'd been almost two weeks since we'd set Breaker up in the quad room, and four since I'd watched my brother walk out of my life. After the day's training, I was looking forward to the curious engineer's long-awaited update. None of us knew what was happening. Breaker had proven quite reclusive, not letting any of us in. The state of the quads was a source of mystery and anxiety, but nowhere near as bothersome as Arjun's unknown status or whereabouts.

Somewhere scattered among the trees ahead was Rho Squad.

I'd grown close to Ondo and his team through platoon training. They were good people, though it wouldn't keep them from kicking my ass. When the Clunkies weren't outside keeping the perimeter clear, they were honing their skills alongside Sigma and the other three squads of Platoon III. I was thrilled it wasn't Xavier in the bushes waiting for me. Every time I looked at him, his icy-blue eyes were electrified by vengeance. I was prepared for the coming day of reckoning, knowing that I couldn't expect a fair fight from him or his ilk.

We had four weeks to get out of here before our thousand-soldier battalion moved out for the Hive. I smirked. *I'm sure five companies of four platoons each was exactly what Memo had in mind when he said small.* Arnav Madan wasn't one for taking advice. He was far too headstrong and militaristic. He couldn't imagine a ten-person force to be as effective as his thousand-person army. The joke would be on him when we rolled out, leaving Pod Bhopal in our tracks. I can't say I'd ever be in a hurry to come across the wronged man again.

I was immensely thankful for the invaluable advanced training we were receiving. Fen was extraordinarily proud of our progress. We'd lived up to our reputation and then some. Everyone in the pod knew who we were, but it hadn't been as bad as we'd thought. For the most part, we were simply greeted with respect and the occasional salute. There were always holdouts like Xavier and his goons, who'd just as soon smear us on the interior wall of the Drome.

I heard the twang of a bowstring and rolled into a cluster of itchy shrubs just as an arrow pinged off the wooden pole next to me. Like all the training weapons, the tip was blunted. Any direct hit to the torso counted as a fatality, not to mention, would leave a nasty bruise. It still hurt to take a really deep breath from a hit I'd taken a week ago. When I came up, I located the Rho soldier and flicked my blunted dagger hilt-first at his chest, knocking the wind out of him. Even a blunted blade could break the skin, something best avoided. A bell's toll rang off the walls, indicating the downed Rho. *Nine to go.*

It wasn't unheard of for someone to win ten-on-one, but it didn't happen often. As a matter of fact, Xavier had been the most recent cadet to accomplish the feat. His dirty fighting style had made him the victor, but he'd put four members of Upsilon in the platoon's medical district. No matter how real the simulations were, everyone held back when their comrades were in the sights—everyone with a soul, at least.

Since I was already crawling in the scratchy brush, I slithered along on my stomach, keeping my eyes lifted towards the trees. Creeping towards the edge of an embankment, I saw another soldier waiting in ambush at the bottom. He spotted me too late as I lept through the air, landing with a soft thud on top of him and muffling his mouth. I popped him in the side with my dagger and spun behind a nearby tree as the bell rang once more.

I took out one more soldier stealthily before I had an open confrontation. I tried to attack one of the female soldiers that'd saved my life from the mud raptors on the boat to Bhopal. The momentary hesitation had almost got me "killed." We ended up fighting it out, her lightning-fast bo staff versus my sluggish sandbag hammer. I won the encounter, but barely. I didn't understand how a stick the size of Ondo's thumb could be so painful. *Speaking of Ondo…* The scuffle brought his attention, his wide-shouldered frame bounding through the trees to defend his teammate. With his hammer poised to deliver a fatal blow, he had the briefest pause to consider the collateral damage to his friend. The opening was just enough for me to slam my hammer into his side. *Funny how our friends endanger us nearly as often as they protect us.*

With only four left, I got the drop on yet another soldier. Miraculously, she hadn't heard my approach. I crept up behind her and readied my war hammer. The sandbag weapon had the same heft as my own but would be far less likely to pulverize bone. *Don't hesitate.* The blow would hurt, so I aimed low where the side armor would dissipate most of the impact's force. I swung with all my might, sending the soldier flying. *A damn dummy!* With no time to react, I felt a cold blade at my neck.

"Just like a boy," whispered Trivia, her breath raising the hairs on my neck. "Too excited about the kill to inspect the target."

The bell tolled the triple ring indicating the end of the round and declaring Rho Squad the victor. I hadn't escaped unscathed. I'd probably feel the blow to my calf for another week.

"Not bad, Cadet Hemant," said Diaz. "Eleven minutes. Not a record, but you took out more than half of Rho Squad before they got you. Lieutenant Fen, good work."

Diaz turned on her glossy boot's heels and vanished through the exit.

"I'd be happy to fight alongside you any day, Hemant," said Ondo, clutching his ribs. "As long as you don't hit me with that hammer again."

I laughed and patted him on the back. "Me too, man. You and Trivia are formidable opponents."

Trivia smiled, blushing at the praise which brought out her freckles.

"You wanna… grab some food or something?" I asked.

She bounced over to me.

"Maybe," she said, with a soft kiss on my cheek, then whispering into my ear, "After you pass the Drome."

"You bet I will," I said to myself, still intoxicated by her spicy scent long after she'd left.

With training over, we excitedly packed into Huck and Ariadne's room before Roque led us to the quad room. My patience had nearly expired waiting for Breaker to meticulously tear down the eight all-terrain quads. They'd need to be in tip-top shape to traverse the grueling surface, but that didn't make the waiting any easier. I was desperate to know if Arjun was okay. I'd put through multiple requests for radio contact with the transporters but had been refused each time. Diaz refused to pass my request higher. In her view, cadets didn't warrant special accommodations. It sucked coming as far as we had, only to feel like a peon again.

We arrived at the tiny hatch in the wall and piled in, one after the other, crawling to our hidden destination. Between the cleaning and regular traffic, I merely needed to dust off when I stood in the low-ceilinged room. The floor was littered with parts, carefully placed into boxes drawn on the floor with chalk. The room reeked of stale coffee and urine, but seeing the straw-colored bottles lining the wall, I no longer suspected the rats. Huck was last through the door and accidentally kicked a small washer which pinged off the wall and rolled who-knows-where.

"Dammit!" said a red-eyed Breaker. "Don't you dare move. Don't even twitch. Did you have to bring them all, Roq?"

"I mean, it's their project," he said.

"I don't care whose project it is, if we lose some of these pieces, it'll be no one's."

"Everyone have a seat right where you're at," said Ariadne. "Breaker, we're here to listen. What do you have for us."

Breaker took a swig of coffee and a deep breath.

"Alright. Good news or bad?"

"Good, please," I said, slowly lowering myself to the floor, groaning as my sore muscles protested the maneuver.

"Everything here is fixable. I've already either tracked down the parts or procured them myself. Managing communications supply has its benefits. The First Builders were smart. They used a ton of shared components, not just between vehicles, but between everything. I suspect you could take apart half the pod with a ten-mil socket. I don't have access to the more engine-specific parts, but I can obtain quite a few others. It'll be pushing it to get it done before we march, but it's possible."

I was lost on the fact that Breaker managed communication supplies.

"Could you build us a radio?" I blurted, pulling everyone's attention.

"Umm… sure," he said. "I'm assuming you mean long-range."

I nodded.

"I'll add it to the list," he sighed. "The quads are each equipped with short-range transmitters to facilitate communication with each other. Historically, if you got more than ten or so meters away from your partner, the interference would choke out the signal. With the antenna bugs gone, optimistically, you might get a few kilometers out of them."

"I need further," I said, standing. "Like thousands of kilometers."

"Hemant—" said Ariadne.

"No! Too many people have kept me from talking to my brother. He's more important than escaping. Than this mission. Than this whole damn war as far as I'm concerned. I need that radio."

"Hemant," said Breaker. "I understand. My sister's my entire world. Look, I'll see what I can do, okay?"

I nodded and looked down at my hands. I was trembling. As I sat, Ariadne scooted close to me and took my hand. My eyes and nose burned as I fought back tears. I wanted to jerk open the exterior door and march off to find my brother. Sensing my feelings, Ariadne squeezed tighter as Breaker continued.

"I'm going to begin reassembly in the morning," he said, handing Ariadne a list. "I've cleaned and repaired all I can. I've already brought up all the parts I could get myself. Here's a list of what I still need if your friend Marie's offer still stands."

"It does," said Marie. "I will do whatever I must."

"No killing, Marie," said Huck.

"Are you willing to be trapped here to stay my hand?"

"Yes," I said. "No one deserves to die for us. Humanity can't afford to lose any more."

"I will honor your request," she said.

"Why is 'plugs' circled?" Ariadne asked.

"You remember what I said about the First Builders using common parts?" asked Breaker.

She nodded.

"Those are unique. Only used by small natural gas engines. They pose a two-fold problem. One, they will be hard to find and expensive. Two, they have the potential to raise some eyebrows."

"Great," I said. "Where do we begin?"

"Start with the respectable businesses," said Breaker. "Enough of these parts are so commonly used, they won't attract attention. Just look for signs of excess wear or shoddy production. Parts aren't what they used to be. And for God's sake, don't pay legit merchants with diamonds. You'd have every merchant in the pod offering you their wares. Now, for the less common items you might need to locate less reputable dealers. Even then, they might take some persuading."

"Can we pay *them* in diamonds?" Krista asked.

"Sure," said Breaker. "If you want to wake up battered and naked in some dark, low-level corridor. If you wake up, that is. Everyone who's not a cadet or elite can barely subsist on support wages. If the unscrupulous even suspect that you have wealth, they won't stop until everything you own has been stripped away."

"Jesus," I muttered.

Everyone turned to look at me as if frozen in time.

"What did I say?" I asked.

I realized while everyone had turned towards me, their eyes were looking past me. I slowly turned my head to find Fen and Mego blocking the entrance tunnel, a scowl draped across their faces.

CHAPTER 41: FEN

"I can explain everything," said Roque, wide-eyed.

"You have twenty seconds," I said, fuming. "Go."

Between losing over half my squad and gaining seven newbies, the last four weeks had seen more upheaval than I cared for. The new cadets hadn't been near as bad as I feared, but I was sorely missing the camaraderie that my old squad had built during our time together. Even Roque and TomTom had become increasingly distant. I'd never let them know, but I was stung by their newfound desire to spend more time with Huck and his friends than with us. Sigma Squad meshed well in training, which was the most important, but I felt like a squad needed a deeper connection between the soldiers with whom they would likely perish arm in arm.

In the interest of bringing us closer together, I dragged Mego from the current installment of his serial down to the dorms of the new cadets. I was hoping to entice them with the prospect of chasing down some greasy food and strong drinks, maybe followed by a few rounds of snooker. When we'd rounded the corner, we saw Roque and TomTom accompanying the rest of Sigma away from Huck's dorm and further down the corridor.

"What the hell are they doing?" I asked.

"Nothing, babe," said Mego. "Having fun, I'm sure. The newbies already have their own little dynamic. It seems they've adopted Roque and TomTom. I doubt it's personal."

"Spare me the psychoanalysis, Mego," I said. "You've been reading too much crime drama again."

He shrugged.

"I love your company. If you're feeling lonely, you're always welcome to take me back to the room and we can—"

"Look at them. Does that look like hanging out to you?"

"You're being paranoid," said Mego. "Look at… Okay, you may have a point."

For cadets trained in the covert arts, they couldn't have looked more obvious. I shook my head at their lack of self-awareness. Every few steps, Roque would glance around suspiciously. If it didn't pose a danger, it would almost be comical how poorly they implemented their training outside of the arena.

"He may be great at tenner, but I'm better," I said, sneaking off after them.

Mego sighed and followed, whispering all the while. "I really don't think this is a great idea. Showing a lack of trust could undermine your leadership."

"They're up to something," I said, turning to face him. "If it involves *my* squad, *I* need to know about it."

We followed them all the way to the stairwell, giving them time to put a few flights between us before following. When we entered the underused stairway, it took my eyes a few moments to adapt to the dim conditions.

"Which way did they go?" whispered Mego, listening.

I heard a clunk above and pointed. Mego nodded and we silently began the climb. The stairway didn't have too many people. The few who lined its peeling walls weren't up to anything good. As long as the elevators worked, most pod residents saw little reason to use the dank passages. Its few occupants gave us apprehensive looks, suspicious of the not one, but two, unusual groups trespassing in their perceived territory.

A few flights from the top, we heard the clang of metal, then nothing. We climbed the remaining steps until we reached a small landing.

"Where'd they go?" I asked, looking around.

It appeared that the landing had been used for storage, its contents long forgotten. A dusty set of rodent-chewed dining chairs were stacked in the corner. Along the wall was a rack of moth-eaten old uniforms and patched evening gowns. Judging by the dry rotting, the items had to have been decades old. Mego and I looked at each other, wondering. With as many officers the pod had lost over the years on Hive missions, it hadn't occurred to me they may have left behind families. Like their belongings, their lives were all but forgotten.

Mego pointed down at the ground, pulling me from my thoughts. There in the dust were tracks from the rack's spherical wheels. Without hesitation, I swung it out, revealing a tiny metal service hatch embedded in the graffitied wall.

"They can't have gone through that, right?" asked Mego.

"That sound wasn't one of the main doors," I said. "You first."

Mego let out a sigh of exasperation. "Fine."

I'd made the commitment to myself when we'd started dating that I'd never ask him to do anything I wouldn't do. Frequently, the lines between our command relationship and our personal one conflicted, but I did my best to keep them separate.

I followed him into the maintenance tunnel, struggling to pull the rack back into place and shut the hatch behind me. With numerous off-chutes, the passage would've been a maze to follow Roque and the others, save for one particular direction always being significantly cleaner. After several minutes of crawling on my hands and knees, I was thankful when I heard the familiar voices of my squad. However, I was totally unprepared for what I saw when I emerged from the tunnel. Vehicle parts were everywhere. My fury rose as their implications set in.

"Okay… Look… Umm... So you remember Huck's mission, right?"

I stared at him. His speech became faster and more nervous.

"So… umm… he was given that mission by Prime Minister Leal, right? Who's equivalent in rank to Madan. Well, Madan isn't letting Huck do the mission the way he's supposed to, so we decided to… help them."

"Help. Them. What?" I asked through clenched teeth.

"Umm… escape," said Roque, bracing himself.

"You what?!" I screamed. "The hell were you thinking? What do you think Madan's going to do when we show up to morning training with our squad missing?"

"I don't… I didn't…"

"That's right! You didn't think about the repercussions. We'd be in the brig, waiting for universe-knows-what terrible punishment Madan came up with. This is insubordination at its finest! And Roque, why didn't you tell me?" I asked, genuinely hurt.

"I wanted you to have deniability," he said, eyes downcast.

"Are you going to report us?" asked Huck, taking Ariadne's hand.

"No!" I said, turning away so they couldn't see the tears forming. "If I report you, Madan will assume I don't have control of my squad. If I show up without you, Madan will assume I don't have control of my squad. And if you're caught, Madan will assume

I don't have control of my squad. There's no good way out of this for me. I've worked too long and hard to get my chance at the Hive. I'm not going to let seven people I barely know take that opportunity away from me!"

"There's got to be some alternative," said Ariadne. "We were sent on this mission by Leal. All we're trying to do is what we were ordered to. You have to see that."

"Of course, I see that!" I said, facing them, tears or no. "But I'm under orders too! If you guys leave, the four of us will be severely punished! And, Breaker, you of all people should know what Madan is capable of. If your superiors knew you were down here…"

"With all due respect, I've made my decision, Lieutenant," said Breaker, raising his eyes to meet hers. "If we can get them back on track, they have a chance to end this god-forsaken war. There will still be a need for us to eradicate the rest, but imagine a war with an end in sight."

I shook my head.

"The only way this ends well is if I shut this down. Madan is a great leader. Under his authority, and with the weapon, we stand to make a difference."

"Or die like every other battalion that's made the trip," said TomTom. "No one likes to talk about it, but that's the reality of the situation. What if Memo's plan actually worked?"

I glared at my friend.

"There's another alternative," said Hemant. "You could come with us."

I wanted to scream! *Who the hell do they think I am?* I'd fought and fought for every single opportunity I had. Twice as hard as half the men in the program. I wasn't going to lose it now, right before we left for the Hive.

"This little crusade is over," I said. "Pack it up. I'll order the hatch locked immediately. None of you are to return to this room.

That's an order! It's not like you'd ever get the bomb out of here anyway. Breaker, I'll report you to your C.O. if I see you anywhere near my squad again. Clear?"

"Yes, sir," he said, looking angry and hurt.

"Everyone out!" I said.

I watched as my squad exited one after another, scowls on their faces. I was their commanding officer, dammit. Sometimes I had to give harsh commands. The face that surprised me the most was Mego's. As he climbed into the tunnel, a brief look of pity and disappointment passed across his face.

"God, I hate being the asshole," I muttered as I crouched down to enter the passage.

●●●●●●●●

Dinner was a quiet affair. I'd gone for the comfort food I'd been set on, but it was doing little to alleviate my darkening mood. Not even the multiple mash beers I'd drained through the course of the meal lowered the growing tension. Mego didn't help matters. I couldn't help but feel like he wasn't on my side. After enough of his intentionally clattering the dishware, I called him out.

"What good could possibly come from allowing them to escape?" I asked, angrily slamming the recycling chute.

"I don't know," said Mego, exasperated. "I thought that the point of this whole thing was to win. Madan sends battalion after battalion to the Hive, but do any of them ever return?"

"God, not you too," I said.

Mego grabbed my by the shoulders, forcing me to look at him.

"Not a bloody one!" he said, eye glistening. "Yes, Madan has a new weapon. Yes, he's leading the charge. But what if nothing changes? Leal's whole idea is predicated on a small force planting the bomb inside. Depending on how you look at it, we're either disobeying Madan's orders or Leal's. We have a chance to make a real difference here. Maybe we *should* sneak out with them. I mean, defeating the Arthropods at their home is what you've always wanted, right?"

I nodded, crying.

"I love you, Fen. I would die if I lost you. If we're not going to survive, I want our loss to have been for something real, not just another name in a list of elites who didn't make it."

I thought about the abandoned items in the stairwell, imagining our jumpsuits on the rack instead of the clothes belonging to the unknown officer and his partner.

"If we do this… If *I* do this and we get caught, our careers are over," I said.

"Then at least we'll be mucking out animal pens together," he said.

I grabbed him, burying my face in his chest and squeezing him tightly.

"This is either the stupidest bloody thing I've ever done or the smartest," I said. "I'm not sure which."

"No. The smartest thing you've ever done will always be nabbing me," he said.

"I love you too, Mego," I said.

•••••••••

Huck's dorm proved to be extremely cramped with our entire squad plus Breaker. None of us could move, and the smell after the day's training was approaching unbearable. The tight confines were one of the few places I felt that we'd have enough privacy for the upcoming discussion.

"I'll make this quick," I said. "I don't want to keep you guys from your showers any longer than I have to."

I struggled to get everyone's attention. Judging by the furtive glances, everyone still harbored resentment toward me over my orders to abandon their pet project.

"First off, I want to make it clear that I didn't appreciate being left out of your plans, deniability or not. We are a squad. If one of us goes down, we all go down. Do I make myself clear?"

I dismissed the lack of respect in their murmurs of understanding.

"Under normal circumstances, I would take punitive measures toward all of you. Seeing as your goal was to help Huck carry out Prime Minister Leal's mission, I don't feel like that's necessary."

There was no sigh of relief. My audience looked just as perturbed as they had when I entered.

"After giving your plan considerable thought, I concluded that your actions were not only warranted but necessary."

Every pair of eyes made contact with me in surprise.

"From this moment forward, I will assume full responsibility for the restoration of the quads, obtainment of the bomb, and our forthcoming escape. *Every* aspect of the plan must be run by me and I will use all means at my disposal to ensure its success and concealment."

Cheers erupted from the cadets as they excitedly slapped each other on the back.

"I expect to be read into the plan before the day is out," I said. "I want to know every detail. Every nuance. We *cannot* be caught. If we're going to do this, we're committing one hundred percent. We *must* succeed."

CHAPTER 42: HUCK

My heart had stopped the moment Fen walked into that room. My throat still went dry thinking back to it. It had been a flood of relief when she'd come to our side. The anxiety of sneaking around was halved. After all that had unfolded, I wanted nothing more than a hot shower. Ariadne and I made plans to meet the others later for dinner and headed for the locker rooms. The pod's communal showers had initially been strange when we'd first arrived, but now it was just another part of life. We cleaned up and got dressed before walking out arm in arm.

"You're beautiful," I said, her hair still damp from the shower.

A smile raced the blush across her face. I took her injured hand and kissed lightly up her arm, stopping at her shoulder.

"What do you think about foregoing dinner?" I asked.

"In favor of…?" she asked.

"I'm sure you can figure it out."

"I can, but sometimes I just want to hear you say it."

"Fine," I said, playing along. "I want to take you to the room, kiss you up and down your body, and strip—"

I froze as a disconcerting face emerged from the shadows.

"What, Huck?" asked Ariadne, seeing the surprise plastered on my face.

"Don't stop now," said Xavier. "It was just getting good."

"Leave us alone, man," I said.

"Or what?" he said, laughing. "Where's your buddy? The femme fan?"

Three other members of Tau Squad loomed behind him. Even if Ariadne and I could take him, we couldn't take all four. Unfortunately for us, Madan had a survival of the fittest mentality when it came to in-fighting. If Xavier and his goons saw it fit to tear us apart, it'd ruin our plans for the Hive.

"Back off, asshole," said Ariadne.

"Tsk, tsk, tsk," he said. "That's no way to talk to a senior officer. I could have you reprimanded for that."

"We both know you won't do anything of the sort," said Ariadne. "You wouldn't risk sounding like a whiny little bitch."

Xavier stepped close to Ariadne, grabbing a lock of her hair and smelling it.

"Women have no place in war, save for servicing the real soldiers," he said.

I couldn't take it anymore. I dove for him, but Ariadne beat me to it, jamming her elbow deep into his ribs. Xavier collapsed to one knee, gasping. His goons rushed forward to defend him but froze when Marie landed between us and them.

"Where the hell did she come from?" one of the guys asked.

Marie glanced up to the level above. Following her gaze, Xavier's minions looked up, giving Marie the opening she desired. In seconds, she had the three of them rolling on the ground.

"Who the hell do you think you are?" Xavier asked, climbing to a knee.

"From the looks of things, your enemy," she said, sauntering towards him.

"Want a piece of me?" he asked, staring her down with a sneer. "Diaz has us running a tenner in the morning. *You* will volunteer."

"Marie, you don't have—"

"I can't wait," she purred.

• • • • • • • •

When Ariadne and I arrived at the observation deck overlooking the mock jungle, the room buzzed with anticipation. Word had spread and the room was already filling with bodies. Several officers I didn't recognize had even joined the spectators. The showdown between Xavier and Marie had kept me tossing and turning through the night. I wasn't so much worried about her as him. If Marie's hemolymph-altered survival instincts kicked in, I didn't trust that she could stop herself before she killed him. I'd seen her fury firsthand and knew she wasn't one to be backed into a corner.

We squeezed through the crowd to join the other members of Sigma, stationed up front for priority viewing because of our member's involvement. I nodded a greeting to Roque and Hemant before turning to look out over the faux forest everyone referred to as the Jungle. Ariadne took my hand.

"Don't tell me you're still worried about Xavier," whispered Ariadne.

"A little," I said. "I'm also worried this'll bring a lot of unwanted attention to our squad."

"What makes you say that?" asked Hemant.

"Them," I said, pointing.

At the entrance to the deck, I watched as the rest of our platoon filed in. Four squads crammed into the room as the fifth prepared to defend the Jungle.

"Hey lovebirds," boomed a familiar voice.

"Ondo," Ariadne and I said in unison as he wrapped us in a bear hug. "What's up with all the spectators?"

"Oh, that would be my fault," he said with a mock sheepishness. "When I heard the crazy chick was taking on Xavier in a ten-on-one, I couldn't help myself. I told everyone! Half the damn company would be up here if Diaz hadn't limited it to Platoon III."

I forced a laugh.

"Relax bud," he said, slapping me hard on the back. "She's going to kick his ass."

"That's what I'm afraid of," I said.

"What? Poor widdle Xavier getting his precious ego bruised?" he asked. "Tell me you're joking."

"When we do the Drome, he'll stop at nothing to avenge whatever happens today. I don't want anyone in Sigma getting killed because he's unhinged."

"The man's always been merciless," said Fen. "If anything, his anger will cloud his judgment."

"Regardless, there's a whole lot of people, elite and cadet both, who want to see Xavier get his comeuppance," said Ondo, rubbing his hands together. "And today, we're going to get it."

"Quiet!" yelled Diaz.

The room fell silent. Diaz took out a long, wooden mallet, battered from years of use, and handed it to our lieutenant. Fen swung hard and fast. The sound of the gong reverberated through the room, signaling the beginning of the exercise. Everyone devoted their attention to the match. I moved forward to the angled glass protecting our vantage point. The former building window was cloudy around the edges from years of exposure in its previous life, but easy enough to see through. I rested my hands on the cool glass as I searched for any sign of Marie.

"You won't see her," said Omar.

"What do you mean?" I asked.

"Think about it. Every time she wanted to disappear, there was no sign. No sound. Only death."

His last words made me shiver. I was carefully examining the fake foliage, seeking out any sign of movement when I heard the first bell. A single tone. She'd made her first "kill." *My God, she's fast.*

"Anyone see her?" I asked.

Everyone shook their heads. Liesel pointed. I followed the gesture to where a Tau elite was perched in a tree. There were signs of movement within the branches, but no sign of my comrade.

"Wait!" said Krista. "Where'd he go?"

I looked where the soldier had been but saw nothing. *Oh. My. God.* It was much the same for the majority of the match. Bell after bell rang, but never the three rapid chimes indicating Marie's defeat. On the rare occasions we could identify one of the Tau elites, they'd disappear before our very eyes. By the time the ninth bell sounded, everyone who could reach had their face plastered against the vintage glass. Even the officers were craning their necks excitedly over one another's shoulders. Diaz responded to something through her hardline, hanging up angrily before confirming our suspicions.

"Xavier is the only member of Tau still standing," she said, then adding under her breath. "I can't believe a damn survivor is handing our ass to us."

When I turned back to the glass, Marie was strolling out of the woods with Xavier held tightly in front of her. Against his neck wasn't the dulled training blade allotted for the exercise but her own sinister dagger. *Oh, crap!* I sprinted to Diaz, but she was already slamming the button for the ramp. Fen quickly sounded the gong declaring Marie the winner and she released Tau's shamed leader. The ramp door lowered slowly, allowing Marie and Xavier to pass up to the observation platform. I smiled at Marie, doing my best to hide my momentary panic. Within seconds, she was surrounded by excited fans. *She didn't even look fazed.*

"She had a bloody knife the whole time!" he screamed.

"Did she actually kill anyone?" asked an officer.

"No, but she stalks through the trees like a bloody Demented. She should be restrained—"

"That's quite enough, Lieutenant Xavier," said Diaz. "Pull yourself together. You're embarrassing yourself."

Xavier turned towards me, his scowl nothing short of a death sentence. I traded an understanding look with Hemant. We had to escape before facing the Drome.

••••••••

"You're sure this guy can get us the plugs we need?" I asked as we descended deeper and deeper into the pod's seedy underbelly.

"This is where Breaker said to go," said Omar.

I pulled out the piece of trash Breaker had drawn his map on. Omar and Hemant had volunteered to join me in case things got dicey, as things frequently did in the lowers. We stepped off on Level 83, making our way past the poorly-stocked market and unhygienic medical districts before taking the indicated corridor. The new jumpsuits, which I'd found so superior to our previous ones, now made me extremely uncomfortable with the negative attention they were drawing.

"Let's get what we need and get the hell out of here," said Hemant.

"I'm trying," I said. "Here it is."

We came to an industrial-strength hatch that looked out of place next to the more typical entryways dotting the residential corridor.

"You sure this is it?" asked Omar.

"It's what's marked on the map," I said. "I'm pretty sure they'll let us know if we're wrong."

"I'm worried about how they 'let us know,'" said Hemant. "I bet Ariadne doesn't want to find your body in a recycling bin."

"Jesus, you two are whiny," said Omar. "You're highly trained fighters. Act like it."

I took a deep breath and knocked on the steel door. It hardly made a sound. Pulling the dagger from my belt, I rapped the hilt against the rough metal a few times. A lingering minute later, someone slid a small panel open, revealing sunken eyes in a withered face.

"Get lost," the gruff voice said.

"We're here—" I began shakily.

"We need combustion plugs for a small block," interrupted Omar.

"I don't know what you think this is, but I'm—" said the man.

"Cut the crap, old man," said Omar. "Just tell us what you want for them."

"Type-As, eh," he said, scratching the side of his face. "Those are scarce. Not on the permitted list neither. How many?"

"Sixteen," I said.

The man loosed a whistle. "I'm more likely to shoot fiery fuzzies out my ass. Not asking for much, are ya?"

"Can you get them?" asked Hemant.

"I reckon I got one er two, but you're gonna have to wait months for quants like that."

"We don't have months," I said.

"Two weeks," said Omar. "Can you get them?"

"Two weeks? Maybe," said the man. "It'll cost ya dearly."

"We have officer tokens," I said.

In addition to ration points, the officers were issued tokens to buy specialized supplies for their squad. Unlike points, the extremely hard-to-come-by tokens carried considerable street value. Fen had been given extra tokens when we'd arrived—tokens she'd offered to obtain the much-needed quad parts. As the dealer said, it would cost us. We'd have to sacrifice some necessities on the trail, but if a plane crash couldn't slow us down, neither would this.

"Fifteen a plug or no deal," said the man.

"Fifteen?" said Omar. "Monterrey would sell us new quads for that!"

I raised my eyebrow at the slip, hoping it wouldn't come back to bite us.

"Be my guest," he said. "But you're not gonna get it in two weeks."

"Fine," said Hemant. "Do we have a deal?"

"One more thing."

"My God, man. What?" said Omar.

"I want chocolate. Anyone who's got that many officer tokens to burn should be able to get me a damn bar of chocolate. Do *that* and we have a deal."

With that, the panel slammed closed.

"Well, that sounds pretty solid on the plugs, but two weeks will be pushing it," I said. "Now how the hell do we steal back Dieter's bomb?"

"This purchase is going to wipe out our tokens," said Hemant.

"Why'd he have to want chocolate?" said Omar, sitting on a rusting bench, loose where it should've been bolted to the concrete.

"What are you talking about?" I said.

"You don't get it, do you?" said Omar, smirking. "Chocolate is a treat for only the wealthiest citizens—the ones who've trampled others to get what they have. I only ever had it two or three times and I was the damn prime minister's son! I don't know how we're going to get our grubby hands on any of it."

"We find a way. We always do," I said. "Let's update Fen and Breaker. They're working the quad room tonight."

We took the elevator as high as we could without raising suspicion and headed for the stairs. When we exited, one of the tube monitors caught my eye. It was playing a staticky, black-and-white feed promoting an upcoming gala, not that anyone watching would be invited. Prime Minister Madan was hosting a send-off party for himself. The top echelon of the city's society would be in attendance. *Different pod, same corruption.* The image got my gears spinning.

"Remember how we knew you were from an upper by your mannerisms?" I asked.

"Yeah," said Omar, arching an eyebrow. "Why?"

"I know how we can get chocolate *and* reclaim the bomb."

CHAPTER 43: KOLYA

I stood leaning against the hard, armored side of the carrier, admiring the strangely regular gigantic mounds amongst disintegrating, derelict train cars. I walked to the base of one of the mounds to give it a closer examination.

"This used to be a hopping place back in the day," said Brick, kicking at the mound and revealing soil so richly black that it devoured all light.

"Coal," I whispered.

"This was a vital shipping hub for the continent before the territory was incorporated. Now, if you're done admiring, get your ass over to Yuze. He's overseeing the cargo transfer and could use another back. Arjun, we could use you as a lookout."

Arjun nodded and began to climb one of the mounds when Ian grabbed his shoulder.

"We haven't seen a bloody invert this whole trip, but don't let your guard down for a second," he said, sniffing the air as though he possessed some preternatural sense of smell. "They're up to something. At least in a straightforward fight, you know what's happening. All this waiting is… unnerving."

I made my way to Yuze. The ill-tempered man unfairly divvied out the loading process, placing as much of the burden on me as he could manage. *We'll be at sea for a long time, Sveta. Plenty of time for even someone with sea legs to fall overboard.* I shouldered yet another heavy bundle of the canvas-wrapped provisions and made my way up the wooden gangplank. I'd looked forward to seeing the ocean for the first time, but hunched over like a pack animal dripping with sweat hadn't been what I had in mind. I stood above the small hatch and passed my load to the transporter manning the ladder and stood erect, stretching my back to the music of my popping joints.

"I'm getting too old for this," I muttered, gazing over the water toward the eastern horizon.

Though the man-made structures had been all but reclaimed by the earth, the seawalls were still intact and teeming with tiny lifeforms, as though the walls themselves were animate.

"Hey!" yelled Yuze. "Admire the view when we're underway!"

"You can admire the sea as you sink to its depths," I mumbled.

••••••••

I vomited again into the cold steel bowl of the boat's head. My first time on the high seas was turning out to be a bloody miserable one. I'd combated motion sickness occasionally in the vehicles, but finding a spot on the horizon to focus on worked wonders. The problem underwater—there was no bloody horizon! I spit out yet more bile, resting my head on the arm I had draped across the bowl. Absentmindedly, I looked left where Yuze was defecating on the next toilet over.

"Need something?" he asked.

My stomach wrenched at the vile odor captured in the abysmally tight space. I could do nothing but collapse against the wall and wait for the nausea to subside.

"I've never had an audience before," said Yuze, smirking.

I mumbled what I thought about him in the tongue of my mother, a language I knew the blowhard couldn't understand. The beastly woman may have been taught United, but had always preferred the language of our roots. He finished and stood, showing me far more of himself than I cared to see.

"If it's any consolation, it'll pass in a day or so," he said. "That or you'll die of dehydration. Either way, your suffering will be over."

As disgusting as it was, I rested my forehead on the cool rim of the toilet, begging the rolling of my stomach to stop. As smooth as the boat's operation was, the subtle back-and-forth motion was enough to bring me to my knees, something the Arthropods hadn't even done.

Once I finally felt well enough to move, I stood slowly, trying to ignore the headache-inducing smell of oil and grease so prevalent on the vessel. I made my way to the control room and asked Brick about getting some fresh air.

"I suppose," he said with an exaggerated sigh. "But I'm not letting you go topside every time you feel woozy."

"What he's saying is that you need to toughen up, old fart," said Ian.

Arjun spotted me on my way to the ladder and joined me on the deck, which floated only a meter or so above the white-capped waterline. Designed to limit tracking by the now-defunct antenna bug network, the boat operated mostly submerged but never left the ocean's surface. I paced back and forth as I watched the sunset, letting the nausea fade with the light.

"Look at the stars, my boy!" I said. "To think, each likely has orbiting planets of its own. Seemingly infinite celestial bodies dispersed across the universe. How many hold intelligent lifeforms?"

"I don't know. I suppose I could calculate a number," he said.

I shook my head. "I don't need a number to appreciate the infinite vastness of space."

"How many of them do you think are aggressive like the Arthropods?" he asked.

"I don't know," I said, rubbing my chin through a mangy beard. "I refuse to believe that a universe so large isn't teeming with life. Good and bad."

"You truly believe that we can reason with the Arthropods?"

I thought for a moment. "Yes. I have no doubt the Queens exist. I'm certain they can not only communicate but reason. I suspect that our blue friend has somehow communicated with the local drones that we are to be spared for an audience with them."

"We're gambling our lives on it," said Arjun. "It must succeed. I want a better life for my brother—a life with less anger and fighting."

"Twin or not, he's short-sighted. If you hadn't left first, he would've abandoned you at the first convenient place. He told me as much, remember?"

Arjun nodded, looking back to where the continent had long since disappeared behind Earth's curvature.

"Don't do it for him. Do it for yourself! You have a gift, Arjun. Something far more valuable to humanity than your fighting. Our names will outlive us. Arjun and Kolya, pioneers of diplomacy and ambassadors of peace," I said with one arm around his shoulder and the other gesturing towards imaginary words in the sky. "Ha! Imagine that."

"If you are quite done, *ambassadors*, Captain Brick would like to see you," said Ian, half out of the hatch.

"I'm not sure how familiar each of you is with how a u-boat operates, but over the next week, you will follow my commands to the letter," said Brick. "Gentlemen, this is the UTE-120-I. Mathilde's been in commission for just over six years. Unlike the ex I named her after, she'll take care of you if you take care of her. You two *will* stay out of the crew's way until we reach Pod Bandung. We clear?"

I gave a conceding shrug, which satisfied Brick.

"I do have one question," I said. "If I'm unable to enter Bandung because of this mark you so willingly gave me, what do you propose I do?"

"You're under my protection as long as you remain outside of the pod. Bandung is a little different. The First Builders designed it linked to a shipyard by underground train. You wouldn't be the first Banished to grace its docks. It's become a giant gray area where banished individuals can have a second lease on life. You and Arjun pulled your weight well enough on this trip. You're also welcome to continue among our ranks."

"Thank you, Captain," I said. "If it's all the same to you, I believe our future lies elsewhere."

"You know where to find us if you change your mind," he said, shrugging. "If you're as good of a scientist as you claim to be, I'm sure you'll make a hell of a shipbuilder."

I smirked and turned towards my berth.

"Can you imagine? Me, a shipbuilder? Ha," I said to Arjun once out of earshot. "Arjun the future lies just before us. Can you see it?"

"I'm afraid I can't, Kolya. I don't understand how we are going to travel from Bandung to the Hive. Since Pod Wagga was never completed, there are no transportation routes that travel to the Australian Territory."

"We have to work on your imagination then!" I said, grabbing his shoulders. "Arjun, we are destiny's tools. A way will present itself. Mark my words."

•••••••••

Five days into the voyage, the seasickness had mercifully waned. When the ocean became particularly choppy, I would have to revisit my polished metal acquaintance. During the day-to-day operation, I'd grown accustomed to ever-present nausea. Learning the boat's inner workings had become an enjoyable way to pass the time. I often toted Arjun along as we discussed the unique physics of the vessel. Provided we stayed clear of the crew—a difficult task given the tight quarters—they didn't mind our hovering and periodic questions. Arjun and I made as many trips to walk the deck as Brick would allow, taking in the salty sea air and hashing out our plans for the Hive.

"What do you think it'll be like?" Arjun asked on one such walk. "You've studied the creatures for longer than I've been alive. How do you think they live?"

"I've pondered this question many times, my boy. Baghdad possessed some ancient tomes—a collection of texts known as encyclopedias. The volumes were grouped by letter and, unfortunately, not a complete set. They were so old, they contained no entries regarding the United Territories of Earth. I was one of the select few with vault access with an interest in the past, which worked out to my benefit," I said, sitting on the deck's edge and draping my arms through the railing. "You know, I really wanted the 'Y' volume? I sent numerous requests to the other pods. One day, my patience was rewarded with not only a 'Y' volume but an 'XYZ' volume. Destiny is not without a sense of humor. It was a children's encyclopedia from circa 1950 America. Imagine that!"

I sat silently for a moment, lost in my memories. *You would've loved it, Sveta—the hand-drawn illustrations that made sinister predators look friendly, flowery descriptions that made slavery sound enjoyable, and a complete lack of perception of global issues.* Mid-1900s America had a knack for seeing the world through a strange dismissive filter. No wonder almost a century later, the Arthropods had taken us by complete surprise. Even then, the leader of the American Territory had been reluctant to identify the threat for what it truly was. The decision to build the pods had been a majority decision by the UTE Council with his begrudging support.

"Kolya?" asked Arjun.

"Hmm?" I asked.

"The Hive?"

"The Hive? Oh, I'm sorry, my boy. Forgive an old man and his nostalgia. What was I saying?"

"Encyclopedias…"

"Oh, right," I said, patting him on the leg. "I studied a number of Earth's native insects. The similarities to the Arthropods are astounding, save for only the size. I believe that's why the early scientists began calling them Arthropods in the first place. It's uncanny, Arjun. It's almost as though they were related, though how I can't begin to imagine."

Arjun cleared his throat.

"Right," I said. "The site of the Arthropod Landing was a little town deep in the Australian Territory called Alice Springs—a name that would be synonymous with their arrival had everyone who remembered the place not perished. I've always wondered, why there? The desolate landscape is mountainous grassland, which must be advantageous to the Arthropods in some way. Much of our earliest information came from a military research installation nearby before it was overrun. You may recall the infamous Last Reports from your education in Horizonte."

"I do," said Arjun, admiring the sun as it merged with the water. "The last thing they documented was seismically-substantial digging."

"Exactly. Thank the universe we had a 'T' in our set. In similar environments, such as the Saharan Territory, there are species of termites that build colonial towers thousands of times larger than themselves. So you ask what I expect the Hive to look like when we arrive? A giant earthen mound the scale of which reaches to the heavens. A modern-day Tower of Babel."

"Inconceivable," said Arjun.

"My thoughts exactly."

I could see the wheels spinning in his mind as he assimilated the revelation. As the sky darkened, revealing the first few stars, I suggested we head below. As Arjun descended the ladder, I awkwardly lowered my foot to the first rung. That's when I heard it. The sound to our aft was just as much moan as a scream. Even from a distance, it was just as Putri had described. I felt the vibration deep within my chest.

"What was that?" asked Arjun, wide-eyed.

"For once I don't wish to know."

CHAPTER 44: ARIADNE

"I don't like this," said Omar as I straightened his bowtie.

"What's the matter?" I said, looking him in the eyes. "Aren't you used to rubbing shoulders with these types?"

"Technically, I was just a candidate, remember? The opportunities I had to enjoy my privileged upbringing were few and far between," he said, making air quotes around privileged. "Carvalho, like those other nepotistic asswipes, knew it would cause a scandal. Guiding their children through the program was common practice among the upper crust, but they didn't exactly flaunt them at parties."

"You've got nothing to fear," said Fen as Mego zipped up her gown. "These people are all the same regardless of their pod of origin. Let them fawn over you, ask their condescending questions, and drone on about themselves while we nab some chocolate."

"I don't understand why I can't be your date, Omar," said Krista, examining Liesel's cocktail dress with a pout. "I am your *actual* girlfriend."

"If it makes you feel better, I'd rather be in my jumpsuit on a sofa than schmoozing with the well-to-do," said Liesel.

"Like I said, these people don't like injuries," said Omar.

"They live in their little perfect bubble. The real world makes them uncomfortable. We need them at ease so they let their guard down. I'm amazed Fen got the four of us in."

"Between your accomplishments, training performance, and, let's be honest, your father, there wasn't much persuasion needed," said Fen.

"Well you and Liesel look stunning in those gowns," I said, smoothing down Mego's collar. "All four of you clean up nice."

"We'd damn well better after what all this cost," said Fen.

It'd taken the last of our squad's resources to buy such fine clothes. The snobbish woman in the pretentious market stall had given us an odd look, but it didn't stop her from selling us her fine apparel. The aged garments didn't match the extravagance of humanity's heyday but were gorgeous by modern-day standards.

Huck and Hemant had just returned with the news that our combustion plug dealer had come through. The two-week wait had been worthwhile. We weren't about to send Omar into a bone arachnid den without confirmation of the operation's value.

"And you're sure this little thing will keep the chocolate from melting?" asked Omar, brandishing a tiny tin. "It doesn't like body heat."

"I'm sure," said Mego. "It should protect against even your nervous sweats."

"Relax and have fun, but keep them distracted while we recover the weapon," I said. "As soon as you guys get back, we'll go trade for the plugs. In a matter of hours, we'll be departing for the Hive."

Roque and TomTom joined us in the squad training room, which was thankfully far more spacious than Huck's and my tiny dorm.

"You two ready?" asked Fen.

"Krista, TomTom, and I will help Breaker assemble everything. The quads will be outfitted in time," said Roque, looking slightly downtrodden. "Once all the final pieces are in place, we'll be ready to roll."

"Then why do you look disappointed?" I asked.

"I have to admit, I had my heart set on tearing up the Drome," he said. "I've spent months idolizing it in a way—*the ultimate challenge*. I mean, none of us would be here if we weren't a little masochistic, right?"

"We're going to the Hive, Roq," said Hemant. "You want *the ultimate challenge*, there it is. I would imagine it's superior to Madan's little creation."

"You're right," TomTom said. "But it would've been nice to see that look of humiliation on Xavier's face again."

"It brought me pleasure as well," said Marie, brandishing her menacing smile.

"Is the extraction team ready?" asked Fen.

"We are," I answered.

"I hope you all got plenty of sleep last night because it's going to be a long time until we rest again," said Fen. "Rendezvous in the quad room at 0100. Move out!"

Accompanied by Hemant and Marie, Huck and I split off from the others, making our way up to the engineering lab on Level 33 where Roque's informant had told us the bomb was being stored. While Roque refused to reveal his source, he assured us that she was trustworthy. It was a relief that it wasn't being stored in the vault. After what Hemant had told us about Baghdad's vault, the news felt fortuitous. The lab would have plenty of security measures and guards but would be far more pregnable than the Nucleus vault.

Once we were on 33, we pushed through the throngs of cadets and residents going about their daily lives. We made our way to the engineering labs, which were nestled in the off-limits research district. I led the others into a nearby bar where we'd wait for the opening our previous stakeouts had detected in the guard's rotation.

The metal chair creaked something awful when I took my seat at the low table, making our arrival anything but inconspicuous. I watched as the guards paced back and forth behind the decorative concrete gear that spanned the entryway.

"What'll it be, cadet?" asked the young waiter, pushing his long hair out of his acne-scarred face.

"Beers and chips around," I said in my best attempt to sound casual.

The waiter smirked before walking away to put in our order.

"You'd look a bit more natural if you didn't put the napkin in your lap," said Hemant, chuckling.

"Shut up," I said, leaning in. "So I'm not great at this sneaking around thing."

"Follow the plan and we'll be fine," said Huck, resting a hand on my knee.

Nearly a half-hour passed before we saw the anticipated gap in the guard's movement. Huck and I rose, making our way towards the guard post, laughing and holding hands. We'd planned to act like overly-intoxicated lovers, which was one thing I could do convincingly with only a few sips of alcohol. We kissed and groped all the way to the vacant alcove where we made out in the shadows. The threat of being caught made the illicit activity all the more exciting and by the time we were discovered, it took more control than I expected to drop the act.

"What are you two—" the guard got out before Marie had him unconscious and folded away in the shadows of the looming sculpture.

The wide-eyed second guard emerged a moment later, but before he could open his mouth, Hemant had him from behind in a choke hold and dropped him next to the first.

"Thank the universe for art," he said. "Let's get a move on before they wake."

I grabbed the slotted badge off the guard and shoved it into the reader by the door. The glass door clicked as its locks disengaged. Huck swung it open as we dragged the two unconscious men inside. We locked them in a broom closet bound and gagged with a few lengths of rope we'd brought along. Making our way deeper inside, we crouched behind the banks of countertops so we wouldn't be seen through the lab's front windows by passersby.

"Where to now?" I whispered.

"The lab we're looking for is at the end of the second hallway on the left," whispered Huck. "Lab 33-02."

In a crouch, we stalked down the corridor under the low orange glow of the pod's nighttime lights, praying no one would catch us by surprise. Roque's informant had claimed that only four guards were on duty at night and alternated two-hour shifts. If she was accurate, the other two would be focused on a card game or napping in the back room. All we had to do was wheel the bomb out of the lab without making a ruckus.

When we arrived at the lab's door, I used the key card again, anxiously waiting for the pins to confirm our entry. There was no guarantee that the guard had access to the inner lab, but my fears were alleviated when the light glowed green. When I opened the door, there it was, just like we'd left it—only cleaner. Dieter's nuclear device was laying on the table. I let the door latch softly behind me as Huck pulled a two-wheeler out from the wall. Marie guarded the entry as Hemant and Huck began to carefully lift the meter-long tube and strap it down. An old clipboard with the engineer's report rested on the side of the workbench, the paper smudged by the greasy fingers that had written it. What I read made me suck in my breath.

"What is it?" Huck whispered.

I quoted the report. "We've identified the problem. The damage wasn't from impact as initially suspected. Multiple wires appear to have been intentionally severed from the nuclear core and chemical charges. It is our opinion that the weapon was sabotaged."

"That bastard!" Hemant said loudly.

The look Marie gave could've sliced steel. We froze, listening for any sign of the guards. After a few agonizing moments, I sighed with relief.

"Sorry," whispered Hemant. "I don't care what you think. I'm going to kill him, Huck."

For the first time, Huck didn't argue.

Smuggling the bomb out of the lab was stress-inducing, but went well. With a blanket over the two-wheeler, no one paid us any mind as we made our way to the maintenance stairway. Once out of sight, Hemant loaded the device on his back for the hike up. Tugging it through the tunnel proved to be quite the ordeal, but we managed it. When we arrived, Roque, TomTom, and Krista were already there, waiting for us with all of our gear. There was no sign of the others.

"They should've been back by now," Breaker said, pacing.

"They're only three minutes late," I said, taking his arm to calm him.

As if in answer, we heard the familiar scuffling through the tunnel. Omar emerged with Liesel just behind, both of them back in their familiar gray jumpsuits, their styled hair and makeup making for an odd juxtaposition. Fen and Mego were right behind them.

"Did you get it?!" I asked.

Omar held up a dented metal box of plugs in one hand and the small tin in the other.

"With chocolate to spare!" he said, grinning from ear to ear.

"I knew you could do it!" I said, planting a kiss on his cheek.

"It was tough," said Omar, passing out the chocolate. "Some drunk old geezer with a handlebar kept talking about his good old days on the surface. I could hardly pry myself away from him."

Breaker took the box of plugs and examined them under his magnifying lamp.

"What's the verdict?" asked Fen with her mouth full, eyes rolling back in near ecstasy. "God, this is the best thing I've ever tasted."

"They're not brand new, but they look good," said the engineer. "You know we won't be able to test them. We have to open the door when we start these things or we'll suffocate. And when we open the door, it better be to get the hell out of here."

"Get them in the quads and go home," said Roque. "You've done us a favor we can never repay you for. I don't want you anywhere close when Madan comes sniffing around."

"With Sylvia safe, there's little else I need," he said. "Good luck at the Hive. If you ever need anything, you know where to find me."

Breaker finished installing the plugs and did every final check he could do. After a few hugs and a tearful goodbye, he disappeared back into the tunnels. I was glad that we'd been able to give him a future with his sister.

"I'm going to miss him," I said.

"He was cranky, but you'd be hard-pressed to find a better guy," said Mego.

For the next twenty minutes, we loaded up the quads. Many of us would have our own, but with only eight of the four-wheelers, three of us would be doubling up. I jumped on my quad as Marie clasped me from behind. My heart nearly beat out of my chest with nervous excitement at the prospect of being on the surface again. My hands were cold from anxiety as I gripped the throttle.

"Want to do the honors, Roq?" asked Fen.

Roque stood by the door's release. He lifted the safety latch and placed his hand on the red knob which would split the doors at the top of the room's ramp.

"Everyone ready?" he asked.

We all nodded. Before his hand could turn we heard the whine of the door. Everyone looked around in confusion. The door ahead wasn't opening. Light streamed in from behind as the primary door to the room parted, revealing the silhouettes of General Madan, Xavier, and Trivia, who Captain Diaz held by the collar.

"Oh, crap," I said.

CHAPTER 45: HEMANT

"I have to admit, I'm disappointed by what I see," said the prime minister, stepping into the faint light of the moon shining down through the porthole. "I knew the moment you set foot in my pod that your reputation was undeserved. Your friend Trivia lives up to her nickname—always sharing pertinent, albeit classified, information. At least she had the decency to admit her mistakes under interrogation."

The look that passed between Roque and Trivia was one of deep hurt on both sides. Everything we'd hoped wouldn't go wrong had. Looking at Madan and the others, I saw the chances of catching Arjun evaporate before my eyes. We'd reached the end of the road and it hadn't even been the inverts that'd stopped us.

"Lieutenant Xavier, return the bomb to the vault," said Diaz, not relinquishing her tight grip on our companion. "Need I reiterate the need for discretion?"

"No, sir," Xavier said, beaming at our misfortune.

"It wasn't hard to track down the leak," explained Madan as Xavier and his goons worked. "Rho Squad was the unit tasked with escorting the bomb down to maintenance. Once Diaz had them gathered, Trivia couldn't keep from fidgeting. Perhaps I should be thankful. On the battlefield, weakness tends to prove far more deadly."

Ondo, who'd stood off to the side, looked chagrined. Another wave of guilt washed over me for all who'd suffered in the preservation of our mission. Sure, Trivia had shared confidential information, but it was because we'd required it. This was our blame to shoulder.

"I'm most disappointed in you, *Cadet* Fen," said Madan. "You were one of our rising stars—one of the youngest female Lieutenants in my tenure. And the exact reason Diaz misplaced her faith in you to train these last-minute additions. It's a mistake I'm prepared to rectify. From this moment on, Sigma Squad is on indefinite probation, all ranks removed."

Fen deflated. She'd lost everything she'd worked so hard for, because of us. With the botched escape, her sacrifice would be meaningless.

"Do you have anything to say for yourself, Cadet?" asked Diaz.

"I stand by my choices," she said, holding her head high. "Everything I've done was to uphold Prime Minister Leal's mission."

"That's not your job, soldier!" shouted the general, showing aggravation for the first time. "I'm your commanding officer. Your duty is to follow orders. Mine above all else's. Is that clear?"

"Yes, sir!" she said, blinking back tears.

"Not that it's any of your business, but I've been in communication with Leal," he said. "And I promised that I would do my damnedest to ensure his team made it to the Hive unscathed. Now, since I'm not in the habit of lying, you will still sail with the battalion."

Xavier's head shot up from latching the bomb to a rolling cart, eyes narrowing. My heart momentarily fluttered. *Maybe this isn't the end of the road after all.*

"Don't get excited. I never said under what pretext you'd be traveling. This mission will continue as planned. As *I* planned. Your repairs to these forgotten quads bought you just enough goodwill that I won't rescind my promise to Memo for your actions. In two weeks, our battalion *will* march to the river. We *will* set sail for the Australian Territory. We *will* carry the bomb. And we *will* prevail."

Madan turned on his combat-booted heel and disappeared, leaving us alone with Diaz. The tension I'd been holding released. Whatever punishment the prime minister would inflict would be infinitely better than being imprisoned here. Maybe Fen was right. Maybe Madan's mission would be the success humanity needed. I'd still have a chance to fight the inverts at their doorstep, track down my brother, and get my hands on that wretched excuse for a man—Kolya. Catching me unaware, Diaz threw Trivia toward us.

"There," she said. "I think that's better. Don't you, Ondo?"

Ondo gave a forced nod, his typical joyful demeanor absent.

"Trust me. You're better off without her," she said, turning to Fen. "The twelve of you can keep each other company in the brig."

"But Madan—" I said.

"These are Madan's orders, Cadet. You didn't think you were going to mosey onto the transport ship as one of us, did you?" she asked without waiting for a response. "You defied orders. You will continue to train daily until which point you can pass the Drome. In the evenings, you will report to the Level 35 brig as your new quarters, where you can be diligently watched until our departure. At that point, you will take a supplementary role cleaning up after the *actual* troops on the mission."

My mouth nearly hit the floor. I was going to the Hive but as a bloody janitor?!

"I don't understand. The Drome?" asked Ariadne.

"Of course, Cadet," she said. "No one leaves Bhopal without demonstrating their mettle and valor. You will join us as elites or not at all. And as your interim squad leader, I'm giving you one week to do so, unless you'd prefer a subservient position here…"

"We'll beat it!" said Fen.

"Good," said Diaz. "You have little other choice."

•••••••••

The next few days were misery. Our beloved, albeit awkward, reputation vanished once word spread of our foiled escape. Salutes changed to spittle, cheers to insults. By attempting to carry on our original mission, we were nothing more than glory hogs. If our situation didn't suck so much, I could almost find it comical. We were immediately instated in custodial roles. Upon waking, our Tau guards fed us a measly breakfast in the barren confines of the brig before we had to wash and sanitize the floor's disgusting recycling chutes. I couldn't understand how the level's two thousand residents could get something so dirty so fast.

If we rushed, we could finish the work before the gong sounded for platoon training. We'd work out as other cadets and elites alike leered and jeered. Training exercises like Ten-on-One, Squad in the Dark, and Invert in the Maze had become agony as other squads relentlessly did everything they could to injure or embarrass us. All traces of platoon camaraderie vanished. The only one who remain unchanged was Xavier, who hated us just as much as ever.

By day's end, we'd drag our bruised bodies and damaged morale back to our graffitied concrete tomb. Our annoyed guards would feed us another crappy meal while harassing us until they got bored or fell asleep, finally giving us a chance to rest. More than one night I'd fallen asleep to the whimpers of another.

With one evening remaining before our date with the Drome, I wanted nothing more than to be alone with the squad on the surface, racing quads to the Hive as intended. The only bright spot of the week had been that Trivia was pretty damn cool. It was easy to forgive her for talking. She'd kept her mouth shut until they threatened her with one of the more nightmarish subservient roles. Then she'd cracked. Who could blame her? War had a habit of blurring the definition of good.

"You doing okay?" I asked Trivia while our guards gambled away.

"I miss my squad," she said. "At least what it used to be. No one, save for Ondo, acts like they even miss me."

"It never ceases to amaze me how fast people can turn on you," I said.

"You have to remember how hard everyone here has trained as an army to lay siege to the Hive," said Mego. "Teamwork is beaten into us from the moment cadets step into Bhopal. It's a collective mindset. *Everything* is for the good of the group. You were heroes for your accomplishments when you arrived, but the second you became individuals, it was over."

"Pack mentality at its finest," said Fen, who hadn't spoken much for days.

"It's just so aggravating," said Ariadne. "We're a pack too! We were roped into Madan's mission and by trying to do *our* duty, all of a sudden we're the bad guys? It's not fair!"

"Little in life is fair, Ariadne," said TomTom.

Ariadne remained silent.

"Our best bet is to keep our heads down from now until we reach the Australian Territory," said Omar. "With any luck, we'll get a chance to do what we've crossed the world to do—kill the damn Queens."

Spoken like a true survivor. I smiled. Omar had an interesting way of looking at the world.

"He's right," I said. "What really matters in the grand scheme? That our names are listed as heroes in the records or that humanity outlasts and rebuilds?"

"You're right, man," said Huck, pulling Ariadne close. "If it's all the same to you, I'd like to survive as well."

"Absolutely," I said, laughing, "But first we have to survive this stupid Drome."

"I think I can help there," said Trivia, turning every head in the two adjoining cells we currently called home.

"Trivia, you realize what you're offering, right?" asked Roque.

"What Hemant said about what really matters stuck with me," she said, taking my hand. "And that's getting us out of here."

For the next several hours, she supplied us with every detail of the Drome that she could remember. The diabolical gauntlet would challenge us in familiar and foreign ways, risking our lives and limbs to prove—what? That we were more badass than when we arrived? If I didn't have anxiety about the challenge before, I certainly did now. It was one thing to run a moving obstacle course, but another to have a squad actively trying to hurt and possibly kill you as you did so.

"And every squad of cadets does this?" I asked.

Mego nodded.

"Surviving it is a point of pride," he said.

"The whole thing is just as ridiculous as Release Day," I said, standing. "Survival of the fittest my ass. Sure, train us, push us, knock us down, but what good is maiming or killing us? We should be out there right now! Fighting our way to the Hive. But no, we're stuck in this god-forsaken cell, waiting to pass a stupid-ass test so we can warm a bench for the *real* soldiers! This is a load of pig—"

"Don't stop on my account," said Xavier through the bars. "The Drome is a tool. It exists to separate the whiners from the warriors. And it's pretty clear which of the two you are. It ensures that every member of our 1,000-man battalion deserves to be there."

"And what of the battalions that have never returned?" asked Huck. "I'm assuming they were all 'warriors.'"

"They weren't us," said Xavier.

"Don't you think that's what they thought too?" asked Fen.

"You forget, I knew many of the last battalion. They weren't as strong, as well led, or as well provisioned."

"The problem isn't the strength, it's the numbers," said Ariadne. "You have to see that!"

"Numbers?! You want to talk to me about numbers?!" screamed Xavier, spitting through the iron bars. "How about 250,000?! That's how many people died in Pod Bogotá where I'm from! Double that to include Baghdad—your last stop! Humanity is down to eight pods. What is that? Two million people? Don't you dare lecture me on numbers!"

"I'm sorry. I didn't—" Ariadne stammered.

"You didn't what?" he yelled, grabbing Ariadne by the jumpsuit and jerking her into the bars. "You didn't think that I cared about something? That we have to treat every damn chance as if it's our last? You disgust me."

"Let her go, man!" I said, jumping up.

Xavier released her and began walking away. Ariadne stumbled back into Huck's awaiting arms, trembling and distraught.

"It's cadets like you we weed out," he said, half-turning. "See you tomorrow."

CHAPTER 46: FEN

I could barely choke down breakfast. The flavorless gruel did nothing to calm my roiling stomach, agitated by the Drome lingering at the forefront of my thoughts. I'd been training for months, almost excited by the prospect of proving myself as a soldier and leader. Now, the anticlimactic pinnacle of training felt more like a sentence. I was done playing their game. I knew who I was and who I could be. Getting caught had only revealed the truth of the machismo culture that surrounded the Clunkies.

Our punishment and subsequent ostracization weren't a matter of doing what was best for humanity. It was bravado—pure and simple. The idea that brute force would always win the day. Well, they were wrong. I'd been brainwashed into thinking our mission would somehow be different, but now I was convinced it wasn't. Prime Minister Leal had the right of it. I didn't know how, but I would do everything I could to make sure that Huck and the others could carry out their mission.

"It's time," said one of the Tau goons.

"Not that I could eat anyway," said Ariadne, flicking her spoon into her bowl.

"Me either," I said, pushing the bowl away.

Save for Marie, not one of us had finished the paste-like slurry.

"Your weapons will be waiting for you at the summit," the guard said.

"Thank you," said Huck.

The guard smirked.

"You'll never reach the bottom," said the guard. "We don't want you on that ship. You're not worthy of cleaning a Clunkie's crap."

"What are you talking about?" I asked, exasperated, as he opened the brig's door, letting us out onto the open walkway of the level.

"You tried to leave us high and dry," he said, putting his finger on my chest. "You're no better than traitors."

Mego flung himself towards the man causing the second guard to rush forward, but Omar grabbed Mego before he could lash out.

"Save it for the Drome," I said.

The guards silently escorted us through the pod to the Drome's summit. The residents parted like a river around a stone, watching on in near silence, as though we were prisoners marching our way to the gallows. The crowd thinned as we neared the restricted area of the Drome. We were greeted by the rest of Tau Squad, including its smug leader, Xavier. Also present were Diaz, a few members of Rho, and unexpectedly, General Madan, who'd taken an interest in our performance.

"Welcome, cadets," said Madan. "This is your chance to prove your competence. It won't put you back in good standing, but it's a step in the right direction. For All!"

"For All!" we echoed as Madan headed for the observation ring encircling the arena.

"Tau Squad, take your places," commanded Diaz.

Half of the members of Tau filed across the narrow, unrailed catwalk to the top of the Drome, flexing the thin metal that spanned the gap, before ducking inside the entrance to the structure's central column. The other half descended ladders, taking places on the platform that spiraled around the cavernous arena's exterior wall facing in towards the foreboding edifice. From there, they would operate the posts, sealing off sections behind us. If any of us were trapped, that person would automatically fail the challenge in addition to risking serious injury.

"The objective is clear. Your goal is to reach the ground level by any means necessary as Tau Squad utilizes every method at their disposal to prevent you from doing so," said Diaz. "Once you reach the sand, you will face live Arthropods as the environment shifts around you. When the inverts are slain, all living members of the squad will be considered elite, but don't expect anyone to refer to you as a Clunkie."

Maybe being a Clunkie isn't all it's cracked up to be.

"Cadets, take your weapons," commanded Diaz. "Then take your places on top of the Drome."

I avoided looking down at the seven-story drop-off to the sand as I walked across the flimsy catwalk. In a whisper, Hemant bemoaned the heights from one side to the other. Once on top of the Drome, I realized that the metal facade felt as dangerously built as it looked. There were as many ways to get hurt by the jagged metal's razor edges and weakly-riveted seams as we'd likely face inside.

With the twelve of us positioned on the roof, Ondo and the other Rhos withdrew the catwalk, leaving us stranded on top of the malevolent construction.

"Good luck," mouthed Ondo.

I nodded my thanks. I spared a glance at Trivia, who held her head high, but trembled nonetheless. This would be her second time in the Drome.

"When you hear the gong, you may enter," said Diaz. "There is no going back. Only forward. Open the hatch."

On the ground next to the central column, which protruded a few meters above the Drome, was a hatch. Huck bent over and opened it, revealing a ladder down into the ominous darkness. I swallowed my fear and readied myself. Lieutenant or not, I would see them through. I positioned myself at the rear and took a deep breath. Without warning or pomp, the gong sounded, echoing off of the arena walls and filling my veins with ice water.

"Go, go, go," I shouted, watching one after another of my squad disappear into the maw before I followed suit.

It took a moment for my eyes to adjust to the darkness, but as soon as they did, I dodged a sharp pole coming directly at my face. I dropped to the ground as another sprouted from the wall, trying to impale me on the ground. *Jesus Christ!* I jerked up and pushed through the maze of spears, coming from all sides. I could hear the muffled yells of Xavier, directing the Tau elites from inside the column.

Like the spiral around the wall outside, the Drome's floor twisted down with each step as unpredictable obstacles and irregular barriers constantly hampered our progress. Behind us, the poles raced to barricade the sections we'd barely escaped. The course behaved like a nightmarish creature, constantly taunting and attacking. While you anticipated one blow, another would nearly take you down. I urged everyone forward as the poles threatened to seal us in behind. Ahead, Liesel screamed.

"You'll be okay!" Huck yelled. "We have to keep going."

It was too dark to see what had occurred, but the floor was slick with blood. I heard a painful groan from Hemant and knew some horror had also befallen him. We finally emerged from obscurity into blinding strobes. I shielded my eyes, unable to see in the bright flashes. A loud bang nearly deafened me as something hard hit me in the chest, expelling every modicum of air from my lungs. *I'm dead.* After the spears, whatever had hit me had to be lethal. Omar rushed to me, jerking me up off the ground as another object impacted his back.

"Aaahhh!" he screamed, arching his back and wincing in pain.

An onion-sized rubber ball rolled away and for the first time, I noticed the air cannons placed in the walls. Tau was shooting at us. I stumbled to my feet, thanking Omar, drawing slow shallow breaths as though Ondo was sitting on my chest. Around me, agonizing screams echoed off the walls as everyone felt the cannons' sting. Another shot took me in the shoulder, numbing my entire arm.

"We'll be in no shape to fight if this keeps up!" I yelled.

"We have to keep pushing!" yelled Ariadne.

Mego looked back at me with concern. He didn't have to say anything. We were barely into the second of seven progressively harder levels. We were fighting for every step as a sadist-led, ill-tempered squad attacked. To top everything off, we were so hated, it was as though fate itself was poised against us. *I'll die before I give up.* Mego saw my determination and the tip of his lips curled up as if to say, "That's my girl."

We made it through the rubber onslaught and plunged back into darkness. With every step, the barricades behind us came faster and faster. With no light filtering in from the seams, our environment was pitch black. Reluctantly, I put my hand out in front of me, hoping that I wouldn't touch anything harmful. I listened as Hemant and Mego tapped the floor with their weapons, searching intently for any pitfalls. The Drome had become silent like the Tau shouts. Suddenly, a burst of steam hit Trivia in the face, causing her to scream in agony. *Dammit!*

"I got her," yelled Ariadne.

"I don't have time for this," said Marie, kicking at the exterior paneling to let in a trace of light.

She picked up one of the rubber balls that had rolled down behind us and shoved it into the steam pipe protruding from the wall. When the Tau elite fired, the steam backfired into the column, scalding the soldiers trapped inside. A small part of me took a twisted pleasure in their screams and curses. Marie returned to the wall and expanded the opening as quickly as possible as the section-closing bars rapidly gained on us. She jerked a lengthy conduit out from the wall, uncoiling it down out of the hole.

"You coming?" she asked, before repelling down.

"Can she do that?!" asked Krista.

"She just… umm… did," said TomTom.

"Diaz said by any means necessary," said Roque, leading himself and TomTom after her example.

"Everybody out!" I screamed.

One by one, each squad member exited the Drome, descending to the sand meters below. By the time I leapt through the hole, I narrowly missed the poles. I landed in the sand with a puff, having to drop the last few meters without the conduit. The ground level was dim, the light from above barely reaching the ground. I could make out the forms around us. Above echoed the yells of frustration at the turn of events.

The bottom level of the arena was open, broken only by the columns supporting the Drome's massive weight above. The floor began to lurch as hexagonal sections rose and fell in a randomized pattern, constantly creating new pits and towers. A strange clicking sound told me that we weren't alone.

"Dammit!" yelled Hemant. "Not them again."

"Not them what?" I asked.

"Wraiths," he said.

All the air vanished from my lungs as though I'd been hit by another ball. In my travels, I'd never encountered a wraith. I'd only heard scattered stories, spoken with reverence for the elusive creatures. It wasn't enough for the room to have automated floors, but someone had chosen one of the most daunting foes as our final enemy. *It's rigged for us to fail.* I slung my arms, letting the inertia draw out my forearm blades, and readied myself as the floor undulated below.

I raised my weapons as the chatter moved closer. Moving with practiced grace, Marie spun towards the vacant space in front of me and sliced through part of the mantis wraith. The invisible beast screamed in fury and lashed out as the floor moved in Marie's favor, blocking its attack. With its attention diverted, Liesel drove her bladed staff into the midst of the screams, delivering a fatal blow. I heard Roque gasp as the carcass grayed into visibility.

No sooner than it appeared, there was a chittering to my right. I spun my blades towards the sound but encountered nothing but empty air. TomTom silently dropped from a column that had risen beneath his feet, blades out, but as stealthy as he was, it wasn't enough. He flew back towards the column as the creature spun its body into him. He crumpled at its base, unconscious.

"No!" screamed Roque, spinning his dual katanas towards the wraith's perceived location in a fit of anger.

Judging by the ear-wrenching cries of agony, he'd landed a blow. Mego sliced at the space, severing the head from the beast.

"How many are there?" Huck yelled.

A vengeful clacking sounded to the left as the floor continued to rise and fall beneath our toes. As Trivia flung a handful of sand in the creature's direction and revealed its sinister shape, Ariadne loosed an arrow directly through its eye, ending it.

The floor froze in place as a slow clap pierced the silence. I turned to see Madan descending with the others only paces behind.

"You put on quite a show," said the general.

"The traitors cheated!" screamed Xavier, emerging from his place of safety in the column, face blistered and pink from the steam explosion.

"What you saw as cheating, I saw as resolve, ingenuity, and survival," said Madan. "You are still on probation, but you have passed all of the challenges I have to offer. You are no longer cadets, but elites."

"Yes!" said Ondo, pumping his fist.

Everyone turned in surprise at his reaction. He stood at attention and tried unsuccessfully to hide his contentment. Xavier looked on in dismay before storming off.

"Well done, Elite Fen," said Diaz. "Keep this up and you'll be an officer again."

For the first time in weeks, I smiled.

CHAPTER 47: KOLYA

"**G**et that bloody hatch closed!" yelled Brick. "I don't give an eight's ass if they're still outside, I'm not jeopardizing my crew."

Ian rushed through the tight corridor, hesitating when he saw us, but forcing himself past to double-check the hatch as ordered.

"Good," said Brick, on seeing us. "Glad you could join us. What the hell is that thing? It's pinging on our sonar like a bloody whale."

"You've never seen a whale, Captain," said Ian, leaning on the map table amidst the chaos, calm as ever.

"Shut up," said Brick, listening intently. "There it is again. How's it closing so fast?"

The captain reached up and grabbed the headset for the ship-wide intercom.

"Emergency engine shutdown," he said. "Mandatory silence. No one moves."

I gripped the table in an attempt to hide my hand's fearful tremors. Everyone stood frozen in place, not uttering a syllable as the creature's cries grew more terrifying. The only other sound was the faint ping of the sonar as it bounced off of the threat's form.

With sweat beading on foreheads, all the attention was directed towards the sonar's decreasing intervals, boding of the Arthropod's proximity. When it was mere meters behind, there was a collective breath as everyone braced for impact.

Screeeeeeeech. The air filled with the horrifying sound of chitin scraping metal from one end of the vessel to the other. I waited anxiously for an impact that never came. After what felt like an eternity, the pings faded as the creature receded back into the depths of the Indian Ocean from whence it came. The crew collectively sighed their earlier breath.

"Make for Bandung. Cruising speed," Brick said onto the com. "Resume normal activity."

"That was insightful," said Ian. "What exactly is it about you two that changed the status quo?"

Brick stared down at the table. In a flash, he had me by the jumpsuit and threw me against a series of exposed pipes. By morning I'd have one or two knob-shaped bruises.

"What are you playing at?" he yelled, as the crew looked on in silence. "We've been running this area for years. You two show up and not only do we not fight a single invert, but the biggest damn one I've ever seen just passed us over like we were putrid meat! And don't you dare tell me it was because we stayed quiet. That was a desperate tactic I *knew* wouldn't work… and yet it did."

"Put me down and we shall speak like gentlemen," I said, trying my best to retain my rage.

Brick lowered me to the floor as Ian looked with curiosity.

"We're acting as a forward team of ambassadors for the rest of our coterie," I lied. "Arjun and I will attempt to coerce the inverts into leaving our planet. It was important to Minister Lafet that a diplomatic effort was made before we erase them from the Earth."

Brick laughed, his hearty guffaw bouncing off the bulkheads.

"Diplomacy? With them? You two are far stupider than you

led me to believe! *If* you get to that god-forsaken place, which I highly doubt, there's no way the inverts are just going to pack up and leave."

"They'll likely paralyze you and eat you alive—toes first," said Ian. "No thanks. I prefer a straight-forward fight to mind games."

"Do you know why the creature didn't attack us?" asked Arjun.

Brick and Ian exchanged looks before shaking their heads.

"The Arthropods know we're coming. They understand our intent and the lack of interference is their way of sending a message."

"What message?" asked Brick.

"That they will grant us an audience."

·······

The remaining days of the voyage passed without incident. After crossing the open ocean, we'd stopped at the northernmost point of the island chain that contained Bandung for fuel. Taking advantage of our ability to repel the inverts, Captain Brick gave the crew a day of shore leave to relax on the beach. With the vessel's inhabitants revitalized, spirits had been high for the rest of the trip to the city.

The ship's crew buzzed with excitement. Within moments, we would be arriving at the Pod Bandung shipyards. Following an old tradition, the majority of the crew would greet the city's gates from the deck of the underwater boat. I followed Arjun up the ladder and stepped out onto the humid deck. The rain that had plagued us for days had finally subsided, but under the sun's intense rays, the evaporating water made the heat unbearable, inside and outside of the boat. Taking my mind off of the discomfort were the giant walls looming in the distance. The shipyard looked more like a fortress than a pod.

"The walls surround the entire yard, sealing it off from attack," explained Ian. "The sea-faring vessels are far too large to build within the confines of the city, so the First Builders made one hell of a barricade. Everything comes in and out of that gate."

"I thought the city would be further inland," said Arjun.

"It is," said Ian. "The actual pod is over forty klicks from here. The First Builders created an underground tunnel to move people and supplies to the pod proper. The pod itself will look much like the others. It's mainly the shipyard that sets Bandung apart."

Escaping first notice, the colossal gates embedded in the aging wall were a foreboding sight, making me wonder if there was anything they couldn't keep out. Leading up to the wall, huge concrete forms pierced the water's surface. They had been reclaimed by nature but still held the geometric form indicative of their human design.

"Why aren't we going in a straight line?" asked Arjun.

"You're very perceptive for such a young man," said Ian. "This area wasn't always a coastal city. Before the invert crisis, humanity was battling a self-inflicted climate crisis. Global temperatures were on the rise, causing the polar regions to melt. Once inhabited low-lying coastal regions of Earth were consumed by the sea."

"So we're maneuvering around hidden underwater structures," said Arjun. "That explains the ruins."

"Mmmhmm," said Ian. "Ironically, when the inverts decimated the global population, the climate crisis resolved itself."

"So why didn't the water recede?" asked Yuze, who'd been listening in to the conversation.

"Icecaps take far longer than several hundred years to refreeze, Yuze," I said.

"Humans irreparably damaged the Earth with their cavalier attitudes," said Arjun. "If humanity survives the Arthropod War, it's critical that we are better inhabitants going forward. That or maybe we're better off extinct."

"Harsh words," said Yuze.

"For too long, we've considered ourselves above nature," I said. "The Arthropods were happy to illustrate otherwise. If we are to have a future, Arjun's right. We must reevaluate our position in nature."

"You lost my interest," said Ian, walking away.

Yuze, looking perplexed, sauntered off.

"I couldn't have said it better myself, Arjun," I said. "Don't fret because the weaker minds don't understand. Our parley with the Queens will be the first step in the reevaluation you spoke of. Imagine a future where Arthropods and humans work together! Think of the places they could take us."

With the relentless rain picking back up, the boat trundled forward on its indirect path to the gates. Recognizing the vessel, the city guards opened the gates, which lumbered along their deep underwater tracks with a groaning squeal.

"My God," I said. "They're meters thick."

"They have to be," said Ian. "I've seen a hook beetle open an armored vehicle like an old can of beans."

I stared at the walls as we neared, the waves lapping against their barnacle-covered sides. Further out at sea, their bleached appearance gave the impression of strength and integrity, but closer in, I saw the walls for what they were—crumbling vestiges of a past age. Like everything else we'd made, it was failing.

Once cleared of the entrance, the gates slowly swung shut once more, resounding with a thump that reverberated through the city. The shipyard was a spectacle to behold. Arjun gasped at my side.

"It's quite something? Isn't it, Arjun?" I said, patting his back.

"I couldn't have imagined we still had facilities like this," he said.

"It's one of a kind," said Ian. "If they'd had the time or resources, every city would have a walled portion like this, but sadly, Bandung is the only one."

The shipyard spanned the width of the walls. Half of the contained area was water. Beyond the docks, the other half appeared to be factories, above ground, yet covered by meters of earth for protection. Under various stages of construction and restoration were underwater boats and smaller watercraft, but what caught my eye was an enormous hybrid wood and metal galleon.

"I had no idea, Sveta," I mumbled.

"What was that?" asked Arjun.

"Nothing, my boy. Just thinking out loud."

Arjun had a question posed just behind his lips, but dismissed it, too busy hashing out the possibilities the vessels before us presented. Green lights lit our way to the u-boat's designated slip. I watched as the practiced deckhands hurled the heavy ropes to awaiting dock workers, guiding us in until we felt the slightest bump against the rubber bumpers. As the vessel was being tied to the bollards, Brick joined us on the deck.

"Nice weather to welcome us, eh?" he said, chuckling. "Just like Bandung, hot as the devil's arse or steamy as a whore's cooch."

"And usually reeking of both," added Ian.

"Ah, the mouths of sailors," said a wisp of a man with facial hair to match.

"Ah, Zimo. As usual, it's not a pleasure," said Brick.

"The feeling's mutual, I assure you," said Zimo. "The minister would like you to join him for an al-fresco lunch at your earliest convenience."

"That might be a problem," said Brick, holding up his hand to shield his face from the constant drizzle. "One of these here men is banished. Is that going to bother him?"

"Is he going to be a problem?" he asked.

"Are you?" Brick asked, turning to me.

"I most certainly will not," I said. "I'm more versed in etiquette than any of you. It's you the minister should be worried about dining with. Need I remind you who—"

"I think he will be a fine companion for the minister," interrupted Zimo. "They seem to have much in common."

He leaned over to one of his aides, who ran off in a sprint across the wet concrete of the docks.

"Al-fresco?" I asked, arching an eyebrow.

"Another gray area," said Brick, pointing at a tower towards the rear of the enclosure.

Seemingly sprouting from the factory below, the stone tower rose above the height of the surrounding walls. Its uppermost floor stretched into a wide veranda with a wooden roof to protect it from the elements.

"Being protected by a perimeter wall has its benefits," said Zimo, noticing my interest. "The minister likes to take his tea with an ocean view, so the guard tower was modified to suit his proclivities. In addition to serving as a guard post, it doubles as a lighthouse. Alas, I forget my manners, I'm Zimo, Chief Advisor to Prime Minister De León."

"I'm Kolya," I said. "This is my friend Arjun."

"A pleasure," said Zimo, gesturing towards the tower. "If you'll follow me."

"Don't you have to worry about the flying Arthropods?" asked Arjun as the short man led us towards the tower.

As if in answer to his question, I heard the distinct sound of a minigun firing a burst.

"Our gunners are quite accurate," said Zimo. "For the most part, the inverts have learned this, but there is the occasional rogue that threatens our boundaries."

"What about mud raptors and dart beaks?" I asked. "They're far too quick to be brought down by guns."

"They both present a substantial threat, but we have small bunker emplacements scattered across the entire yard," said Zimo, pointing. "In addition to manning the weaponry, the gunners also serve as lookouts, sounding the sirens. We always suffer some loss, but we minimize it as best we can. We don't usually miss those too slow to make it to a bunker."

Brick rolled his eyes at the advisor's dismissive nature of human life, but there was something to be said about promoting the survival of the fittest. If humanity was going to regrow in a partnership with the Arthropods, it would be fitting to start with the best seeds.

By the time we reached the tower, there wasn't a dry bit of clothing on any of our number. I could hear Arjun's teeth chattering inside his head. Despite the warm climate, the rain had a tendency to suck the warmth right out of your body. On the first level, we were shown to rooms with fresh clothing, where aides took my dirty clothes and traded them for ornate robes, more befitting for a guest of the minister.

From there, we were guided up the spiraling staircase up the interior of the tower to the veranda we'd seen from the docks. Copious amounts of food lined the lengthy table, at the head of which was a round-bellied man with a pencil-thin, black mustache. He was dressed as if he thought himself a sixteenth-century ruler.

"I must say, the weather leaves something to be desired," said the man. "Brick, my good man, what is this I hear about a Banished joining us for lunch? I'd hate it if lunch became… troublesome."

"That would be this one," said Brick, gesturing towards me.

"Here to work the docks, no doubt?" the man said, bemused. "You must be more interesting than Brick lets on. Oh, very well. What's your name, sir?"

Dockhand my ass, Sveta. I wonder if he'd be so cheerful with an ice pick buried in his skull? I put on a friendly smile as I answered.

"Kolya the Banished. Formerly Researcher Kolya from Pod Baghdad."

"You will address the minister as 'milord,'" said Zimo.

I took everything in me not to roll my eyes. Someone had been consuming far too much of the ancient stories. There was only one being I referred to as my lord, and it wasn't this pompous bastard.

"I think I know this name, Kolya," said the man, tapping his chin with a finger that had never seen labor. "I'm Prime Minister Rodolfo De León. Zimo has been kind enough to keep me abreast of the new discoveries and developments regarding the Arthropods. Your name has been mentioned on numerous occasions. Correct me if I'm wrong, Zimo, but some of our new designs have been based on your work."

"You are correct, milord," said Zimo.

"I knew it!" said the minister, slapping his knee.

There was a bark and a small stray dog ran out and jumped up on the minister's legs. Instead of kicking the dog away as expected, the man picked it up and let the vile little creature lick his face. Worse, he seemed to enjoy it! I looked away in disgust. *What type of place have we found ourselves, Sveta?*

"What's the matter?" asked Brick. "Didn't you have pets in Baghdad, Kolya?"

Only the low-level scum kept animals. Ironic given that they had the least food to share with them. Pets only served as a nuisance to humanity. They were better off outside of the cities.

"I've not had the privilege of meeting an animal so… refined, milord," I said, biting my tongue.

"Oh, I think we'll get along splendidly, Kolya," said the minister. "Everyone have a seat and let's eat before we catch our death of cold from this miserable rain."

•••••••

Back on the boat, I wrapped up in as many blankets as I could scrounge. The vessel was unnaturally quiet with its crew enjoying their shore leave. Aside from the occasional engineers working on the boat's systems, only Arjun had joined me in the tight confines.

The lunch had been much of the same. The minister spent the meal making deprecating comments about himself or the city, then waiting for one of his minions to spout the obligatory contradiction. Throughout the entire meal, the dog sat in his lap, receiving morsels directly from the table. *How can some with such a pretentious air, be so… unsophisticated?*

Arjun sat in the berth next to me, swaddled in nearly as many blankets as I was. We'd each had to change back out of the posh robes for our return walk to the dock.

"I'll be glad when we're free of this wretched city, my boy," I said.

"Once we find this Francisco, that will happen," said Arjun, taking notes from the ship's map, which he borrowed from the command room and sprawled across his bunk.

I rolled onto my back, thinking back to the awkward conversation.

"And what is it that you intend to do, if not remain here, Mr. Kolya?" asked Rudolfo. "Surely your banished status would prevent you from such futile notions as pursuing asylum in another pod."

"We're heading—" began Arjun.

I lifted my hand to halt him. Speaking of this matter with a gentleman such as De León required a deft hand, something that Arjun was sorely missing.

"We seek transportation to the Australian Territory," I said, taking a sip of the fine wine the minister had provided.

Once De León and Zimo had finally stopped their hysterical laughter, I continued.

"We wish to engage the Arthropods' hierarchy in a civil discourse."

"You can't be serious," said Rudolfo, struggling for breath between fits of giggles. "To what ends?"

"To end the war," said Arjun.

"You cannot think the good minister would spare a vessel and crew only to have it senselessly destroyed by the inverts," said Zimo, still chuckling, dabbing a tear from his eye with a long embroidered handkerchief.

"We will take whatever you have to offer, provided it's seaworthy," I said. "I would need someone to teach me how to sail."

"And how do you intend to pay for this vessel?" asked Zimo. "Or your training?"

"Arjun, you mentioned you have experience as an engineer," said Brick. "You and Kolya could work off the cost in the yards."

"We haven't the time. Our mission is urgent," I said. "Prime Minister, would you consider loaning us a vessel? Perhaps one you could afford to lose. If we're successful, you could brag that you inspired the voyage."

Rudolfo tugged at his mustache thoughtfully. "As tempting as that sounds, I cannot spare a seaworthy vessel for your idealistic endeavor. I'm afraid the answer is still no."

Zimo leaned over and whispered something into Rudolfo's ear.

"Maybe," said the minister. "My thoughtful advisor has reminded me that there may yet be an avenue for your request."

"What is it?" Arjun asked excitedly.

"Seek out Boatmaster Francisco," said Zimo. "He's an impoverished fisherman who lives down by the docks. He's been begging for rights to fish on the open seas."

"These peasants," said Rudolfo, "Never content with their lot in life. Are there not plenty of fish within the confines of the port?"

"For reasons you can imagine, we've refused his requests," said Zimo. "Opening the gates with any regularity would prove… problematic."

"But how will we convince a fisherman to spare his boat?" I asked.

"Not spare it, but rather take you," said Rudolfo, his smug grin revealing his yellowing teeth.

"The question still remains, how can we convince him?"

"I'll draft a letter," said Zimo, matching the minister's grin. "We'll promise him the position of…"

"Boatmaster General!" said Rudolfo, stomping his feet as he was overcome with laughter. "Full fishing rights outside of the city! A fleet to command!"

The two guffawed until tears rolled down their cheeks. *We'll show them, won't we, my dear?*

"The minister isn't an idiot, Arjun. Neither he nor his advisor expects the three of us to return."

"Our mission has been successful thus far," he said, not lifting his eyes from the map. "We're only asking death to stay its hand a little longer."

"In the most hostile environment on the planet," I said, letting out a laugh in a vain attempt to ease my tension.

"First thing in the morning, we'll track down Francisco," said Arjun, beaming. "With any luck, we'll be underway in the next few days. The Hive, Kolya. We're actually going to see it."

CHAPTER 48: HUCK

The day of the battalion's departure came even quicker than expected. It seemed like only yesterday when we'd arrived in the militaristic pod, the months having disappeared in a blink. Leaving the pod without Arjun felt… wrong. Hemant was nearly twitching with anticipation as we took the elevator up to the top floor. Our probationary squad would be one of one hundred in the battalion, totaling up to approximately a thousand elite soldiers.

When we stepped into the staging area, a wave of anxiety almost overtook me. Memories of Release Day flooded my memory as we pushed through the sea of bodies filling the space. This was bigger than any release had ever been and would be far less of a slaughter. The exterior area had been patrolled regularly by the elites eagerly waiting for the next mission. Now that mission was departing, we would be doing so in a lengthy chain of armored vehicles.

Over the heads of the elites (of which I was now one, though didn't feel like it), I could see a fleet of familiar vehicles, many more of them than I'd ever laid eyes on. Between the people and vehicles, the room was shoulder to shoulder. I held Ariadne's hand as we pressed our way through the throngs to where Platoon III had assembled.

"…should've been back by now," I overheard Diaz say, struggling to be heard over the crowd.

"If Brick's unusual last transmission is to be believed, they'd encountered something in the water," said a bearded stranger sporting a burgundy beret. "That or they were going crazy. He kept going on about…"

The man's words froze on his lips when he saw me eavesdropping. I hadn't realized I wasn't making any effort to hide my interest. Diaz turned towards me with a look of reproach. Out of the corner of my eye, I saw that Ariadne had been equally interested in the conversation.

"Elite Huck," she said. "I see manners weren't one of the skills taught in your training, either here or in Horizonte."

"Forgive me, Captain," I said. "We're desperate for news of our friend, Arjun. Did something happen to the transporters?"

At the mention of his brother's name, Hemant had tuned out all other distractions and made his way toward us.

"Did someone say Arjun?" he asked.

Captain Diaz rolled her eyes. "Elites, this is our deputy prime minister, Jonas Kohler."

"A pleasure," the man said, snapping a militaristic bow. "Regretfully, we lost contact with Captain Brick and his team while they were making their return voyage across the sea."

"No, no, no," Hemant began to mutter, his legs failing underneath him.

"Do you know anything of the two new people he took with him?" I asked, desperate for information.

"As a matter of fact, I do," he said. "For whatever reasons, your two companions chose to remain at Pod Bandung. Whatever fate that has befallen our transporters wouldn't seem to include your friends."

"Thank God," Hemant said, releasing a long-held breath.

Diaz arched an eyebrow.

"But I hope Captain Brick and the others are okay," he added.

"At this point, it's uncertain," said Kohler. "They were due in earlier this week. We were hoping when we lost communication, their radio had simply gone out. Apparently, that's not the case."

With a nod to Diaz, the deputy prime minister headed towards the temporary stage that'd been erected in the center of the assembly. Arjun was an entire pod ahead of us if not further. I rubbed Hemant on the back as he recovered his composure. Our stay in Bhopal had been filled with highs and lows, but Hemant's had been compounded by Arjun's absence.

"Form up," yelled Diaz over the commotion.

Sigma and the other four squads of our platoon took our places, assembling for the main address. I scanned over the sea of faces. Unlike Release Day, many of the soldiers would survive the expedition, only to perish somewhere deep within the Australian Territory. Another lost battalion on a growing list. At that moment, overflowing with pessimism, I couldn't help but think humanity was nearing its end. General Madan took his place on the stage as everyone snapped to attention. The hall reverberated with the thunder of boots slamming into place.

"Welcome elites!" he yelled.

"Ooh-rah!" came the choral reply of a thousand voices.

"Today, we set forth on our journey to the Hive!" he said to raucous cheers. "With the newest addition to the fleet—a retrofitted borer—we will deliver our newest weapon deep within the Hive and hit the inverts where it hurts. Prepare yourselves, soldiers. After this, we will all be heroes!"

The room exploded in excitement. Hemant turned to me, mouthing "our weapon?" I shrugged. It was already clear what the prime minister thought of our original mission. None of Sigma was quite as excited as the rest of the battalion. Not only had our mission been jerked away from us, but Arjun's status was still unknown, and the duties that awaited us included cleaning toilets. If there was a bright side to the mission, it was that this old well borer they lugged up from the pod's depths might be capable of depositing the nuclear weapon deep enough underground to decimate the invert's hierarchy and reproduction.

"To the cadets and residents viewing throughout the pod, I leave you under the leadership of Deputy Prime Minister Kohler, who will execute the duties of the office with dignity. I vow to you this: We will return victorious! For All!"

Fist pumps filled the air with the echoing reply.

"To your vehicles!" said Madan.

The pod vibrated with energy, every inhabitant in the pod united in the hope that *this* would be the mission that would restore humanity to Earth's surface. Even plagued by negative feelings, I couldn't help but embrace the excitement. Being part of a thousand-man force will do that. I pulled Ariadne close and snuck a kiss on her forehead.

"I love you," I said. "Regardless of what happens, I want you to know that."

"I love you, too," she said, pulling me close.

"And I love you guys!" said TomTom, laughing.

"Platoon III!" yelled Diaz. Company G is assigned to Carriers 3 and 4. Make your way to them. See Colonel Ribeiro for your assignments."

"Two carriers for two hundred people?" asked Upsilon's lieutenant.

"How astute," said Diaz, mockingly. "Monterrey doesn't have the resources to equip battalion after battalion. They've already supplied us with everything they had in hopes we can end this bloody war. Now, get a move on!"

The staging area was chaos, but eventually, Platoon III made it to where Company G was forming. The clean-cut Colonel Ribeiro stood on a crate barking out orders.

"Platoon III, you'll be sharing Carrier 4 with Platoon IV," he ordered. "I'll leave it to your captains to determine who's walking, who's riding, and who's hanging. P3, you'll be responsible for the tanker. P4, you've got the supply truck. Take care of both, they've got our fuel, food, and medicine. Now, who's got wheel time? If you're lying, I'll drag your ass from here to the coast."

I traded a look with Hemant and we raised our hands.

"Names?" he asked, pointing at each extended arm in turn.

"Huck," I said, pointing. "This is Hemant."

If the colonel recognized our names or knew of our fall from grace, it wasn't obvious. With the drivers accounted for, he began vehicle assignments. Driving skills were scant among the elites, forcing Kohler to split Hemant and me up. Each of us would be responsible for training a secondary driver. I was tasked with driving the sluggish tanker truck while Hemant would be handling the supply truck. With our uncommon skills, we would have the best seats available for the duration. Our single perk of the trip. If not for the danger that my friends would be in, I would've taken pleasure in the privilege. Judging from the sideways glances, many took issue with the placement.

"Go on," said Ariadne. "I'll be fine."

"Make ready for departure," yelled the colonel.

"You heard him," she said.

I gave her a lingering hug before turning to Fen.

"Take care of them," I said.

"Is that an order?" she said, smiling.

"More of a request."

"Don't worry. I'll keep everyone out of harm's way," said TomTom, laughing. "Go enjoy your cushion."

I made my way to the tanker, but Marie approached me first.

"This method of travel makes me deeply uncomfortable," she said. "It stands against my experience with the creatures. This is wrong. It will get everyone here killed."

"I have to believe Madan knows what he's doing," I said. "Our way isn't going to work out. Let's—"

"Get in your vehicle, driver!" yelled Ribeiro. "The time for chit-chat is over."

"I've got to go," I said. "We just have to… adapt."

I paced backward from her. For some reason, I was reluctant to turn away from her. The look on her face was one of distrust and hurt. A pit opened in my stomach as I realized our path together may have reached its conclusion. Once she'd vanished into the crowd, I turned to climb into the cab and saw Xavier mounting a quad. He gave me a sly grin as he saw my recognition. It was one of Breaker's. I ignored him and climbed into the cab of the truck with two others. So much for comfort. The bench was cramped with three bodies, especially when one was Ondo's. His muscular bulk barely gave me enough room to operate the pedals, shifter, and levers.

"Hey, Huck," said Ondo. "I was hoping you could teach us how to drive."

"Umm… Sure." I said. "It'll be hard to miss when I change gears between your thighs."

Ondo looked down and cackled.

"Can you manage it?" he asked.

"I think so. We just might get a little closer than either of us care for."

Ondo roared with laughter.

"This is Andre," said Ondo. "He's one of mine."

"Good to meet you," I said.

"Same," he said, chuckling. "If it's all the same to you. I'll learn from over here."

If it was going to be a long, cramped ride, at least I was in good company. I was thankful Yanus had forced Hemant and me to learn to drive, and even more thankful for a patient teacher like Taha. I would miss being able to talk to the others as I drove. Instead of a cargo bed full of my companions behind me, there were thousands of liters of compressed natural gas. I could barely see the chain of vehicles behind me for all the elites clinging to bars mounted on the tank's sides.

"Clunkies," began Madan, standing on the lead carrier.

The room fell silent as a thousand mouths clamped shut.

"We march into history!" he yelled.

One by one, each vehicle started its engine as the primary gates parted, letting the afternoon rain pour in. By the end of the day, there were going to be a lot of drenched people. I wasn't looking forward to my first time back in the seat pitting my driving skills and the tanker's tracks against the muddy terrain.

"We headed southeast, Ondo?" I asked, who doubled as my navigator.

"Nope," he said. "The transporters have enough vehicles to make the drive. That'd wear out the marchers and take us a damn month. We're heading northeast to the lake."

"How's a lake going to get us to the Australian Territory?" asked Andre.

"Boy, didn't they teach you geography when you were a candidate?"

Andre looked abashed as I put the truck into gear and pulled along slowly behind Hemant's supply truck in front of me.

"There's some lake up there where they keep a troop transport ship. We'll drive the vehicles on, then sail down the river to the coast. From there, Andre, we'll cross the ocean to the Australian Territory. It's a much shorter journey, but getting to the lake will still take us damn near two weeks."

"Two weeks!" I said, feeling the inclination change as I drove the truck up the ramp.

"You may as well get comfortable," said Ondo, leaning his head against the rear of the cab and shutting his eyes.

CHAPTER 49: ARIADNE

Man, *was I wrong.* I'd thought traveling under such large numbers was going to be easier. *More soldiers, better odds, right? Nope.* By the time we made camp the first night, we'd already lost more than fifty soldiers to attacks. The thunderous marching of our battalion on the old road's sun-baked surface had drawn every invert for kilometers, flooding the first line of defenders. Their attacks would come in waves. Eventually, we'd kill enough to run them off, but they'd return with reinforcements. If the convoy hadn't been composed of such highly-trained warriors, everyone outside of the vehicles would've been dead by the first day's end.

The most disappointing revelation came when I realized that Marie was nowhere to be found. I was sure, as was Huck, that she couldn't have fallen in battle. Whether true or not, the unusual woman somehow seemed invincible. It didn't make the sadness of her disappearance any less profound. When Huck shared the last conversation he'd had with her, it hit me—she'd snuck away, not in cowardice, but in self-preservation. She was right. The attention the battalion was drawing with every step was exactly what Memo had hoped to avoid. We were better off alone. I knew it. Memo knew it. Marie knew it.

We pushed on, day after day, much to the same end. The list of names on each platoon's roll call grew shorter with each passing day. The worst attack had come on our eighth day of travel as we slogged through the treacherous mountainous terrain. A slew of inverts stormed out of the jungle like a tsunami, washing over a carrier, supply truck, and the soldiers surrounding it. More than a hundred Clunkies died in an instant, vanishing with the tidal wave as it receded. A hook climbed on top of Carrier 6, sawing it open with its aquiline beak. The surrounding troops watched powerlessly as eights climbed in and pulled its occupants out one by one, ripping them apart and flinging them asunder. No one had the heart to sound off that night. Even Madan's eyes were clouded with doubt, though he'd be loath to admit it.

By the time we reached the arid region of the lake, we'd already lost nearly four-hundred men. We hadn't even reached the ocean and forty percent of our battalion was just… gone. As we made camp for our last night on land, the members of Sigma split off to perform our obligatory cleaning roles. I meandered around the campsite picking up after the other soldiers, already feeling demeaned by the labor, when a member of Tau threw his plate at my feet.

"Clean that for me, puppet," the boy said.

Huck, nearby, observed the situation, hands tied in the matter. This was the duty Madan had relegated us to. In two months' time, we'd gone from being world heroes to indentured servants. I stooped to pick up the plate.

"Check out that backside," said another Tau. "What exactly can we order her to do?"

Before I could react, Ondo grabbed my arm, stopping me from picking up the plate.

"Pick up your own damn plate, Squid. Ariadne's saved you ass more than once this trip," he said, turning to the others in the vicinity. "As a matter of fact, Sigma has proven its worth on this trip time and time again. They may still be in the muck, but I for one ain't going to ask them to do a damn thing. And if you know what's good for you, you won't either."

"I second that," said Andre, taking a place at Ondo's side.

A tear ran down my cheek at the show of support. Before it was over, most of the soldiers in the clearing were standing in solidarity with Sigma, whose other members had gathered around me. Only a few scattered elites and the members of Tau remained seated.

"They might not stand, but I doubt they'll ask you to do anything else," said Ondo.

"I don't know how to thank you," said Huck. "You stood up for us when no one else would."

"There's not a person here who doesn't have a reason to be grateful to you," said Ondo. "If nothing else, we can see the stars more clearly than ever."

"You don't hold anything against us for trying to run off with the bomb?" asked Fen.

"Hell no!" he said. "If I was under orders, I would've done the same thing. Now I don't know how we can change much, but I'll do everything I can to uphold your mission, provided it doesn't conflict with my orders."

"Thank you," said Huck. "You can't know how much that means."

"I knew you guys were alright the moment I met you," said Ondo, pulling me into a side hug. "And plus, you guys are taking care of Trivia for me. I need her back at my side. Without her around, I don't know half the stuff I'm looking at out here."

"I know the feeling," said Hemant, downtrodden.

"Yeah, Huck's been regaling me with your stories while he teaches us to drive," said Ondo. "Arjun sounds like one hell of a dude. I wish I could've spent some time with him."

"I think he would've liked you," I said.

"Alright," said Fen. "I may not be your lieutenant, but it's getting late. And something tells me that tomorrow won't be a stroll around the shaft. Let's get some shut-eye."

Taking her up on her advice, Huck and I headed back to our bivvies. We'd set them up side by side, nestled in the crook of two carriers parked bumper to bumper. All around the encampment, the vehicles formed a protective circle for the occupants within. A roving perimeter of guards protected the convoy's exterior. Self-dubbed the Night Owls, the volunteer group did their best to sleep in their allotted carrier as it trundled along during the day. They were the only reason any of us could get any rest. As Huck unzipped his bivvy, I put my hand on his.

"Stay with me tonight," I said.

Fen's concerns about the upcoming day loomed in my mind. I didn't want to lose another moment with Huck should the coming day prove fatal for either of us. He climbed into the tight confines of the single-person tent. We lay there for a while, softly kissing. Tangled together, all I could think about was how incomplete I'd felt without him. When the lure of sleep became too powerful, Huck held me from behind, softly kissing my neck as I drifted off into the world of dreams.

••••••••

The camp buzzed with energy as what was left of the battalion readied itself to roll out for the lake. Our last day of marching would be spent reaching the troop transport ship, which would ferry us and our vehicles to the Hive. It was refreshing to feel a modicum of our respect returning, something that had been sorely lacking since our probation. No one forced me to clean, load, or prepare anything outside of the normal duties carried out by all battalion members. Surprisingly, we were even offered a shift inside the carrier. We piled into the vehicles, grinning at each other. The day was off to a great start.

"You think we'll still have to clean the latrines on the ship?" asked Liesel over the noise of the tracks beneath the carrier's bed.

"I don't know," I said. "Ondo seems to have intimidated anyone from asking, but that doesn't mean Madan won't order it flat out."

"Everyone seems to have embraced us," said Krista, bracing against the wall as we rolled over some particularly rough terrain. "I mean, a guy called Omar a Clunkie last night."

Omar tried to hide his smile. He, in particular, hadn't taken the subservient role well and had fallen into a bit of a slump. Thankfully, he was quickly returning to his old, cranky self. Outside, I could hear the sounds of yet another skirmish as the inverts harried our passage. It was the first time on the trip that I hadn't formed part of the defensive force. I felt a pang of guilt, riding in relative comfort as others fought to the death. I still couldn't shed the haunting images of the carrier being ripped open and I was washed by a sudden wave of claustrophobia. *The carrier's not all it cracked up to be.* We weren't marching, but it was stifling hot, miserably humid, and obnoxiously loud. Hours later, screams of elation began to pierce the sides of the carrier.

"We're here!" said Mego, turning from the narrow viewing slat. "I can see the lake!"

"And the ship!" shouted Liesel. "My god! It's the biggest thing I've ever seen."

"How did they get enough metal to build that?" asked Roque.

"Most of the larger vessels were built before the Arthropod Landing," said Trivia, her freckled face healed but bearing the scars of her run-in with the steam. "It's taken every resource Bandung has to keep the ancient things afloat. Didn't Mego or TomTom tell you this? They're the ones from Bandung."

"It never came up," said TomTom, shrugging.

"Well, what can you tell us about it now?" I asked, wishing Huck could be part of the conversation.

"To be honest, I was never interested in shipbuilding," said TomTom. "That's why I left. I learned enough to tell the basics, though. It's a catamaran hull, meaning it's pretty fast. It'll hold all of us, plus our vehicles. It's got a shallow draft, which is why it can come this far inland."

"That sounds awesome," said Krista.

"It's far from perfect," said Mego. "They're notorious for not liking bad weather."

"You mean like we might encounter on the ocean?" asked Omar, suddenly interested.

Mego nodded.

"Hemant's going to love that," I said.

The carrier slowed to a crawl as we neared the lake. I wondered if the vehicle would drive on board or if we'd have to get out. Madan's voice answered my question as it erupted through the lead vehicle's speakers.

"Everyone out!" he boomed. "They're coming from everywhere!"

Omar thrust the carrier's rear door open as we piled out of the vehicle. Inverts plowed through the trees, converging on us as though they had no intention of letting us leave. Madan stood on top of his command vehicle, barking orders at the multiple companies of the battalion.

"G, I, J Companies, defend the convoy and the ship! H Company, ready the boat for departure! K Company, get these vehicles stowed."

"You heard the man," yelled Colonel Ribeiro, our company commander. "Stand your ground!"

Everywhere I looked was an endless torrent of inverts,

writing and climbing over each other to reach us. Not even the vehicle turrets held any effectiveness against the deluge. We'd never overcome numbers like these. *How are we ever going to survive the Hive?* A multipede barreled towards me with the momentum of a twentieth-century locomotive. I slung the bow from my shoulders and pulled an arrow back to my cheek. With barely enough time, I released, watching the arrow soar, burrowing deeply into the pede's eye. The blow brought the creature to the ground where it plowed up the earth, coming to rest mere meters away.

TomTom spun next to me with the agility of a bone arachnid and sliced a hook beetle's sides open, spilling its entrails at my feet and saving my life in the process. I nodded my thanks and moved on, targeting an eight attacking Krista and Liesel. I fired arrow after arrow into the invert's abdomen, continually missing its weak, velvety patch. It was Liesel's guandao that delivered the killing blow to the vulnerable spot on its belly, bringing it down.

Explosions pummeled the battlefield as the first polies dropped from squadrons of powder moths, a silent command to don dust masks. The tidbit of knowledge we'd brought to Pod Bhopal was now saving countless lives.

"Archers, target those pill bugs!" yelled Madan from his post.

I swung my bow up and after leading the target just enough to compensate for the duster's air speed, loosed an arrow. *Direct hit!* The polie exploded, bringing the duster carrying it spinning and smoldering to the ground.

"Fall back to the ship!" yelled Diaz, for the first time looking disheveled, a light spray of hemolymph soiling her normally impeccable uniform.

Clunkies continued to fall, caught in the barrage of attacks, as we retreated up the ramp into the ship. When the last soldiers who stood a chance were on board, Ribeiro slammed the button to raise the ramp, sealing the fate of the remaining Clunkies still dealing out death on the battlefield and covering our exit. Ribeiro turned to us with a look of exhaustion and dismay. Just as the gates were moments from closing, a hook slammed its gnashing beak through the gap, clamping it shut on the top half of Ribeiro, who disappeared out the opening.

As soldiers continued to fend off the attackers, I couldn't take my eyes off the bottom half of our colonel as it fell, blood pooling on the deck. I almost didn't notice when an arm grasping a crooked blade slapped over the ramp's uppermost edge. Marie pulled herself up and over, rolling into the center of the floor. The ramp closed with a thud, smashing invert appendages around the edges. I frantically scanned the cargo area for Huck and almost collapsed with relief when his eyes met mine.

"Marie!" shouted Hemant. "You're alive?!"

"You didn't think I was going to let you catch that bastard before me, did you?" she said, wiping the blood splatters from her pale face.

It was good to have her back. She was quite possibly the fiercest warrior amongst us. She must have followed the convoy from a distance, fairing far better alone than with hundreds of soldiers trampling through the jungle. I felt the vibration of the boat's engines through the metal-clad decking and the sensation of movement as the boat lurched forward. *Safety.* I couldn't believe it. We'd survived.

"Archers, to the deck!" ordered one of the colonels. "They're scaling the sides!"

CHAPTER 50: HEMANT

I stormed up the ship's steep ladder to the upper deck of the loading bay, racing behind Ariadne. In addition to archers, they'd called for soldiers to defend them. The sight that greeted me when I ran through the wide steel doors onto the deck nearly brought me to my knees. Over the sides, bone arachnids lapped onto the deck like waves and washed away everything in their paths. The sky was filled with hovering hook beetles, eager for an opening to make off with yet another soldier. I covered my ears as one of the ship's guns opened fire.

"Archers, clear the sides!" yelled a colonel over the din. "Everyone else, give them cover!"

Ariadne, Trivia, and the other archers began to slowly pick at the writhing pile of eights, their off-white exoskeletons lashing out in a cloud of fury. At this rate, they'd run out of arrows long before making a dent. Hooks flew in, picking off archers one by one. I swung fruitlessly at them as they dove, but even the slow fliers were too quick for my cumbersome hammer. With the guns concentrating on the airborne nemeses, I focused on the eights escaping the archers' barrage.

Within minutes, I was weary from exertion with no end in sight. The boat was struggling to move, stuck in the mire under the excess weight of the inverts piled on the vessel's hull. Just when I was thinking we had traded one hell for another, several soldiers emerged from the ship's belly, laden with tanks and unusual weapons tipped with fire. *Flamethrowers!* They looked like smaller versions of what Hera had used on the *Sekhmet.*

"Move or fry with them!" Lieutenant Xavier yelled.

No one hesitated. With the elites clear, the flamethrower team loosed their fire, scorching the deck and igniting the undulating masses of inverts. The intense heat radiating from the flames nearly set my skin ablaze. Most of the burning inverts threw themselves into the murky water below, leaving behind only the most hostile foes. Pissed and fearless, the smoldering army slowly advanced toward us.

"What are you waiting for?" shouted Ariadne. "Light them up!"

"I'm out!" yelled Xavier. "These tanks only last seconds!"

I rushed towards the nearest eight, but the heat radiating off of its exoskeleton forced me back. Unbelievably, the eight hadn't succumbed to the fire. Taking advantage of my hesitation, the eight lunged forward nearly taking Xavier's head with its razor-sharp leg. Just in time, Mego slammed his double-bladed staff through the creature's leg before jerking back in pain. Blisters were already rising on the side of his face from the burn. Ariadne crouched and sent an arrow deep into the arachnid's velvety patch, causing it to spasm violently before collapsing off the deck.

As I spun around, frantically searching for the next enemy. I saw nothing but injured humans, dead inverts, and the warm sun, finally peeking through the overcast sky. Beneath me, I felt the ship pick up momentum as it broke loose from the quagmire.

"We did it!" I screamed.

Cheers erupted from the others. We'd lost several more, but we were escaping the onslaught. The remaining inverts were busy consuming the dead—Arthropod and human alike—before retreating into the woods. Ariadne crouched next to Mego, administering treatment when Xavier approached them.

"Without you guys, I suppose I wouldn't be alive," he said, looking down at his feet before raising his gaze. "So, thanks… Clunkies."

Before the situation could become awkward, Xavier turned and began belting out orders to anyone in decent enough shape to help get the injured and deceased below deck. In a state of shock, I made my way to one of the few edges of the deck that wasn't blackened and smoking and collapsed onto one of the ship's wide cleats. I looked back in the direction of our embarkation. Aside from the marred ground, the inverts had all but vanished, taking most of the evidence of battle with them.

"It's unreal," I said as Huck came to check on me. "Some days I almost feel like we understand our enemy and other days… I realized we don't know the first damn thing. It's like when all those inverts marched to their deaths to ambush us back in the Latin Territory. You saw that eight a minute ago. There was zero instinct of self-preservation. The damn thing was on fire, Huck! They will stop at nothing—nothing—until we're all annihilated."

"That's why we have to exterminate them first," said Fen, "But for now, Hemant, there's a lot of injured who could use your help."

Just because everyone had embraced us as part of the Clunkies didn't mean Madan was going to let us eke by without punishment. No sooner had we transferred the injured to the medics and the dead into cold storage for later burial at sea, Madan already had cleaning duties waiting. Yet another harsh reality of the surface, there was no time for grieving.

Everyone had chipped in to scour the deck after the initial attack, but it was Omar's and my responsibility to see to the day-to-day deck cleaning. The task didn't sound too bad until we realized how much pipe ash and tobacco spittle constantly dirtied every surface of the ship's exterior. *My god, how can people be so nasty?* Before long, I grew grateful for the assignment. The ability to see the horizon from the deck helped with my seasickness more than anything. Even drifting down the relatively small river, haunted only by spring tongues and wake striders, I couldn't shake the annoying nausea.

Liesel and Fen tended to the officers' quarters, a pleasure by comparison to some of the squad's other duties. While much cleaner than the general population of the ship, the officers were far more anal in their attention to cleanliness. The two often had to clean and reclean until the officer in question found their work to be satisfactory.

"You'd think they'd have something better to do than complain about dust," said Fen one evening. "From what you guys have told me, Pod Bhopal was already the neatest of the previous pods you've seen."

It was only our second of three nights on the river before we reached the coast and our evenings had become nothing more than a gripe session about our daily duties.

"It was impressively clean," said Ariadne. "Save for the uppermost levels, the pods we visited were pretty dingy and falling apart."

"Oh, Bhopal is falling apart alright," said Mego "Madan had us do everything we could to mitigate it though. Structurally speaking, it was a borderline disaster."

"Well I'd rather be recleaning some nitpicky officer's quarters than the nastiness we've been seeing," said Krista. "They might be marksmen with bows, but they can't hit the toilets to save their lives."

Roque, Huck, and Ariadne all nodded, laughing in agreement at their abysmal chore.

"What I find most distressing is the food Trivia and I have to clean up," said TomTom. "I don't mind the work, especially when I hear about what you guys have to contend with, but seeing the waste is appalling. Madan did a good job at covering it up, but people were starving in Bhopal's lower levels. Pod Pittsburgh, on the other hand, is living up to humanity's motto. They are doing their damnedest to stretch resources and increase nutrition for everyone. Meanwhile, these knuckleheads are throwing out food that the Failed Ones— excuse me, the Recouping—would be gracious for."

I was having to get used to the changes in vocabulary as well. Memo was making a lot of positive changes back in Horizonte, including renaming many of the people groups with terms that evoked more optimistic connotations. Failed ones, those critically injured, were now called the recouping. Laborers, generally stereotyped as convicts and outcasts, were now the skilled. Lastly, the unabled, those people with genetic or acquired disabilities, were now referred to as the aided. Despicable people like Zabu were still in power, but the world was changing. People were awakening from their apathy and just in time too.

"Makes me feel like complaining about the grease under my fingernails is stupid by comparison," said Mego. "The smell still gives me a headache though."

"I don't know," said Marie. "I like the smell of the engine room. There's something soothing about the way the vibrations penetrate your bones. Between the tight confines and the heat, it's almost like a womb."

"I don't know about all that," said Mego, "but it's fine, I suppose."

"What's the plan for tomorrow," I asked Fen.

"You always ask me like I'm still included in the platoon briefings," she said. "Fortunately for you, there's enough gossip that I can parse it out. We'll reach the coast sometime in the afternoon. We're stopping just long enough to refuel. For obvious reasons, Madan doesn't want to sit idle a second longer than we have to."

"Then the ocean?" I asked.

"Then the ocean," she said.

• • • • • • • •

The following afternoon, General Madan ordered all non-essential personnel up to the deck of the *Spearhead*, anticipating another attack as we neared the anticipated fuel stop. As we reached the delta where the river poured into the ocean, the water changed from a murky greenish-brown to a beautiful, rich blue. I took a deep breath of the salty air as Huck and Ariadne took their usual places at my side, wishing only that my brother could join us.

"You remember the first time we saw the ocean together?" I asked. "Did you ever imagine we'd come this far?"

"I was naively optimistic," said Huck. "Looking back, though, I'm amazed by what we've done. We've only made it this far because we've had each other."

"And Arjun," I added. "For that matter, all the people who've helped us every step of the way. We couldn't have done this without them."

"I feel like we should have a toast," said Ariadne. "Shame we're on duty."

There we stood, watching the hinterlands carefully for any sign of encroaching inverts. When the men far below began rolling up the hoses from the abandoned pump house, I breathed a sigh of relief.

"If there's one thing I'm glad the inverts and I have in common, it's that we both dislike water," I said. "I don't know what I'd do if I had to face an irrational fear at the same time as a real one."

Huck patted me on the back.

"Next thing you know, we'll be pulling into Bandung," said Ariadne. "With any luck, Arjun will still be there."

I shook my head as Fen and the others joined us.

"No," I said. "Kolya was far too motivated to reach the Hive. I suspect we'll arrive there only to find them long gone."

"We're not stopping long anyway," said Fen. "Madan's heading straight for the Hive."

"Good," I said. "Better chances of catching up with my brother."

"And to the despicable one," said Marie, hatred burning like a bonfire behind her eyes.

I listened to the whine as the ramps lifted into their place in the hull. The engines restarted with renewed vigor as the massive vessel pushed itself slowly out to sea. Within moments, the rocking increased as the meandering currents of the river exchanged for the wilder ones of the ocean. I took a deep breath. Trivia noticed and took my hand in hers.

"I used to get seasick too," she said, extending her free hand. "Chew on this."

I put the yellowish-brown chunk in my mouth, struggling to get around its pulpy, wooden texture and spicy taste. Eventually, I noticed the nausea subsiding.

"Ginger?" asked Ariadne.

Trivia nodded.

"If you know where to dig, it's all over the place around here," she said. "I picked up several roots the last night we camped."

"You'll have to tell me what else you know about local flora," said Ariadne, excitedly.

"Thank you," I said, looking down into her azure eyes.

Before I could react, she popped up on her toes and kissed my lips, then wandered off with Ariadne.

"She just… she…" I stuttered, feeling the huge grin spanning my face.

Huck and the others chuckled and left me to my thoughts. I dropped to a seat on the ship's bow, still chewing on the ginger and enjoying the moment of solace. Trivia was right. I *was* starting to like it. I felt warm and fuzzy, and not just from the gift. I stared out at the expanse, still bracketed by land into the horizon, but knowing there was nothing but open water between us and the island chain that was home to Pod Bandung.

"I'm coming for you, brother."

CHAPTER 51: FEN

I didn't mind cleaning Captain Diaz's stateroom. The woman was as tidy as she was immaculate in appearance. Aside from restitching the seams in her aging spare uniform and picking the ceiling's flaking paint chips from the floor, the woman took care of herself. Colonel Richelieu, on the other hand, could barely make it out the door with his shirt buttoned. Keeping his stateroom in working order required elbow grease and patience. It amazed me in so few days how someone of his high stature could make a place so filthy. It must have been a challenge that he'd obviously accepted. Thankfully, aside from living in squalor, the older man proved to be quite friendly.

Colonel Richelieu, or Pilot Jules when at the helm, was one of three officers trained to operate the *Spearhead*. Under Madan's command, he and the other pilots ran the ship day and night, dividing the day into shifts. I desperately wished I could have opened the two portholes in his room to allow in the fresh sea air. His compact room (though far less compact than our berths) always reeked of stale tobacco and the mint he used to mask the fact he wasn't fond of showers. As I folded his clothes on the evening of our second day at sea, he returned to his berth earlier than expected.

"Oh, so sorry, Lieu— Elite Fen," he said, correcting himself.

"Looking for this?" I asked, handing him his pipe.

"Why, yes. You are a doll, looking after a messy old man like me."

I looked at his hair and beard, once thick and brown, now intertwined with gray yellowed by his excessive smoking. The colonel was far from old. In a pod like Bhopal that held physical prowess in such prestige, his middle age must have felt ancient by comparison to the youth comprising the bulk of its population. He smiled his thanks, turning to head back to the bridge.

"Colonel Richelieu?" I asked.

"As long as we're alone, call me Jules. You've earned that right, lieutenant or not."

"Jules," I said, the name feeling far too informal in my mouth. "I often look out the window as I fold your clothes. Occasionally I see red lights blinking in the distance. Is that my imagination?"

"No, dear," he said. "Those are rescue buoys. A former prime minister of Pod Bandung had the bright idea to restore a bunch of those from some long-forgotten war. They dot the way from the coast to the pod. Should anything unfortunate befall mariners, they'll find much-needed help there. Waste of good metal if you ask me. The Arthropods have many ways to kill us, but on the water doesn't seem to be one of them."

"What about the stories of a water beast?" I asked. "I've heard that—"

"Pay no mind, dear," the pilot said, snorting. "Nothing but old sailor myths. When we stare out at the water for too long, our eyes tend to play tricks on us."

"What about Captain Brick's team? Wasn't their last transmission on the water?"

"Hmm," the man pondered. "With or without the Arthropods, the seas can be a treacherous place. Brick was a sharp one. I'm sure he'll turn up eventually."

With that, he left, closing the hatch behind him. I looked out over the water, lit only by the moon, and saw another red twinkle in the distance. *I hope they're just made-up sea stories.* I finished my duties and met up with the rest of Sigma at the ship's cantina. It was after hours, so the only thing available were drinks. Nestled up next to Mego, I sipped my mediocre coffee as Krista regaled us with tales of how disgusting the members of Upsilon could be. There, surrounded by friends and the warmth of the ship, I dozed off contentedly. When I was jostled awake some time later, all hell had broken loose.

"Mego?! Mego?!" I shouted, groggy and confused.

"I'm here!" he yelled, his face visible in the strobing light as the ceiling fluorescents' power came and went.

In the flashes, I could see blood draining down his face from an impact. A bloody gash crossed his forehead. Overhead, a burst pipe was loudly hissing steam, the condensation collecting on a nearby bulkhead.

"What happened?" I yelled.

"I don't know," he said.

"Something hit us!" shouted Ariadne.

The ship groaned loudly and my sense of equilibrium skewed.

"We're listing!" shouted Omar. "We need to get higher, now!"

"What? Why?" asked Krista.

"Because we're taking on water," he yelled.

"No, no, no," said Hemant. "We can't be taking on water. This thing is solid metal. It'll go right to the bottom."

The light flashed long enough for me to see the deadly serious look on Omar's face.

"Oh," said Hemant. "Everybody move!"

We piled out of the cantina's narrow hatch and into the crowded hallway. Everyone, it seemed, had the same idea.

"All hands, man your stations!" said Madan over the ship's intercom. "We've got a hull breach on the port side. We can make it to land if—"

A second blow smashed into the ship, slamming me into a wall with such force it nearly rattled my teeth from my skull.

"You okay?" asked Huck, lifting me up.

I nodded, freeing up Huck to move down the hall to help TomTom. Either my head was swimmier than I thought or the ship was already listing further. We located the ladder and took it up to the next deck, which was packed tight with bodies. The ship protested the shift in weight with a loud moan of the metal hull.

"What do we do?" asked Roque.

"There are lifeboats on the deck," said Omar. "If we can get to those before the ship sinks…"

"Lifeboats?" I asked. "Madan said—"

"Madan is wrong," said Omar. "With the speed we're listing, it won't be long before we capsize. And that'll be well before we reach land."

"Bloody hell," I said. "Then let's get to the lifeboats!"

"There's another problem," said Hemant. "I'm no good at math, but I'm pretty sure there aren't enough boats for several hundred soldiers."

"How many do you think there are enough for?!" I yelled.

"Maybe half our number *if* they're packed tight," he answered.

"Jesus Christ!" shouted Ariadne. "So what? Our mission is going to end with us drowning because there aren't enough freaking boats?!"

Xavier nearly knocked me down, sprinting down the hallway, just in time to hear Ariadne's conclusion. Time momentarily froze as he and the two Tau elites with him came to the inevitable conclusion. In a moment of self-preservation, he shoved Hemant and Omar to the side and the three of them bolted up the ladder to the deck above.

"Selfish prick!" I yelled up after him.

The words echoed pointlessly off the metal-clad hull. Ariadne and I helped the two up. I looked down as the dim, battery-powered emergency lights kicked on and nearly found myself standing on the wall.

"Keep moving!" shouted Omar.

"There you guys are!" screamed Ondo, joining us. "I was getting worried about you!"

We ascended the remaining flights to find ourselves in the midst of pure chaos unfolding under the nighttime flood lights. On the deck, instead of practiced bravery and camaraderie, it was every soldier for himself. Clunkies were shoving and punching to obtain placement in one of the few lifeboats. One had already launched and was barely over half full.

"My God in heaven," said TomTom, astounded by the surrounding scene. "It's like everything we trained for is worthless."

"It makes me sad to be a human being," said Liesel.

I could feel the tears burning my face. For a brief moment, I wanted all those selfish bastards to die. Here I was, standing with the most honorable people on the ship and we're relegated to cleaning the heads.

"If we're not going to have our escape, I will die defending theirs," said Marie. "Whether they deserve it or not."

Pnk. Pnk. Pnk. Pnk. Pnk. One after another, the strange sound rang from the starboard hull. Each followed by a faint vibration denoting an impact. *Pnk. Pnk. Pnk. Pnk. Pnk.* Almost identically, the sound repeated on the lower port side.

"What the hell was that?" asked Ondo, a look of fear in his eyes.

"There's something out there," I said, bile rising in my throat. *Old sailor myths, my ass.* "Something in the water. And I think it just latched onto our hull."

"Oh, hell no!" said Hemant, shaking his head. "Sometimes I wonder why I ever let you haul my ass along on this damn mission, Huck."

"Me?! You were the one—"

"Shut up!" yelled Omar, pacing towards the open stairway leading down into the belly of the ship.

I froze, listening for whatever it was that had captured his attention. I didn't hear anything and was about to speak when I heard it. A chittering. Not like the wraiths, but like hundreds of tiny feet tinging on the walls as they converged on our position.

"Watch your backs!" Omar boomed as loudly as he could manage. "We have incoming!"

Over the cries and fights of the deck, everyone's attention focused on the open stairway as the noise grew in volume. I started backing up.

"Guys, I think we should fall back to the bridge," I said, knowing it might be the most fortified place on the sinking vessel.

"I think you're right," said Huck, pulling Ariadne in that direction.

Before we could get close, it happened. Tiny, fast-moving creatures poured from the opening, climbing out from the ground, the sides, even the ceiling of the opening. Overwhelming the nearby Clunkies, the critters washed over the men, leaving behind flayed corpses before moving on to the next. In a scuffle to escape, Roque was thrown to the deck, leg twisted at an unnatural angle. Mego and TomTom hoisted him up. In a sprint, Ondo and the members of Sigma Squad stormed up the ladder to the bridge slamming the port door behind us.

"Lock the doors!" I screamed to a perplexed bridge crew.

After a moment's hesitation, Captain Diaz dove towards the starboard door, locking it just as the semi-transparent brownish inverts covered the windows, blocking our visibility of the deck.

"What about the others?" asked Jules. "We have to help them!"

"There are no others!" screamed Roque, sobbing. "Those… those things… they didn't stand a chance!"

I looked at the windows, now covered in tiny spider-like bodies, jaws gnashing at the windows trying to break through.

"We're safe here," said Madan, unusually calm even for him. "That's armored glass. The old militaries were quite fond of the material."

"Safe?!" I yelled at my superior. "Safe?! The ship is sinking, *General.* We can either drown in here or let them eat us out there, but we sure as hell aren't safe!"

"No. I suppose you're right," he whispered.

I felt Ariadne's hand on my bicep and turned to her.

"The Shock," she mouthed.

It wasn't just Madan. The entire bridge was struggling to comprehend the moment. All the physical training in the world couldn't prevent the Shock. Like Pod Bhopal, masking the underlying problems did little to resolve them. I heard a crack and whirled around in time to see a streak arc across the window.

"They're breaking through!" shouted Liesel.

As soon as she spoke, the bridge was engulfed by flame. Scorching heat radiated through the walls, bringing on an instant sweat. The inverts screamed and writhed in agony as they roasted within their exoskeletons which turned opaque in the heat. I struggled to breathe as the fire seemed to pull all the oxygen from the room. Just when I thought that I was going to pass out, I felt an arm at my shoulder. I craned my neck up to see Xavier, battered and bleeding, holding a sputtering flamethrower.

"I knew you weren't all bad," I muttered weakly.

CHAPTER 52: HUCK

"**D**id anyone survive?" I managed to ask, surprised as hell to see Xavier not only alive but saving us.

Xavier shook his head forlornly. Ariadne covered her mouth in shock. We knew running into the bridge that it was going to be a massacre, but that didn't make hearing it any easier.

"And the lifeboats?" asked Omar.

"They're pretty banged up, but the creatures were far more interested in us than them," he said. "Just so you know, it's not a pretty sight out here."

I helped Diaz usher the other officers out from the bridge. Save for her, every one of them was so dissociated, I was amazed they could stand upright. Xavier led us down to the deck using his weapon to dispatch any remaining inverts. The boat remained at its steep cant, but for the moment, had stopped sinking. I stepped in something soft and looked down, expecting to find one of the dead inverts. I almost leapt back when I realized it was human viscera. Behind me, Liesel vomited. The deck, virtually spotless when we arrived, was now coated in a thick layer of blackened inverts and what was left of our fallen comrades.

"I don't think they were as afraid of water as we thought," said Mego, holding the back of his hand to his mouth and trying not to gag.

"Is there anyone alive out here?" yelled Ariadne between racking sobs. "Anyone I can help?"

I took her hand in mine. Xavier looked at her, shaking his head.

"Oh. God," muttered Hemant as we saw the boats.

The ones not destroyed in the fracas appeared to be in working order but were covered in recognizable parts. It was too much. I leaned over the side and threw up until my body was shaking from exhaustion. I pinched my eyes closed, doing all I could to stop the torrent of tears. I felt a comforting pat from Ondo's giant hand.

"We've got to get off this boat," he said. "It's still sinking."

I was about to reply, but then I saw something shiny underwater, illuminated by the moonlight. My stomach rolled again as I realized what it was. Clamped onto the boat were six volcanic-looking protuberances, each with a single eye, facing up towards the moonlight. I knew without a shadow of a doubt, I'd find the same on the other side. I forgot all about my nausea.

"Trivia, you need to see this," said Ondo.

She looked over the side and gasped.

"They look like barnacles," she said. "But the biggest I've ever seen."

"Can they see us?"

"I doubt it," she said. "I think they're just photoreceptors."

"What? Photo as in light?" asked Hemant.

"Yeah," she said, running over to one of the small inverts, almost slipping on the blood slathering the deck.

"These are their nauplii," she shouted. "They must have drilled into the boat and deposited their young."

"Is it safe to get in the boats with them nearby?" asked Diaz.

"I have no way of knowing, Captain," said Trivia, shaking her head.

The boat suddenly groaned and listed a few more degrees. No one hesitated. I sprinted to the boat, trying not to think about what I was throwing out to the sides. There would be time for mourning later. Using the wenches, we lowered the lifeboats the short distance to the water, tethering them to the railing until we were ready to disembark. We carefully loaded the surviving officers into the first boat, before we helped Roque and ourselves into the second.

"I'll take care of them," said Xavier. "But I'll need some help."

"I'll go," said Mego, climbing in as the launch rocked back and forth on the waves.

"Me too," said TomTom, lowering himself into the boat as Xavier evenly distributed its dazed occupants.

"TomTom," said Roque from his reclined position on the seat, "be careful."

"I will, my love," he replied.

Madan stared at the sinking ship, forlorn, then turned to me.

"The bomb, Huck," he said, pensively, before removing a key from around his neck.

"Go!" I said to Xavier, grabbing the key and looking at Hemant.

"On it," he said, already jumping out alongside me.

We thundered into the bridge, making our way to the ship's locker and wrenching it open with the help of Madan's key. It took both of us to lift it out of its compartment, but from there, Hemant and I were able to carry it down to the remaining boat. In the time that the side trip had taken, the deck had reached the waterline. We carefully loaded the weapon and loosened the mooring lines, slowly paddling away from the transport ship and after the others. The ship's hull bubbled as it disappeared further and further into the dark water. Once its last light winked out, we could see the *Spearhead* no more.

"Is this why no one ever returns from the Hive?" I asked, trying to sync my stroke with Hemant's.

"I don't know," said Fen, sitting on the bow. "We didn't even make it to Bandung."

"It's so dark, I can't even tell which direction the coast is," said Omar.

"I know what to do!" said Fen, yelling to the other boat. "Mego, make for the blinking red light!"

"What blinking red— Oh," he said. "I see them!"

I stopped rowing long enough for our boat to turn and continued paddling the indeterminable distance to the light's origin.

"Where are we going?" asked Trivia.

"You mean there's something you don't know?" said Ondo, forcing a chuckle.

"Rescue buoys," said Fen. "Jules was just telling me about them this morning."

"I'm not sure who Jules is, but I could kiss him right now," said Hemant.

"Coming over to our side now, Hemant?" asked Roque.

Hemant harrumphed.

"There's one thing I don't understand," I said.

"What's that?" said Ariadne, shifting to face me from her bench.

"We felt those barnacles hit the boat," I said. "It was nothing like the first impact that started us sinking."

"Huck's correct," said Marie. "If anything, the barnacles slowed the leak."

"Then what caused the first impact?" asked Hemant, his chestnut face as white as a matriarch's hat.

From deep beneath the water rose a devilish roar, rocketing a chill up my spine the likes of which I'd never felt before. With one glance at Hemant, we dramatically increased the speed of our rowing, as did Xavier's crew. I turned back over my shoulder to gauge our distance from the buoys. *Still half a kilometer away, dammit.* I increased my speed yet again as Hemant matched, adrenaline fueling the physiological demands.

Illuminated by the moonlight, the otherwise calm ocean water began to mound as something underneath the water tempted the surface with its breach. Moving towards us at great speed, the girth of the creature became strikingly apparent. *It's bigger than a bloody desert borer!* Liesel tapped my shoulder encouraging me to pour on more speed.

"Must go faster, must go faster," repeated Roque, favoring his injured leg.

At last, we were close enough to the buoy to see its sun-bleached yellow form. Meters ahead of us, the traumatized officers had become aware of the impending danger. In a panic, they were rocking the boat side to side as Mego, TomTom, and Xavier struggled to keep them under control. The rise in the water changed directions, pursuing the disturbance. Fen tensed as she watched on, unable to act. The sea creature collided with Mego's boat, sending the officers and our friends careening into the ocean water.

"We have to get them!" Fen screamed.

"There's not enough room," I said, rowing meters away from the others. "We'll come back for you!"

My eyes burned, watching the others flounder in the infested water. I felt the impact as our boat bumped into the buoy, almost knocking me into the floor.

"Everyone out!" I said as loudly as I dared, not knowing what exactly attracted the creature. "Tread lightly!"

"Mego!" shouted Fen, as Omar wrapped his large hands around her mouth.

Fen flailed, slamming her heavy boots into the buoys wide deck, biting Omar's hand in an attempt to call to her lover. Omar held her tightly, knowing the risk she posed. As I dragged him up onto the buoy, Roque looked on in horror as TomTom struggled to keep his head above water among the others' thrashing.

"Hemant, get the hatch open!" I said, dodging Fen's kick. "Once everyone's in, we'll rescue the others!"

Hemant crouched down next to the rusted wheel that operated the hatch and tried with all his might to spin it. Even with the adrenaline throbbing through his system, it wouldn't budge.

"Use your hammer for leverage," said Trivia, tapping him on the back.

Hemant pulled off his war hammer and jammed it through the wheel, but it still wouldn't twitch. Ondo took a knee to help.

"Look!" said Ariadne.

I turned back towards the capsized boat just as the monstrous invert reached them. The water exploded in a violent spray of pink mist as the mysterious clawed creature pulverized everyone in the water. When the water settled, the moonlit sea was silent. *No!* Inside I was screaming.

In a moment of shock, Omar dropped Fen, who began screaming for Mego. Roque was frozen in silence, mouth agape. Hemant fell to the deck, bracing himself against the railing as he and Ondo pushed against his hammer with all their might. The creature made the sweeping turn for us, drawn by the noise. With the speed of an arrow, it drove towards the buoy while we looked on in terror. I did all I could think to do. I picked up the paddle and walloped Fen upside the head, knocking her unconscious. I held my finger to my lips as the others looked at me, horrified. *I'll apologize when we survive.* With everyone silent as the grave, the invert was still barreling towards us. I held my breath as it neared, but at the last moment, it passed harmlessly underneath us.

A slight squeal pierced the air as Hemant wrenched the hatch open. Ariadne climbed down first and had Omar lower Fen's unconscious frame to her. One after another, everyone went inside, leaving Hemant and I alone on its surface. We pulled the bomb from the boat and carefully brought it inside, leaving the boat moored to the railing.

The buoy was cramped, but we were alive and presumably safe, provided we were quiet. I muttered a silent prayer as I activated the buoy's emergency beacon, hoping to the universe someone was out there listening. Since the buoys had gone this long without attracting the drill barnacles, hopefully they could go a little longer. As best as I could tell, the buoy contained a box of medical supplies; several week's rations; a case of bottles, presumably water; a carton of pipe tobacco; and a compact toilet.

"Whoever built this place was a hell of an optimist," I whispered, hearing only my own sounds echo off the walls back to me.

Everyone looked at me as though it was my fault the others were dead. I slunked off into a corner, sitting in one of the bunks next to Ariadne, who was in no hurry to meet my eyes. As my adrenaline dissipated, my mood spiraled downward. I leaned back against the cold metal of the buoy's interior, heartbroken from the day's incalculable losses.

In a disturbing way, we'd gotten our wish. We were alone once again, closer to the Hive than ever. Like our Release Day, so many had unwillingly perished for our cause. I sat in near silence, surrounded by disappointed companions, trapped in a room-sized buoy, floating somewhere in the Indian Ocean, as god-knows-what lurked outside.

CHAPTER 53: FRANCISCO

"**B**oatmaster Francisco?" asked a skinny young man on the dock. The fellow, not much older than a boy, had the same complexion as the fisherman on the far side of the wharf. Bhopali, if I remembered correctly. I nodded as I continued sewing the damaged net that'd caught on submerged debris the day prior.

"Do you understand United?" asked a portly, bedraggled man with browning teeth as he stepped awkwardly onto my boat uninvited.

I nodded again, further frustrating the older fellow.

"Give him the paper, Arjun," the man said.

The fellow called Arjun passed me a small slip of paper. Paper was a rare resource, not usually wasted on the likes of poor fisherfolk. *Must be important.* I unrolled the paper, written in both United and the common language of the harbor, taking in its contents slowly so as to absorb their meaning and purpose. *Boatmaster General, eh? They really don't expect my return.*

I was barely making ends meet as it was. Demand for fish was high, as one of the few fresh resources in the entire pod. With each boat that passed through the gates, new fish would partially replenish the bay, but single-handedly feeding a family while competing with the larger vessels was becoming more challenging by the day. But taking these two to the Australian Territory? It was hard to see how it wasn't suicide.

I rubbed the coarse stubble lining my face, tossing the decision from side to side. If I didn't survive, my family would be on their own. Yadira likely slaving away in a sweatshop while the kids still went hungry. *Perhaps it's not worth the risk. But if I succeeded... everything would change.* If the letter was to be believed, these unlikely fellows were on a quest to end the war.

A wrinkled face stared back at me from the blade of my rigging knife, weathered and dark from where the sun had taken its toll. Though an honorable profession, fishing wasn't the life I desired for my children. I threaded the last line through the net and tied it off, catching another glimpse of my reflection as I sliced the thin rope. Could I still face myself if I didn't act in humanity's hour of need? Whether the pair standing in front of me was successful or not, if I returned, I would do so as Boatmaster General. *I believe I'll do it.* More for my kids than humanity, but I would do it.

"This what the minister thinks of our duty? A fisherman who can't understand United and skiff that hardly looks seaworthy?" asked the man, a researcher named Kolya according to De León's letter—a *bajingan* if you ask me. "I wouldn't be surprised if he pulls out oars."

"Can we leave in the morning?" asked Arjun, pantomiming a sunrise.

I nodded, rerolling the paper and placing it inside my wicker satchel for safekeeping.

"At least it's something," said Kolya. "Let's see if we can find some tolerable food before we head back to our berths.

"Thank you," said Arjun, placing a hand over his heart as his companion climbed onto the dock.

I watched as my would-be passengers strode down the quay, disappearing between the fisherman heading to their homes. I didn't trust the prime minister to stay true to his word without documentation. I'd give the letter to my brother for safekeeping. I stepped carefully out of the boat, timing the leap with the boat's sway so that I could land on my good leg.

Making my way through the crowded thoroughfare, I quickly arrived home. Despite the structure being little more than a shack, I did all I could to keep the house in good repair just as my wife kept it immaculately clean. I hobbled through the door and kissed her before picking up my toddling twins.

"I've been given a task from the minister, Yadira," I said in perfect United, hanging my wide-brimmed straw hat on the hook by the door. "He's finally agreed to let me fish outside the city."

The grin across her face was replaced by suspicion.

"And what is he expecting in return?" she asked.

I sat down placing my son on one knee and my daughter on the other.

"Your father's going to have to go away for a while," I said, squeezing them tightly.

"Are you coming back?" asked Tio.

I looked at my wife's eyes, glistening in the lantern light with tears.

"Yes, my son. One way or another."

"Mother, why are you crying?" asked my daughter.

"Because I'm going to miss your father terribly while he's gone, Tia," she said, wiping her eyes with her tattered apron, stained from transforming the most mundane ingredients into the most delectable dishes.

"Why are you going?" asked Tio, rubbing his soft fingers across my calloused hands.

"My, aren't you full of questions," I said, laughing. "I'm carrying some friends across the sea. When I return, I'll be able to change some things for the better."

"I don't want better, Father. I want you," said Tia, pouting, her tiny, half-toothed smile warming my heart.

"I have to," I said, picking them up and placing them in their bed across from ours. "I'll be gone when you wake, but I'll be back before you know it."

"Promise?" they said in unison.

"I promise," I said, removing the chipped sand dollar necklace and handing it to my awaiting son.

"Your necklace?" he asked. "Didn't your father give this to you?"

"Yes. It symbolizes the leader of the family and I'm trusting you with it. Can you take care of your mother and sister until I return?"

He nodded vigorously. I kissed them each on the forehead and tucked them in before closing the door to the bedroom. Removing my wooden limb, I gently lowered myself to a floor cushion in the living area, which shared space with the kitchen.

"So tell me true, husband. Where are you going?"

"De León has asked me to carry two strangers to the Australian Territory. In return—"

"The Australian Territory?!" she said, voice raised, then looking towards the bedroom, dropped into a whisper. "Are you mad?!"

"This is a chance to change our lives, Yadira."

"Listen to your daughter," she pleaded, kneeling next to me. "We don't need change. We need you! Not even the Bhopali soldiers come back from there! What chance does a one-legged fisherman have?"

I clutched her as she sobbed away in my arms.

"I'm not going to fight, just to deliver cargo. I've been on the water as long as the land, perhaps longer. I know how to be stealthy. Yadira, I watched my grandfather and father work themselves to death, barely having enough to feed and clothe their families. I don't need an extravagant life, but I want more for my children."

"And if you fail? What then? Will you have your children fatherless while their mother works as a whore?"

"That will never happen. Your brother will find work for you mending. The children could even help. With one less mouth to feed, you might even have more to eat."

Yadira let out a chuckle sob and smacked me.

"I want to hate you for running off, but you always have to be so selfless. Go, then. But you better come back here—alive," she said, giving me a lingering kiss.

She stood, slowly untying the string which barely kept the coarse fabric from falling off of her thin frame, and let her clothes fall to the floor. I drank in her beauty for a moment before pulling off my own tunic and trousers. She curled up next to me, holding my head in her hands as she gazed into my eyes.

"You come back to me, my Francisco," she whispered.

•••••••••

Before the first golden rays of the sun rose above the city wall and baked the morning mist off of the harbor, my sailboat was laden with the provisions the minister had provided. *He must have some faith in me, providing enough supplies for a return trip.* In addition to medicine and water, the list Zimo had rattled off included dried fruit and pickled vegetables. The ocean, it seemed, would be responsible for the bulk of our diet. I triple-checked the boat from bow to stern, making sure everything was sea-ready. I'd even been supplied with a fresh sail, drawing a few envious glances from other boatmasters as they set off into the bay. The patchwork fabric I'd replaced had been in no condition for such a long journey.

I climbed out of the hold and tacked in the last nail, further securing the railing that had come loose the day before. I had too much respect for myself to host passengers on an ill-maintained vessel. I sat on the deck, awaiting my charges, chewing on a piece of sugar cane harvested from the fields adjacent to the docks.

"There he is," said the older one, pointing. "I don't understand how anyone finds a damn thing here. Every damn boat and fisherman look alike."

"Morning," said Arjun.

I responded with my typical nod.

Yadira always had a sense about people, noticing things that others wouldn't—mannerisms, expressions, gestures—that might evade the casual observer. Over the years, I'd learned to trust her judgment when it came to strangers. In the case of Arjun's friend, I didn't need Yadira to recognize him for the spineless eel he was.

"Us. Go," said Kolya, gesturing to the three of us before pointing towards the gates.

I nodded, ignoring his condescending tone, and began collecting the ropes anchoring us to the dock. When Arjun saw what I was doing, he jumped in to help. At least one of the two had redeeming qualities.

"I'm sure he knows how to handle his own boat," said the man, moving supplies around to make himself more comfortable.

"I'm sure he does, Kolya, but it's going to be a long voyage as it is. If he's willing, I'll learn his craft and be better for it."

"Suit yourself, Arjun," said Kolya, sitting on the aft bench and reclining awkwardly. "I can't imagine that it would take more than a day to master the man's skills."

It was going to be a long voyage like Arjun predicted, though not for the reason he thought. It'd be tempting to swing the boom "accidentally" and knock the pompous man into the ocean for a much-needed bath. It was a feat to have a stronger odor than the fishy docks. Once everything was prepared and the final checks were complete, we were ready to get underway. Taking a deep breath, I raised the sail and manned the tiller.

I took one last look back and was surprised to see my wife and children watch my departure. As my kids waived excitedly, I blew them kisses, smiling to mask the crack forming across my heart. For a moment, I doubted that I could go so long without them. *I will return.* Kolya twisted his thick neck back to see what had my attention.

"Your family?" he asked, gesturing.

I nodded.

"She's cute, your wife."

I felt the weight at my side where I kept my razor-sharp rigging knife. The man had been a guest for mere minutes and I was already itching to be rid of him. Being a man of my word, I would see this filthy ingrate and his unlikely friend to the dangerous territory they were so anxious to reach. As a frequent betrayer himself, De León constantly guarded against the threat of betrayal. His message had said the men carried a passcode. Only upon reaching the Australian Territory, would they divulge it. On my return with said code, I would receive De León's promised reward.

Every day as my bow had swung towards the gates, I dreamt of sailing beyond them. Today was the day I would finally be able to do so. An almost magnetic attraction lured me to the foreboding portal separating us from the dangers of the open ocean. Out on the water, there'd be nothing to protect us from the Arthropods or the elements, the wooden hull a flimsy barrier to any creature with ill intentions. Low and slow would be our motto, all the way to the foreign lands.

High up in the wall, the guard nodded, forewarned of my early-morning departure. With a clang and a grind, one side of the gate began to lurch open, my humble boat braving a passage meant for far sturdier vessels. As soon as the hull cleared the monstrous walls, my aching heart nearly burst with excitement for the unknown. I took a deep breath of the briny air, adjusting my course toward the rising sun, dodging the scraping fingers that hid just under the rippling surface. As the air currents began pounding my sail, I locked the tiller just long enough to make the necessary adjustment.

"Here. Can I do it?" asked Arjun as Kolya rolled his eyes.

I handed him the loose rope and demonstrated how to ease the tension. He looked back at me with a subtle grin of accomplishment.

"I have a new appreciation for the skill it takes to operate a boat like this," he said. "It must take constant tweaking."

I nodded, smiling as the lush landscape drifted by in the distance. Ironic as it was, land meant safety. Provided we stayed close, we supposedly had little to fear. It was the deeper waters where the rumored creature was said to lurk. I saw little truth in the sailors' myths, but that didn't mean I wouldn't play it safe.

"We'll have safe passage," said Arjun, reading my thoughts.

I looked at him, puzzled.

"We sent a chemical message ahead of us to the Hive. As best as we can tell, it's been received and understood. The Arthropods haven't made a hostile move towards us since."

"Don't waste your breath, my boy" said Kolya. "I doubt he understands."

Arjun sauntered off to check the ropes for the umpteenth time. He was a quick study in the art but had as much to learn about when to leave well enough alone as what to do. *Safe Passage? Chemical message?* What had I stuck my harpoon in this time?

I shook my head and chuckled to myself, wrapping my hand around the backstay for balance, its hemp weave as comforting to me as the smoothest silk. I was standing at the threshold of destiny, gazing out over the azure sea that stretched to the edges of the Earth. Somewhere out there was my destination—the most perilous place known to humanity—home to the Hive. I was going closer than the bravest dared. All for family. I hadn't let my mounting fear show, but I'd be stupid not to be afraid.

"Arjun," I said. "I would like to hear more of this chemical message."

ACKNOWLEDGEMENTS & AUTHOR'S NOTE

Writing a book is hard. Writing a series is even harder. As I finish the third book of the Release Day Saga and begin the final installment, I am ever humbled by the writing process. My appreciation for my favorite authors and their work grows as my own fictional universe expands.

I couldn't have gotten as far as I have without my wonderful support system. I want to thank my wife and daughters first, who continually sacrifice their time so that I can focus on the writing, design, and promotion of the series. A special thanks goes to my editor, Ariel Wells, who generously agreed to edit the manuscript during her busiest time of the year. I also want to thank my test readers: Jessica Matthews, Deshea Surratt, Emily Wan, and Missy Wood. Their editing and feedback are invaluable.

Thank you to all of the people who've bought and reviewed my work, believing in me from the beginning. It is the coolest and most humbling experience to have supportive fans who want to see me succeed. I look forward to every event and the opportunity to meet each of you. Don't ever hesitate to drop by, even just to say, "Hi!"

As always, it's important to me to tell this story with authentically diverse voices from an inclusive perspective as they experience the harsh realities of this corrupt, dystopian world. The characters represent varying ethnicities, genders, sexualities, religions, body types, and abilities. I did my best to handle this with care and hope it is reflected.

On one final note, remember to respect each other, regardless of our differences. I enjoy writing about a violent and dystopian world, but I never wish for it to become reality.

—Ryan

RYAN MATTHEWS

The Release Day Saga is the debut series of Ryan Matthews, an English as a Second Language (ESL) teacher and graphic designer. In addition to writing and teaching, he enjoys spending time with his family, taking insect and mushroom pictures on hikes, and plowing through his extensive reading list. He also dabbles in foreign languages, open-world video games, and the French horn. Ryan holds a Bachelor's Degree in Art and a Master's Degree in Education. He lives in Tennessee with his wife, daughters, and the family pets, Luna and Coda.

@ryanmatthews501
ryanmatthewsauthor.com

NEWSLETTER

For the latest updates, events, and behind-the-scenes information, visit Ryan's website and subscribe to his newsletter.

RATE & REVIEW

If you wish to support authors like Ryan, please leave reviews on sites like Amazon and Goodreads for all of your favorite books.